THE SKY-LINERS
&
GALLOWAY

D0191548

Bantam Books by Louis L'Amour
ASK YOUR BOOKSELLER FOR THE BOOKS YOU HAVE MISSED.

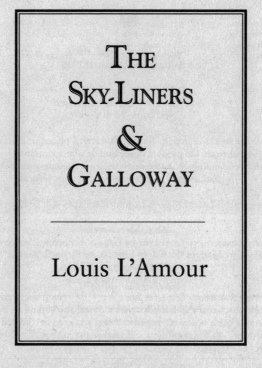

THE
SKY-LINERS
&
GALLOWAY

Louis L'Amour

BANTAM BOOKS

THE SKY-LINERS / GALLOWAY
A Bantam Book / March 2008

Published by Bantam Dell
A Division of Random House, Inc.
New York, New York

These are works of fiction. Names, characters, places, and incidents
either are the product of the author's imagination or
are used fictitiously. Any resemblance to actual persons, living
or dead, events, or locales is entirely coincidental.

Photograph of Louis L'Amour by John Hamilton—Globe Photos, Inc.

All rights reserved
The Sky-Liners copyright © 1967 by Louis & Katherine L'Amour Trust
Galloway copyright © 1970 by Louis & Katherine L'Amour Trust
Cover image by Fred Pfeiffer
Cover design by Yook Louie

If you purchased this book without a cover, you should be aware
that this book is stolen property. It was reported as "unsold and
destroyed" to the publisher, and neither the author nor the publisher has received any payment for this "stripped book."

Bantam Books and the rooster colophon are registered trademarks
of Random House, Inc.

ISBN 978-0-553-59178-1

Printed in the United States of America
Published simultaneously in Canada

www.bantamdell.com

OPM   10 9 8 7 6 5 4 3 2

THE SKY-LINERS

SOUTHERN APPALACHIA

OHIO
INDIANA
St. Louis
Sedalia
ILL
Ohio River
Louisville
W. VA.
MISSOURI
Smithland
Green River
Barren R.
Scaggs Cr.
Cumberland Gap
VA
Cumberland R.
Caney Fk.
Tazewell
Sinking C
Nashville
N.C.
ARKANSAS
Bald Knob
TENNESSEE
Tennessee R.
S.C.
MISSISSIPPI
ALABAMA
Atlanta
GEORGIA

Pueblo
Goodnight
Arkansas River
St. Charles River

SOUTH-CENTRAL COLORADO
Contour interval 500 feet
Scale of Miles
0   5   10   15

Greenhorn
Huerfano River
Cucharas River

Walsenburg
Goodnight Trail

Santa Fe Trail

Purgatoire River

Trinidad

Map by Alan McKnight

CHAPTER 1

EVERYBODY IN OUR part of the country knew of Black Fetchen, so folks just naturally stood aside when he rode into town with his kinfolk.

The Fetchen land lay up on Sinking Creek, and it wasn't often a Sackett got over that way, so we had no truck with one another. We heard talk of him and his doings—how he'd killed a stranger over on Caney's Fork, and about a fair string of shootings and cuttings running back six or seven years.

He wasn't the only Fetchen who'd worked up to trouble in that country, or down in the flat land, for that matter. It was a story told and retold how Black Fetchen rode down to Tazewell and taken some kin of his away from the law.

James Black Fetchen his name was, but all knew him as Black, because the name suited. He was a dark, handsome man with a bold, hard-shouldered way about him, as quick with his fists as with a gun. Those who rode with him, like Tory Fetchen and Colby Rafin, were the same sort.

Me and Galloway had business over in Tazewell or we'd never have been around those parts, not that we feared Black Fetchen, or any man, but we were newly home from the western lands and when we went to Tazewell we went to pay off the last of Pa's debts. Pa had bad luck several years running and owed honor debts we were bound to pay, so Galloway and me rode back from the buffalo plains to settle up.

We had taken off to the western lands two years before, me twenty-two then and him twenty-one. We worked the Santa Fe Trail with a freight outfit, and laid track for a railroad mountain spur, and finally went over the trail from Texas with a herd of steers. It wasn't until we went buffalo hunting that we made our stake.

About that time we heard some kinfolk of ours, name of William Tell Sackett, was herding up trouble down in the Mogollon, so we saddled up and lit out, because when a Sackett has trouble his kin is just bound to share it with him. So we rode down to help him clean things up.*

This debt in Tazewell now was the last, and our last cent as well. After two years we were right back where we started, except that we had our rifles and hand guns, and a blanket or two. We'd sold our horses when we came back to Tennessee from the hunting grounds.

We walked across the mountain, and when we got to town we headed for the town pump. Once we'd had a drink we started back across the street to settle our debt at the store that had given Pa credit when times were bad.

We were fairly out in the middle of the street when hoofs began to pound and a passel of folks a-horse-back came charging up, all armed and loaded for feudin' or bear-fightin'.

Folks went high-tailing it for shelter when they

---

* *The Sackett Brand*

saw those riders coming, but we were right out in the middle of the street and of no mind to run. They came a-tearing down upon us and one of them taken a cut at me with a quirt, yelling, "Get outen the street!"

Well, I just naturally reached up and grabbed a hold on that quirt, and most things I lay a hand to will move. He had a loop around his wrist and couldn't let go if he was a mind to, so I just jerked and he left that saddle a-flying and landed in the dust. The rest of them, they reined around, of a mind to see some fun.

That one who sat in the dust roosted there a speck, trying to figure what happened to him, and then he came off the ground with a whoop and laid at me with a fist.

Now, we Sacketts had always been handy at knuckle-and-skull fighting, but Galloway and me had put in a spell with Irish track-layers and freighting teamsters who did most of their fighting like that. When this stranger looped a swing at my face, I just naturally stepped inside and clobbered him with a short one.

I fetched him coming in on me, and his head snapped back as if you'd laid the butt end of an axe against it. He went into the dust and about that time I heard Galloway saying, mild-like, "Go ahead, if you're a mind to. I'm takin' bets I can empty four, five saddles before you get me."

Me, I'd held my own rifle in my left hand this while, so I just flipped her up, my hand grasped the action, and I was ready. The two of us stood there facing the nine of them and it looked like blood on the ground.

Only nobody moved.

The big, handsome man who had been riding point for the outfit looked us over and said, "I'm Black Fetchen."

Galloway, he spoke over to me. "Black Fetchen, he says. Flagan, are you scared?"

"Don't seem to be, now that I think on it. But I've been scared a time or two. Recall that Comanche out there on the short grass? There for a minute or two I figured he had me."

"But you fetched him, Flagan. Now, what all do you figure we should do with this lot?"

"Well, he made his confession. He owned up fair and honest who he was. He never tried to lie out of it. You got to give credit to a man who'll confess like that."

"Maybe"—Galloway was almighty serious—"but I think you're mistaken in this man. He owned up to the fact that he was Black Fetchen, but there wasn't the shame in him there should have been. I figure a man who can up and say 'I'm Black Fetchen' should feel shame. Might at least hang his head and scuff his toe a mite."

Black Fetchen had been growing madder by the minute. "I've had enough of this! By the—!"

"Hold off, Black." That was Colby Rafin talking. "I seen these two before, over nigh the Gap. These are Sacketts. I heard tell they'd come home from the buffalo range."

Now, we Sacketts have been feuding up and down the country with one outfit or another for nigh on to a hundred years, and nobody could say we hadn't marked up our share of scalps, but nobody could say that we hunted trouble.

When Rafin said that, we could just sort of see Black Fetchen settling down into his saddle. We weren't just a pair of green mountain boys putting on a show. He was a brave man, but only a fool will chance a shot from a Winchester at forty feet. Knowing who we were, he now knew we would shoot, so he sat quiet and started to smile. "Sorry, boys, but a joke is a joke. We've come to town on business and want no trouble. Shall I say we apologize?"

That was like a rattlesnake stopping his rattling while keeping his head drawn back to strike.

"You can say that," I agreed, "and we'll accept it just like you mean it; but just so's there's no misunderstanding, why don't you boys just shuck your artillery? Just let them fall gentle into the street."

"I'll be damned if I will!" Tory Fetchen yelled.

"You'll be dead if you don't," Galloway told him. "As to being damned, you'll have to take that up with your Lord and Maker. You going to shuck those guns, or do I start shooting?"

"Do what he says, boys," Black said. "This is only one day. There'll be another."

They did as ordered, but Galloway is never one to let things be. He's got a hankering for the fringe around the edges.

"Now, Gentlemen and Fellow-Sinners, you have come this day within the shadow of the valley. It is well for each and every one of us to recall how weak is the flesh, how close we stand to Judgment, so you will all join me in singing 'Rock of Ages.'"

He gestured to Black Fetchen. "You will lead the singing, and I hope you are in fine voice."

"You're crazy!"

"Maybe," Galloway agreed, "but I want to hear you loud and clear. You got until I count three to start, and you better make sure they all join in."

"Like hell!" Tory was seventeen, and he was itching to prove himself as tough as he thought he was... or as tough as he wanted others to think he was.

Galloway fired, and that bullet whipped Tory's hat from his head and notched his ear. "Sing, damn you!" Galloway said; and brother, they sang.

I'll say this for them, they had good strong voices and they knew the words. Up in the mountains the folks are strong on goin' to meetin', and these boys all knew the words. We heard it clear: *"Rock of ages, cleft for me, Let me hide, myself in thee."*

"Now you all turn around," Galloway advised, "and ride slow out of town. I want all these good people to know you ain't bad boys—just sort of rambunctious when there's nobody about to discipline you a mite."

"Your guns," I said, "will be in the bank when it opens tomorrow!"

So James Black Fetchen rode out of town with all that rowdy gang of his, and we stood with our rifles and watched them go.

"Looks like we made us some enemies, Flagan," Galloway said.

"Sufficient to the day is the evil thereof," I commented, liking the mood, "but don't you mind. We've had enemies before this."

We collected the guns and deposited them in the

bank, which was closing, and then we walked across the street and settled Pa's account.

Everybody was chuckling over what happened, but also they warned us of what we could expect. We didn't have cause to expect much, for the fact was we were going back to the buffalo prairies. Back home there was nothing but an empty cabin, no meat in the pot, no flour in the bin.

We had done well our first time west, and now we would go back and start over. Besides, there were a lot of Sackett kinfolk out there now.

We started off.

Only we didn't get far. We had just reached the far end of town when we sighted a camp at the edge of the woods, and an oldish man walked out to meet us. We'd talked with enough Irish lads whilst working on the railroad to recognize the brogue. "May I be havin' a word wi' you, boys?"

So we stopped, with Galloway glancing back up the street in case those Fetchen boys came back with guns.

"I'm Laban Costello," he said, "and I'm a horse-trader."

More than likely everybody in the mountains knew of the Irish horse-traders. There were eight families of them, good Irish people, known and respected throughout the South. They were drifting folk, called gypsies by some, and they moved across the land swapping horses and mules, and a canny lot they were. It was in my mind this would be one of them.

"I am in trouble," he said, "and my people are far away in Atlanta and New Orleans."

"We are bound for the buffalo lands, but we would leave no man without help. What can we do?"

"Come inside," he said, and we followed him back into the tent.

This was like no tent I had ever seen, with rugs on the ground and a curtained wall across one side to screen off a sleeping space. This was the tent of a man who moved often, but lived well wherever he stopped. Out behind it we had noticed a caravan wagon, painted and bright.

Making coffee at the fire was a girl, a pretty sixteen by the look of her. Well, maybe she was pretty. She had too many freckles, and a pert, sassy way about her that I didn't cotton to.

"This is my son's daughter," he said. "This is Judith."

"Howdy, ma'am," Galloway said.

Me, I merely looked at her and she wrinkled her nose at me. I turned away sharp, ired by any fool slip of a girl so impolite as to do such as that to a stranger.

"First, let me say that I saw what happened out there in the street, and you are the first who have faced up to Fetchen in a long while. He is a bad man, a dangerous man."

"We ain't likely to see him again," I said, "for we are bound out across the plains."

Personally, I wanted him to get to the point. It was my notion those Fetchens would borrow guns and come back, loaded for bear and Sacketts. This town was no place to start a shooting fight, and I saw no cause to fight when nothing was at stake.

"Have you ever been to Colorado?"

"Nigh to it. We have been in New Mexico."

"My son lives in Colorado. Judith is his daughter."

Time was a-wasting and we had a far piece to go.

Besides, I was getting an uneasy feeling about where all this was leading.

"It came to me," Costello said, "that as you are going west, and you Sacketts have the name of honorable men, I might prevail upon you to escort my son's daughter to her father's home."

"No," I said.

"Now, don't be hasty. I agree that traveling with a young girl might seem difficult, but Judith has been west before, and she has never known any other life but the camp and the road."

"She's been west?"

"Her father is a mustanger, and she traveled with him."

"Hasn't she some folks who could take her west?" I asked. Last thing I wanted was to have a girl-child along, making trouble, always in the way, and wanting special treatment.

"At any other time there would be plenty, but now there is no time to waste. You see Black Fetchen had put his mind to her."

"*Her?*" I was kind of contemptuous. "Why, she ain't out of pigtails yet!"

She stuck out her tongue at me, but I paid her no mind. What worried me was that Galloway wasn't speaking up. He was just listening, and every once in a while he'd look at that snip of a girl.

"She will be sixteen next month, and many a girl is wed before the time. Black Fetchen has seen her and has told me he means to have her ... in fact, he had come tonight to take her, but you stopped him before he reached us."

"Sorry," I told him, "but we've got to travel fast,

and we may have a shooting fight with those Fetchens before we get out of Tennessee. They don't shape up to be a forgiving lot."

"You have horses?"

"Well, no. We sold them back in Missouri to pay up what Pa owed hereabouts. We figured to join up with a freight outfit we once worked with, and get west to New Mexico. There's Sacketts out there where we could get some horses until time we could pay for them."

"Suppose I provide the horses? Or rather, suppose Judith does? She owns six head of mighty fine horses, and where she goes, they go."

"No," I said.

"You have seen Fetchen. Would you leave a young girl to him?"

He had me there. I wouldn't leave a yeller hound dog to that man. He was big, and fierce-looking for all he was so handsome, but he looked to me like a horse- and wife-beater, and I'd met up with a few.

"The townsfolk wouldn't stand for that," I said.

"They are afraid of him. As for that, he says he wishes to marry Judith. As far as the town goes, we are movers. We don't belong to the town."

It wasn't going to be easy for us, even without a girl to care for. We would have to hunt for what we ate, sleep out in the open, dodge Indians, and make our way through some of the worst possible country. If we tied on with a freight outfit we would be with rough men, in a rough life. Traveling like that, a girl would invite trouble, and it appeared we would have a-plenty without that.

"Sorry," I said.

"There is one other thing," Costello said. "I am prepared to give each of you a fine saddle horse and a hundred dollars each to defray expenses on the way west."

"We'll do it," Galloway said.

"Now, see here," I started to protest, but they were no longer listening. I have to admit that he'd knocked my arguments into a cocked hat by putting up horses and money. With horses, we could ride right on through, not having to tie up with anybody, and the money would pay for what we needed. Rustling grub for ourselves wouldn't amount to much. But I still didn't like it. I didn't figure to play nursemaid to any girl.

"The horses are saddled and ready. Judith will ride one of her own, and her gear will be on another. And there will be four pack horses if you want to use them as such."

"Look," I said. "That girl will be trouble enough, but you said those horses of hers were breeding stock. Aside from the geldings you'll be giving us, we'll have a stallion and five mares, and that's trouble in anybody's country."

"The stallion is a pet. Judith has almost hand-fed it since it was a colt."

"Ma'am," I turned on her. "That stallion will get itself killed out yonder. Stallions, wild stock, will come for miles to fight him, and some of them are holy terrors."

"You don't have to worry about Ram," she replied. "He can take care of himself."

"This here girl," I argued, "she couldn't stand up to it. West of the river there ain't a hotel this side of the Rockies fit for a lady, and we figure to sleep under the stars. There'll be dust storms and rainstorms, hail the like of which you never saw; and talk about thunder and lightning..."

Costello was smiling at me. "Mr. Sackett, you seem to forget to whom you are talking. We are of the Irish horse-traders. I doubt if Judith has slept under a roof a dozen times in her life, other than the roof of a caravan. She has lived in the saddle since she could walk, and will ride as well as either of you."

Well, that finished me off. Ride as well as me? Or Galloway? That was crazy.

"Look," I said to Galloway, "we can't take no girl."

"Where else are we going to get horses and an outfit?" he interrupted.

He was following Costello out the back way, and there were eight horses, saddled, packed and ready, standing under the poplars. And eight finer animals you never did see. Nobody ever lived who was a finer judge of horseflesh than those Irish traders, and these were their own stock, not for trading purposes.

Right off I guessed them to be Irish hunters with a mite of some other blood. Not one of them was under sixteen hands, and all were splendidly built. The sight of those horses started me weakening almighty fast. I'd never seen such horses, and had never owned anything close to the one he'd picked for me.

"Irish hunters," he said, "with a judicious mixture of mustang blood. We did the mustanging ourselves, or rather, Judith and her father and his brother did. They kept the best of the mustangs for breeding, because we wanted horses with stamina as well as speed, and horses that could live off the country. Believe me, these horses are just what we wanted."

"I'd like to," I said, "but—"

"Fetchen wants these horses," Costello added, "and as they belong to Judith and her father, they would go with her."

"That makes sense," I said. "Now I can see why Fetchen wanted her."

She was standing close by and she hauled off and kicked me on the shin. I yelped, and they all turned to look to me. "Nothing," I said. "It wasn't anything."

"Then you had better ride out of here," Costello said; "but make no mistake. Black Fetchen will come after you. Today was the day Fetchen was coming after Judith."

When I threw a leg over that black horse and settled down into the leather I almost forgave that Judith. This was more horse than I'd ever sat atop of. It made a man proud. No wonder Fetchen wanted that fool girl, if he could get these horses along with her.

We taken out.

Galloway led the way, keeping off the road and following a cow path along the stream.

When we were a mile or so out of town, Galloway edged over close to me. "Flagan, there's one thing you don't know. We got to watch that girl. Her grandpa whispered it to me. She thinks highly of Black Fetchen. She figures he's romantic—dashing and all that. We've got to watch her, or she'll slip off and go back."

Serve her right, I thought.

CHAPTER 2

NOW, THERE'S NO accounting for the notions of womenfolks, particularly when they are sixteen. She came of good people. We Sacketts had dealt with several generations of Irish horse-traders, and found them sharp dealers, but so were we all when it came to swapping horseflesh. There were several thousand of them, stemming from the eight original families, and it was a rare thing when one married outside the clans.

I thought about Black Fetchen. To give the devil his due, I had to admit he was a bold and handsome man, and a fine horseman. He was hell on wheels in any kind of a fight, and his kinfolk were known for their rowdy, bullying ways. Judith had seen Fetchen ride into town, all dressed up and flashy, with a lot of push and swagger to him. She knew nothing of the killings behind him.

We rode a goodly distance, holding to mountain trails. Judith rode along meek as a lamb, and when we stopped I figured she was plumb wore out. She ate like a hungry youngster, but she was polite as all get out, and that should have warned me. After I banked the fire I followed Galloway in going to sleep. Judith curled up in a blanket close by.

The thing is, when a man hunts out on the buffalo grass he gets scary. If he sleeps too sound he can lose his hair, so a body gets fidgety in his sleep, waking up every little while, and ready to come sharp awake if anything goes wrong.

Of a sudden, I woke up. A thin tendril of smoke lifted from the banked fire, and I saw that Judith was gone. I came off the ground, stamped into my boots, and grabbed my pistol belt.

It took me a minute to throw on a saddle and cinch up, then I lit out of there as if the devil was after me. The tracks were plain to see. There was no need to even tell Galloway, because when he awakened he could read the sign as easy as some folks would read a book.

She had led her horse a good hundred yards away from camp, and then she had mounted up, held her pace down for a little bit further, and then started to canter.

At the crossing of the stream the tracks turned toward the highroad, and I went after her. For half a mile I let that black horse run, and he had it in him to go. Then I eased down and took my rope off the saddle and shook out a loop.

She heard me coming and slapped her heels to her horse, and for about two miles we had us the prettiest horse race you ever did see.

The black was too fast for her, and as we closed in I shook out a loop and dabbed it over her shoulders. The black was no roping horse, but when I pulled him in that girl left her horse a-flyin' and busted a pretty little dent in the ground when she hit stern first.

She came off the ground fighting mad, but I'd handled too many fractious steers to be bothered by that, so before she knew what was happening I had her hog-tied and helpless.

For a female youngster, she had quite a surprising flow of language, shocking to a man of my sensibilities, and no doubt to her under other circumstances. She'd been around horse-trading men since she was a baby, and she knew all the words and the right emphasis.

Me, I just sat there a-waiting while she fussed at me. I taken off my hat, pushed back my hair, settled my hat on my head again, all the time seeming to pay her no mind. Then I swung down from the saddle and picked her up and slung her across her horse, head and heels hanging. And then we trotted back to camp.

Galloway was saddled up and ready to ride. "What all you got there, boy?" he called to me.

"Varmint. I ketched it down the road a piece. Better stand shy of it because I figure it'll bite, and might have a touch of hydrophoby, judgin' by sound."

Wary of heels and teeth, I unslung her from the saddle. "Ma'am, I'm of no mind to treat anybody this-away, but you brought it on yourself. Now, if you'll set easy in the saddle I'll unloose you."

Well, she spoke her piece for a few minutes and then she started to cry, and that done it. I unloosed her, helped her into the saddle, and we started off again, with her riding peaceable enough.

"You just wait," she said. "Black Fetchen will come. He will come riding to rescue me."

"You or the horses," I said. "I hear he's a man sets store by good horseflesh."

"He will come."

"You'd best hope he doesn't, ma'am," Galloway

suggested. "We promised to deliver you to your pa in Colorado, and that's what we aim to do."

"If he really loves you," I said, "he'd think nothing of riding to Colorado. Was I in love with a girl, that would seem a short way to go."

"*You!*" she said scornfully. "Who would ever love *you?*"

Could be she was totally right, but I didn't like to think it. Nobody ever did love me that I could remember of, except Ma. Galloway, he was a rare hand with the girls, but not me. I never knew how to sit up and carry on with them, and likely they thought me kind of stupid. Hard to find two brothers more alike and more different than Galloway and me.

Both of us were tall and raw-boned, only he was a right handsome man with a lot of laughter in him, and easy-talking except in times of trouble. Me, I was quieter, and I never smiled much. I was taller than Galloway by an inch, and there was an arrow scar on my cheekbone, picked up on the Staked Plains from a Comanche brave.

We grew up on a sidehill farm in the mountains, fourteen miles from a crossroads store and twenty miles from a town—or what passed as such. We never had much, but there was always meat on the table. Galloway and me, we shot most of our eatin' from the time I was six and him five, and many a time we wouldn't have eaten at all if we couldn't shoot.

Ma, she was a flatland schoolma'am until she up and married Pa and came to live in the mountains, and when we were growing up she tried to teach us how to talk proper. We both came to writing and figuring easy enough, but we talked like the boys around us.

Although when it came right down to it, both of us could talk a mite of language, Galloway more than me.

Mostly Ma was teaching us history. In the South in those days everybody read Sir Walter Scott, and we grew up on *Ivanhoe* and the like. She had a sight of other books, maybe twenty all told, and one time or another we read most of them. After Ma died, me and Galloway batched it alone until we went west.

GALLOWAY AND ME were Injun enough to leave mighty little trail behind us. We held to high country when possible, and we fought shy of traveled roads. Nor did we head for Independence, which was what might have been expected.

We cut across country, leaving the Kentucky border behind, and along Scagg's Creek to Barren River, but just before the Barren joined the Green we cut back, west by a mite south, for Smithland, where the Cumberland joined the Ohio. It did me good to ride along Scaggs' Creek, because the Scaggs it was named for had been a Long Hunter in the same outfit with one of the first of my family to come over the mountains.

We bought our meals from farms along the way, or fixed our own. We crossed the Mississippi a few miles south of St. Louis.

No horses could have been better than those we had. They were fast walkers, good travelers, and always ready for a burst of speed when called upon.

Judith was quiet. Her eyes got bigger and rounder, it seemed to me, and she watched our back trail. She was quick to do what she ought and never complained, which should have been a warning. When she did talk it was to Galloway. To me she never said aye, yes, or no.

"What is it like out there?" she asked him.

"Colorado? It's a pure and lovely land beyond the buffalo grass where the mountains r'ar up to the sky. Snow on 'em the year 'round, and the mountains yonder make our Tennessee hills look like dirt thrown up by a gopher.

"It's a far, wide land with the long grass rippling in the wind like a sea with the sun upon it. A body can ride for weeks and see nothing but prairie and sky... unless it's wild horses or buffalo."

"Are the women pretty?"

"Women? Ma'am, out in that country a body won't see a woman in months, 'less it's some old squaw or an oldish white woman... or maybe a dancing girl in some saloon. Mostly a man just thinks about women, and they all get to look mighty fine after a while. A body forgets how mean and contrary they can be, and he just thinks of them as if they were angels or something."

We saw no sign of Black Fetchen nor any of his lot, yet I'd a notion they were closing in behind us. He didn't look like a man to be beaten, and we had stood him up in his own street, making him lose face where folks would tell of it, and we had taken his girl and the horses he wanted.

There was more to it than that, but we did not know it until later.

From time to time Judith talked some to Galloway, and we heard about her pa and his place in Colorado. Seems he'd left the horse-trading for mustanging, and then drifted west and found himself a ranch in the wildest kind of country. He started breeding horses, but kept on with the mustanging. Judith he'd sent back to be with his family and get some education. Only now he wanted her out there with him.

Now and again some of the family went west and often they drove horses back from his ranch to trade through the South. But now he wanted his daughter, and the stock she would bring with her.

Back of it all there was a thread of something that worried me. Sizing it up, I couldn't find anything that didn't sound just right, but there it was. Call it a hunch if you like, but I had a feeling there was something wrong in Colorado. Galloway maybe felt the same, but he didn't speak of it any more than me.

We camped out on the prairie. It was Indian country, only most of the Indians were quiet about that time. Farmers were moving out on the land, but there were still too many loose riders, outlaws from down in the Nation, and others no better than they should be. This was a stretch of country I never did cotton to, this area between the Mississippi and the real West. It was in these parts that the thieves and outlaws got together.

Not that Galloway or me was worried. We figured to handle most kinds of trouble. Only thing was, we had us a girl to care for...one who would grab hold of a horse any time she saw a chance and head for home...and Black Fetchen.

One night we camped on the Kansas prairie with a moon rising over the far edge of the world and stars a-plenty. We could hear the sound of the wind in the grass and stirring leaves of the cottonwoods under which we had camped. It was a corner maybe half an acre in extent, at a place where a stream curled around a big boulder. There was a flat place behind that boulder where we shaped our camp; here there was a fallen tree, and firewood from dead limbs.

We built up a small fire, and after we'd eaten our beef and beans we sat about and sang a few of the old songs, the mountain songs, some of them reaching back to the time when our folks came across the water from Wales.

Judith was singing, too, and a clear, fine voice she had, better than either of us. We liked to sing, but weren't much account.

The horses moved in close, liking the fire and the voices. It was a mighty fine evening. After Judith turned in, Galloway did likewise. I had the first watch. Taking up my rifle, I prowled around outside the trees of the small woods.

Second time around I pulled up short over on the west side. Something was moving out yonder in the dark, and I squatted down to listen, closer to the ground, to hear the rustle of the grass.

Something was coming slow . . . something hurt, by the sound of it. The sound was a slow, dragging movement, and a time or two I heard a faint groan. But I made no move, for I was trusting no such sound.

After a bit, I made him out, a crawling man, not many yards off. Carefully, I looked all around at the night, but I saw nothing.

I slipped back to camp. "Galloway," I whispered, "there's a man out yonder, sounds to be hurt bad. I'm going to bring him in."

"You go ahead. I'll stand by."

If it was a trick, somebody would wish it wasn't. I

walked out there, spotted the man again, and spoke to him quiet-like, so's my voice wouldn't carry.

"What's the trouble, *amigo*?"

The crawling stopped, and for a moment there was silence. Then the voice came, low, conversational. "I've caught a bad one. Figured I glimpsed a fire."

"You bein' sought after?"

"Likely."

Well, I went up to him then and picked him up and packed him into camp. He was a man of forty or so, with a long narrow face and a black mustache streaked with gray. He had caught a bad one through the body and he looked mighty peaked. The slug had gone on through, for he was holed on both sides. Whilst I set to, plugging him up, Galloway he moved out to keep an eye on the prairie.

Judith, she woke up and set to making some hot broth, and by the time I'd patched him up she was about ready with it. I figured he'd lost blood, so I mixed up some salt water and had him drink that. We had been doing that for lost blood for years back, and it seemed to help.

He was game, I'll say that for him. Whilst Judith fed soup into him, I had a look at his foot.

"Wagon tongue fell on it," he said. "Rider jumped his horse into camp and knocked the wagon tongue over and she hit me on the instep."

His foot was badly swollen, and I had to cut the boot off. He stared at me between swallows of soup. "Look at that now!" he worried. "Best pair of boots I ever did have! Bought 'em a month back in Fort Worth."

"You a Texan?"

"Not reg'lar. I'm an Arkansawyer. I been cookin' for a cow outfit trailin' stock up from the Nueces country. Last evenin' a man stopped by our wagon for a bite of grub. He was a lean, dark, thin sort of man with narrow eyes. He was rough-dressed, but he didn't look western." He glanced up, suddenly wary. "Fact is, he talked somewhat like you boys."

"Don't be troubled. There's no kin of ours about here."

"He wore a sort of red sash and carried a rifle like he was born to it—"

"Colby Rafin!" Judith said.

"You called it, I didn't," I said.

"Anyway, he et and then rode off. About the time we'd been an hour abed, they come a-hellin' out of the night. Must've been a dozen of them or twenty. They come chargin' through camp, a-shootin' and a-yellin' and they drove off our herd, drove them to hell off down the country."

"You'd better catch some rest. You look done in."

He looked straight at me. "I ain't a-gonna make it, *amigo*, an' you know it."

Judith, she looked at me, all white and funny, but I said to him, "You got anybody you want us to tell?"

"I got no kin. Bald-Knobbers killed them all, a long time back. Down Texas way my boss was Evan Hawkes, a fine man. He lost a sight out there this night—his herd, his outfit, and his boy."

"Boy?"

"Youngster . . . mebbe thirteen. He had been beggin' the boss to let him ride north with us instead of on the cars. We were to meet Hawkes in Dodge."

"Are you sure about the boy?"

"Seen him fall. A man shot right into him, rode over him. If any of our outfit got away it was one of the boys on night herd."

He sat quiet for a while, and I stole a glance at Judith. She was looking almighty serious, and she had to realize that bunch of raiders that stole the herd and killed the boy had been the Fetchen outfit. Colby Rafin was never far from Black.

"They know they got you?"

"Figured it. They knew I was knocked down by the wagon tongue, and then one of them shot into me as he jumped his horse over."

As carefully as I could, I was easing the biggest sticks away from the fire so it would burn down fast. One thing was sure. That Fetchen outfit had followed us west. But this was no place or time to have a run-in with them.

The man opened his eyes after a bit and looked at Judith. "Ma'am? In my shirt pocket I got a gold locket. Ain't much, mebbe, but my ma wore it her life long, and her ma before her. I'd take it kindly, if you'd have it as a present."

"Yes . . . thank you."

"You got tender hands, ma'am, mighty gentle hands. Been a long time since a woman touched me . . . gentlelike. It's a fine thing to remember, ma'am."

I'd moved off to the edge of the darkness, listening for trouble riding our way, but I could faintly hear him still talking. "That tall man here," he said, "he carries the look of an eagle. He'll make tracks in the land, ma'am. You better latch onto him, ma'am, if you ain't spoke for. His kind run mighty scarce."

After a moment, he opened his eyes again. "You knowed that man come to my camp?"

"Colby Rafin." She was silent for a moment, and then she said, "They were looking for us, I think."

"For *him*?" he half-lifted a hand toward me. "They're crazy!"

Galloway came in out of the dark, and I whispered to him about Rafin and how the herd was lost.

"It's like them—outlaws always. Now they've turned cattle thieves."

Neither one of us had much to say, because we were both thinking the same thing. The Fetchens had come west, all right, and they had come a-hunting us. The trouble was they had us outnumbered by a good bit, and running off this herd showed they'd taken the full step from being rowdies and trouble makers to becoming genuine outlaws. From now on it would be a fight to the death against an outfit that would stop at nothing...and us with a girl to watch out for.

That Colorado ranch began to look mighty far away, and I was cursing the hour when I first saw Costello or Judith.

Not that we minded a fight. We Sacketts never had much time for anything else. If we weren't fighting for our country we were fighting men who still believed in rule by the gun, and no Sackett I ever heard of had ever drawn a gun on a man except in self-defense, or in defense of his country or his honor.

Right then I was glad Galloway stood beside me. Nobody ever needed an army when they had Galloway, and maybe one other Sackett...it didn't make much difference which one.

CHAPTER 3

WE HIT TRAIL before sunup, keeping off the skyline as much as possible, but always moving westward, riding sidewise in the saddle so as we could look all around, Galloway facing one way, me the other.

There was a look to the sky that spelled a weather change, but we didn't pay it no mind, figuring only to get distance behind us.

Short of noon a man came up from the south riding a paint pony and hazing about thirty head of cattle. When he put eyes on us he rode his pony around the cattle and came up to us, keeping his Winchester handy and studying us careful-like.

"You pass anybody back yonder? I'm huntin' my outfit."

The brand on his pony and those cattle spelled the story for me—a Half-Box H. "You got stampeded a while back," I said, "and one of your outfit died in our camp."

"Which one?"

"Said he was the cook. Come to think on it, he never did give us his name. Said he rode for Evan Hawkes, and he told us Hawkes's boy got killed in the stampede."

The man's face showed shock. "The boy's dead? That'll go hard on the boss. He set store by the lad."

Me, I curled one leg around the pommel and pushed my hat back. "Mister, looks to me like your herd was scattered hell to breakfast. We covered some miles back yonder and seen nobody. What you figure to do?"

"Drive these cattle into Dodge an' report to Evan Hawkes. All I can do."

He told me his name was Briggs. "Might as well ride with us," I said to him. "It's one more gun for each of us."

"What's that mean?"

"That was James Black Fetchen's outfit from Tennessee who jumped your herd. They're hunting us. If we meet up with them there'll be shooting, and you can lay to it that if they see you're alive they'll be after you, too."

"I'll ride along," he said.

During the next hour we picked up thirteen head of scattered cattle wearing the Hawkes brand. By nightfall we had close to fifty head more. We'd scarcely made camp when we were hailed out of the night...in those days no man in his right mind rode up to a strange camp without giving them a call.

"That'll be Ladder Walker," Briggs said. "I know the voice."

Walker was an extra tall, extra lean man, which was why they called him Ladder. He was driving six head of steers, and he had a lump on his skull and a grouch over what happened. "You catch sight of any of that bunch?" he asked Briggs. "All I ask is a sight down a gun barrel at them."

"You stand easy, friend," Galloway said. "That's a

mean outfit. If they can help it you'll not get a shooting chance."

The upshot of it was that of the herd of fifteen hundred cattle the Half-Box H sent up the trail, we drove into Dodge with a hundred and twenty, picked up along the way. No doubt a few more riders could have combed twice that number out of the breaks along the creeks and the coulees, scattered stuff left behind from the stampede.

Now, we Sacketts carried a name known in Dodge. Tyrel, Orrin, and some of the others had come into Dodge long before, Tyrel and Orrin being there when the town was mighty young. They were the first Sacketts to go west to settle. Their pa had come west earlier than that, riding and trapping fur along with Bridger, Carson, and Joe Meek. He'd never come back from his last trip, so it was always figured that some Blackfoot had raised his hair, back up in Montana. We'd heard the story as youngsters, but had never known any of that branch of the family until we bumped into Tyrel and Orrin down in the Mogollon, where they'd gone to lend a fighting hand to their brother Tell.

Knowing that if the other riders had come through the stampede alive, they would head for Hawkes at his hotel, we went along with Walker and Briggs. Three other riders had already come in, which left seven missing.

Evan Hawkes was a tall, broad-shouldered but spare-built man with darkish red hair. The build of him and the way he combed his hair reminded a body of Andy Jackson, and he had a pair of gray eyes that advised a man he'd make a better friend than an enemy.

"They've got that herd to sell," Hawkes said, "and we will be there when they try. I'll pass the word around."

"Mr. Hawkes," I said, "you got to remember that Fetchen is no fool. From all I hear, he's mighty shrewd, as well as mean. He may not sell that herd at all."

"What do you mean?"

"From what I've seen of those we gathered, you had quite a bit of young breeding stock. Fetchen could push that herd west into Wyoming, peddle the steers to Indians or the army or some beef contractor. Then he could use the young stuff to start his own outfit."

"You believe he has come west to stay?"

"I've been wondering about that. It doesn't seem reasonable they'd all come west without reason. I figure something happened back there after we left."

Judith had been standing by getting madder by the minute, and now she let go at all of us. "You've no right to suppose anything of the kind! And you've no evidence that Black Fetchen stole that herd!"

Hawkes looked at her, kind of surprised. "It seems to be there's a difference of opinion among you."

"The little lady doesn't think Black is all that mean," Galloway said.

"I certainly do not!"

"The way we figure it," Galloway went on, "what happened to you is mostly our fault. You see, the Fetchens came west hunting us. Black wants the little lady here, and he wants her horses, some of the finest breeding stock you ever did see. Back there in Tazewell—"

"Tennessee?" said Hawkes. "I know it well. I'm from Kentucky."

"Well, we had a run-in with those boys, sort of calmed 'em down when they were about to show their muscle. They been used to having things their own way."

Leaving Hawkes with his riders, the three of us went downstairs to the dining room. Judith had her nose up, and her cheeks were flushed and angry. When we'd found seats at a table she said, "You have no right to talk that way about Mr. Fetchen. He is an honorable man."

"I hope so," Galloway commented, "because if he wasn't, and you went to him, you'd be in a kind of a fix, wouldn't you? This far from home, and all."

We ordered, and then she started to look around some, and so did we. Neither me nor Galloway had been to many towns. We had seen Santa Fe, Dodge, Abilene, and Sedalia, Missouri, and both of us liked to see folks around us.

There were cattle buyers, land speculators, officers from the army post, cattle drivers, gamblers and such like around. All of them were dressed to the nines, and were looking almighty fancy. Galloway and me had taken time before coming in to brush up a little, but somehow we didn't shape up like these folks. We looked like a pair of mountain boys still, and it shamed me. As soon as we got some money, I thought, we'd buy us some proper clothes.

"You been to big towns, Judith?" Galloway asked her.

"I have been to Atlanta and Nashville, and to New Orleans, Mobile, and Louisville... oh, lots of towns. My folks traded in all of them."

I'd had no idea she was such a traveled girl, but it followed. The Irish traders were folks that got about a good bit. There for a few minutes she forgot all about Black Fetchen and took to telling us about the big towns, and believe me, we listened to every word.

The restaurant door opened while she was talking and I turned my head. It was Black Fetchen.

He had surely changed. He wore a brand-new black broadcloth suit, a white shirt, and black tie. His boots were polished like all get out, and he carried a new black hat in his hand. His hair was all slicked down with bear grease or the like, and I'll have to admit he was a handsome sight. Tory came in behind him, with Colby Rafin and another one of their outfit known as Ira Landon.

Fetchen walked right over to our table, the others sitting down across the room with their backs to us.

"Why, Judith! How nice to see you!" Then he turned to me and said, "I hope you boys carry no grudge against us. We're certainly not about to hunt trouble with you. Back there we were just a-funnin'— we didn't mean no trouble."

Judith was beaming. It made me mad to see so much sparkle in her eyes over such a no-account rascal. Me, I didn't buy that flannel-mouth talk, and he knew it. All the time he was talking I could just see the taunting in his eyes; but Judith, she was all excited and happy.

"Why, sure!" Galloway was the smooth-talking one of the two of us. "Why don't you pull up a chair and set? We'd enjoy talking a while. Maybe you could tell us something about a herd of cattle somebody stampeded and run off back down the trail."

Judith's face went white and her lips tightened up. She was both mad and scared . . . scared something was going to happen.

"Cattle? Since when did you two go into the cattle business?"

"They weren't our cattle," Galloway said as smooth as silk. "They belong to a friend of ours, name of Evan Hawkes . . . a good man. His herd was stampeded by some rustlers . . . murderers, too, because they killed his boy, and some of his men."

Fetchen never batted an eye. Oh, he was a coo' one! He just smiled and said, "Come to think of it, we did see a few stray cattle. We even drove in half a dozen and turned them over to the marshal."

He pulled back a chair and sat down, easy as you please. "As a matter of fact, I didn't just come over to say howdy to some old friends from the home state. I came over to see Judith. Seems you boys aren't going to give me a chance to be alone with her, so I'll have to speak my piece right here before all of you."

Judith's eyes were shining and her lips were parted. I didn't like it to see her getting so flustered. Before I could say anything, Black Fetchen, still smiling like the cat sizing up the canary, says, "Judith, will you marry me?"

And before either of us can say aye, yes, or no, she ups and says, "Yes, James—yes, I will!"

"I'm honored, ma'am, right honored." Then he says, "I don't think it is really the right thing for a man's betrothed to be spending so much time with two men, single men who are no kin to her, so I've taken a room for you here at the hotel until we're married."

We sat there, caught flat-footed. This here was something we hadn't expected, nor did we know what to do. It was Galloway who spoke first. "That's right nice, Black," he said, "but her grandpa asked us most particular to take her to her pa in Colorado. Now, it ain't so many miles from here, so why don't you two figure on being married there where her pa can attend? After all, she's his only daughter."

Fetchen never stopped smiling. "Mr. Sackett, I wouldn't expect you to understand, but I am in love. I do not want to wait."

"Nor do I!" Judith said. "We can be married right here in Dodge."

Galloway didn't show any ire, even if he felt it. He just said, "It would be nice if your pa knew, Judith. Do you care so little for him?"

That got to her, and she sobered up, suddenly so serious I thought she might cry.

"It's a noble sacrament," I said, "and a rare thing for a man to see his daughter wedded to the man of her choice."

She looked up at Fetchen. "James...maybe we should wait. After all, it isn't very far."

Black's lips tightened and his eyes squinted just a mite. I'd always heard he carried a fearful temper, liable to burst out whenever he was thwarted, and it was edging toward the surface now. Maybe if she saw him in a rage it would help. Me and Galloway must have been thinking the same thing. Only trouble was,

I up and made a damn fool of myself. I said the wrong thing.

"Besides," I said, "Judith is only a youngster. She's not old enough to marry."

Judith ran up her flag and let go with all her guns, she was that mad. "Flagan Sackett, you wouldn't know a woman if you saw one! I am so old enough! We'll just show you how old I am! James, if you're ready we can be married tomorrow morning."

Fetchen straightened up. Of course, that was all he wanted all the time. He threw me a look that was what a body might call triumphant. "I would be honored, Judith. If you'll come with me I'll show you to your room."

Judith got up and turned her back squarely to me. I started to speak, but what could I say?

Fetchen turned and looked back at us. "Gentlemen, I'll send a couple of the boys over for my fiancée's clothing and her horses—all of them."

"What do you mean, all of them?"

"I mean those you two have been riding. They are Costello horses."

"For which we have a bill of sale," I said calmly, but I was fighting mad underneath.

"That's right, James," Judith said. "Those horses belong to them."

"We will look into that a bit further," Fetchen replied. "I do not think those bills of sale, as you call them, will stand up in court."

They walked away together and left us sitting there, and of a sudden I no longer had any appetite. Youngster she might be, but I had no wish to see any girl in the hands of Black Fetchen.

"Galloway, we can't let him do it. We got to stop him."

"You tell me how. She wants to marry him, and we can't prove a thing against him."

"Do you suppose he really drove in some Half-Box H cattle?"

"I'd lay a bet on it. Oh, he's a smart one! If anybody saw him with cattle of that brand, he's now got himself an alibi. Also, it makes him look good with the other cattlemen around."

"What's he see in her, do you suppose?"

Galloway, he gave me an odd look. "Why, you damn' fool, that's a right pretty little girl. Shapes up like pretty much of a woman. And in case you forget, Ma was no older when she married Pa."

He was right, only I didn't like to admit it. That Judith seemed like a youngster... all those freckles and everything. Only when I started reminding myself of that everything, I got to remembering that what Galloway had been saying was right. She was nigh to being a woman, even if she wasn't one yet... in my judgment, anyway.

"Flagan, what are we going to do?"

Upshot of it was, we went to see the marshal, Wyatt Earp, but he said he could do nothing. "Sorry, boys." He was kind of abrupt. "Mr. Fetchen brought in some of the Hawkes cattle and turned them over at the corral. That certainly doesn't make him seem a thief. Also, there seems to be no evidence that he had anything to do with running off the herd. As for the girl, she is old enough to marry, and she wants to marry him. I am afraid I can do nothing."

Bat Masterson was sheriff of Ford County, and we

went next to see him. He was a right handsome young man about twenty-four or -five years old, wearing a dark suit and black derby hat. You had to be quite a man to wear a hard hat in those days; it was such a temptation for some half-drunk cowpoke to try to shoot it off your head. Bat's didn't carry any bullet marks that I could see.

He listened to what we had to say, then shook his head. "Sorry, boys, there's nothing I can do. The girl has a right to marry, and there's no warrant out for any of that crowd." He paused a minute. "Although I've got some good ideas of my own."

"Anything we can tie to?" Galloway asked.

"No. But a man who rode in the other day said he saw the Fetchen outfit driving about fifty head of cattle. They didn't turn in but half a dozen scrubs."

"Ain't that evidence?"

"Not exactly. Rufe was drunk when he saw them. Now, I'd take his word for how many head he saw, drunk or sober—Rufe's an old cowhand. But I doubt if you could make it stick in a court of law."

"What can we do?"

Masterson tipped back in his chair and considered the question. "I'd say you might wire her grandfather. Get authority from him to hold up the wedding. And wire her father too."

Well now. Neither one of us had even thought of that, because we'd had no truck with telegraph wires. We'd heard about them, and seen the wires along the railroad tracks, but the idea of sending a message to Costello never occurred to us.

"If you'd write us out a message, we'd be obliged,"

I said, "and you'd be helping a mighty nice girl from a bad marriage."

So Bat taken up a pen and scratched out the message. I had figured a body would have to write it some special way, but nothing of the kind.

He wrote it out, slick as you please: *Fetchen here. Proposed marriage, Judith accepted. Wire authority to stop marriage.*

"If we get a wire from Costello saying he refuses permission," Masterson said, "I'll stop it."

When we had sent the message we stood on the boardwalk in front of the Long Branch and considered the situation. Of a sudden, Galloway had an idea. "This sort of town," he said thoughtfully, "I wonder how many preachers it's got?"

"Three, four, maybe."

He was looking at me kind of funny-like and I began to read the sign of what he was thinking. "Now, that there," I said, "is what comes of contemplating. I think we better ask around."

"Ladder Walker, Harry Briggs, and them," Galloway said, "they owe us a favor, and Hawkes told me this morning that they were holding what cattle they'd found about fifteen miles north of here. I figure one of those boys should talk to a preacher. Ladder, f'r instance. If he was dyin' he would surely want a preacher."

About that time Bat came walking down the street headed for the Long Branch, carrying the cane from which he had taken his name.

"Mr. Masterson," I said, "how many preachers in Dodge?"

Bat's eyes started to twinkle. "You're lucky," he

said. "They're all out of town but one." And then he added, "Don't forget the justice of the peace."

Galloway, he rounded up his horse and headed for the camp on the run to set up the deal at that end. Me, I mounted up, taken my horse out of town for a good run, and brought him back into town and up to the preacher's house, all lathered up.

"Reverend," I said, "there's a man in a bad way out to a cow camp, and he's bound to make his peace with the Lord. Will you ride out to him?"

Now, that sky pilot was a right fine gentlemen who put down his coffee cup, wiped his mouth, and harnessed his team. I hooked up the traces whilst he slipped into his coat. In less time than it takes to tell about it, he was ready.

"One more thing," I said, "he wishes to make a will, and he said the man he wanted to draw it up for him was the justice of the peace. Said he didn't know whether the J.P. was a proper lawyer or not, but he doesn't care. He believes he's an honest man."

Well, with me riding alongside the buckboard we made it to the J.P.'s house and he was quick enough to go. It looked like a good fee and he was ready. They went dusting out of town in that buckboard, riding on their mission of mercy, and I tailed behind them.

When we rode up to the camp it was nothing but a corral, a spring, and a sod shanty that was half dugout. Ladder Walker was a-lying on his back with a blanket pulled up over him, and he looked sicker than anybody I ever did see. Those others cowpokes were all standing around with their hats off, talking in low voices.

As soon as all was going well, Galloway and me

slipped out and rode back to Dodge. It looked to me as if Ladder was shaping up to one of the longest death scenes in history.

Although the preacher said he was a Protestant, and confession was not necessary, Ladder couldn't miss a chance like that. So he started off by confessing to several hours of the most lurid sinning a body ever heard tell of. He had confessed to all he had done, which was a-plenty, all he had wanted to do, which was a sight more, and then he began inventing sins the like of which you never heard. I'll say one thing for him. He had him an audience right from the word go. They never even looked up when we went out.

"You can bet your bottom dollar," Galloway said, "they'll never get out of there tonight."

The thing that worried us, suppose one of those sky pilots who had been out of town should return?

Only they didn't.

CHAPTER 4

GALLOWAY AND ME, we rode up to the hitch rail in front of the Lady Gay and stepped down from our saddles. We were hungry and tired, and it was coming on to storm. As we stood on the boardwalk sizing up the town, lightning flashed out over the prairie.

"Looks to be a gully-washer," Galloway said. "I've been watching those clouds all the way in."

"You go ahead. I'll put up the horses." I hesitated there a moment, then added, "You might look to see if Judith has switched her gear over to that room Fetchen got for her."

The street was empty. I could hear boots on the walk down half a block or so, but could see nobody. The saloons were all lit up, going full blast, but there were few horses or rigs around because of the storm a-coming.

Leading both horses, I walked across the street and went on down to the livery stable. On the corner I held up for a moment, watching a tumbleweed rolling down the street and thinking of that Judith. Of all the contrary, ornery, freckle-faced...Trouble was, I missed her.

There was a lantern over the livery stable door, the flame sputtering in the wind. Nobody was around, so I led the horses back to their stalls and tied them, then went up a ladder into the loft and forked hay down to both of them. I was finishing off the last fork of hay when I thought I heard a step down below, a slow, careful step.

The loft where I was covered the whole top of the barn, and there were three ladders up to it—three that I'd seen, two on one side, one on the other. Come to think of it, there should be a fourth ladder, but if there was it must come down in an empty stall at the back of the barn where the liveryman hung spare bits of harness, tools, and suchlike.

All the time I was thinking of that, I was listening. Had somebody followed me in? Or was it some drunk hunting a place to sleep away from the storm? Or maybe somebody coming to get his horse?

The way those footsteps sounded made me think it was surely not one of the last two. My Winchester was down there beside my saddle and my slicker, waiting to be picked up before I went to the hotel. Likely that man down there had seen them and was just a-playing 'possum, waiting for me to come down and pick them up. And whatever lead he could throw at me.

Now, some folks might think me a suspicious man, and they'd be right. Many's the time I've suspected something when I was wrong; but there were other times I'd been right, and so I was still among the living.

Slipping the rawhide thong off the hammer of my six-shooter, I put that pitchfork down as easy as I could. Then I straightened up to listen. If he knew I was up here I'd best stir around a mite, or he'd be suspicious.

Many a cowpoke slept in a livery stable, and that was the idea I hoped to give him. What I figured on was getting him to come up that ladder, instead of him catching me coming down.

All the same, I started figuring. Seems to me a man can most usually take time to contemplate, and if he does it will save him a lot of riding and a lot of headaches.

Now, suppose I was down there and wanted to shoot a man on one of those ladders? Where would I take my stand so's I could watch all three to once?

It didn't leave much choice. Two ladders were on one side of the loft, opposite to him; the other ladder he knew of was on his side of the loft, up toward the front. If the man below wanted to keep all of them under cover, he had to be somewhere on the right side of the stable, toward the rear. If there was another ladder, which went up from that empty stall, one long unused, it would be behind the watcher.

If I made a try at coming down any one of the three ladders now, I'd be climbing down with my back to the gunman—if that was what he was.

The first thing I did was to sit down on some hay. I fluffed some of it around as if I was shaping a bed, and not being careful about noise; then I took off my boots and dropped them on the floor. After that I picked them up, tied them together with a piggin string, and slung them around my neck. Then, just as carefully as I could, I stood up in my sock feet. The floor was solid and not likely to squeak, so I eased across, soundlessly as I was able. And I waited.

There was not a sound from below. Near me was a bin full of corn, unshelled corn waiting to be fed to some of the local horses. I tossed an ear of that corn over to where I had taken off my boots, and it hit the boards near the hay. I hoped he would believe I'd dropped something, or something had slipped from my pockets. Then I eased along the side of the loft till I was over that empty stall. Sure enough, there was an opening there, with a ladder leading down.

It was well back in the stall and in a dark corner. The chances were that few of the stable's customers had any idea that this ladder was there.

Crouching by the opening, I listened, but heard no sound. I drew my Colt and carefully lowered my head until I could see into the lower level. . . . Nothing.

Swinging my feet down, my Colt gripped in my right hand, I felt for the first rung of the ladder, found it, and then the second. Lowering myself down, clinging to the ladder, I searched for him but could see nothing. I came down a step further, and heard a shout.

"Got you, damn it!" A gun blasted not over thirty feet away. The bullet smashed into the frame of the ladder, stabbing my face with splinters, and I fired in return, my bullet going slightly above and left of the flash. I realized even as I fired that my shot was too high, and I triggered a second shot lower down.

At the same instant I let go and dropped, landing on the balls of my feet, but I tumbled forward with a crash of harness and a breaking chair; and then came the bellow of a gun, almost within inches of me. Rolling over, I fired again.

Outside I heard a shout, heard running feet, and I sprang up. Down the far side of the stalls near the horses a man was staggering. He was bent far over, clutching at his stomach, and even as I saw him he stumbled forward and fell on his face.

The running feet were coming nearer.

Ducking out the back door of the barn, I slid between the corral bars and, still in my sock feet, ran lightly along the area back of the buildings until I was close to the hotel. I paused for just a moment and got my boots on, and then I went up the back stairs of the hotel, and along the hall.

Several heads appeared from doorways, and one of them was Judith's. She saw me, and for a moment I thought I saw relief on her face. "Flagan, what is it? What's happened?" she asked.

"Some drunken cowhand," I said. "You've got to expect that in Dodge."

She still stood there in the door of her room. She was fully dressed, although it was very late. "I will be married tomorrow," she said, almost tentatively.

"I wish you luck."

"You don't really mean that."

"No, ma'am, I don't. I think you're doing the wrong thing, and I know it isn't what your grandpa wanted . . . nor your pa, either, I'm thinking."

"Mr. Fetchen is a fine man. You'll see."

We heard voices from down below, and then boots on the stairs. Colby Rafin was suddenly there, Black Fetchen behind him, with Norton Vance and Burr Fetchen coming up in the rear.

"There he is!" Colby yelled.

He grabbed for his gun, but I had him covered. Back in Tennessee those boys never had to work at a fast draw, and the way that gun came into my hand stopped them cold.

"I don't know what you boys are looking for," I said, "but I don't like being crowded."

"You killed Tory!" Burr shouted.

Before I could open my mouth to speak, Judith said, "How could he? He's been standing here talking to me!"

That stopped them, and for the moment nobody thought to ask how long I'd been there. After that moment they never got the chance, because the marshal pushed by them.

"What happened down there?" he asked me.

"Sounded like some shooting. These boys say Tory Fetchen got killed."

Just then Bat Masterson came up the steps. "Everything all right, Wyatt?" Then he saw me standing there at Judith's door. "Oh, hello, Sackett."

Earp turned on him. "Do you know this man, Bat?"

"Yes, I do. He brought Evan Hawkes's cattle in, and helped round up some strays. He's a friend of mine."

Earp glanced down at my boots. "Mind if I look at your boots? The man who did that shooting had to come along behind the buildings. It's muddy there."

I lifted one boot after the other. Both were as slick as though they'd never stepped on anything but a board floor.

Colby Rafin was sore. He simply couldn't believe it. "He's lyin'!" he shouted. "It had to be him! Why, Tory was—"

"Tory was what?" Masterson demanded. "Laying for him? Was that it?"

It was Burr who spoke up. "Nothin' like that," he protested, "Tory just went after his horse."

"At this hour?" Earp asked. "You mean he was riding out of town this late, with a storm brewing?"

"Sure," Burr replied easily. "He was riding out to join some of our outfit."

"Gentlemen," Earp said coldly, "before we ask any further questions or you give any more answers, let me tell you something. Your friend Tory Fetchen wore new boots, boots with a very distinctive heel pattern. He left enough tracks down there at the stable for a man who was doing a lot of waiting, a man crouched down or standing beside one of the support posts. From those tracks, I'd say he was waiting for somebody and trying to keep out of sight. He was either nervous or he waited a long time. In any case, his gun was fired twice, and he was hit twice . . . looked to me like a third shot cut the top of his coat's shoulder. We've no case against the man who shot him. Both men were armed, both were shooting. It's nothing but a matter of clearing up the details."

"Just a question, gentlemen," Masterson said. "You came up here, apparently headed for Sackett's room. Did you have some idea of finishing the job Tory tried to do?"

"Aw, it was nothing like that!" Burr Fetchen waved a careless hand. "Only we had some trouble back in Tennessee, and—"

"Then I suggest you go back to Tennessee and settle it," Earp interrupted. "I won't have shooting in Dodge."

"I give you my word, Marshal," I said, "I won't shoot unless I'm shot at."

"That's fair enough, Sackett. All right, you boys go about your business. If there's any more trouble I'll lock you up."

When they had gone, I said, "Judith, I'm sorry I got you into this."

"You were standing here with me!" she insisted. "Why, I must have come out of my door just as those shots died away."

She had been quick enough. The trouble is that a running man can cover a good distance, and folks just never calculate time as well as they think. In any event, she had stopped a nasty shooting in a crowded place where she or others might have been hurt, and for that much I was glad.

"They didn't tell the truth," she said then. "Tory wasn't going out of town. He was going to have dinner with James and me."

"Late for dinner, isn't it?"

"James said he would be busy. He wanted to eat late. He said the restaurant would not be so crowded."

"I'd better go," I said. I backed off a few steps. "If you change your mind, you can always come back and join us. We'll take you on to your pa."

She smiled a little. "Flagan, I shall not change my mind. I love James, and he loves me."

"You keep telling yourself that. Maybe after a while you'll come to believe it," I said.

"Flagan Sackett, I—"

Maybe it isn't right for a gentleman to walk away whilst a lady is talking, but I did. This was an argument where I was going to have the last word, anyway...when they found no preacher in town.

There was a corner at the head of the stairs where a body couldn't be seen from above or below, and I stopped there long enough to reload my gun.

Galloway was sitting in the lobby holding a newspaper. He looked up at me, a kind of quizzical look in his eyes. "Hear there was a shooting over to the livery," he said.

"Sounded like it," I agreed, and sat down beside him. In a low tone I added, "That Tory laid for me whilst I was putting hay down the chute. He come close to hangin' up my scalp."

"Yeah, and you better start pullin' slivers out of your face. The light's brighter down here than in that hallway upstairs."

Something had been bothering my face for several minutes, but I'd been too keyed up and too busy talking to notice it much. Gingerly, I put my hand up and touched the end of a pine sliver off that post. Two or three of them I pulled out right there, getting them with my fingers, but there were some others.

We walked down the street to the Peacock, just to look around, and Bat was there. He came over to us, glanced at the side of my face and smiled a little. "I hope you had time to change your socks," he said. "A man can catch cold with wet, muddy socks on."

Me, I had to grin. "Nothing gets by you, does it?"

"I saw you go into the barn. I also saw Tory follow you. I saw the track of a sock foot just back of the barn. I kicked straw over it."

"Thanks."

"When I take to a man, I stand by him. I have reason to believe that you're honest. I have reason to believe the Fetchens are not."

But, no matter how good things looked right at that moment, I was worried. Black Fetchen was not one to take Tory's shooting lying down, and no matter what anybody said, he would lay it to me or Galloway. I'd had no idea of killing anybody; only when a man comes laying for you, what can you do? The worst of it was, he'd outguessed me. All the time, he knew about that other door from the loft, and he figured rightly that I'd find it and use it. That he missed me at all was pure accident. I'd been mostly in the dark or he'd have hit me sure, and he'd been shooting to kill.

After a bit Galloway and me went back to the hotel and crawled into bed. But I slept with a Colt at my hand, and I know Galloway did, too.

Tomorrow two things would happen, both of them likely to bring grief and trouble. First would be Tory's funeral, and second would be when they tried to find somebody to marry Judith and Black Fetchen.

Anybody could read a funeral sermon, but it took a Justice of the Peace or an ordained minister to marry somebody.

CHAPTER 5

THERE WAS A light rain falling when we went down to the restaurant for breakfast. It was early, and not many folks were about at that hour. The gray faces of the stores were darkened by the rain, and the dust was laid for a few hours at least. A rider in a rain-wet slicker went by on the street, heading for the livery stable. It was a quiet morning in Dodge.

We stopped at the dining-room door, studying the people inside before we entered, and we found a table in a corner where we could watch both doors. Galloway had the rawhide thong slipped back off his six-shooter and so did I, but we were hunting no trouble.

Folks drifted in, mostly men. They were cattlemen, cattle buyers, a scattering of ranch hands, and some of the business folks from the stores. A few of them we already knew by sight, a trick that took only a few hours in Dodge.

There were half a dozen pretty salty characters in that room, too, but Dodge was full of them. As far as that goes, nine-tenths of the adult males in Dodge had fought in the War Between the States or had fought Indians, and quite a few had taken a turn at buffalo hunting. It was no place to come hunting a ruckus unless you were hitched up to go all the way.

We ordered scrambled eggs and ham, something a body didn't find too much west of the Mississippi, where everything was beef and beans. Both of us were wearing store-bought clothes and our guns were almost out of sight. There was a rule about packing guns in town unless you were riding out right off, but the law in Dodge was lenient except when the herds were coming up the trail, and this was an off season for that. Evan Hawkes had been almost the only one up the trail right at that time.

Nowhere was there any sign of the Fetchen crowd, nor of Judith.

"You don't suppose they pulled out?" Galloway asked.

" 'Tisn't likely."

Several people glanced over at us, for there were no secrets in Dodge, and by now everybody in town would know who we were and why we were in town; and they would also know the Fetchen crowd.

It was likely that Earp had figured out the shooting by this time, but as had been said, Tory was armed and it was a fair shooting, except that he laid for me like that. He'd tried to ambush me, and he got what was coming to him. Dodge understood things like that.

We ate but our minds were not on our food, hungry as we were, for every moment we were expecting the Fetchens to show up. They did not come, though. The rain eased off, although the clouds remained heavy and it was easy enough to see that the storm was not over. Water dripped from the eaves and from the signboards extending across the boardwalk in some places.

We watched through the windows, and presently a man came in, pausing at the outside door to beat the rain from his hat and to shake it off his raincoat. He came on in, and I heard him, without looking at us, tell Ben Springer, "They had their buryin'. There were nineteen men out there. Looked to be a tough lot."

"Nineteen?" Galloway whispered. "They've found some friends, seems like."

We saw them coming then, a tight riding bunch of men in black slickers and mostly black hats coming down the street through the mud. They drew up across the street and got down from their horses and went to stand under the overhang of the building across the street.

Two turned and drifted down the street to the right, and two more to the left, the rest of them stayed there. It looked as if they were waiting for us.

"Right flatterin', I call it," Galloway said, picking up his coffee cup. "They got themselves an army yonder."

"Be enough to go around," I commented. Then after a minute I said, "I wonder what happened to Judith?"

"You go see. I'll set right here and see if they want to come a-hunting. If they don't, we'll go out to 'em after a bit."

Pushing back my chair, I got up and went into the hotel and up the stairs. When I got to her door, I rapped . . . and rapped again.

There was no answer.

I tried rapping again, somewhat louder, and when no answer came I just reached down and opened the door.

The room was empty. The bed was still unmade after she'd slept in it, but she was gone, and her clothes were gone.

When I came back down the stairs I came down moving mighty easy. Nothing like walking wary when a body is facing up to trouble, and I could fairly smell trouble all around.

Nobody was in the lobby, so I walked over to where I could see through the arch into the dining room.

Galloway was sitting right where I'd left him, only there were two Fetchens across the table from him and another at the street door, and all of them had guns.

The tables were nigh to empty. Chalk Beeson was sitting across the room at a table with Bob Wright; and Doc Holliday, up early for him, was alone at another table, drinking his breakfast, but keeping an eye on what was happening around.

Black Fetchen was there, along with Burr and a strange rider I didn't know, a man with a shock of hair the color of dead prairie grass, and a scar on his jaw. His heels were run down, but the way he wore his gun sized him up to be a slick one with a shootin' iron, or one who fancied himself so. A lot of the boys who could really handle guns wore them every which way, not slung down low like some of the would-be fast ones.

"It was your doing," Black was saying, "you and that brother of yours. You got that preacher out of town. Well, it ain't going to do you no good. Judith is ridin' west with us, and we'll find us a preacher."

"I'd not like to see harm come to that girl,"

Galloway commented calmly. "If harm comes to her I'll see this country runs mighty short on Fetchens."

"You won't have the chance. You ain't going to leave this room. Not alive, you ain't."

About that time I heard a board creak. It was almost behind me, and it was faint, but I heard it. Making no move, I let my eyes slant back. Well, the way the morning sunlight fell through the window showed a faint shadow, and I could just see the toe of a boot—a left boot.

Just as I sighted it, the toe bent just a mite like a man taking a step or swinging a gun to hit a man on the head. So I stepped quickly off to the right and back-handed my left fist, swinging hard.

When he cut down with that six-gun barrel he swung down and left, but too slow. My left fist smashed him right in the solar plexus, right under the third button of his shirt, and the wind went out of him as if he'd been steer-kicked. His gun barrel came down, his blow wasted, and by that time my right was moving. It swung hard, catching him full in his unprotected face, smashing his nose like a man stepping on a gourd.

The blood gushed out of his nose and he staggered back, and I walked in on him.

Now, there's a thing about fighting when the chips are down. You get a man going, you don't let up on him. He's apt to come back and beat your ears down. So I reached out, caught him by one ear and swung another right, scattering a few of his teeth. He turned sidewise, and I drove my fist down on his kidney like a hammer, and he hit the floor.

Now, that all amounted to no more than four or

five seconds. A body doesn't waste time between punches, and I wasn't in anything less than a hurry.

Nor was I making much noise. It was all short and sharp and over in an instant, and then I was facing back toward that room.

Galloway was sitting easy. Nobody ever did fluster that boy. He was a soft-talking man, but he was tough, and so rough he wore out his clothes from the inside first. There were Fetchens ready to fire, but Galloway wasn't worried so's a body could see, and I was half a mind to leave it all to him. It would serve them right.

One time when he was short of thirteen we were up in the hills. We'd been hunting squirrels and the like, but really looking for a good razor-back hog, Ma being fresh out of side-meat. Well, Galloway seen a big old boar back under the brush, just a-staring at him out of those mean little eyes, and Galloway up and let blast at him. That bullet glanced off the side of the boar's shoulder and the hog took off into the brush. We trailed him for nigh onto two miles before he dropped, and when we came upon him there was a big old cougar standing over him.

Now, that cougar was hungry and he'd found meat, and he wasn't figuring on giving up to no mountain boy. Galloway, he'd shot that wild boar and we needed the side-meat, and he wasn't about to give it up to that big cat. So there they stood, a-staring one at the other.

Galloway was carrying one load in that old smooth-bore he had, and he knew if he didn't get the cat with one shot he would be in more trouble than

he'd ever seen. A wounded cougar is something nobody wants any truck with, but if that cougar'd
known who he was facing he'd have taken out running over the hills.

Galloway up and let blast with his gun just as that
cougar leaped at him. The bullet caught the cat in
the chest but he was far-off from dead. He knocked
Galloway a-rolling and I scrambled for a club, but
Galloway was up as quick as the cougar, and he
swung the smooth-bore and caught that cat coming
in, with a blow on the side of the head. Then before
the stunned cougar could more than get his feet under
him, Galloway outs with his Arkansas toothpick and
then he and that cat were going around and around.

Blood and fur and buckskin were flying every
which way, and then Galloway was up and bleeding
but that cat just lay there. He looked at Galloway and
then just gave up the ghost right there before us.

Galloway had his ribs raked and he carries the
cougar scars to this day. But we skinned out the
cougar and toted the hide and the side-meat home.
We made shift to patch Galloway up, and only did
that after he lay half naked in a cold mountain stream
for a few minutes.

What I mean is, Galloway was nobody to tackle
head-on without you figured to lose some hide.

Galloway, he just sat there a-looking at them, that
long, tall mountain boy with the wide shoulders and
the big hands. We two are so much alike we might
be twins, although we aren't, and he's away the best-
looking of the two. Only I can almost tell what he's
thinking any given time. And right then I wouldn't
have wanted to be in the shoes of any Fetchen.

"I'm going to leave this room, Fetchen," he said, "and when I please to. If I have to walk over Fetchens I can do it. I figure you boys are better in a gang or in a dark barn, anyway."

Black came to his feet as if he'd been stabbed with a hat pin. "It was you, was it?"

"Don't push your luck." Galloway spoke easy enough. "The only reason you're alive now is because I don't figure it polite to mess up a nice floor like this. Now, if I was you boys I'd back up and get out of here while the getting is good. And mind what I said, if one hair of that girl's head is so much as worried, I'll see the lot of you hang."

Well, they couldn't figure him. Not one of them could believe he would talk like that without plenty of guns to back him. He was alone, it seemed like, and he was telling them where to get off, and instead of riding right over him, they were worried. They figured he had some sort of an ace-in-the-hole.

Burr glanced around and he saw me standing back from the door, but on their flank and within easy gun-range—point-blank range, that is. I was no more than twenty or twenty-five feet away, and there was nothing between us. Not one of them was facing me. For all they knew, there might be others, for they'd seen us around with some of the Half-Box H outfit.

Black got up, moving easy-like, and I'll give it to him, the man was graceful as a cat. He was a big man, too, bigger than either Galloway or me, and it was said back in the hills that in a street fight he was a man-killer.

"We can wait," he said. "We've got all the time in

the world. And the first preacher we come upon west of here, Judith and me will get married."

They went out in a bunch, the way they came in, and then I strolled over from the door. Galloway glanced up. "You have any trouble?"

"Not to speak of," I said.

We walked out on the street, quiet at this hour. Somewhere a chicken had laid an egg and was telling the town about it. A lazy-looking dog trotted across the street, and somewhere a pump was working, squeaking and complaining—then I heard water gush into a pail.

A few horses stood along the street, and a freight wagon was being loaded. Right then I was thinking of none of these things, but of Judith. It seemed there was no way I could interfere without bringing on a shooting. She'd consented to marry James Black Fetchen, and we'd had no word from her folks against it. The law couldn't intervene, nor could we, but I dearly wished to and so did Galloway.

We knew there'd be more said about Tory Fetchen. That was no closed book. The Fetchens were too canny to get embroiled in a gun battle with the law when the law is such folks as Wyatt Earp, Bat Masterson, and their like. West of us the plains were wide, and what happened out yonder was nobody's business but theirs and ours. We all knew that west of here there'd be a hard reckoning some day.

We saw them coming, riding slow up the street in that tight bunch they held to, Judith out in front, riding head up and eyes straight ahead, riding right out of town and out of our lives, and they never turned a head to look at us, just rode on by like a pay car passing a tramp. They simply paid us no mind, not even Judith.

She might at least have waved good-bye.

When they disappeared we turned around and walked back inside. "Let's have some coffee," Galloway said gloomily. "We got to contemplate."

We'd no more than sat down before Evan Hawkes came in. As soon as he spotted us he walked over.

"Have you boys made any plans? If not, I can use you."

He pulled a chair around and straddled it. "If we are correct in assuming that the Fetchen crowd stampeded and stole my cattle, it seems to me they will be joining the herd somewhere west of here. No cattle have been sold that we know of, beyond a possibility of some slaughtered beef at Fort Dodge. We now have about three hundred head rounded up that I was planning on pushing to Wyoming, but I mean to have my herd back."

"How?"

"Why not the same way they got it?"

Well, why not? Fetchen had stolen his herd, so why not steal it back? There was sense to that, for nobody wants to have nigh onto fifty thousand dollars' worth of cattle taken from under his nose.

"We're riding west," I told him. "We figured to sort of perambulate around and see they treat that girl all right."

"Good! Then you boys are on the payroll as of now—thirty a month and food."

He sat there while we finished our coffee. "You boys know the Fetchens better than I do. Tell me, do they know anything about the cattle business? I mean *western* cattle business?"

"Can't see how they could. They're hill folk, like we were until we came west the first time. Howsoever, they might have some boys along who do know something . . . if they dare show their faces."

"What's that mean?"

"I figure they've tied in with some rustlers."

"That's possible, of course. Well, what do you say?"

Me, I looked at Galloway, but he left such things to me most of the time. "We're riding west, and we'd find the company agreeable," I said. "You've hired yourselves some hands."

We moved out at daybreak, Evan Hawkes riding point, and ten good men, including us. He had Harry Briggs and Ladder Walker along, and some of the others. A few, who were married men or were homesick for Texas, he paid off there. In our outfit there were, among others, two who looked like sure-fire gunmen, Larnie Cagle was nineteen and walked as if he was two-thirds cougar. The other was an older, quieter man named Kyle Shore.

Wanting to have our own outfit, Galloway and me bought a couple of pack horses from Bob Wright, who had taken them on a deal. Both were mustangs, used to making do off prairie grass, but broken to saddle and pack. Evan Hawkes was his own foreman, and I'll say this for him: he laid in a stock of grub the like of which I never did see on a cow outfit.

He had a good, salty remuda, mostly Texas horses, small but game, and able to live off the range the way a good stock horse should in that country.

The outfit was all ready to move when we reached

the soddy where his boys had been holed up, so we never stopped moving.

Hawkes dropped back to me. "Flagan, I hear you're pretty good on the trail. Do you think you could pick up that outfit?"

"I can try."

There were still clouds and the weather was threatening. A little gusty wind kept picking up, and the prairie was wet without being soggy. Galloway stayed with the herd and I cut out, riding off to the south to swing a big circle and see what I could pick up.

Within the next hour I had their sign, and by the time a second hour had gone by I had pegged most of their horses. I knew which one Judith rode and the tracks of all her other horses, and I also knew which one was Black Fetchen's. It had taken me no time at all to identify them.

This was wide-open country, and a body had to hang back a mite. Of course, they were well ahead of me, so it was not a worrisome thing right away, but it was something to keep in mind. Of course, a man riding western country just naturally looks at it all. I mean he studies his back trail and off to the horizon on every side. Years later he would be able to describe every mile of it. As if it had been yesterday.

First place, it just naturally had to be that way. There were no signposts, no buildings, no corrals, or anything but creeks, occasional buttes, sometimes a bluff or a bank, and a scatter of trees and brush. As there wasn't much to see, you came to remember what there was. And I was studying their sign because I might have to trail the whole outfit by one or two tracks.

There was one gent in that outfit who kept pulling off to one side. He'd stop now and again to study his back trail, plainly seen by the marks of his horse's hoofs in the sod. It came to me that maybe it was that new rider with the scar on his jaw. Sure enough, I came upon a place where he'd swung down to tighten his cinch. His tracks were there on the ground, run-down heels and all. Something about it smelled of trouble, and I had me an idea this one was pure poison.

And so it turned out...but that was another day, and farther along the trail.

CHAPTER 6

THE LAND LAY wide before us. We moved westward with only the wind beside us, and we rode easy in the saddle with eyes reaching out over the country, reading every movement and every change of shadow.

Now and again Galloway rode out and took the trail and I stayed with the herd, taking my turn at bringing up the drag and eating my share of dust. It was a job nobody liked, and I didn't want those boys to think I was forever dodging it, riding off on the trail of the Fetchens.

OF A NOON, Galloway rode in. He squatted on his heels with those boys and me, eating a mite, drinking coffee, then wiping his hands on a handful of pulled brown grass. "Flagan," he said, "I've lost the trail."

They all looked up at him, Larnie Cagle longest of all.

"Dropped right off the world," Galloway said, "all of a sudden, they did."

"I'll ride out with you."

"Want some help?" Larnie Cagle asked. "I can read sign."

Galloway never so much as turned his head.

"Flagan will look. Nobody can track better than him. He can trail a trout up a stream through muddy water."

"I got to see it," Cagle said, and for a minute there things were kind of quiet.

"Some day you might," I said.

We rode out from the herd and picked up the trail of that morning. It was plain enough, for an outfit of nineteen men and pack horses leaves a scar on the prairie that will last for a few days—sometimes for weeks.

Of a sudden they had circled and built a fire for nooning, but when they rode away from that fire there wasn't nineteen of them any longer. The most tracks we could make out were of six horses. We had trouble with the six and it wasn't more than a mile or two further on until there were only three horses ridden side by side. And then there were only two . . . and then they were gone.

It made no kind of sense. Nineteen men and horses don't drop off the edge of the world like that.

In a little while Hawkes rode over with Kyle Shore. Shore could read sign. Right away he began casting about, but he came up with nothing.

"The way I figure it, Mr. Hawkes," I said, "those boys were getting nigh to where they were going, or maybe just to those stolen cattle, so they had it in their mind to disappear. Somebody in that lot is almighty smart in the head."

"How do you think they did it?" Shore asked.

"I got me an idea," I said. "I think they bound up their horses' hoofs with sacking. It leaves no definite print, but just sort of smudges ground and grass.

Then they just cut out, one at a time, each taking a different route. They'll meet somewhere miles from here."

"It's an Apache trick," Galloway said.

"Then we must try to find out where they would be apt to go," Hawkes suggested.

"Or just ride on to where they'll likely take that herd," Shore added. "Maybe we shouldn't waste time trying to follow them."

"That makes sense," I agreed.

"Suppose they just hole up somewhere out on the plains? Is there any reason why they should go farther?"

"I figure they're heading for Colorado," I said. "I think they're going to find Judith's pa."

They all looked at me, probably figuring I had Judith too much in mind, and so I did, but not this time.

"Look at it," I said. "Costello has been out there several years. He has him a nice outfit, that's why he wanted Judith with him. What's to stop them taking her on out there and just moving in on him?"

"What about him? What about his hands?"

"How many would he have on a working ranch? Unless he's running a lot of cattle over a lot of country he might not have more than four or five cowboys."

They studied about it, and could see it made a kind of sense. We had no way of telling, of course, for Fetchen might decide to stay as far from Judith's pa as possible. On the other hand, he was a wild and lawless man with respect for nothing, and he might decide just to move in on Judith's pa. It would be a good hide-out for his own herd, and unless Costello had some salty hands around, they might even take over the outfit.

Or they might do as Hawkes suggested and find a good water hole and simply stay there. In such a wide-open country there would be plenty of places.

The more I contemplated the situation the more worried I became, and I'm not usually a worrying man. What bothered me was Judith. That girl may have been a fool about James Black Fetchen; but she was, I had to admit, a smart youngster. I had an idea that, given time and company of the man and his kin, she'd come to know what he was really like. The more so since he would think he had everything in hand and under control.

What would happen if she should all of a sudden decide she was no longer inclined to marry Black Fetchen?

If she could keep her mouth shut she might get a chance to cut and run; but she was young, and liable to talk when she should be listening. Once she let Black know where he stood with her, the wraps would be off. She would have to cut and run, or be in for rough treatment.

"They don't want to be found," I told Hawkes. "They've buried the ashes of their fires. And I trailed out two of them today, lost both trails."

"What do you figure we can do?"

"Let me have Galloway, Shore, and maybe one or two others. You've got hands enough. Each one of us will work out a different trail. Maybe we can come up with something."

"You mean if the trails begin to converge? Or point toward something?"

"Sooner or later they've got to."

So it boiled down to me an' Galloway, Shore, Ladder Walker, and an old buffalo hunter named Moss Reardon. We hunted down trails and started following them out. They were hard enough to locate in the first place.

The idea didn't pan out much. By the end of two days Walker's trail petered out in a bunch of sand hills south of us. Galloway lost his trail in the bed of a river, and Shore's just faded out somewhere on the flat. Only Reardon and me had come up with anything, and that was almighty little. Both of us lost the trail, then found it again.

When we'd joined up again with the others, I drew on the ground with a bit of stick and tried to point out what I'd found. "Right about here—and there was no trail, mind you—I found a place where the grass was cropped by a horse. It's short grass country, but the horse had cropped around in a circle, so figuring on that idea and just to prove out what I'd found, I located the peg-hole that horse had been tied to. It had been filled up, and a piece of grass tucked into the hole—growing grass."

Hawkes sort of looked at me as if he didn't believe it.

"Only there wasn't one of them, there were three. I sort of skirted around, looking for another cropped place and I found two more, further out from camp."

"You found their *camp*?"

"Such as it was. They'd dug out a block of sod,

built their coffee fire in the hole, then replaced the sod when they got ready to move."

Hawkes sat back on his heels and reached for the coffeepot. He studied the map I had drawn, and I could see he was thinking about all we had learned.

"What do you think, Moss? You've hunted buffalo all over this country."

"Sand Creek," he said, "or maybe Two Buttes."

"Or the breaks of the Cimarron," Kyle Shore suggested.

Moss Reardon threw him a glance. "Now, that might be," he said. "It just might be."

We moved westward with the first light, keeping the small herd moving at a good pace. As for me, just knowing that Judith was out there ahead of us gave me an odd feeling of nearness. Up to now we hadn't been exactly certain which way she was taking, but now I had the feeling that if I was setting out to do it I could come up to them by sundown.

That night we camped on the north fork of the Cimarron, and scarcely had coffee boiling when a rider hailed the fire. In those days, as I've said before, nobody just rode up out of the dark. If he wanted to live to see grandchildren he learned to stop off a piece and call out.

When he was squatting by the fire and the usual opening talk was over, such as how did he find the grass, and how beef prices were, or had he seen any buffalo, he looked across the fire at me and said, "You'll be Flagan Sackett?"

"That I am."

"Message for you, from Bat Masterson."

He handed me a folded paper. Opening it, I found another inside.

The first was a note from Bat: *If we had known this!*

The second was an answer to our telegram sent to Tazewell: *J. B. Fetchen, Colby Rafin, Burr Fetchen and three John Does wanted for murder of Laban Costello. Apprehend and hold.*

"So they killed him," Galloway said. "I had a thought it might be so."

"We got to get that girl away from them, Galloway," I said.

"If what you surmise is true," Hawkes said, "they might want her for a bargaining point with the old man. Look at it this way. They've got a big herd of cattle and no range. They could settle on free range most anywhere, but there will be questions asked. Mine is a known brand, so if they haven't altered it, they must."

"They ain't had the time," Walker said. "Takes a spell to rope and brand that many head."

"We're wastin' time," Larnie said. "Let's locate the herd and take it from them."

"There's nineteen of them," Briggs objected. "Taking a herd from such an outfit wouldn't be that easy. A man's got to be smart to bring it off."

"Larnie's right about one thing," Hawkes said. "We've got to find the herd."

In a wide-open land like this where law was a local thing and no officer wanted to spread himself any further than his own district, a man could do just about what he was big enough to do, or that he was fast enough with a gun to do. The only restraint there was on any man outside of the settled communities was his own moral outlook and the strength of the men with him.

Black Fetchen and his kin had always ruled their roost about as they wanted, and had ridden rough-shod over those about them, but they had been kind of cornered by the country back there and the fact that there were some others around that were just as tough as they were.

The killing of Laban Costello had made outlaws of them and they had come west, no doubt feeling they'd have things their own way out here. They started off by stealing Hawkes's herd, killing his son, and some of his men as well, and seeming to get away with it.

They had been mighty shrewd about leaving no tracks. Galloway and me were good men on a trail, and without us Hawkes might never have been on to them. That's not to say that Kyle Shore and Moss Reardon weren't good—they were.

But the West Fetchen and his men were heading for wasn't quite what it had been a few years before, and I had an idea they were in for a surprise. Circumstances can change in a mighty short time where the country is growing, and the West they had heard about was, for the most of it, already gone.

For instance, out around Denver a man named Dave Cook had gotten a lot of the law officers to working together, so that a man could no longer just run off to a nearby town to be safe. And the men who rode for the law in most of the western towns were men who weren't scared easy.

James Black Fetchen was accounted a mighty

mean man, and that passel of no-goods who rode with him could have been no better. I had an idea they were riding rough-shod for grief, because folks in Wyoming and Colorado didn't take much pushing. It's in their nature to dig in their heels and push back.

This was an uncomplicated country, as a new country usually is. Folks had feelings and ideas that were pretty basic, pretty down to earth, and they had no time to worry about themselves or their motives. It was a big, wide, empty country and a man couldn't hide easy. There were few people, and those few soon came to know about each other. Folks who have something to hide usually head for big cities, crowded places where they can lose themselves among the many. In open western country a man stood out too much.

If he was a dangerous man, everybody knew it sooner or later; and if he was a liar or a coward that soon was known and he couldn't do much of anything. If he was honest and nervy, it didn't take long for him to have friends and a reputation for square-dealing; he could step into some big deals with no more capital than his reputation. Everybody banked on the man himself.

Once away from a town, a man rode with a gun at hand. There were Indians about, some of them always ready to take a scalp, and even the Indians accounted friendly might not be if they found a white man alone and some young buck was building a reputation to sing about when he went courting or stood tall in the tribal councils.

A rustler, if caught in the act, was usually hung to the nearest tree. Nobody had time to ride a hundred miles to a court house or to go back for the trial, and there were many officers who preferred it that way.

———

NOW, ME AND Galloway were poor folks. We had come west the first time to earn money to pay off Pa's debts, and now we were back again, trying to make our own way. And the telegram from Tennessee had changed everything.

We had made no fight when Black Fetchen claimed Judith, because she had said she was going to marry him, and we had no legal standing in the matter. But the fact that he had killed her grandpa changed everything, and we knew she'd never marry him now, not of her own free will.

"We got to get her away from them, Flagan," Galloway said, "and time's a-wasting."

But things weren't the way we would like to have them around the outfit, either. That Larnie Cagle was edgy around us. He had heard of the Sackett reputation, and he reckoned himself as good with a gun as any man; we both could see he was fairly itching to prove it.

Kyle Shore tried to slow him down, for Kyle was a salty customer and he could read the sign right. He knew that anybody who called a showdown to a Sackett was bound to get it, and Shore being a saddle partner of Cagle's, he wanted no trouble.

Half a dozen times around camp Larnie had made comments that we didn't take to, but we weren't quarrelsome folks. Maybe I was more so than Galloway, but so far I'd sat tight and kept my mouth shut. Larnie was a man with swagger. He wanted to make big tracks, and now he had a feeling that he wasn't making quite the impression he wanted. A body could see him working up to a killing. The only question was who it would be.

Like a lot of things in this world, it was patience that finally did it for us. Galloway and me were riding out with Moss Reardon. We had followed a faint trail, picking up where we'd left off the day before, as it had run along in the same direction we were taking. On that morning, though, it veered off, doubled back, turned at right angles, switching so often it kept Galloway and me a-working at it.

All of a sudden we noticed Moss. He was off some distance across the country but we recognized that paint pony he was riding; we hung to our trail, though, and so did he. And then pretty soon we found ourselves riding together again.

"I think we've got 'em," Moss said. "As I recall, there's a hole in the river yonder where water stays on after the rest dries up. There'd be enough after a rain to water the herd."

We left the trail and took to low ground, keeping off the sky line but staying in the same direction the trail was taking. Every now and again one of us would ride out to see if we could pick up track, and sure enough, we could.

Moss Reardon's bronc began to act up. "Smells water," he said grimly. "We better ride easy."

We began to see where the grass was grazed off in the bottoms along the river. Somebody had moved a big bunch of cattle, keeping them strung out in the bottoms, which no real cattleman would do because of the trouble of working them out of the brush all the while. Only a man whose main idea was to keep a herd from view might try that.

We found a place in the river bed where there had been water, all trampled to mud by the herd, but now the water had started to seep back. We pulled up and watered our horses.

"How far do you figure?" Galloway asked.

Reardon thought a minute or two. "Not far... maybe three, four miles."

"Maybe one of us ought to go back and warn Hawkes."

It was coming on to sundown, and our outfit was a good ten miles back. Nobody moved. After the horses had satisfied themselves we pulled out.

"Well"—I hooked a leg around the saddlehorn—"I figure to Injun up to that layout and see how Judith is getting along. If she's in trouble, I calculate it would be time to snake her out of there."

"Wouldn't do any harm to shake 'em up a mite," Moss suggested, his hard old eyes sharpening. "Might even run off a few head."

We swung down right there and unsaddled to rest our horses giving them a chance to graze a little. Meanwhile we sort of talked about what we might do, always realizing we would have to look the situation over before we could decide. The general idea was that we would Injun up to their camp after things settled down and scout around. If the layout looked good we might try to get Judith away; but if not, we'd just stampede that herd, or a piece of it, and drive them over to join up with the Hawkes outfit.

All the while we weren't fooling anybody. That outfit had acted mighty skittish, and they might be lying out for us. They had men enough to keep a good guard all the while, and still get what sleep they needed.

After a while we stretched out to catch ourselves a few minutes of sleep. Actually, that few minutes stretched to a good two hours, for we were beat.

Me, I was the first one up, as I am in most any camp. There was no question of starting a fire, for some of their boys might be scouting well out from camp.

I saddled up and then shook the others awake. Old Moss came out of it the way any old Indian fighter would, waking up with eyes wide open right off, and listening.

We mounted up and started off, riding easy under the stars, each of us knowing this might be our last ride. Lightly as we talked of what we might do, we knew we might be riding right into a belly full of lead.

It was near to midnight when we smelled their smoke, and a few minutes later when we saw the red glow of their fire. We could make out the figure of a man sitting on guard, the thin line of his rifle making a long shadow.

CHAPTER 7

WE HAD COME up to their camp from down wind so the horses wouldn't get wind of us. The cattle were bedded on a wide bench a few feet above the river, most of them lying down, but a few restless ones still grazing here and there.

There would be other guards, we knew, and without doubt one was somewhere near us even now, but we sat our horses, contemplating the situation.

About midnight those cattle would rise up, stretch, turn around a few times and maybe graze for a few minutes, and then they would lie down again. That would be a good time to start them.

We figured to start the stampede so as to run the cattle north toward our boys, which would take it right through the camp Fetchen had made, or maybe just past it. And that meant that we had to get Judith out of there before the cattle started running.

The upshot of it was that I cut off from the others and swung wide, working toward the camp. I could see the red eye of the dying fire all the while. Finally I tied my horse in a little hollow surrounded by brush. It was a place where nobody was likely to stumble on the horse, yet I could find it quickly if I had to cut and run.

Leaving my rifle on the saddle, I started out with a six-shooter, a spare six-gun stuck down in my pants, and a Bowie knife. Switching boots for moccasins, which I carried in my saddlebags, I started easing through the brush and trees toward the camp.

Now, moving up on a camp of woods-wise mountain boys is not an easy thing. A wild animal is not likely to step on a twig or branch out in the trees and brush. Only a man, or sometimes a horse or cow, will do that, but usually when a branch cracks somewhere it is a man moving, and every man in that camp would know it.

Another distinctive sound is the brushing of a branch on rough clothing. It makes a whisking-whispering sound the ear can pick up. And as for smells, a man used to living in wild country is as keenly aware of smells as any wild creature is. The wind, too, made small sounds and, drawing near to the camp, I tried to move with the wind and to make no sudden clear sound.

The guard near the fire could be seen faintly through the leaves, and it took me almost half an hour to cover the last sixty feet. The guard was smoking a corncob pipe and was having trouble keeping it alight. From time to time he squatted near the fire, lifting twigs to relight his pipe, and that gave me an advantage. With his eyes accustomed to the glow of the fire, his sight would be poor when he looked out into the darkness.

The camp was simple enough. Men were rolled up here and there, and off to one side I could see Judith lying in the space between Black Fetchen and Burr. At her head was the trunk of a big old cottonwood, and Fetchen lay about ten feet to one side, Burr the same distance on the other. Her feet were toward the fire, which was a good twenty feet away.

There was no way to get her without stepping over one of those men, or else somehow getting around that tree trunk. Unless... unless the stampede started everybody moving and for the moment they forgot about her.

It was a mighty big gamble. But I thought how out on the plains a man's first thought is his horse, and if those horses started moving, or if the cattle started and the men jumped for their horses, there might be a minute or so when Judith was forgotten. If, at that moment, I was behind that tree trunk...

We had made no plans for such a thing, but I figured that our boys would take it for granted that I'd gotten Judith, so they would start the stampede after a few minutes. The best thing I could do would be to slip around and get back of that tree trunk, so I eased back from where I was, and when deep enough into the woods I started to circle about the camp.

But I was uneasy. It seemed to me there was something wrong, like maybe somebody was watching me, or laying for me. It was a bad feeling to have. I couldn't see anybody or hear anything, but at the same time I wasn't low-rating those Fetchen boys. I knew enough about them to be wary. They were such a tricky lot, and all of them had done their share of hunting and fighting.

When I was halfway to where I was going I eased up and stayed quiet for a spell, just listening. After a while, hearing no sound that seemed wrong, I started circling again. It took me a while, and I was getting scared they'd start those cattle moving before I could get back of that tree trunk.

Of a sudden, I heard a noise. Somebody had come into their camp. By that time I was right in line with the tree trunk, so I snaked along the ground under the brush and worked my way up behind it.

I could see Black Fetchen standing by the fire, and Burr was there too. There were three or four others with them, and they were all talking together in low tones. Something had happened...maybe they had seen the boys, or maybe some of their lot had seen our outfit off to the north.

About that time I saw Judith. She was lying still; her eyes were wide open and her head was tilted back a mite and she was looking right at me.

"Flagan Sackett," she whispered, "you go right away from here. If they find you they will kill you."

"I came for you."

"You're a fool. I am going to marry James Black Fetchen."

"Over my dead body."

"You stay here, and that's the way it will be. You go away."

Was I mistaken, or did she sound less positive about that business of marrying Black? Anyway, it was now or never.

I had no idea whether anything had gone wrong or not, but that stampede should have begun before this. It was unlikely I'd ever get this close again without getting myself killed, so I said, "Judith, you slip back here. Quiet now."

"I will do no such thing!"

"Judith," I said, for time was slipping away and I'd

little of it left, "why do you think the whole Fetchen outfit came west?"

"They came after me!" she said proudly.

"Maybe . . . but they had another reason, too. They ran because the law wants them for murder!"

The Fetchen boys were still standing together, talking. Another man had gotten up from his blankets and gone over to join them. About that time one of the group happened to move and I saw why they were all so busy.

Standing in the center was someone who didn't belong with them, but someone who looked familiar. He turned suddenly and walked off toward his horse. I couldn't see his face, but I knew that walk. It was Larnie Cagle.

"I don't believe you!" Judith whispered.

Me, I was almighty scared. If Cagle was talking to them he would have told them we were close by, for from the way they welcomed him you'd have thought he was one of the family.

"I've got no more time to waste. Black Fetchen, Burr, and them killed your grandpa, and I've got a telegram from Tazewell to prove it."

She gasped and started to speak; then suddenly she slipped out of her blankets, caught up her boots, and came into the brush. And I'll give her that much. When she decided to move she wasted no time, and she made no noise. She came off the ground with no more sound than a bird, and she slid between the leaves of the brush like a ghost.

We scrambled, fear crawling into my throat at being scrooched down in that brush. Suddenly behind us somebody yelled, "Judith!...Where's that fool girl?"

Behind us I heard them coming, and we got to our feet and started to run. Just at that moment there was a thunder of hoofs, a wild yell, a shot; then a series of yells and shots and we heard the herd start.

Glancing over my shoulder to get my direction from their fire, I could see the clearing where they were camped. Everybody had stopped dead in their tracks at those yells, and even as I looked they ran for their horses. And then the cattle hit the brush in a solid wall of plunging bodies, horns, and hoofs,... maddened, smashing everything down before them.

My horse was safely out of line, but we had no chance to reach him. I jumped, caught the low branch of a cottonwood and hauled myself up, then reached and grabbed Judith, pulling her up just as a huge brindle steer smashed through beneath me, flames from the fire lighting his side.

Behind us at the camp there were shots and yells as they tried to turn the herd, then I heard a scream, torn right from the guts of somebody trampled down under churning hoofs. Then the cattle were sweeping by under us, and I could feel the heat of their bodies as they smashed through.

It could have been only a few minutes, but it seemed a good deal longer than that.

As the last ones went by, I dropped to the ground, caught Judith by the hand, and she jumped down beside me. We ran over the mashed-down brush where the cattle had passed. Running, it taken us no time at all to reach my horse, and he was almighty glad to see me. I swung up, and took Judith with me on the saddle. She clung to me, arms around my waist, as I hit out for our camp where we'd planned to meet.

Yet all I could think of at the moment was Larnie Cagle. He had sold us out.

It was nigh on to daylight when I met Moss and Galloway. They came riding up, leading one of the Costello mares and a pinto pony.

Judith switched to the mare's saddle and we headed north for Hawkes's camp, rounding up what cattle we saw as we rode. By the time we reached the camp we had at least five hundred head ahead of us. The four of us had spread out, sweeping them together and into a tight bunch. Here and there as we rode, other cattle came out of the gray light of morning to join the herd.

Kyle Shore was the first man out to meet us, and right behind him came Ladder Walker.

I looked over at Shore, measuring him, and wondering if he had sold us out too. Or how far he would go to back his partner.

We walked the cattle up to the camp. Evan Hawkes, in his shirtsleeves and riding bareback, came to meet us, too.

He glanced from the cattle to Judith. What he said was, "You boys all right?"

"Yeah," I said. "But the Fetchens may be hurting. The stampede went right through their camp."

"Serves them right," Walker said.

The cattle we'd brought moved in with our herd, and we swung our horses to the fire. When I got down I stood back from the fire where I could see them all. "Who's with the herd?" I asked.

"Cagle, Bryan, and McKirdy. Briggs just rode in to build up the cook fire."

"You sure?"

They looked at me then, they all looked at me. "Anybody seen them?" I asked.

Briggs looked around from the fire. "Everybody's all right, if that's what you mean."

"Did you talk to any of them, Briggs?"

"Sure. Dan McKirdy and me passed by several times. What are you getting at?"

There was a sound of singing then, and Larnie Cagle rode in. "How about some coffee?" he said. "I'll never make no kind of a night hawk."

I stepped forward, feeling all cold and empty inside. "I don't know about that," I said. "You did a lot of riding tonight."

Of a sudden it was so still you could almost hear the clouds passing over.

He came around on me, facing me across the fire. Nobody said anything for a moment, and when one of them spoke it was Kyle Shore.

Even before he spoke I knew what he would say, for I knew other men who had ridden other trails, men like Shore who were true to what they believed, wrong-headed though it might be.

"Larnie Cagle is a friend of mine," he said.

"Ask him where he was tonight, and then decide if he is still your friend."

"You're talking," Cagle said. "Better make it good."

"Before we start talking," I said, "let every man hold a gun. The Fetchens are coming for us, and they know right where we are. They should be here almost any minute."

Harry Briggs turned suddenly from the group. "I'll tell Dan and the boys," he said, and was gone.

Kyle Shore had been looking at me, only now he was turning his eyes upon Cagle. "What's he mean, Larnie?"

"He's talkin', let him finish it."

"Go ahead, Sackett," Shore said. "I want to hear this."

"Larnie Cagle slipped away from night-herding and rode over to the Fetchen camp. He told them all they wanted to know. He told them about Galloway, Moss, and me, and if we hadn't made it sooner than expected, we'd have been trapped and killed. They'd have followed with an attack on this camp."

Cagle was watching me, expecting me to draw, but he was stalling, waiting for the edge.

"Nobody is going to believe that," he said, almost carelessly.

"They will believe it," Judith said suddenly. It was the first thing she had said since coming into camp. "Because I saw you, too. And that wasn't the first time. He had been there before."

Suddenly all the smartness had gone out of him. Cagle stood there like a trapped animal. He had not seen Judith, and had no idea she was in camp.

"What about it, Cagle?" Hawkes's tone was cold.

"Mr. Hawkes," Kyle Shore said, "this here is my deal. I rode into camp with him, we hired on together."

He turned to Cagle. "Larnie, when I ride, I ride for the brand. I may sell my gun, but it stays sold."

Briggs rode up to the edge of the firelight. "They're comin', Mr. Hawkes. They're all around us."

"You ain't got a chance!" Cagle said with a sneer in his voice. "You never had a chance."

"You've got one," Kyle Shore said. "You've got just one, Larnie, but you got to kill me to get it."

They looked at each other across the fire, and Shore said, "I never rode with no double-crosser, and never will. I figure you're my fault."

Cagle gave a laugh, but the laugh was a little shrill. "You? Why, you damn' fool, you never saw the day you—"

He dropped his hand, and he was fast. His gun cleared the holster and came up shooting. The first shot hit the dirt at Shore's feet and the second shot cut a notch from his hat brim.

Kyle Shore had drawn almost as fast, but his gun came up smoothly, and taking his time he shot . . . just once.

Larnie Cagle took a teetering step forward, then fell on his face, dead before he touched the ground.

"Damn' fool," Shore said. "He surely fancied that fast draw. I told him he should take time. Make the first shot count. He wouldn't listen."

Out upon the plains there was a shot, then another. We ran for our horses, bunching them under the trees. Galloway dropped to one knee near a tree trunk and fired quickly at a racing horse, then again. Taking Judith by the hand, I pushed her down behind a big fallen tree. Then I knelt beside her, rifle up, hunting a target.

There was a flurry of hammering shots and then the pound of racing hoofs, and they were gone. When

Black saw there was no surprise, he just lit up the night with a little rifle fire and rode off, figuring there'd be another day ... as there generally is.

———

DAYLIGHT TOOK ITS time a-coming, and some of us waited by the fire nursing our coffee cups in chilly fingers, our shoulders hunched. Others dozed against a fallen log, and a few crawled back into their blankets and catnapped the last two hours away.

Me, I moved restlessly around camp, picking up fuel for the fire, contemplating what we'd best do next. Evan Hawkes would be wanting to get the rest of his cattle back; but now that we had Judith again, it was our duty to carry her west to her pa.

There was a sight of work to do, and some of the cattle would be scratched or battered from horns or brush, and unless they were cared for we'd have blowflies settling on them. A cowhand's work is never done. He ropes and rides before sunup and rarely gets in for chow before the sun is down.

Judith, she slept—slept like a baby. But she worried me some, looking at her. She didn't look much like a little girl any more, and looking at a girl that-away can confuse a man's thinking.

My fingers touched my jaw. It had been some time since I'd shaved, and I'd best be about it before we got to riding westward again.

Kyle Shore wasn't talking. He was sitting there looking into the fire, his back to the long bundle we'd bury, come daybreak. I had Shore pegged now. He was a good, steady man, a fighter by trade, with no pretense to being a real gunman. He was no fast-draw artist, but his kind could kill a lot who thought they were.

Thinking about that, I went for coffee. It was hot, blacker than sin, and strong enough to float a horse-shoe. It was cowboy's coffee.

CHAPTER 8

MORNING, NOON, AND night we worked our hearts out, rounding up the scattered herd, and when we had finished we still lacked a lot of having half of what Evan Hawkes had started with when he left Texas. The Fetchen outfit had made off with the rest of them.

After a week of riding and rounding them up we started west once more.

Judith was quiet. She pulled her weight around camp, helping the cook and generally making herself useful, and when she was on the range she showed that she not only could ride the rough string but that she could savvy cattle.

Much as I wanted to pay her no mind, it was getting so I couldn't do that. She was around camp, stirring pots, bending over the fire, and looking so pretty I wondered whether I'd been right in the head when I first put eyes on her back yonder in Tazewell.

Nonetheless, I kept my eyes off her as much as I could. I rode out from camp early, and avoided sitting nigh her when it was possible. Only it seemed we were always winding up sitting side by side. I never talked or said much. First off, I'm simply no hand with women. Galloway now, he had half the girls in the mountains breathing hard most of the time, but me, I was just big and quiet, and when I was seated by womenfolks all the words in me just lost themselves in the breaks of my mind. No matter how much I tried, I couldn't put a loop over even one sentence.

Besides, there was the land. A big, grand, wide country with every glance lost in the distance. There was a special feeling on the wind when it blew across those miles of grass, a wind so cool, so deep down inside you that every breath of it was like a drink of cool water. And we saw the tumbleweeds far out ahead of us, hundreds of them rolling south ahead of the wind, like the skirmish line of an army.

At first they made the cattle skittish, but they got used to them, as we did. I never knew where they came from, but for three days the wind blew cool out of the north and for three days they came in the hundreds, in the thousands.

Trees grew thicker along the streams, and the grass was better. From time to time we saw scattered buffalo, three or four together, and once a big old bull, alone on a hilltop, watching us pass. He followed us for two days, keeping his distance—wanting company I suppose.

Twice we saw burned-out wagons, places where Indians had rounded up some settlers. Nobody would ever know who they were, and folks back home would wonder about them for a while, and then time would make the memories become dimmer.

Like Galloway and me. We had no close kinfolk, nobody keeping account of us. If we were to get killed out here nobody would ask who, why, or whatever. It made a body feel kind of lonesome down inside, and it set me to wondering where I was headed for.

Once, far ahead of the herd, I heard a galloping

behind me, and when I turned in the saddle I saw it was that Judith girl. She rode sidesaddle, of course, and looked mighty fetching as she came up to me.

"You'd be a sight better off with the rest," I said. "If we met up with Indians, you might get taken."

"I'm not afraid. Not with you to care for me."

Now, that there remark just about threw me. I suppose nobody had ever said such a thing to me before, and it runs in the blood of a man that he should care for womenfolk. It's a need in him, deep as motherhood to a woman, and it's a thing folks are likely to forget. A man with nobody to care for is as lonesome as a lost hound dog, and as useless. If he's to feel of any purpose to himself, he's got to feel he's needed, feel he stands between somebody and any trouble.

I'd had nobody. Galloway was fit to care for himself and an army of others. He was a man built for action, and tempered to violence. Gentle, he was most times, but fierce when aroused. You might as well try to take care of a grizzly bear as of him. So I'd had nobody, nor had he.

"I'd stand up for you," I said, "but it would be a worrisome thing to have to think of somebody else. I mean, whilst fighting, or whatever. Anyway, you'd take off after that Fetchen outfit if they showed up."

"I would not!"

She put her chin up at me, but stayed alongside, and said nothing more for a while.

"Mighty pretty country," I ventured after a bit.

"It is, isn't it? I just can't wait to see Pa's ranch." She sobered down then. "I hope he's all right."

"You worried about the Fetchens?"

"Yes, I am. You've no idea what they are like. I just

never imagined men could be like that." She looked quickly at me. "Oh, they were all right to me. James saw to that. But I heard talk when they didn't think I was listening." She turned toward me again. "The happiest moment in my life was when you came from behind that tree trunk. And you might have been killed!"

"Yes, ma'am. That's a common might-have-been out here. There's few things a man can do that might not get him killed. It's a rough land, but a man is better off if he rides his trail knowing there may be trouble about. It simply won't do to get careless.... And you be careful, too."

A pretty little stream, not over eight or ten inches deep, but running at a lively pace, and kind of curving around a flat meadow with low hills offered shelter from the north, and a cluster of cottonwoods and willows where we could camp...it was just what we needed.

"We'll just sort of camp here," I said. "I'll ride over and get a cooking fire started."

"Flagan!" Judith screamed, and I wheeled and saw three of them come up out of the grass near that stream where they'd been laying for me.

Three of them rising right up out of the ground, like, with their horses nowhere near them, and all three had their rifles on me.

Instinctively, I swung my horse. He was a good cutting horse who could turn on a dime and have six cents left, and he turned now. When he wheeled about I charged right at them. My six-shooter was in my hand, I don't know how come, and I chopped down with it, blasting a shot at the nearest one while keeping him between the others and me.

Swinging my horse again, I doubled right back on my heels in charging down on the others. I heard a bullet nip by me, felt a jolt somewhere, and then I was firing again and the last man was legging it for the cottonwoods. I taken in after him as he ran, and I came up alongside him and nudged him with the horse to knock him rolling.

I turned my horse again and came back on him as he was staggering to his feet. I let the horse come alongside him again, and this time I lifted a stirrup and caught him right in the middle with my heel. It knocked him all sprawled out.

One of the others was getting up and was halfway to his horse by the time I could get around to him, but I started after him too. He made it almost to the brush before I gave him my heel, knocking him face down into the broken branches of the willows.

Judith had now ridden up to me. "Are you hurt?" she asked.

"Not me. Those boys are some upset, I figure." I looked at her. "You warned me," I said. "You yelled just in time."

Three riders had come over the hill, riding hell bent for election. They were Galloway, Kyle Shore, and Hawkes himself, all of them with rifles ready for whatever trouble there was.

There was only blood on the grass where the first man had fallen. He had slipped off into the tall grass and brush, and had no doubt got to his horse and away. One of the others was also gone, but he was hurting—I'd lay a bit of money on that. The last man

I'd kicked into the brush looked as if he'd been fighting a couple of porcupines. His face was a sight, scratched and bloody like nothing a body ever saw.

"You near broke my back!" he complained. "What sort of way is that to do a man up?"

"You'd rather get shot?"

He looked at me. "I reckon not," he said dryly, "if given the choice."

"You're a Burshill by the look of you," I said.

"I'm Trent Burshill, cousin to the Fetchens."

"You might be in better comp'ny. But I know your outfit. You folks have been making 'shine back in the hills since before Noah."

"Nigh to a hunert years," he said proudly. "No Burshill of my line never paid no tax on whiskey."

"You should have stayed back there. You aren't going to cut the mustard in these western lands. Now you've mixed up in rustling."

"You got it to prove."

Kyle Shore looked hard at him. "Friend, you'd best learn. Out here they hold court in the saddle and execute the sentence with a saddle rope."

"You fixin' to hang me?"

"Dunno," Shore said, straight-faced. "It depends on Mr. Hawkes. If he sees fit to hang you, that's what we'll do."

Trent Burshill looked pretty unhappy. "I never counted on that," he said. "Seemed like this was wide-open land where a man could do as he liked."

"As long as you don't interfere with no other man," Shore said. "Western folks look down on that. And they've got no time to be ridin' to court, maybe a hundred miles, just to hang a cow thief. A cotton-wood limb works better."

Trent Burshill looked thoughtful. "Should be a way of settling this," he said. "Sure, I lined up with Black, him being my cousin an' all."

"Where's Black headed for?" I asked.

He glanced around at me. "You're one of them Tennessee Sacketts. I heard tell of you. Why, he's headed for the Greenhorns—some mountains west-ward. He's got him some idea about them."

Burshill looked at me straight. "He aims to do you in, Sackett. Was I you, I'd be travelin' east, not west."

The rest of the outfit were trailing into the bottom now with the herd. I spotted a thick limb overhead. "There's a proper branch," I said. "Maybe we ought to tie his hands, put the noose over his neck, and leave him in his saddle. Give him a chance to see how long his horse would stand without moving."

Trent Burshill looked up at the limb over his head. "If you boys was to reconsider," he said, "I'd like to ride for Tennessee. These last few minutes," he added, "Tennessee never looked so good."

"That puncher with the scar on his face," I said to him, "that newcomer. Now, who would he be?"

Burshill shrugged. "You can have him. I figure he deserves the rope more than me. Personal, I don't cot-ton to him. He's snake-mean. That there is Russ Menard."

Kyle Shore looked at me. "Sackett, you've bought yourself trouble. Russ Menard is reckoned by some to be the fastest man with a gun and the most danger-ous anywhere about."

"I knew a man like that once," I said.

"Where is he?"

"Why, he's dead. He proved to be not so fast as another man, and not so dangerous with three bullets in him."

"Russ Menard," Shore said, "comes from down in the Nation. He killed one of Judge Parker's marshals and figured it was healthier out of his jurisdiction. He was in a gun battle in Tascosa, and some say he was in the big fight in Lincoln, New Mexico."

Evan Hawkes, who had ridden over to locate his chuck wagon and crew, now came back. Judith Costello rode beside him. Harry Briggs and Ladder Walker drifted along, leading a horse.

"Found his horse," Hawkes said.

"Tie him on it," Walker said, "backwards in the saddle, and turn him loose."

"Now, see here!" Burshill protested.

"Then take his boots off and let him walk back. I heard about a man walked a hundred miles once, in his bare feet!"

"Way I heard it," Burshill said, "was there would be land and cattle and horses for the taking. A man could get rich, that's what Black said. I never figured on no rope."

"The land's for the taking," Hawkes said, "but the cattle and the horses belong to somebody. You have helped in rustling, and you were about to dry-gulch my men. What have you to say for yourself?"

"I made good whiskey. It was 'shine, but it was good whiskey," Burshill said. "I wouldn't want to grieve my kinfolk back in Tennessee."

"I'll let you have your horse," Evan Hawkes said, "but if we see you west of here we'll hang you."

"Mister, you let me go now, and you'll have to burn the stump and sift the ashes before you find me again."

"All right," Hawkes said, "let him go."

Trent Burshill let out of there as if his tail was afire, and that was just as well. I wasn't strong on hanging, anyway.

When the night fire was burning and there was the smell of coffee in the air, I went to Evan Hawkes.

"Mr. Hawkes, Galloway and me, we figure we'd best light out of here and head for Costello's ranch in the Greenhorns. If the Fetchens come on him unprepared they might ride him down. We can make faster time free of the herd."

"All right. I'm sorry to lose you boys, but we're heading the same way." He paused. "I'm going to get my herd back, so you boys figure yourselves still on the payroll. When you get that girl back to her father, you roust around and locate my cattle for me."

By daylight we had the camp well behind us. The horses we rode were good, fast ones with a lot of stamina. Judith was a rider, all right, and we stayed with it all day, riding the sun out of the sky, and soon we could see the far-off jagged line of mountains. The stars came up.

We slept in a tiny hollow under some cottonwoods, the horses grazing, and the remains of a small fire smoking under the coffeepot. Me, I was first up as always, putting sticks and bark together with a twist of dried grass to get the flame going, but keeping my ears alert for sound. At times I prowled to the edge of the hollow and looked around.

Back at camp Galloway still slept, wrapped in his

blanket, but Judith lay with her cheek pillowed on her arm, her dark hair around her face, her lips soft in the morning light. It made a man restless to see her so, and I turned back to my fire.

Judith Costello . . . it was a lovely name. But even if I was of a mind to, what could I offer such a girl? Her family were movers, they were horse-traders and traveling folks, but from all I'd heard they were well-off. And me, I had a gun and a saddle.

My thoughts turned to the ranch in the Greenhorns. The Fetchens had killed Judith's grandpa back in Tennessee, more than likely in anger at Judith and because of the loss of the horses. But suppose there was something more? Suppose the Fetchen outfit knew something we did not even surmise?

First of all, it was needful for us to ride west to that ranch, and not come on it unexpected, either. It was in my mind to circle about, to look the place over before riding right in. I had no idea what sort of a man Costello was, or how much of an outfit he had, but it would do no harm to sort of prospect around before making ourselves known.

We put together a breakfast from provisions we'd brought from Hawkes's outfit, then saddled up and rode west, keeping always to low ground.

The Greenhorns were a small range, a sort of offshoot of the towering Sangre de Cristos. It was Ute country, and although the Utes were said to be quiet, I wasn't any too sure of it, and I was taking no chances.

First off, we had to locate Costello's ranch, for all we had in the way of directions was that it was in the Greenhorns. The nearest town I knew of was

Walsenburg, but I wanted to avoid towns. Sure as shootin', the Fetchens would have somebody around to let them know of us coming. North of there, and about due west of us, was a stage stop called Greenhorn, and at the Greenhorn Inn, one of Kit Carson's old hangouts, we figured it was likely we'd hear something.

Big a country as it was, most everybody knew of all the ranchers and settlers around, and the place was small enough so we could see about everything in it before we rode into town—if town it could be called.

We made our nooning on the Huerfano River about ten miles east of Greenhorn, and made a resting time of it, for I wanted to ride into the place about sundown.

Galloway was restless, and I knew just what he felt. There was that much between us that we each knew the other's feelings. He could sense trouble coming, and was on edge for it. We both knew it was there, not far off, and waiting for us like a set trap.

There was a good deal of hate in the Fetchens, and it was in Black most of all; and they would not rest until they'd staked our hides out to dry, or we had come it over them the final time.

When noon was well past, we mounted up and pushed on to Greenhorn. The mountains were named for an Indian chief who had ruled the roost around there in times gone by. It was said of the young buck deer when his horns were fresh and in velvet that he was a "greenhorn," for he was foolishly brave then, ready to challenge anything. The chief had been that way, too, but the Spanish wiped him out. So the name greenhorn was given to anyone young and braver than he had right to be, going in where angels fear to tread, as the saying is.

The Greenhorn Inn was a comfortable enough place, as such places went—a stage stop and a hotel with sleeping quarters and a fair-to-middling dining room. We rode up, tied our horses out of sight, and the three of us checked the horses in the stable, but we saw none we recognized as Fetchen horses.

The place was nigh to empty. One old codger with a face that looked as if it was carved out of flint was sitting there, and he looked at us as if he'd seen us before, although I knew no such face. He was a lean, savage-looking old man, one of those old buffalo hunters or mountain men, by the look of him—nobody to have much truck with.

The man behind the bar glanced at Judith and then at us. We found a table and hung our hats nearby, then sat down. He came over to us.

"How are you, folks? We've got beans and bacon, beans and bear meat, beans and venison. You name it. And we've got fresh-baked bread...made it my ownself."

We ordered, and he brought us coffee, black and strong. Tasting it, I glanced over at Judith. For a girl facing up to trouble, she looked bright and pretty, just too pretty for a mountain boy like me.

"This here," I said to her, "is right touchy country. There's Indians about, both Utes and Comanches, and no matter what anybody says there's angry blood in them. They don't like white men very much, and they don't like each other."

"I can't think of anything but Pa," she said. "It has

been such a long time since I've seen him, and now that we are so close, I can hardly sit still for wanting to be riding on."

"You hold your horses," Galloway advised. "We'll make it in time."

Even as he spoke, I had an odd feeling of foreboding come over me. It was such a feeling as I'd never had before. I looked across at Galloway, and he was looking at me, and we both knew what the other felt.

What was going to happen? What was lying in wait for us?

When the man came back with our food I looked up at him and said, "We're hunting the Costello outfit, over in the Greenhorns. Can you tell us how to get there?"

He put the dishes down in front of us before we got an answer. "My advice to you is to stay away from there. It will get you nothing but trouble."

Judith's face went pale under the tan, and her eyes were suddenly frightened.

When I spoke, my voice was rougher than I intended, because of her. "What do you mean by that?"

The man backed off a step, in no way intimidated, simply wary. "I mean that's a tough outfit over there. You go in there hunting trouble and you're likely to find it."

"We aren't seeking it out," I said, more quietly. "Costello is this lady's pa. We're taking her home."

"Sorry, ma'am," he said quietly. "I didn't know. If I were you, I'd ride careful. There's been trouble in those hills."

It was not until we had finished eating that he

spoke to us again. "You boys drop around later," he said, "and I'll buy you a drink."

At the door, hesitating before going to her room, Judith looked from Galloway to me. "He's going to tell you something, isn't he? I mean that's why he offered to buy you a drink, to get you back there without me."

"Now, I don't think—" Galloway interrupted.

She would have none of it. "Flagan, you'll tell me, won't you? I've got to know if there's anything wrong. I've simply got to! After all, I haven't seen Pa in a long time."

"I'll tell you," I said, though I knew I might be lying in my teeth, for I figured she'd guessed right. That man had something to relate, and it was likely something he didn't want Judith to hear.

She turned and went to her room, and we stayed a minute, Galloway and me, hesitating to go back.

CHAPTER 9

WE STOOD THERE together, having it in our heads that what we would hear would bring us no pleasure. The night was closing in around us, and no telling what would come to Greenhorn whilst we were abed. Whatever it was, we could expect nothing but grief.

"Before we go to bed," Galloway suggested, "we'd better take a turn around outside."

"You sleep under cover," I said. "I'll make out where I can listen well. I'd not sleep easy otherwise."

"I ain't slept in a bed for some time," Galloway said, "but I'm pining to."

"You have at it. I'll find a place where my ears can pick up sound whilst I sleep."

We walked back into the saloon, two mountain boys from Tennessee. The old man still sat at his table, staying long over his coffee. He shot a hard glance at us, but we trailed on up to the bar.

The bartender poured each of us a drink, then gestured toward a table. "We might as well sit down. There'll be nobody else along tonight, and there's no sense in standing when you can sit."

"That's a fine-looking young lady," he said after we were seated. "I'd want no harm to come to her, but there's talk of trouble over there, and Costello is right in the midst of it."

We waited, and there was no sound in the room. Finally he spoke again, his face oddly lighted by the light from the coal-oil lamp with the reflector behind it. "There's something wrong up there—I don't know what it is. Costello used to come down here once in a while...the last time was a year ago. I was over that way, but he wouldn't see me. Ordered me off the place."

"Why?"

"Well, it was his place. I suppose he had his reasons." The bartender refilled the glasses from the bottle. "Nevertheless it worried me, because it wasn't like him...He lives alone, you know, back over on the ridge."

He paused again, then went on, "He fired his hands, all of them."

"He's alone up there now?"

"I don't think so. A few days back there were some men came riding up here, asked where Costello's layout was."

"Like we did," I said.

"I told them. I had no reason not to, although I didn't like their looks, but I also warned them they wouldn't be welcome. They laughed at me. One of them spoke up and said that they'd be welcome, all right, that Costello was expecting them."

"They beat us to it, Flagan," Galloway said. "They're here."

The bartender glanced from one to the other of us. "You know those men?"

"We know them, and if any of them show up again, be careful. They'll kill you as soon as look at you...maybe sooner."

"What are you two going to do?"

"Go up there. We gave a fair promise to see the young lady to her pa. So we'll go up there."

"And those men?"

Galloway grinned at him, then at me. "Why, they'd better light a shuck for Texas before we tie cans to their tails."

"Those men, now," I said, "did they have any cattle?"

"Not with them. But they said they had a herd following." He paused. "Is there anything I can do? There's good folks in this country, and Costello was a good neighbor, although a man who kept to himself except when needed. If it comes to that, we could round up a goodly lot who would ride to help him."

"You leave it to us. We Sacketts favor skinning our own cats."

The old man seated alone at the table spoke up then. "I knowed it. I knowed you two was Sacketts. I'm Cap Rountree, an' I was with Tyrel and them down on the Mogollon that time."

"Heard you spoken of," Galloway said. "Come on over and set."

"If you boys are ridin' into trouble," Rountree said, "I'd admire to ride along. I been sharin' Sackett trouble a good few years now, and I don't feel comfortable without it."

We talked a spell, watching the night hours pass, and listening for the sounds of riders who did not come.

Black Fetchen must have sent riders on ahead, and those riders must have moved in fast and hard. He might even have gone on ahead himself, letting the herd follow. We would have ridden right into a trap had we just gone on ahead without making inquiries, or being a mite suspicious.

"Hope he's all right," I said. "Costello, I mean. It would go hard with Judith to lose her pa as well as her grandpa all to once, like that."

"Well, I'll see you boys, come daylight," Rountree said. "I'm holed up in the stable should you need me."

"I'll be around off and on all night," I told him. "Don't shoot until you see the whites of my eyes."

Cap walked outside, stood there a moment, and then went off into the darkness.

"I like that old man," Galloway said. "Seems to me Tyrel set store by him."

"One of his oldest friends. Came west with him from eastern Kansas, where they tied up on a trail herd."*

"We'll need him," Galloway added. "We're facing up to trouble, Flagan."

"You get some sleep," I advised. "I'll do the same."

Outside it was still. Off to the west I thought I could see the gleam of snow on the mountains. I liked the smell of the wind off those peaks, but after a minute I walked tiredly across the road, picked up my blanket and poncho, and bedded down under a cottonwood where I could hear the trail sounds in the night. If any riders came up to the Greenhorn Inn I wanted to be the first to know.

Tired as I was, I didn't sleep, my thoughts wandering, just thinking of Galloway and me, homeless as

*The Daybreakers

tumbleweeds, drifting loose around the country. It was time we found land, time we put down some roots. It did a man no good to ride about always feathered for trouble. Sooner or later he would wind up dead, back in some draw or on some windy slope, leaving his carcass for the coyotes and buzzards to fight over. It doesn't matter how tough a man becomes, or how good he is with a gun, there comes the time when his draw is a little too slow, or something gets in the way of his bullet.

We were rougher than cobs, Galloway and me, but in this country many a tough man had cashed in his chips. It wasn't in me to think lightly of Black Fetchen. He was known throughout the mountains for his fist fighting and shooting, a man of terrible rages and fierce hatreds . . . we weren't going to come it over him without grief.

Suddenly, I came wide awake. I had no idea just when I'd dozed off, but my eyes came wide open and I was listening. What I heard was a horse walking . . . two horses.

My hand closed on my gun butt.

There was no light showing anywhere in any of the four or five buildings that made up Greenhorn. The inn was dark and still.

The first thing I made out was the shine of a horse's hip, then the glisten of starlight on a rifle barrel. Two riders had pulled up in the road right in front of the inn. A saddle creaked . . . one man was getting down.

Our horses were out back, picketed on a stretch of meadow. Unless those riders scouted around some they'd not be likely to find them, for the meadow was back beyond the corral and stable.

Noiselessly I sat up, keeping the blanket hunched around my shoulders, for the night was chill. I held my .45 in my hand, the barrel across my thigh.

After a bit I heard boots crunching and the rider came back. By now I could almost make him out—a big man with a kind of rolling walk. "Ain't there," I heard him whisper. "At least, their horses aren't in the stalls or the corral."

He stepped into the saddle again and I listened as they walked their horses down the road. Beyond the buildings they stepped them up to a trot, and I wondered where they figured to lay up for the night. It seemed to me they might have a place in mind. Come daylight, if they didn't find our tracks on the trail, they might just hole up and wait for us.

I dozed off, and when next I awakened the sky was getting bright. I rolled my bed and led the horses in, gave them an easy bait of water, and had all three horses saddled before Galloway came out of the inn.

"They're a-fixing to eat in there," he said. "It smells almighty nice."

Cap Rountree came from the stable, leading a raw-boned roan gelding, under a worn-out saddle packing two rifle scabbards. He glanced at me and I grinned at him.

"I take it your visitor wasn't talking much," I said.

"Didn't see me," Cap said, "an' just as well. I had my old Bowie to hand, and had he offered trouble I'd have split his brisket. I don't take to folks prowlin' about in the dark."

"Fetchen men?" Galloway asked.

"I reckon. Leastways, they were hunting some-body. They went on up the road."

Rountree tied his horse alongside ours. "You boys new to this country? I rode through here in the fall of 1830, my first time. And a time or two after that." He nodded toward the mountains. "I brought a load of fur out of those mountains two jumps ahead of a pack o' Utes.

"Ran into Bridger and some of his outfit, holed in behind a stream bank. I made it to them, and those Utes never knew what hit 'em. They'd no idea there was another white man in miles, nor did I.... Good fighters, them Utes."

He started across the street toward the inn. "Point is," he stopped to say, "I can take you right up to Costello's outfit without usin' no trail."

Judith was waiting for us, looking pretty as a bay pony with three white stockings. We all sat up, and the bartender, innkeeper, or whatever, brought on the eggs and bacon. We put away six eggs apiece and most of a side of bacon, it seemed like. At least, Galloway and me ate that many eggs. Judith was content with three, and Cap about the same.

An hour later we were up in the pines, hearing the wind rushing through them like the sound of the sea on a beach. Cap Rountree led the way, following no trail that a body could see, yet he rode sure and true, up and through mountains that reminded us of home.

Presently Cap turned in his saddle. "These Fetchens, now. You said they rustled the Hawkes herd. You ever hear talk of them hunting gold?"

"We had no converse with them," Galloway said, "but I know there was some talk of a Fetchen going to the western mountains many years back."

"Fetchen?" Cap Rountree puzzled over the name.

"I figured I knowed most of the old-timers, but I recall no Fetchen. Reason I mentioned it, this here country is full of lost mines. The way folks tell it, there's lost mines or caches of gold all over this country."

He pointed toward the west and south. "There lie the Spanish Peaks, with many a legend about them of sun gods an' rain gods, and of gold, hidden or found.

"North of here there's a cave in Marble Mountain, called the Caverna del Oro, where there's supposed to be gold. I never did hear of gold in a natural cave unless it was cached there, but that's possible. Those old Spanish men rode all over this country.

"There's a man named Sharp lives over there yonder," he went on. "Got him a place called Buzzard Roost Ranch and he's made friends with the Utes. He probably knows more about those old mines than anybody, although I don't rec'lect him wastin' time a-huntin' for them."

Half a mile further he drew up to let the horses take a blow. "I was thinkin' that maybe the Fetchen outfit knew something you boys don't," he said. He threw a sharp glance at Judith. "You ever hear your grandpa talk of any gold mines or such?" he asked her.

Then he said to us, "You told me the Fetchens murdered him. D' you suppose they wanted something besides this here girl? Or the horses?"

He grinned slyly at Judith. "Meanin' no offense, ma'am, for was I a younger man I might do murder myself for such a pretty girl."

"That's all right," Judith said. "I'm used to it."

After a moment, she shook her head. "No, there's nothing that I can recall."

"Now, think of this a mite. Yours is a horse-tradin' family, and they stick together. I know about the Irish traders—I spent time in country where they traded. Seems unusual one of them would cut off from the rest like your pa done. D' you suppose he knew something? Maybe when he got to swappin' around, he took something in trade he didn't talk about."

The more I considered what Cap was saying the more I wondered if he hadn't made a good guess. That Fetchen outfit were a murdering lot by all accounts, but why should they kill Costello? What could they hope to gain?

It was possible, trading around like they had done, that one of the Costellos might have picked up a map or a treasure story in trade. Maybe thrown in as boot by somebody who did not believe it themselves.

Now here was a new idea that would account for a lot.

"You consider it," I said to Judith. "Come morning, you may recall something said or seen."

There were a lot of folks scattered through the East who had gone west and then returned to the States— some to get married, some because they liked the easier life, some because they figured the risk of getting their hair lifted by a Comanche was too great. It might be that one of them had known something; or maybe some western man, dying, had sent a map to some of his kinfolk.

We had been following Rountree up an old Indian trail through the high country, but now we saw a valley before us, still some distance off. He drew up again and pointed ahead.

"Right down there is Sharp's trading post, the Buzzard Roost. Closer to us, but out of sight, is the town of Badito.

"Some of the finest horseflesh you ever did see, right down in that valley," he added.

"Costello's?"

"His an' Sharp's. Tom Sharp went back to Missouri in seventy-one and bought himself about thirty, forty head o' stock, a thoroughbred racer among them. Then he sent north into Idaho and bought about two hundred head of appaloosa's from the Nez Percé. He's bred them together for some tough, hardy stock."

"That's what Pa and Grandpa were doing," Judith said.

Well, I looked over at her. "Judith, was your pa in Missouri in seventy-one? I mean, it might have been him or some of his kinfolk who made a deal with Sharp. The tie-up might be right there."

"I don't know," she said doubtfully. "I was just a little girl. We were in Missouri in that year or the next, I think, but I never paid much attention... we were always moving."

We camped in the woods that night, smelling the pines, and eating venison we'd killed ourselves. It was a good night, and we sat late around the fire, just talking and yarning of this and that. Galloway and me, we sang a mite, for all we mountain boys take to singing, specially those of Welsh extraction like us.

It was a fine, beautiful night, and one I'd not soon forget, and for once we felt safe. Not that one or the other of us didn't get up once in a while and move away from the fire to prowl around and listen.

Tomorrow we were heading down into the valley, for we had decided to talk to Tom Sharp. Cap knew him, and he had been a friend to Costello. If there was anything to be found out, we would learn it from him.

But I was uneasy. I'd got to thinking about that girl too much, and it worried me. When a man gets mixed up in a shooting affair he'd best keep his mind about him, and not be contemplating a girl's face and a pair of lovely lips.

When we tangled with the Fetchens again they would be out for blood. They had got where they were going, but we had won several hands from them . . . now they would try to make us pay for it. We were few, and there was nowhere about that we could look for help.

Cap gestured off toward the western mountains. "Just over there Tell Sackett an' me had quite a shindig a while back. Believe me, they know the name of Sackett in that country."

I knew about Tell. I'd heard all that talk down in the Mogollon. The trouble was, mostly we Sacketts were noted for our fighting ways, except maybe for Tyrel, who had become a rancher, and Orrin, who was in politics. It was time some of us did something worthwhile, time we made a mark in the country for something besides gunplay.

A man who rides a violent road comes to only one end—up a dry creek somewhere, or on Boot Hill.

CHAPTER 10

TOM SHARP WAS a fine-looking man, the kind you'd ride the river with. He was pushing forty. He had been wounded in the War Between the States, had come west, hunted meat for the mining camps, and cut telegraph poles on contract for the Union Pacific. Finally he'd traveled up the old Ute trail to Huerfano River and opened a trading post in the valley in a big adobe building.

Right off, he started to improve both his horses and cattle by bringing in blooded stock from the States. He was not one of those who came west to get rich and get out; he came to stay and to build. The town of Malachite grew up around his trading post.

As we came riding up to the trading post, he came outside and stood on the steps to meet us, giving us a careful study. All I needed was one glimpse of Sharp to know that he was a man who would stand for no nonsense, and he certainly would not cotton to the likes of Black Fetchen.

"Mr. Sharp?" I said. "I'm Flagan Sackett, this here is my brother Galloway, and our friend, Cap Rountree. The young lady is Judith Costello."

Now, mayhap that wasn't just the way to introduce folks, but I wanted Tom Sharp to know who we were right off, for if a lot of tough strangers had been coming into the country, he would not be in a trusting mood.

He ignored me, looking first at Judith, for which I didn't blame him. "How are you, Judith? Your father has spoken of you."

"Is he all right? I mean...we haven't heard, and those men..."

"He was all right the last I saw of him, but that's been over a month ago. Will you get down and come in? The wife will be wanting to talk to you, and I'm sure you could all do with some food."

Whilst the rest of them went in, I led the horses to water. After a bit Tom Sharp came out, and gave a look at the horses. "Fine stock," he said. "Is that some of the Costello brand?"

"Yes, it is. We've taken the responsibility of bringing Judith out here to her pa, but there's been trouble along the way. With the Fetchens."

"I have heard of them," Sharp said grimly, "and nothing good. And it isn't the first time."

I gave him a surprised glance. "You've run into them before? You surely ain't from Tennessee?"

"From Missouri. No, it wasn't back there. A few years ago we had a sight of trouble over east and north of here with the Reynolds gang, and one of the gang was a Fetchen. They were some connection of the Reynolds outfit, I never did know what it was. The Reynolds outfit were wiped out, but Fetchen wasn't among those killed."

"Which one was he?"

"Tirey Fetchen. He'd be about my age now. He was a wanted man even before he tied up with the Reynolds gang. I'd had wanted circulars on him when

I was a deputy sheriff up in Wyoming, maybe twelve years back, and I recall they listed killings back before the war. He was with the Reynolds gang during the war."

We stabled the horses, and then I went inside. The rest of them were gathered around a table eating, and that food surely smelled good.

"We've seen them come in," Sharp told us over coffee, "but not to stay around. They'd show up, then head for the hills." He looked around at me. "If they've gone up to Costello's place, he may be in real trouble."

"If Judith can stay here," I suggested, "we'll ride up and look around."

"I'll not stay!" Judith exclaimed.

"Now, ma'am," Sharp protested.

"I mean it. I have come all the way to see my father, and I won't wait any longer. I'm going with you." Then she added, looking right at me, "If you don't take me I'll go by myself."

Well, I looked over at Galloway and he shrugged, and that was all there was to it. Both of us knew there was no time to be gained arguing with a woman, and we'd both had a try before this at arguing with Judith.

She went off with Mrs. Sharp, and Sharp sat down with us. "You boys better ride careful," he said. "That's a bad outfit."

So we told him about the trip west and the loss of the Hawkes herd, the Half-Box H.

Sharp was thoughtful. When he looked up at us he said, "I'd better warn you, and when Hawkes comes along you'd better warn him. Fetchen registered a brand in his own name, the JBF Connected."

Cap chuckled. "Ain't takin' him a while to learn. A JBF Connected would fit right over a Half-Box H, fit it like a glove. If Hawkes ain't right careful he'll find all his herd wearin' the wrong brand."

I looked at Sharp. "How are folks hereabouts? Are they understandin'?"

"That depends."

"Maybe the only way we can get those cattle back is to rustle them," I said. "If he can misbrand cattle, we can just brand 'em over."

"What about that?" Galloway said. "What would cover a JBF Connected?"

"When we were ridin' through Texas," I suggested, "we saw a man down there who had a Pig-Pen brand. And I heard tell of one with a Spider-Web. They would cover most anything you could dream up."

"You would have to be careful," Sharp said. "And if you will forgive me, I would have to see Hawkes's papers on the herd."

"He's got 'em, and he'll be showing up right quick." I paused a minute, giving it thought. "What we figured, would be to sort of let the word get around. I mean, about Hawkes's herd and what he figures to do about it."

Sharp chuckled. "Now, that could be right amusing. But you'd have to move fast. It is about roundup time."

"So much the better. A lot of things can happen during a roundup. Only thing we want is to have it understood this is strictly between us and the Fetchen crowd."

"Serve them right," Sharp said. "You just wait until word gets around. You'll have the whole country on your side."

Nevertheless, I was worried. We had to get back into the hills and scout around the Costello outfit, and we had to see Costello himself, but Galloway and me, we knew that every step of the way would be a step further into trouble. Whatever the Fetchens were up to, they were also laying a trap for us, and we were riding up there, maybe right into the trap.

The more we learned, the more we had to worry about. Evan Hawkes was still far behind us, whilst the Fetchens were here, and in considerable strength. Along the line they had picked up more men, outlaws and the like.

But what was it that Black Fetchen was really after? What lay behind their move west? Had it been simply because of their killing of Laban Costello? And for revenge on us? Or was there some deeper cause that began even before we showed up? Was it something they wanted even more than Judith, more than the horses, more than Costello's ranch, if that was what they aimed for?

The thing that stuck in my mind was that Tirey Fetchen had stirred about in these parts before any of us came west, and with the Reynolds gang. Now, there was something about that...I couldn't recall what it was, but something I'd heard about that Reynolds outfit.

They had been a gang of outlaws who passed it off that they were robbing to get money for the Confederacy, or that was the tale I'd heard. They had been caught up with, and some of them had been tied to a tree and shot. I had nothing to say about that part of it to anybody, because I wanted to recall what it was about the Reynolds gang that made me remember them ... some item I'd forgotten.

We went into the hills, climbing high up by an old Ute trail that Sharp told us of, and we skirted about to reach the valley where Costello's outfit lay.

No horse tracks showed on the trail we rode. No sound came from anywhere near. There were, of course, birds talking it up in the bushes, and a slow wind that stirred the trees as we rode along. Nothing else but once in a while the rattle of a spur or the creak of a saddle as a horse took strain in climbing, or a rider shifted weight in the saddle. Sunlight dappled the trail with leaf shadows.

We did not talk. We listened as we rode, and from time to time we paused to listen more carefully.

Cap, who was riding point, drew up suddenly, and we closed in around him. Before us was an opening among the branches of the trees lining the trail. Several miles away we could see a green valley, perhaps five hundred feet lower down, and from it sunlight reflected from a window.

"That will be it," Cap commented. "The way Sharp told it, we will be ridin' Costello range at almost any minute."

We pushed on, circling the smaller valleys that made a chain through the hills. Now, from time to time, cattle tracks showed among those of deer and elk.

The ranch, when we came upon it, lay cupped in the hills, a small but comfortable house set back on a green meadow where a stream curled through. There was slow smoke rising from the chimney, and a good lot of horses in the corrals. Sitting on the stoop in front of the house was a man with a rifle across his knees. We saw no other folks around.

In the meadow a dozen or so head of horses were grazing, the sun gleaming from their smooth flanks. It made a handsome sight, but the man on the stoop looked mighty like a guard.

Galloway sat his horse, giving study to the place, and I did likewise. "Looks too easy," Galloway said after a bit. "I don't like it."

"It's a nice morning," Cap commented. "They might just be idling about."

"Or hid out, waiting for us," I said.

We waited, but Judith was impatient. "Flagan, I want to go down there. I want to see Pa."

"You hold off," I said. "You'll see him soon enough ... when we know it's safe."

"But he may be in danger!" she protested. "They killed my grandfather, you told me so yourself."

"Yes, but it won't ease your pa's mind to have you in their hands, too. You just wait."

The valley where the ranch lay opened into another, wider valley that we could see as we moved along. There were a few cattle in the first one, and we could see more beyond. The grass was green and rich, and running down the streams there was all the snow water that any rancher could want for his stock. Costello had found a good place.

"They're hid out," Galloway said finally. "I have it in mind they're expecting us. No ranch is quiet like that, this time of day. Not with so many men somewhere about."

We had moved along to a lower bench among the trees, a place not forty feet from where the mountain dropped off into the valley. We saw a man come from the ranch house, saw the screen door shut behind him. From where we were, we could hear it slam.

This man, after a few minutes of talk, seated himself on the steps, while the first man went inside, apparently relieved from guard duty.

"Your pa," Cap surmised, "must be in the house. Certain sure, there's something or somebody down there to be watched over."

Nobody was saying what we had been thinking, that it would make little sense to keep Costello alive ... unless they were worried for fear some neighbor might insist on seeing him. By this time the Fetchens would know about Tom Sharp, a man not likely to be put off, nor one to trifle with. Yet time would be running out.

They might hold Costello as they had planned to hold Judith, one to be used in controlling the other. If Black Fetchen could get hold of Judith, marry her, and so establish legal claim to the Costello ranch, then Costello might be made to disappear, leaving them in control. It was a likely thing, but there was much that was puzzling about the whole affair, and about their possible connection with the Reynolds gang.

We waited under the trees, moving as little as possible, and keeping wary for fear we would be discovered. The whole thing was growing irksome, and Judith had my sympathy. Her pa was down there, and it was natural she should want to see him. Only we needed to know a few more things before we could act against them. We needed to know if Costello was alive, and how they were holding him, and we needed to know what they were after.

By now we were all pretty sure that the cattle had been incidental. They had the Half-Box H herd, and they would try to hold it, but I felt certain there was more to it than the herd, or even the ranch.

We had to wait them out. I knew they were not patient men and would soon tire of lying around in the brush, doing nothing.

"We've got to know more about this setup," I said. "Cap, do you know the story of the Reynolds outfit?"

"No more than everybody hereabouts knows. They gave it out that they were Confederate sympathizers, and began robbin' some gold trains and the like, letting it be known they were gettin' the gold to hold for the South. But most folks thought they had no such idea—not after the gold started pilin' up. They figured they planned to use it for themselves."

"What happened to the gold?"

"I can't say as I ever heard, although no doubt folks who lived round here could tell you."

"Sharp would know," Galloway suggested.

In the fading afternoon the Costello ranch looked mighty pretty. Shadows were stretching out, but down there the light was mellow and lovely. I could see why a man, even a mover like Costello, would like to settle in such a place. And there was good grazing in the hills around.

But we saw nothing of Costello, nor of anyone else at all.

The stars came out and the wind grew cool. Restlessly, I walked out to a place where the valley could be seen in more detail. There were lights in the ranch house, and shadows moved before some of the windows. Suddenly the door opened and someone went in. It was open long enough to admit two or three men.

Judith came up beside me. "Do you think Pa is down there, Flagan?"

"Uh-huh."

She said nothing more for some time, and then wondered out loud, "Why did this happen to us?"

"I reckon folks have wondered that always, Judith. In this case it's no accident, I'm thinking. Your pa or your grandpa knew something somebody else wanted to know, or else for some reason they need this ranch."

"Flagan, I've been thinking about what you wanted to know...you know, if Pa had been in Missouri in seventy-one. I am sure he was, because I've just remembered something."

"What?"

"Pa had an uncle who wasn't much good. He'd gone off and left us after he got into some trouble with the family, and he went out west. Nobody would talk about him much, but he got into more trouble... in Denver, I think it was."

"And so?"

"He came back one night. I remember I woke up and heard talking in a low voice, in Pa's side of the tent. I heard another man's voice, a man who sounded odd...as if he was sick or something."

That was all she remembered right then, but it was enough to start me thinking.

Maybe what the Costellos knew was nothing they picked up in trade. Maybe it was something that renegade told them that night in Missouri.

That renegade had been in or around Denver. So had Tirey Fletchen. And so had the Reynolds gang.

CHAPTER 11

WE RODE AWAY down the mountain to a hollow in the hills, sheltered by overhanging cliffs and a wall of pines, and made camp there where we could have a fire.

"I figure if we go down to the ranch we'll get so shot full of holes our hides wouldn't be worth tanning," Galloway said. "That outfit's all laid out for an ambush, so let's leave 'em wait."

"Seems to me a likely time to be thinkin' of them cattle," Cap suggested.

"Now, there's a good thought. Let's dab a loop on some and check out the brand."

So we settled down over coffee and bacon to consider. It stood to reason that if most of their crowd were waiting for us to show up, there would be only a few watching the cattle, if any at all. In these mountain valleys, with plenty of grass and water, cattle needed no watching.

The upshot of it was that when the sky lightened with another day coming, we saddled up and went off. The only one who was upset by our decision was Judith.

"This isn't taking me any closer to Pa!" she objected. "I wish I could find a man like Ivanhoe or the Black Knight! He would ride right down there and bring Pa back!"

"You know," I said, "I don't carry any banners for the Fetchen boys, but if the Black Knight was to ride down amongst them in his tin suit he'd have a sieve for an overcoat. Those Fetchens may run short on morals, but morals don't win no turkey-shoots! I know those boys, and they could part your hair with the first bullet and trim around your ears with the next two.

"If you want to choose up heroes to help you, you'd be a sight better off to pick on Robin Hood or Rob Roy. My pa always said you should never walk into a man when he's set for punching. Better to go around him and work him out of balance.

"Well, while they're waiting for us to come down on 'em, we'll simply round up and drive off a few head of cattle. Then we might sort of scout around down to Sharp's place at Buzzard Roost. I'll lay a bet Fetchen has somebody staked out down there to bring him word."

By the time the sun was high we were at Buzzard Roost and sitting alongside the stove eating crackers and sardines, and I mentioned the Reynolds outfit. I'd scarcely said the name before Sharp was giving us the story.

The Reynolds gang had buried a treasure, some said, somewhere near the Spanish Peaks. They were right over there to the south of us, only a few miles away.

Contrary to what some folks said, they hadn't been a very bloody outfit. Fact was, it was claimed they'd killed nobody in their robberies. Reynolds had some reputation as an outlaw before the war began, and then supposedly he was recruited by the South to loot

Colorado of its gold and silver shipments. "There's been a lot of talk about how much he stole," Sharp said, "and how much they buried when the law caught up with them; but no matter what anybody says there's small chance they had over seventy thousand dollars."

"That's a lot," Galloway said, kind of dryly. "That's more money than I'm likely to see in this lifetime."

"Do you think it's there?" Cap asked.

Sharp shrugged. "It's certain they hadn't anything on 'em when they were caught, and they hadn't much time to hide it unless they hid it very soon after taking it—which could be."

Judith wasn't talking, she was just sitting there looking solemn and kind of scared too, yet knowing her I had a feeling she was scared less for herself than for her Pa. It came to me that I should try, by some trick, to get him away from the ranch.

That was easy said, but the little valley was bounded by pretty high mountains, and getting in and out of such a guarded place would be next to impossible.

Cap drifted off somewhere, and Galloway did, too, while I sat with Judith. I said to her, "Don't you worry. He's all right, and we'll have him out of there in no time."

"Flagan, I just couldn't imagine he would be like this—James Fetchen, I mean."

For a minute I couldn't place James Fetchen, we were so used to calling him Black. Then I said, "How could you know? All you'd seen of him was a tall, fine-looking man riding by on a horse. Believe me, you can't always tell a coyote by his holler. But that Fetchen outfit was known all over the mountains by the trouble they caused, by the shootings and cuttings they'd been in."

Judith left me, to talk with Sharp's wife, and I walked out on the stoop, looking about for Galloway and Cap, but I saw neither one of them. I don't know what made me do it, but I reached my fingers back and slipped the rawhide loop off my six-gun, freeing it for quick use, if need be.

There's times when nothing is more companionable than a six-shooter, and I had an uneasy feeling, almost as if somebody was walking on my grave, or maybe digging one for me.

The sunlight was bright on Buzzard Roost, and on the mountains all around. A dog trotted lazily across the dusty road, and far up the valley I could see cattle feeding on the grass on the lower slopes of Little Sheep. Everything looked peaceful enough.

There seemed no particular reason why I should feel this way just now. Black Fetchen and his kin had reason for wanting to stake out my hide, but it seemed to me they were in no hurry. That outfit was sure of itself. They'd been in shooting scrapes before and they had come out on top, and they figured they would again. Winning can make folks confident... or it can make them cautious.

Here and there I'd come out ahead a few times, but it only made me careful. There's too much that can happen—the twig that deflects your bullet just enough, the time you don't quite get the right grasp on the gun butt, the dust that blows in your eyes....

Anyway, there's things can happen to the fastest of men and to the best shots. So I was cautious.

And then there's the gun itself. No man in his right mind will play with a gun. I've seen show-offs doing fancy spins and all that. No real gun-fighter ever did. With a hair-trigger, he'd be likely to blow a hole in his belly. The gun-fighter knows enough of guns to be wary of them. He treats them with respect. A pistol was never made for anything except killing, and a gun-fighter never draws a gun unless to shoot, and he shoots to kill. And he doesn't go around trying to gun up a score. That's only done by tin-horns. Nor does he ever notch his gun, another tin-horn trick.

All the while these thoughts were sort of in the back of my mind, I had my eyes searching for a lookout, if there was one. It seemed likely that the Fetchens would have somebody around who could keep a watch on Buzzard Roost, for anybody coming or going in that country just naturally rode by there, or stopped off.

I gave thought to where I'd hole up if I was to keep a watch on the place. It would be best to find a place on a hillside, or somewhere a man could keep out of sight while seeing all who came and went. That naturally cut down on the possibilities.

I began to feel that somebody was watching me—I could feel it somehow in my bones. Judith, she came out and walked up to me. "Flagan—" she began, but I cut her off.

"Go back inside," I said. "Take your time, but you get inside and stay there till I come."

"What's wrong?"

"Judith! Damn it, get inside!"

"Flagan Sackett, you can't talk to me like that! Who do you think—"

Sunlight made a slanting light on a gun barrel in the brush not a hundred and fifty feet away. It was a far shot for a six-gun, but I'd hit targets at a greater distance than that.

With my left hand I swept Judith back toward the door, and my right went down for my gun just as the other gun muzzle stabbed flame. It was the movement to push Judith out of the way that saved my bacon, for that bullet whipped by my ear, stinging me as it went.

My six-gun was up and hammering shots. I was holding high because of the distance, and I let three bullets go in one roll of sound, as fast and slick as I could thumb back the hammer and let it drop.

Then I ran forward three steps, and took one to the side and fired again, holding a mite higher because he might be up and running. I was firing at the place I'd seen the flare of the gun muzzle, but was scattering my shots to have a better chance of scoring a hit.

The battering explosion of the shots died away, leaving a sudden silence, a silence in which the ears cried out for sound. I stood there, gun poised, aware that it was empty, but hesitating to betray the fact to my enemy, whoever he was.

Slowly I lowered the gun muzzle, and as unobtrusively as possible I opened the loading-gate with my thumb and worked the ejector, pushing the empty shell from the cylinder. Instantly, I fed a cartridge into place, then ejected another, and repeated this until the gun was reloaded. In all that time there was no sound, nor was there any movement in the brush.

Unwilling to take my eyes from the brush, I wondered where Cap and Galloway might be.

And had Judith been hit? I felt quite sure she had not, but a body never knew, when there was shooting taking place.

Warily, I took a step toward the brush, but nothing happened.

Off on my right Galloway suddenly spoke. "I think you got him, boy."

Walking slowly toward the brush, I had to make several climbing steps as I got close to it. There was an outcropping of rock, with thick, thorny brush growing around and over it, and several low trees nearby. The whole clump was no more than thirty or forty yards across, and just about as deep.

First thing I saw was the rifle. It was a Henry .44 and there was a fresh groove down the stock, cut by a bullet. There was blood on the leaves, but nothing else.

Gun in hand, I eased into the brush and stood still, listening. It was so quiet I seemed to be hearing my own heart beat. Somewhere off across country a crow cawed; otherwise there was silence. Then the door of the trading post opened and I heard boot heels on the boards.

My eyes scanned the brush, but I could see no sign of anyone there. Parting the branches with my left hand, I stepped past another bush. On a leaf there was a bright crimson spot . . . fresh blood. Just beyond it was a barely visible track of a boot heel in the soft earth. I was expecting a shot at any moment. It was one of those places where a man figures he's being watched by somebody he can't see.

Then I saw a slight reddish smear on the bark of a tree where the wounded man had leaned. He was hit pretty good, it looked like, although a man can sometimes bleed a good bit from a mighty inconsiderable wound.

I could tell that the man I hunted had gone right on through the brush. I followed through and suddenly came to the other side.

For about fifty yards ahead the country was open, and a quick glance told me that nothing stirred there. Standing under cover of the brush, I began to scan the ground with care, searching every clump of grass or cluster of small rocks—anywhere a man might be concealed.

The ground on this side of the knoll sloped away for several feet, and this place was invisible from the trading post. A man might slip down from the mountain, or come around the base and ease into the brush, leave his horse and get right up to that knoll without anybody being the wiser.

Pistol ready, I walked slowly toward the further trees, my eyes scanning the terrain all around me. Twice I saw flecks of blood.

Beyond the trees, on a small patch of grass, I saw where a horse had been tied on a short rope. By the look of the grass he had been tied there several times, each time feeding close around him. Whoever tied the horse had allowed him just enough rope to crop a little grass without giving him more rope than a man could catch up along with the reins, in one quick move.

Whoever had been watching there must have suddenly decided to try his shot. It must have seemed like a copper-riveted cinch, catching me out like that. Only my move in getting Judith out of the way had saved me.

Galloway had come up behind me. "You're bleedin', Flagan," he said.

I put my hand to my ear, which had been smarting some, and brought it away bloody. From the feel of it, the bullet had just grazed the top of the ear.

We followed the rider back into the hills a short way, then lost his trail on a dusty stretch. We found no more blood, and from the way he'd moved in going to his horse I figured he hadn't been hurt more than I had been.

When we got back to the trading post, Evan Hawkes was there, making plans with Tom Sharp for the roundup.

It turned out they had friends in common, stock-buyers and the like. There were eight or ten other cattlemen around the country who were all close friends of Sharp, and all of them had come to be wary of the Fetchen boys.

"One thing I want understood," Hawkes said. "This is our fight. They opened the ball, now we're going to play the tune and they'll dance to our music."

"Seems to me you're outnumbered," said Dobie Wiles. He was the hard-bitten foreman of the Slash B. "And it seems to me that JBF Connected brand will cover our brand as well as yours."

"They left blood on the Kansas grass," Galloway said, "blood of the Half-Box H. I figure Hawkes has first call."

He gave a slow grin. "And that includes us."

CHAPTER 12

THE CATTLE CAME down from the hills in the morning, drifting ahead of riders from the neighboring ranches. They moved out on the grass of the bottom land and grazed there, while the riders turned again to the hills.

At first only a few riders were to be seen, for the land was rough and there were many canyons. The cowboys moved back into the hills and along the trails and started the cattle drifting down toward the valley.

The chuck wagon was out, and half a dozen local cattlemen, all of whom rode out from time to time only to return and gather near the wagon. James Black Fetchen himself had not appeared, although several Fetchens were seen riding in the hills. Once, Evan Hawkes roped a young steer and, with Tom Sharp as well as two other cattlemen beside him, studied the brand. It was his Half-Box H worked over to a JBF Connected.

"They do better work down in Texas," Breedlove commented. "There's rustlers down there who do it better in the dark."

Rodriguez looked around at Hawkes. "Do you wish to register a complaint, Señor?"

"Let it go. That steer will be wearing a different brand before this is over."

"As you will."

"When this is over, if there is any steer you want to question we can either skin him and check the brand from the reverse side, or turn him into a pool for it to be decided. I want no cattle but my own, and no trouble with anyone but Fetchen."

"And that trouble, Señor—when does it come?"

"I hope to delay it until after the roundup. There's a lot the Fetchens don't know about cattle and rustling. If I figure it right, they're going to come up short and never know what hit them." He glanced around at them. "Gentlemen, this is my fight, mine and the Sackett boys'. There's no reason to get mixed up in it if you don't have to."

"This is our country," Sharp replied, "and we don't take to rustlers. We'll give you all the room you want, but if you need a hand, just lift a yell and we'll be coming."

"Of course, Señor," Rodriguez said mildly, "but there may have to be trouble. A rider from the Fetchen outfit was drinking in Greenhorn. It seems he was not polite to one of my riders. There were seven Fetchens, and my man was alone. At the roundup he will not be alone."

Hawkes nodded. "I know...I heard some talk about that, but shooting at a roundup might kill a lot of good men. Let's take it easy and see what happens when the tally is taken."

I listened and had no comment to offer. It was a nice idea, if it worked. It might work, but there were a few outsiders riding with the Fetchen gang now, and they might know more about brand-blotting than the Fetchens did. That scar-faced puncher with the blond hair, for example. What was his name again? ... Russ Menard.

I spoke the name out loud, and Rodriguez turned on me. "*Russ Menard?* You know him?"

"He's here. He's one of them."

The Mexican's lips tightened, then he bared his teeth in a smile that held no humor. "He is a very bad *hombre,* this Menard. I think no faster man lives when it comes to using the pistol. If he is one of them, there will surely be trouble."

The cattle had scattered so widely in the hills that it was brutally hard work combing them out of the brush and canyons. This was rugged country— canyons, brush, and boulders, with patches of forest, and on the higher slopes thick stands of timber that covered miles. But there was water everywhere, so most of the stock was in good shape. Aside from Hawkes's rustled herd, there were cattle from a dozen other outfits, including those of Tom Sharp. By nightfall several hundred head were gathered in the valley.

Most of the riders were strangers, men from the ranches nearby, good riders and hard-working men. They knew the country and they knew the cattle and so had an advantage over us, who were new to the land. Most of them were Mexicans, and they were some of the best riders and ropers I ever did see. Galloway and me were handy with ropes but in no way as good as most of those around us, who had been using them since they were knee-high to a short pup.

Most of the stock was longhorn, stuff driven in from Texas over the Goodnight Trail. The cattle from New Mexico were of a lighter strain when unmixed with longhorn blood; and there was a shorthorn or whiteface stock brought in from Missouri or somewhere beyond the Mississippi. Both Costello and Sharp had been driving in a few cattle of other breeds, trying to improve their stock to carry more beef.

The longhorn was a good enough beef critter when he could get enough to eat and drink, but in Texas they might live miles from water, drinking every two or three days, in some cases, and walking off a lot of good beef to get to water.

But in these mountain valleys where there was water a-plenty, there was no need to walk for it and the eastern stock did mighty well. And nowhere did we see the grass all eaten down. There was enough feed to carry more stock than was here.

———

THE ONLY TWO Fetchens I saw were men I remembered from that day in Tazewell. Their names I didn't learn until I heard them spoken around the roundup fire.

Clyde Fetchen was a wiry man of thirty-five or so with a narrow, tight-lipped look about him. He was a hard worker, which was more than I could say of the others, but not a friendly man by any way of speaking. Len Fetchen was seventeen or eighteen, broad-shouldered, with hair down to his shoulders. He didn't talk at all. Both of them fought shy of Galloway an' me—no doubt told to do so by Black.

Others came to the fire occasionally, but those were the only two I saw. Them and Russ Menard.

Meanwhile we were doing a sight of work that a body couldn't see around the branding fire. We were doing our work back in the hills, wherever we could find Half-Box Hitch cattle. All their brands had been altered by now, some of the changed brands so fresh the hide was still warm, or almost. Wherever we found them we dabbed a loop over their horns, threw them, and rebranded with a Pig-Pen, which was merely a series of vertical and horizontal lines like several pens side by each. A brand like that could cover everything we found, but we were only hunting stolen Hawkes cattle. We took turn and turn about bringing cattle to the fire, and the rest of the time we roamed up and down the range, sorting out Hawkes cattle.

Russ Menard spent mighty little time working cattle, so he didn't notice what was going on. The Fetchen boys brought in cattle here and there, mostly with their own brand. At night Briggs and Walker could usually manage to cut out a few of them and brand them downwind from the wagon, out of sight in some creek bed or gully.

By the third day half the hands on the range had fallen in with the game and were rebranding the rustled cattle as fast as we were. On the fifth day, James Black Fetchen came riding down from the hills with Russ Menard and six of his riders.

Evan Hawkes was standing by the fire, and when he saw Fetchen coming he called to Ladder Walker. The tall, lean Half-Box H puncher looked up, then slid the thong off his six-gun. The cook took another look, then slipped his shot-gun out of his bedroll and tucked it in along his dried apples and flour.

Cap Rountree and Moss Reardon were both out

on the range, but it so happened I was standing right there, taking time out for coffee.

Fetchen rode on up to the fire and stepped down, and so did Menard and Colby. Fetchen turned his hard eyes to me, then to Walker at the fire. The cook was busy kneading dough. Tom Sharp was there, and so were Rodriguez and Baldwin, who was repping for a couple of outfits over on the Cucharas.

"I want to see the tally list," Fetchen said.

"Help yourself." Hawkes gestured to where it lay on a large rock, held down by a smaller rock.

Fetchen hesitated, and looked hard at Hawkes.

Russ Menard was looking across the fire at me. "You one of them gun-fighting Sacketts?" he asked.

"Never paid gun-fighting no mind," I said. "Too busy making a living. Seems to me a man's got mighty little to do, riding around showing off his gun."

He got kind of red in the face. "Meaning?"

"Meaning nothing a-tall. Just commenting on why I don't figure myself a gun-fighter. We Sacketts never figured on doing any fighting unless pushed," I added.

"What do you carry that gun for?" he demanded.

I grinned at him. "Seems I might meet somebody whose time has come."

Black Fetchen had turned around sharply, his face red and angry. "What the hell *is* this? You've only got thirty-four head of JBF cattle listed."

"That's all there was," Hawkes said quietly, "and a scrubby lot, too."

Fetchen stepped forward, the color leaving his face, his eyes burning under his heavy brows. "What are you trying to do? Rob me? I came into this valley with more than a thousand head of cattle."

"If you have a bill of sale," Sharp suggested, "we might check out the brands and find out what's wrong. Your bill of sale would show the original brands, and any stolen cattle would have the brands altered."

Fetchen stopped. Suddenly he was cold, dangerous. Me, I was watching Menard.

"You can't get away with this!" Fetchen said furiously.

"If you have any brand you want to question," Sharp said, "we can always shoot the animal and skin it. The inside of the hide will show if the brand has been altered."

Fetchen glanced at him, realizing that to check the brand would reveal the original alteration, the change from Hawkes's Half-Box H to his JBF Connected. Frustrated, he hesitated, suddenly aware he had no way to turn.

Hawkes, Sharp, and Rodriguez were scattered out. Baldwin stood near the chuck wagon, and all of them were armed. Ladder Walker had released the calf he had been branding and was now standing upright, branding iron in his left hand.

And there was me.

To start shooting now would mean death for several men, and victory for nobody. Fetchen started to speak, then his eye caught the dull gloss of the shotgun stock, inches from the cook's hand.

"While we're talking," I suggested, "you might tell Costello he should be down here, repping for his brand. We have business to discuss with him."

"He's not well," Fetchen replied, controlling his anger. "I'll speak for him."

"Costello is a very good friend of mine," Sharp said, "and a highly respected man in this country. We want to be sure he stays well. I think he should be brought down to my place where he can have the attention of a doctor."

"He's not able to ride," Fetchen said. He was worried now, and eager to be away. Whatever his plans had been, they were not working now. His herd was gone, taken back by the very man from whom it had been stolen, and the possibility of his remaining in the area and ranching was now slim indeed.

"Load him into a wagon," Sharp insisted. "If you don't have one, I'll send one up, and enough men to load him up."

Fetchen backed off. "I'll see. I'll talk to him," he said.

Right at that moment I figured him for the most dangerous man I'd ever known. There'd been talk about his hot temper, but this man was cold—cold and mean. You could see it in him, see him fighting down the urge to grab for a gun and turn that branding fire into a blaze of hell. He had it in him, too, only he was playing it smart. And a few moments later I saw another reason why.

Moss Reardon, Cap Rountree, and Galloway had come up behind us, and off to the left was Kyle Shore.

Fetchen's gang would have cut some of us down, but not a one of them would have escaped.

Russ Menard looked at me and smiled. "We'll meet up, one of these days."

"We can make it right now," I said. "We can make it a private fight."

"I ain't in no hurry."

James Black Fetchen looked past me toward the chuck wagon. "Judith, your pa wants you. You comin'?"

"No."

"You turnin' your back on him?"

"You know better than that. When he comes down to Mr. Sharp's, at Buzzard Roost, I'll be waiting for him."

The Fetchens went to their horses then, Russ Menard taking the most time. When he was in the saddle, both hands out in plain sight, he said, "Don't you disappoint me, boy. I'll be hunting you."

They rode away, and Tom Sharp swore softly. With the back of his hand, he wiped sudden sweat from his forehead. "I don't want to go through that again. For a minute there, anything could have happened."

"You sleep with locked doors," Galloway said, riding up. "And don't answer no hails by night. That's a murdering lot."

The rest of the roundup went forward without a hitch. The cattle were driven in from the hills and we saw no more of the Fetchens, but Costello did not come down from the hills. Twice members of the gang were seen close to the Spanish Peaks. Once several of them rode over to Badito.

The roundup over, Rodriguez announced a fandango. That was their name for a big dancing and to-do, where the folks come from miles around. Since no rider from the Fetchen crowd had come down to claim the beef that still wore their brand over the

Half-Box H, it was slaughtered for a barbecue...at least, the three best steers were.

Rodriguez came around to Galloway and me. "You will honor my house, Señores? Yours is a name well known to me. Tyrel Sackett is married to the daughter of an old friend of mine in New Mexico."

"We will come," I said.

Nobody talked much of anything else, and Galloway and me decided we'd ride down to Pueblo or up to Denver to buy us new outfits. Judith was all excited, and was taking a hand in the planning.

We rode off to Denver, and it was two weeks before we got back, just the night of the big shindig. The first person we saw was Cap Rountree.

"You didn't come none too soon," he said. "Harry Briggs is dead...dry-gulched."

CHAPTER 13

IT HAD BEEN a particularly vicious killing. Not only had Briggs been shot from ambush, but his killers had ridden over his body and shot into it again and again.

There could be no doubt as to why it had been done. Briggs was a hard-working cowhand with no enemies, and he carried no money; of the little he could save, the greater part was sent to a sister in Pennsylvania. He had been killed because he rode for the Half-Box H, and it could just as easily have been any of the other hands.

And there was no doubt as to who had done it, though there didn't seem to be any chance of proving it. It was the Fetchen crowd, we knew. There was no other possibility. From the fragments of tracks found near the body, they could tell that more than one killer was involved; he had been shot with at least two different weapons—probably more.

"We've done some scoutin' around," Reardon told us. "The Fetchen riders have been huntin' around the Spanish Peaks. We found tracks up that way. Sharp figures they're huntin' the Reynolds treasure."

Ladder Walker was glum. "Briggs was a good man. Never done harm to nobody. I'm fixin' to hunt me some Fetchens."

"Take it easy," Reardon warned. "Those boys are

mean, and they ain't about to give you no chance. No fair chance, that is."

Judith was standing on the porch when I rode up. "Flagan, I'm worried about Pa. All this time, and no word. Nobody has seen him, and the Fetchens won't let anyone come near the place."

I'd been giving it considerable thought, and riding back from Denver, Galloway and me had made up our minds to do something about it. The trouble was, we didn't know exactly what.

Nobody in his right mind goes riding into a bottlenecked valley where there's fifteen to twenty men waiting for him, all fixing to notch their guns for his scalp. And the sides of that valley allowed for no other approach we knew of. Yet there had to be a way, and one way might be to cause some kind of diversion.

"Suppose," I suggested, "we give it out that we've found some sign of that Reynolds gold? We could pick some lonely place over close to Spanish Peaks, let out the rumor that we had it located and were going in to pick it up."

"With a big enough party to draw them all away from the ranch?"

"That's right. It wouldn't do any harm, and it might pull them all away so we could ride in and look around."

We finally picked on a place not so far off as the Spanish Peaks. We rode over to Badito—Galloway, Ladder Walker, and me—and we had a couple of drinks and talked about how we'd located the Reynolds treasure.

Everybody for miles around had heard that story,

so, like we figured, there were questions put to us. "Is it near the Spanish Peaks?" one man asked.

"That's just it," Galloway said. "Everybody took it for granted that when Reynolds talked about twin peaks he meant the Spanish Peaks. Well, that was where everybody went wrong. The peaks Reynolds and them talked about were right up at the top of the Sangre de Cristos. I mean what's called Blanca Peak."

"There's three peaks up there," somebody objected.

"Depends on where you stand to look at them. I figure that after they buried the loot they took them for landmarks—just looked back and saw only two peaks, close together."

"So you think you've found the place?" The questioner was skeptical. "So have a lot of others."

"We found a knife stuck into a tree for a marker, and we found a stone slab with markings on it."

Oh, we had them now. Everybody knew that Reynolds had told of thrusting a knife into a tree to mark the place, so we knew our story would be all around the country in a matter of hours. Somebody would be sure to tell the Fetchens, just to get their reaction.

"We're going up there in the morning," Walker said, making out to be drunker than he was. "We'll camp in Bronco Dan Gulch, and we'll be within a mile of the treasure. You just wait. Come daylight, we'll come down the pass loaded with gold."

Now, Bronco Dan was a narrow little gulch that headed up near the base of Lone Rock Hill, only three or four miles from the top of the rim. It was wild country, and just such a place as outlaws might choose to hide out or cache some loot. And it wasn't but a little way above La Veta Pass.

Anyway a body looked at it, the place made a lot of sense. La Veta Pass was the natural escape route for anybody trying to get over the mountains from Walsenburg to Alamosa, and vice versa.

Of course, they knew about the knife. That was the common feature of the stories about the Reynolds treasure—that he had marked the place by driving a knife into a tree. The stone marker was pure invention, but they found it easy to accept the idea that Reynolds might have scratched a map on a slab of rock.

That night Cap Rountree went up the mountain and hid in the brush where he could watch the Costello place, and when we arrived shortly after daybreak he told us the Fetchens had taken out in a pack just before daylight.

"They took the bait, all right. Oh, yes, I could see just enough to see them ride out."

"How many stayed behind?"

"Two, three maybe. I don't know for sure."

Galloway went to his horse, and I did the same. You can lay a couple of bets I wasn't anxious to go down there, but we had set this up and this was the chance we'd been playing for.

Cap started to follow along, but I waved him back. "You stay here. No use all of us getting boxed in down there. If you see them coming back, give a shout."

Ladder Walker was along with us—there was no leaving him out of it. So the three of us went down the mountain, following the trail where cattle had crossed a saddle, and we came into the valley within two hundred yards of the ranch, just beyond the corral.

"Stay with the horses, Ladder," I said. "And keep an eye on the opening. I don't like this place, not a bit."

"You figure it for a trap?"

"Could be. Black Fetchen is a wily one, and we've had it too easy so far. We've had almost too much luck."

Galloway and me, spread apart a little, walked toward the house.

We played it in luck this time too. Nobody seemed to be around until we stepped up on the porch. Then we could hear voices coming from the back of the house.

"Don't get any ideas, old man. You just set tight until the boys come back. Then maybe Black will let you go. If'n he can find that gold and them Sacketts all to once, he might come back plumb satisfied."

"He won't find the Sacketts," I said, stepping from the hallway into the room where they sat. It was the kitchen, and on my sudden entrance one of the men stood up so quick he almost turned over the table.

"Get your hat, Mr. Costello," I said. "We've come to take you to Judith."

I hadn't drawn my gun, being of no mind to shoot anybody unless they asked for it. There were two of Fetchen's men in the room and our arriving that way had taken the wind out of them. They just looked at us, even the one who had stood up so quick.

Costello, who was a slim, oldish man with a shock of graying hair, got up and put on his hat.

"Here, now!" The Fetchen man standing up had gotten his senses back, and he was mad. "Costello, you come back and set down! The same goes for you Sacketts, unless you want to get killed. Black Fetchen is ridin' up to this ranch right now."

"We needn't have any trouble," I said calmly.

"I'll get a horse," Galloway said, and ducked out of the door, Costello following him.

"Black will kill you, Sackett. He'll fill your hide with lead."

"I doubt if he's got the guts to try. You tell him I said that."

"I hear tell you're a fast man with a shootin' iron." I could just see the gambler stirring around inside him, and it looked as if it was gettin' the better of his common sense. "I don't think we need to wait for Black. I'd sort of like to try you on myself."

"Your choice."

Meanwhile I walked on into the room, and right up to him. Now, no man likes to start a shooting match at point-blank range, because skill plays mighty little part in it then, and the odds are that both men will get blasted. And anyhow, nobody in his right mind starts shooting at all unless there's no other way, and I wasn't planning on shooting now, if I could help it.

So I just walked in on him and he backed off a step, and when he started to take another step back, I hit him. It was the last thing he was expecting, and the blow knocked him down. It was one quick move for me to slip his gun from its holster and straighten up, but the other man hadn't moved.

"You shuck your guns," I told him. "You just unbuckle and step back, and be careful how you move your hands. I'm a man mighty subject to impressions, and you give me the wrong one and I'm likely to open you up like a gutted sheep."

"I ain't figurin' on it. You just watch it, now." He moved his hands with great care to his belt buckle, unhitched, and let the gun belt fall.

The man on the floor was sitting up. "What's the matter, you yella?" he said to his companion.

"I'm figurin' on livin' a mighty long time, that's all. I ain't seen a gray hair yet, and I got my teeth. Anyway, I didn't see you cuttin' much ice."

"I should've killed him."

"You done the right thing, to my thinkin'. Maybe I ain't so gun-slick as some, and maybe I ain't so smart, but I sure enough know when to back off from a fire so's not to get burned. Don't you get no fancy notions now, Ed. You'd get us both killed."

Well, I gathered up those guns and a rifle I saw in the corner by the door, then I just backed off.

Galloway and Costello were up in their saddles, holding my horse ready.

There wasn't any move from the house until we were cutting around the corral toward the trail down which we had come, and then one man ran from the house toward the barn. Glancing back, I was just in time to see him come out with a rifle, but he took no aim at us; he just lifted the rifle in one hand and fired two quick shots, a space, and then a third shot . . . and he was firing into the air.

"Trouble!" I yelled. "That was a signal!"

Ladder Walker, who had hung back, wanting a shot at anyone who had helped to kill Briggs, now came rushing up behind us. The trail to the saddle over which he had come into the valley was steep, and a hard scramble for the horses, but much of it was among the trees and partly concealed from below.

We heard a wild yell from below and, looking back, I saw Black Fetchen, plainly recognizable because of the horse he rode, charging into the valley, followed by half a dozen riders.

Even as I looked, a man ran toward him, pointing up the mountain. Instantly there was firing, but shooting uphill is apt to be a tricky thing even for a skilled marskman, and their bullets struck well behind us. Before they had the range we were too far away for them, and they wasted no more shots.

But they were coming after us. We could hear their horses far below, and saw the men we had caught in the house catching up horses at the corral, ready to follow.

Deliberately, Galloway slowed his pace. "Easiest way to kill a horse," he said, "running it uphill. We'll leave that to them."

Riding close to Costello, I handed him the gun belt and rifle I'd taken from the cabin. When I'd first run out I had slung the belt over the pommel and hung onto the rifle.

Up ahead of us we heard the sudden boom of a heavy rifle . . . Cap Rountree and his buffalo gun. A moment later came a second shot. He was firing a .56 Spencer that carried a wicked wallop. Personally, I favored the Winchester .44, but that big Spencer made a boom that was a frightening thing to hear, and it could tear a hole in a man it hit so that it was unlikely a doctor would do him much good.

Cap was in the saddle when we reached him, but he made us pull up. "Flagan," he said, "I don't like the look of it. Where's the rest of them?"

There were six or seven behind us, that we knew, but what of the rest?

"You figure we're trapped?" I asked.

"You just look at it. They must know how we got up here, and they can ride out their gap and block our way down the mountain before we can get there."

I was not one to underrate Black Fetchen. Back at the Costello place that man had said Fetchen was due to come riding in at any moment, and at the time I gave it no credit, figuring he was trying a bluff, but then some of the outfit had showed up.

Ladder Walker turned his mount and galloped to a spot where he could look over part of the trail up which we had come in first arriving at our lookout point. He was back in an instant. "Dust down there. Somebody is movin' on the trail."

"Is there a trail south, toward Bronco Dan?"

Cap Rountree chewed his mustache. "There's a shadow of a trail down Placer Creek to La Veta Pass, but that's where you sent some of this outfit. Likely the Fetchens know that trail. If you try it, and they're waitin', it's a death trap."

I gave a glance up toward those peaks that shut us off from the west, and felt something like fear. It was almighty icy and cold up there against the sky, up there where the timber ran out and the raw-backed ridges gnawed the sky. My eyes went along the east face of those ridges.

"What about west?" I asked.

"Well," Cap said reluctantly, "there's a pass off north called Mosca Pass. It's high up and cold, and when you come down the other side you're in the sand dunes."

"We got a choice?" Galloway asked.

"Either run or fight," Walker said, "and if we fight we'll be outnumbered three or four to one."

"I like the odds," Galloway said, "but somebody among us will die."

I looked over at Costello. "Do you know that pass?"

"I know it. If there's any trail there from here, it's nothing but a sheep trail."

"Let's go," I said. Below us we could hear them coming—in fact, we could hear them on both trails.

Costello led off, knowing the country best. Cap knew it by hearsay, but Costello had been up to the pass once, coming on it from the ancient Indian trail that led down Aspen Creek.

We started up the steep mountainside covered with trees, and followed a sort of trail made by deer or mountain sheep.

Mosca Pass had been the old Indian route across the mountains. Later it had been used by freighters, but now it was used only by occasional horsemen who knew the country, and sheepherders bringing their flocks to summer grazing.

Beyond the pass, on the western side, lay the great sand dunes, eighty square miles of shifting, piled-up sand, a place haunted by mystery, avoided by Indians, and a place I'd heard talk of ever since entering Colorado, because of the mysterious disappearances of at least one train of freight wagons and a flock of a thousand sheep, along with the herder.

We didn't have any choice. Black Fetchen undoubtedly had gone himself or had sent riders to look into the story of the Reynolds gold, but at the same time he'd kept riders close to Costello's place to move in if we tried to rescue him. I thought the only thing they hadn't guessed was the trail down the mountain from the saddle. Their missing that one was enough to get us a chance to free Costello; but now they were pushing us back into the mountains, leaving us mighty little room in which to maneuver.

The ridge along which we now rode was a wall that would shut us in. We had to try for one of the passes, and if we succeeded in getting across the mountain we would be on the edge of the sand dunes.

Suppose Black could send those riders who had gone to Bronco Dan Gulch on through La Veta Pass? They could close in from the south, and our only way of escape would be into the dunes. It began to look as if we were fairly trapped, cornered by our own trick, trying to get rid of the gang for a few hours.

From time to time we had to shift our trail. Sometimes it simply gave out, or the ground fell away too steep for any horse to travel. There was no question of speed. Our horses sometimes slid down hill as much as ten to twenty feet, and at times the only thing that saved us were outcroppings of rock or the stands of pine growing on the slope.

But most of the way was under cover and there was no chance of dust, so anybody trying to track us could not be sure exactly where we were.

"We could hole up and make a stand," Walker suggested.

"They'd get above us," Galloway said. "They'd have us trapped on a steep slope so we couldn't go up or down."

Once, breaking out of the timber, we glimpsed the smoke rising from the trading post near the Buzzard Roost Ranch. It was miles away, and there was no chance of us getting down there without breaking through a line of guns. We could make out riders below us, traveling on the lower slopes, cutting us off.

Suddenly there was a bare slope before us, a slope of shale. It was several hundred yards across and extended down the mountain for what must be a quarter of a mile.

Galloway, who was in the lead at the moment, pulled up and we gathered near him. "I don't like it, Flagan," he said. "If that shale started to slide, a man wouldn't have a chance. It would take a horse right off its feet."

We looked up, but the slope above was steep and rocky. A man afoot could have made it with some struggling here and there, but there was no place a horse could go. And downhill was as bad...or worse.

"Ain't much of a choice," Cap said.

"I'll try it," I said. Even as I spoke I was thinking what a fool a man could be. If we tried going back we'd surely run into a shooting match and somebody would get killed—maybe all of us—but if my horse started to slide on that shale I'd surely go all the way; and it was so steep further down that the edge almost seemed to break off sharply.

Stepping down from the saddle, I started toward the edge of the slope, but my horse wanted no part of it. He pulled back, and I had to tug hard to get him out on that shale.

At my first step I sank in over my ankle, but I didn't slide. Bit by bit, taking it as easy as I could, I started out over the slide area. I was not halfway across when I suddenly went in almost to my knees. I struggled to get my feet out of the shale, and felt myself starting to slide. Holding still, I waited a moment, and then I could ease a foot from the shale and managed a step forward. It was harder for my horse, but a good hold on the reins gave him confidence and he came on across the stretch. It took me half an hour to get to the other side, but I made it, though twice my horse went in almost to his belly.

It was easier for the next man, who was Cap Rountree. Cap had been watching me, and I had found a few almost solid places I could point out to him. Before he was across, Walker started, then Costello. All told, that slide held us up a good two hours, but once across we found ourselves on a long, narrow bench that carried us on for over a mile, moving at a good gait.

The top of the pass was open, wind-swept and cold. The western side of it fell steeply away before us. Hesitating, we looked back and glimpsed a bunch of riders, still some miles off, but riding up the pass toward us.

Black Fetchen had planned every move with care. Now we could see just how he must have thought it out, and it mattered not at all whether he went to Bronco Dan or not, he could have trapped us in any case. I was sure they had sent up a smoke or signaled in some manner, and that when we reached the foot of the pass he would have men waiting for us.

The others agreed, so we hunched our shoulders against the chill wind and tried to figure a way out.

It looked as if we either had to fight, facing enemies on both sides, or we had to take our chances in the waterless waste of the sand dunes.

Black Fetchen had taken setbacks and had waited; and then, like a shrewd general, he had boxed us in.

Harry Briggs was dead...murdered. And now it would be us, trapped in the dunes where the sand would cover our bodies. And then Fetchen could go back to get the others...to get Evan Hawkes and his men.

To get Judith....

CHAPTER 14

GALLOWAY URGED HIS horse close to mine and pointed down the mountain. "Riders coming!" he said.

There were two of them, out in the open and coming at a good clip, considering they were riding uphill. We could not make out who they were, but they came on, and no shots were fired.

When they topped out on the ridge we saw they were Kyle Shore and Moss Reardon.

"There's been a shooting over at Greenhorn," Kyle said. "Black Fetchen killed Dobie Wiles in a gun battle—an argument over cattle."

"You boys have ridden right into a trap," Walker told them. "The Fetchens have us boxed in."

They looked around, seeing nobody. "You sure?"

"We'd better get off the ridge," Galloway advised. "Here we're sitting ducks."

"We didn't see anybody," Reardon said doubtfully.

"Try going back," Cap told him. "They're out there, all right."

So now Dobie, foreman of the Slash B, and an outspoken enemy of the Fetchens, was dead. Whatever had brought the Fetchens into this country, it was an all-out war now.

Pushing my horse to the lead, I rode over the rim and started down the steep trail toward the dunes. As

I rode, I was trying to figure some way out of this corner without a fight. Not that I was dodging a fight with the Fetchens. That had to come, but right now the odds were all against us and nobody wants to begin a fight he stands to lose. What I wanted was to find a place we could fight from that would come close to evening things up.

"Keep your eyes skinned," I said over my shoulder. "Unless I've got it wrong, there'll be more Fetchens coming in from the south."

Galloway looked back up the mountain. "They're up there, Flagan," he said, "right on the rim."

Sure enough, we could count eight or nine, and knew there were twice that many close by.

"Flagan," Cap said, "look yonder!"

He pointed to a dust cloud a couple of miles off to the south, a dust cloud made by hard-ridden horses.

It looked to me as if we were up the creek without a paddle, because not far below us the trees scattered out and the country was bare all around, with no kind of shelter. We'd have to stand and fight, or run for the dunes. Well, I just pulled up, stopping so short they all bunched in around me.

"I'll be damned if we do!" I said.

"Do what? What d'you mean?"

"Look at it. He's heading us right into those dunes. We could get boxed in there and die of thirst, or maybe he's got a couple of boys perched on top of one of those dunes with rifles. Just as we get close to them, they'd open fire."

Riders were now on the trail behind us, but some distance back.

"What do you figure to do?"

"We've got to get off this trail. We've got to make our own way, not ride right down the trail he's got set for us."

We walked our horses on through the trees, searching for some kind of way we could take to get off the trail. Knowing the ways of wild game, we figured there might be some trail along the mountainside. Of course, a man on horseback can't follow a deer trail very far unless he's lucky, the way we had been earlier. A deer will go under tree limbs, over rocks, or between boulders where no horse could go. We scattered about as much as the trail and the terrain would allow, and we hunted for tracks.

We were under cover now, out of view from both above and below, but that would not last long.

Ladder Walker came back up the trail from where he had scouted. "They're closin' in, Flagan. They'll be under cover an' waitin' when we show up."

The forest and the mountains have their own secret ways, and in the changing of days the seemingly changeless hills do also change. Fallen snow settles into crevices in the rock and expands in freezing, and so cracks the rock still further. Wind, rain, and blown sand hone the edges of the jagged upthrusts of rock, and find the weak places to hollow them away.

In the passing of years the great cliffs crumble into battlements with lower flanks of talus, scattered slopes of rock, and debris fallen from the crumbling escarpment above.

There upon the north side of the trail I saw a fallen pine, its roots torn from the earth and leaning far over, exposing a narrow opening through the thick timber and the rocks into a glade beyond. It might be no more than a dead end, but it was our only chance, and we took it.

Swiftly, I turned my horse up into the opening, scrambling around the roots, and down through the narrow gap beyond into the glade.

"Cap, you and Moss fix up that trail, will you? We're going to need time."

Maybe we had run into an even worse trap, but at least it was a trap of our own making, not one set and waiting for us. A blind man could sense that Black Fetchen was out for a kill. He did not want just Galloway and me, although no doubt we topped his list: he wanted us all.

While we held up, waiting for Cap and Moss to blot out our trail, I scouted around.

There was a narrow aisle among the pines that followed along the slope toward the north. A body could see along it for fifty or sixty yards. When Cap and Moss came up, we pushed on.

We rode on no trail except one we made, and we found our way with difficulty, weaving among trees and rocks, scrambling on steep slopes, easing down declivities where our horses almost slid on their hind quarters. Suddenly we came upon a great slash on the mountain, came upon it just where it ended.

A huge boulder had torn loose hundreds of feet up the mountain and had come tumbling down, crushing all before it, leaving a steep but natural way toward the higher slopes.

Costello glanced up the mountain. "We'll never make it," he said, seeing my look. "It's too steep."

"We'll get down and walk," I said. "We'll lead our horses. It's going to be a scramble, but it'll be no easier for those who follow, and we'll have the advantage of being above them."

Swinging down, I led off. Mostly it was a matter of finding a way around the fallen trees and rocks, scrambling up slopes, pushing brush or fallen trees out of the way. In no time at all we were sweating, fighting for breath from the work and the altitude.

We were topping out at the head of our long corridor when Ladder kind of jerked in the saddle and gave an odd grunt. Almost at the same instant, we heard the shots.

We saw them at once. They were below us, in the open beyond some trees. They had lost our trail until we came into sight on the slope, and they had fired . . . from a good four hundred yards off.

Scrambling into the trees, I swung around on Ladder. "You hurt?"

"I caught one. You boys keep going. I can handle this."

"Like hell." I got down.

Cap and Galloway had already moved to the edge of the trees and were returning the searching fire the Fetchens were sending into the trees. We had bullets all around us, but most of them were hitting short . . . shooting up or down hill is always a chancy thing.

Ladder Walker had caught a .44 slug on the hip bone—a glancing shot that hit the bone and turned off, tearing a nasty gash in the flesh. It was not much more than a flesh wound, but he was losing blood.

We made a sort of pad with a patch of moss ripped from a tree trunk, binding it in place with his torn shirt.

We were under cover now, and our return fire had

made them wary, so with Walker sitting his saddle, we worked our way along the slope and across Buck Creek Canyon.

There was nothing about this that a man could like. We had broken the trap, but we were far from free. They were wasting no shots, moving in carefully, determined to make an end of us. We had them above and below us, others closing in, and no doubt some trying to head us off.

Pulling up suddenly, I stood in my stirrups and looked off down through the trees toward the sand dunes. If they tried to follow along the side of the mountain below us, we might be able to drive them into the dunes.

Cap rode up beside me. "Flagan, there's a creek somewhere up ahead that cuts through the mountain, or nearly so. I figure if we could get up there we could ride up the creek and cross the mountain; then we could come down behind the Buzzard Roost ranch."

We moved along, taking our time, hunting out a trail as we rode. There was a good smell of pines in the air, and overhead a fine blue sky with white clouds that were darkening into gray, sort of bunching up as if the Good Lord was getting them corralled for a storm.

The traveling was easier now. We wound in and out amongst the fallen trees, most of them long dead, and the boulders that had tumbled down from the mountain higher up. The ground was thick with pine needles or moss, and there were some damp places where water was oozing out.

For about half a mile we had cover of a sort. We couldn't see any of the Fetchen gang, nor could they shoot at us, but there was no chance to make time. Had we slipped from their trap, maybe only to get into a worse one, I wondered. We all rode with our Winchesters in our hands, ready for the trouble we knew was shaping up.

On our right the mountains rose steeply for more than two thousand feet, their peaks hidden in the dark clouds. The air grew still, and the few birds we saw were flying low, hunting cover. A few scattering drops of rain fell.

There came a puff of wind, and then a scattering shower, and we drew up to get into our slickers. The grass on the mountain slope seemed suddenly greener, the pines darker.

Glancing at Ladder Walker, I saw he looked almighty drawn and pale. He caught my eyes and said, "Don't you worry your head, Sackett. I'm riding strong."

It was no easy place to travel. Because the mountainside was so steep we had to pick our way carefully, stopping from time to time to give the horses a breathing spell. We were angling up again now, hunting for the cover of scattered trees that showed higher up. Thunder rumbled back in the peaks, sounding like great boulders tumbling down a rocky corridor. Lightning flashed, giving a weird light.

Galloway, who was riding point at the moment, caught the movement of a man as he was lifting his rifle, and Galloway was not one to waste time. He shot right off his saddle, his rifle held waist-high...and nobody ever lived who was better at off-hand shooting than Galloway.

We heard a yelp of pain, then the clatter of a rifle

falling among rocks; and then there was a burst of firing and we left our saddles as if we'd been shot from them. We hit ground running and firing, changing position as we hit grass, and all shooting as soon as we caught sight of something to shoot.

They'd caught us in the open, on the slope of a rock-crested knoll crowned with trees. We were short a hundred yards or so of the trees, but Cap and Galloway made the knoll and opened a covering fire. Costello helped Walker to a protected spot, whilst Moss and me gathered the horses and hustled them behind the knoll.

We stood there a moment, feeling the scattering big drops before an onrush of rain. The back of that knoll fell away where a watercourse made by mountain runoff had cut its way. There was shelter here for the horses, but there was a covered route down to the next canyon.

"They aren't about to rush us," I told Moss. "You stay here with the horses. I'm going down this gully to see if we can get out of here."

"You step careful, boy," Reardon said. "Them Fetchens have no idea of anybody getting home alive."

The Fetchens were going to be wary, and all the more so because they probably figured they'd either killed or wounded some of us when we left our saddles like that. Now they were getting return fire from only two rifles, with occasional shots from Costello, so they would be sure they were winning and had us nailed down.

Rifle in hand, I crept down that gully, sliding over wet boulders and through thick clumps of brush. All the time I was scouting a route down which we could bring our horses as well as ourselves.

Suddenly, from up above, a stick cracked. Instantly I froze into position, my eyes moving up slope. A man was easing along through the brush up there, his eyes looking back the way I had come. It seemed as if the Fetchens were closing in around my friends, and there wasn't much I could do about it.

Going back now was out of the question, so I waited, knowing a rifle shot would alert them to trouble up here. When that man up there moved again ... He moved.

He was a mite careless because he didn't figure there was anybody so far in this direction, and when he moved I put my sights on him and held my aim, took a long breath, let it out, and squeezed off my shot. He was moving when I fired, but I had taken that into account, and my bullet took him right through the ribs.

He straightened up, held still for a moment, and then fell, head over heels down the slope, ending up within twenty feet of me.

Snaking through the brush, I got up to him and took his gun belt off him and slung it across my shoulders. Also taking up his rifle, I aimed it on the woods up above, where there were likely some others, and opened fire.

It was wild shooting, but I wanted to flush them out if I could, and also wanted to warn my folks back there that it was time to get out.

There were nine shots left in the Winchester, and I dusted those woods with them; then I threw down the rifle and slipped back the way I had come. A few shots were fired from somewhere up yonder, fired at the place from which I'd been shooting but I was fifty yards off by that time and well down in the water-course where I'd been traveling.

Waiting and listening, it was only minutes until I heard movement behind me and, rifle up, I held ready for trouble.

First thing I saw was Moss Reardon. "Hold your fire, boy," he said. "It's us a-comin'."

Me, I went off down the line and brought up on the edge of a small canyon; it was no trouble to get down at that point. When the others bunched around, I pointed down canyon. "Yonder's the dunes. And there seems to be a creek running along there. I take it we'd better reach for the creek and sort of take account of things."

"Might be Medano Creek," Cap said.

"What's that amount to?"

"If it's Medano, we can foller it up and over the divide. I figure it will bring us out back in the hills from Buzzard Roost."

Once more in the saddle, I led off down the canyon, and soon enough we were under the cottonwoods and willows, with a trickle of water at our feet. There was a little rain falling by then, and lightning playing tag amongst the peaks.

Ladder seemed to be in bad shape. He was looking mighty peaked. He'd lost a sight of blood, and that crawling and sliding hadn't done him any good.

The place we'd come to had six-foot banks, and there was a kind of S bend in the stream that gave us the shelter of banks on all sides. Just beyond were the dunes. From a high point on the bank we could see where the creek came down out of the Sangre de Cristos.

"We might as well face up to it," Galloway said. "We're backed up against death. Those boys are downstream of us and they're up on the mountain, and they surely count us to be dead before nightfall."

"One of them doesn't. I left him stretched out up yonder. This here's his gun belt."

"One less to carry a rifle against us," Moss said. He leaned back against the bank. "Gol durn it. I ain't as young as I used to be. This scramblin' around over mountains ain't what I'm trimmed for. I'm a horse-and-saddle man myself."

"I'd walk if I could get out of here," Galloway said.

Costello was saying nothing. He was just lying yonder looking all played out. He was no youngster, and he'd been mistreated by the Fetchens. So we had a wounded man and one in no shape to go through much of this traveling, and we were a whole mountain away from home.

That Medano Creek might be the way, but I didn't like the look of it. It opened up too wide by far for safety.

"Make some coffee, somebody," I suggested. "They know already where we are."

Moss dug into his war-bag for the coffee and I poked around, picking up brush and bark to build us a fire. It took no time at all to have water boiling and the smell of coffee in the air. We had a snug enough place for the moment, with some shelter from gunfire, and water as we needed it.

Galloway and Cap had gone to work to rig a lean-to shelter for Ladder Walker.

There were willow branches leaning out from the bank and they wove other branches among them until they had the willows leaning down and making a kind of roof for those who would lie down. Where the creek curved around there were two or three big old cottonwoods and we bunched the horses there.

We sat around, shoulders bent against the rain, gulping hot coffee and trying to figure what we were going to do.

The Fetchens had us bunched for the kill. They were good mountain fighters, and they had herded us right into a corner. Maybe we could ride up Medano Creek and get clean away, but it looked too inviting to me. It would be a death trap if they waited for us up there where the cliffs grew high.

If we got out of this alive we'd have to be lucky. We'd have to be hung with four-leaf clovers—and I couldn't see any clover around here.

CHAPTER 15

THE WORST OF it was, we weren't getting much of a look at those boys. They were playing it safe, slipping about in the trees and brush as slick as Comanches.

"Galloway," I said, "I'm getting sort of peevish. Seems to me we've let those boys have at us about long enough. A time comes when a man just can't side-step a fight no longer. We've waited for them to bring it to us, and they've done no such thing, so I figure it's up to you and me to take it to them."

"You give me time for another cup of coffee," Galloway said, "and I'll come along with you."

Cap Rountree looked at us thoughtfully. "What you expect *us* to do . . . mildew?"

Me, I just grinned at him. "Cap, I know you're an old he coon from the high-up hills, but the fewer we have out there the better. You boys can stay right here. They'll be expecting us to move on pretty quick, and they'll be settled down waiting for it. Well, me and Galloway figure to stir them up a mite.

"Anyway," I went on, "Ladder's in no shape to travel more'n he's going to have to, getting out of here. Costello's in pretty bad shape, too. I figure you and Moss can hold this place if they try to attack you, which I doubt they will."

Galloway and me, we picked up our rifles and just

sort of filtered back into the brush. "You thinking the same thing I am?" I said.

"Their horses?"

"Uh-huh. If we set them afoot we've got a free ride...after we get through that valley yonder."

We'd been timber-raised, like most Tennessee mountain boys, so when we left our horses we swapped our boots for moccasins, which we always carried in our saddlebags.

The weather was clouded up again and it was likely to rain at any moment. We found no sign of the Fetchens until I came upon a corn-shuck cigarette lying on the moss near the butt end of a fallen tree. It was dry, so it must have been dropped since the last shower. After scouting around we found tracks, and then we worked our way up the mountain, moving all the quieter because of the rain-soaked ground.

Suddenly, high up on the mountain, there was a shot.

A voice spoke so close we both jumped in our skins. "Now what the hell was *that*?"

Galloway and me froze where we stood. The speaker couldn't be much more than twenty feet off from us.

"Do you s'pose one of them slipped out?" another man said.

"Naw! That's gotta be somebody else. Huntin', maybe."

"In this rain?"

We eased up a step, then another. In a sheltered place in the lee of a rock stood two of the Fetchen outfit. I knew neither one of them by name, but I had seen them both before. In front of them was a grassy slope that fell gradually away for about fifty feet, then dropped off sharply.

The two stood there, their rifles leaning against the rock wall, well to one side, and out of the wet. They were sheltered by the overhang, but could watch a good distance up and down the canyon. One man was rolling a cigarette, the other had a half-eaten sandwich in his hand.

Taking a long step forward, rifle leveled, I turned squarely around to face them. Galloway stepped up beside me, but several feet to my right. One of them noticed some shadow of movement or heard some sound and started to turn his head.

"Just you all hold it right where you stand," I said. "We got itchy fingers, and we don't mind burying a couple of you if need be."

Neither of them was in shape to reach for a gun fast, and they stood there looking mighty foolish. "Go up to 'em, Galloway," I said, "and take their hardware. No use tempting these boys into error."

Galloway went around behind them, careful to keep from getting between my rifle and them. He slipped their guns from the holsters, and gathered their rifles. Then we backed them into the full shelter of the slight overhang and tied them hand and foot.

"You boys set quiet now. If any of the Fetchens are alive when this is over, they can come and turn you loose. But if we should happen to see you again, and not tied—why, we'd just naturally have to go to shootin'."

"If I ever see you two again," one of them said, "I'll be shootin' some my own self!"

So we left them there, scouted around, found their

horses, and turned them loose. Then we went on up the mountain, careful-like. It wasn't going to be that easy again, and we knew it.

Suddenly, from up the mountain there came another rifle shot, and then a scream of mortal agony. And then there was silence.

"What's going on up there, Flagan?" Galloway said. "We got somebody on our side we don't know about?"

He pointed up the hill. Three men were working their way down the hill toward us, but their attention was concentrated on whatever lay behind them. Once one of them lifted his rifle to fire, then lowered it, as if his target had vanished.

Again he lifted his rifle, and as he did so I put my rifle butt to my shoulder. If we had a helper up yonder he was going to find out it worked both ways.

"Hold your fire!" someone called.

It was Colby Rafin, and with him was Norton Vance and two other men. They had us covered, and were close upon us.

This was no time to be taken prisoner, so I just triggered my shot and spun around on them. Galloway knew I wasn't going to be taken, and he hadn't waited. He had his rifle at his hip and he fired from there. It was point-blank range and right into the belly of Norton Vance.

He snapped back as if he'd been rammed with a fence post, then sat down and rolled over, both hands clutching his midsection.

A bullet whipped by my ear, burning it a little, but I was firing as fast as I could lever the shots. I missed a couple even at that range, for I was firing fast into the lot of them with no aim, and I was moving so as to give them no target, but I scored, too.

I'd shot at Rafin and missed him, the bullet taking the man who stood behind and to his right, and Rafin dived into the brush with lead spattering all around him. As soon as Colby Rafin got turned around he'd have us dead to rights, so we scrambled out of there and into the brush.

We moved in further, then lay still, listening.

For a time we heard no sound. Then behind us we heard a groan, and somebody called for Rafin, but he wasn't getting any answer.

We moved on, angling up the hill toward the edge of the pass. Then a burst of firing sounded below us where we'd left the rest of our party, and we stopped to look back down the hill. We could see nothing from where we were, but the firing continued. It made a body want to turn and go back, but what we had to do was what we'd started to do.

They hit us just as we started to go on. During those distracting moments, few as they were, they had somehow moved down on us, and they weren't asking questions. They just opened fire.

A bullet caught me on the leg and it buckled, probably saving my life, for there was a whipping of bullets all around me, and another one turned me sideways. I felt myself falling and tucked my shoulder under so I could roll with it, and I went over twice on the slope before I stopped.

What had happened to Galloway, I didn't know. I did know that I'd been hit hard, and more than once, and unless I moved from where I was I'd be dead within minutes. Somehow I'd clung to my rifle—I'd needed to hang onto something. Now I began to inch my way along the steepening face before me.

Instinctively, for I surely can't claim to much thinking just then, hurting the way I was, I worked back toward those hunting me. They would be off to my right, I was sure, and would think I'd try to get away, which was the smart and sensible thing. But I wanted to stay within shooting distance at any cost, and my best chances of getting away free would be to work right close to them.

But then I almost passed out. For a moment there consciousness faded, and when I snapped out of it I knew I couldn't risk that again. I had to find a place to hole up.

Crawling on, I'd gone no more than a dozen feet before I saw what I wanted, maybe sixty feet further along. It was at a steep place on the mountainside where a boulder had jarred loose and tumbled off down the slope into the pass below, leaving a great empty socket overgrown by brush that had once hung over the boulder. If I could only get into that hollow...

Hours later I awakened, shaking with chill. I was curled up in that hollow and I still had my rifle. I had no memory of getting there, no idea how long it had taken me. It was nighttime now, and I was cold and hungry, and hurt.

There was room to sit up. Easing myself around, I touched my leg gingerly, feeling for the wound. One bullet had gone through my leg about five or six inches above the knee and had come out on the other side.

In here I had a hole about six feet either way,

and though it was raining outside it was snug and dry here. The branches in front hung almost to the ground and, breaking off some of those on the underside, I wove them into a tighter screen. There was some bark and dry wood around the base of the tree back of the hole, but I didn't want to chance a fire.

Try as I might, there was just no way I could get comfortable. Hour after hour I lay there, huddled in the cold and the damp, trying to see my way out of this trouble. Come daylight, those Fetchen boys would be hunting my hide, and unless the rain washed out the mess of tracks I must have laid down by crawling and losing blood, they'd have me for sure.

The night and the rain are often friendly things to fugitives, but it gave me small comfort to sit there with my teeth rattling like ghost bones in a hardwood cupboard, and a gnawing pain in my thigh and another in my side.

After a time I dug out a mite more of dirt with my hands, made a hollow for my hipbone, and snuggled down on my unwounded side. I must have slept then, and when I woke up it was still dark but there was no rain—only a few drops falling from leaves. I felt that I was living on short time.

But the thing that worried me most was Galloway. Had they killed him right off? That I couldn't believe. But where could he have gotten to?

Right then I taken out my six-shooter and checked every load. I did the same with my Winchester, and added a few rounds to bring her up to capacity. If the Fetchen boys found me they were going to lose scalps rooting me out of here.

Then I sat back to wait. I would have liked a cup of coffee...four or five cups, for I'm a coffee-drinking man. But all I could do was wait and think.

That Judith girl, now. She was a mighty pretty thing, come to think of it. How could I have been so dumb as not to see it...Mighty contrary and ornery, though. And those freckles...She was pert, too pert....

Other thoughts were in my mind, too. How long could those boys hold out down below—Moss, Cap, and the others?

I had to hand it to Black Fetchen. He was a general. We seemed to be winning a round or two, but all the while he was baiting trap for us.

I wished I knew what had happened to Galloway. He might be dead, or he might be lying up somewhere, worse off than me. Far down the slope I heard a long "halloo"—no voice I knew. All right, let them come.

I twitched around and studied my layout by the coming daylight. They couldn't get at me from behind, and nobody was coming up that slope in front of me. What they had to do was come right along the same way I had. Taking sight down the trail, I figured I had it covered for fifty yards; then there was a bend which allowed them cover. I had the side of the canyon for a hundred yards further along.

It started to rain again, a cold drizzle that drew a sheet of steel mesh across the morning. The grass and the trees were greener than I had ever seen them, the trunks of the trees like columns of iron. For a long time I saw no movement. When I did see it down the trail I saw it half asleep, but I was startled into wakefulness.

On a second look I saw nothing, yet something had moved down there, something black and sudden, vanishing behind a bend in the trail even as it registered on my consciousness.

I lifted my rifle muzzle, and rested it on my half-bent knee. My hand was on the action as I watched the trail. My ears were alert to catch any sound, and I waited for what would come....

Supposing I could get out of this jam—and all the time I knew how slight my chances were—what could I do with my future? Well, Tyrel had no more when he came west, and now he was a well-off man, a respected man, with a fine wife and a ranch.

My eyes had not wandered from the trail, and now a man came into view down there. He was following some sort of a trail, although mine must have washed out long since, and he was edging closer. From his manner, it seemed to me that he fancied he was close upon whatever he was hunting.

Once, while my rifle held him covered, he paused and started to lift his own weapon. He was looking at something above and back of me, but evidently he was not satisfied with his sight picture or else he had been mistaken in his target, for he lowered the rifle.

He came on another step, seemed then to stagger, and he started to fall even as the sound of a shot went booming down the canyon, losing itself in the rain.

The man went down to the ground, his rifle still gripped in his hand, and he lay there sprawled out not sixty yards away from me. I could see the bright stain of blood on his skull and on the trail beside him.

Who had fired?

Waiting for a minute, I saw no one, but suddenly I knew I could not stay where I was. I had taken time to plug and bind my wounds as best I could, but I desperately needed help. So, using my rifle for a crutch, I crawled from my shelter and hobbled into the cold rain.

For a few moments I would be invisible to whoever was up there. With care I worked around and started to go on up the narrow trail. I could not see anybody, but visibility was bad; I knew that shot could not have come from far off.

The trail became steeper. Hobbling along, I almost fell, then I pulled up under some trees.

"Flagan?" came the voice.

It was Judith.

She was standing half behind the black trunk of a spruce, partly shielded by its limbs. She wore a man's hat and a poncho. Her cheeks glistened in the rain and her eyes seemed unnaturally large. She must have been out on the mountain all night long, but I never saw anybody look so good.

"Be careful," she warned. "They are all around us."

"Have you seen Galloway?" I asked.

"No."

I moved up toward her, but stopped to lean against a tree. "I've been hit, a couple of times," I said. "How is it above us?"

"They are all along the ridge. I don't know how I managed to slip through," she said.

Looking up toward the ridge through the branches, I could see nothing but the trees, the rain, and the low rain clouds.

"I've got a place," she said. "We'd better get to it."

She led the way, and before she'd taken half a dozen steps I could see she knew what she was about, holding to cover and low ground, taking no chance of being seen. It was obvious she had used the route before, and that worried me. With a canny enemy against you, it never pays to go over the same ground twice. Somebody is likely to be waiting for you.

"How do you happen to be over here?" I asked her.

"Nobody came back, and we were worried. Finally I couldn't stand it any longer, so I slipped away and came in this direction."

The place she had found wasn't much more than a shelter from the rain. A lightning-struck tree had fallen almost to the ground before being caught between two others. Wedged there, it formed a shelter that she had improved by breaking off small branches on the underside and weaving them into the top.

The steep bank behind and the trees kept it dry, and she could enter it without being seen. The trees lower down the slope screened it in front, and we felt we could even have a small fire without it being seen or the smoke attracting attention.

"Flagan?" She was on the ground beside the fire, waiting for coffee water to boil.

"Yes?"

"Let's just ride away from here. I don't want to fight any more. I don't want trouble."

"Your pa's down there." I gestured toward the base of the mountain, almost within view from here. "He's almighty tired, but when I left them they were holed up in a good spot."

"I want to see him, but I'm scared for you. Black will never rest until he's killed you, Flagan. You and Galloway."

"We don't kill easy."

When the coffee was ready, we drank some, and nothing ever tasted so good. But I was worried. The Fetchens were close around somewhere on this mountain, and I knew I wasn't going to get another chance. The next time we met, it had to be all or nothing. Hurt as I was, I knew I couldn't last very long.

Putting down my coffee cup, I checked my guns. Just then somewhere up the slope a branch cracked, and we both heard it.

Taking up my cup again in my left hand and keeping my six-gun in my right hand, I looked over at her. "You get down behind that mess of branches. This here is going to be a showdown."

"You scared, Flagan?"

"I guess I am. I'm not as sharp as I should be, this here wound and all." I finished my coffee. "That tasted good."

With my rifle I pushed myself up, holstered my gun, and wiped off the action of my rifle, flicking the water away. Standing on a small mound of dirt pushed up by the roots of the fallen tree, I looked down the slope.

They were coming all right. I counted five of them. And there were others up the slope, too, closing in. There must have been fourteen or fifteen in all.

"This here's going to be quite a fight," I said. "You got a pistol besides that rifle?"

She tossed it to me and I caught it left-handed and put it back of my belt.

"What are you going to do?"

"Wait until they get closer. They want a show-down, they'll have it. When they get up close I'm going to step out and go to shooting."

There wasn't anything else to do. I wasn't able to go any further, and I wasn't of a mind to. Right here we would settle it, Black and me and the rest of them.

Right here, on this wet ground we were going to fight . . . and some of us would die.

CHAPTER 16

AT A TIME like that you don't count the odds, and I had the odds against me, no matter what. It wasn't as if I had a choice. This was one time when there was no place to run. It was root hog or die, and maybe both.

But seeing them coming at me, I didn't feel like dying, and I wasn't even feeling that the odds were too great. I'd come to a place and a time where it no longer mattered, and I was only thinking about how many I could take, just how I ought to move, and which targets I should choose first.

My eyes searched for Black. He was the one I most wanted to get into my sights. And in the back of my mind I was thinking: Where was Galloway?

Judith waited there behind me, and I could feel her eyes upon me. "Flagan?" she said.

"Yes?"

"Flagan, I love you."

Turning my head, I looked at her. "I love you, too," I said. "Only we haven't much time.... When this fuss begins, Judith, you stay out of it, d' you hear? I can make my fight better if I know you're out of harm's way."

"All right." She said it meekly enough, and I believed her.

They came on, carrying their rifles up, ready to throw down on anything that moved.

It gave me time to pick my targets—to figure my first shot, and to see just how much I'd have to move my rifle for a second. The way I figured, I had two shots before they could get me in their sights, and if I fired those two and then threw myself down I could move along the ground and get at least one more before they located me. What followed would depend on how they came up shooting, and whether they took shelter or came on.

There was no way of telling whether they had located us yet or not, only they knew we were somewhere along that slope. At first I'd been ready to step out and go to shooting as soon as they got within easy range, but then I began to figure if there wasn't some way to make the situation work for me. So much of any fight depends on the terrain and how a body uses it.

They were coming up from below and coming down from above, and we had the canyon behind us and no way out that we could see. But there was a dip of low ground running diagonally down the mountainside. It was shallow, and partly cloaked with brush, but it was deep enough so a crouching man might slip along it unseen.

If I did step out and go to shooting, I could start downhill, fire my shots, then drop into that hollow and go back up the mountain on an angle, under cover. From where they were, I doubted if they could see that low place, which had likely been scooped out by a rock slide with a lot of snow and weight behind it. With luck, I might make the hollow, get under cover, and come out where they least expected me.

All the time my thoughts kept shifting to Galloway. Common sense told me he must be dead, but there was something in me that refused to accept it. I knew Galloway, who was a tough man to kill.

The men below were well out in the open now, and they were coming along slow. Looking up, I could see the line of the ones above, spaced at intervals and coming down slope, but they could not see each other yet.

"I want to come with you," Judith said.

With my rifle, I pointed the way. "See that long gouge? If there's a way out, it will be up that way. When I shoot, or anybody else does, you hit the ground and scramble. Just keep going up that low place—there's brush all around it and they may not realize it's there. I'll be right behind you."

The time was now.

Rifle up and ready, I stepped out. Judith scooted by me and was into that shallow place before they could glimpse her. I took another quick step, brought up my rifle just as they saw me, and caught a man in my sights who wore a gray Confederate coat The rifle jumped in my hands, the report came smashing back, and I was already shifting aim. My timing was right, and my second shot was following the first before the report died away; and then, with lead flying all around me, I took a running dive into the brush.

Branches tore at my face. I hit rolling, came up in a crouch, and made three fast steps before I caught a glimpse of an opening and a Fetchen with his rifle on me. There was no time for aiming, so I simply turned my body slightly and fired from the hip. A rifle bullet hit the tree near me and splattered my face with bark, but my bullet scored a hit...not a killing hit, but it turned that man around in his tracks, and I was off and running, going up hill with great leaps. Twice I fell, once I lost hold my rifle, grabbed it again, and ran on. My breath tore at my lungs...it was the going uphill and the altitude. I slipped and fell again, felt the hammer of bullets in the earth ahead of me, rolled over under a bush, and wormed out on the other side.

That time I made three steps, but they were closing in on me. Half raised, I fired blind, left and right, and drew a smashing hail of bullets; I was just hoping they would kill each other.

Somebody hollered, and the shooting eased off. I heard them calling back and forth. They had me located, but I kept on squirming along the hollow. It seemed almost like a deer or varmint trail.

A rifle blasted somewhere up ahead, somebody cried out, and I slid across a wet boulder, hit a stretch of sand in the watercourse beyond, and managed four plunging steps before I fell, mouth open—my lungs seemed to be tearing apart.

Fear had wiped out the pain from my wounded leg, but I realized it was bleeding again. My pants leg was soaked and I could feel the squishing in my shoe, although a part of it was rain water.

There was a lot of shooting now. Judith must have opened fire from some place above me. Bleeding or not, exhausted or not, I knew it was death to stay where I was, so I scrambled. I could hear them all around me.

As I squirmed between two boulders, one of the Fetchen men reared up right before me and I hit him with my rifle butt. It wasn't much of a blow, because I held the rifle one-handed and I just swung it up from where it was.

He grabbed the rifle with both hands. But instead of trying to pull it away, I held it hard against him and swung my foot and kicked him under the chin. He went over backwards and I jerked the rifle away. He looked up at me for one black, awful instant, but it was kill or be killed, and I gave him the rifle butt in the face with both hands.

Holding up there, gasping for breath, I fed a few cartridges into the magazine of my rifle. My belt was running shy, so I reached down and ripped the belt off the Fetchen man.

Rain was pouring down, and the firing had let up. Nobody seemed to be moving, and I worked my way slowly ahead, nearing the crest of the ridge. Here and there the bottom of the gorge was choked with brush, and there were many rocks, polished by running water and the abrasion of other tumbling stones.

Once, crawling through the brush, I suddenly felt myself growing weaker, and almost blacked out. I fought against the dizziness for a moment, and then somehow I came out of it, and crawled on.

They had come in behind me now, closing off the way back, even if I had been willing or able to take it. I could hear them coming on, taking their time, checking every clump of brush or rocks.

There was no longer any question of running. I could pull myself up, and by using the rocks and brush I could remain erect long enough to move forward a few feet.

Then the ridge was close above me. I could see the bare wet rocks, the stunted cedars, and the occasional bare trunks of pines shattered by lightning.

At that moment I looked around. Four men were standing not much more than fifty feet away, aiming their rifles at me. Desperately, I threw myself to one side and fired my rifle at them. Fired, worked the lever, and fired again.

Bullets smashed into the ground around me. My hat was swept from my head, blood cascaded into my eyes, and my rifle was struck from my hand. I grabbed for it, and through the haze of blood from a scalp wound I saw that the action was shattered and useless.

Throwing the rifle down, I grabbed my six-shooter. Somehow, in throwing myself to one side, I had gotten into the cover of a rock.

A man came running down the gully, but the earth gave way and he slid faster than he expected, stones and rubble crashing down before him. I shot at point-blank range, my bullet striking the V of his open shirt and ranging upward through him.

He fell forward. I grabbed at his rifle, but it slipped away and fell down among the rocks.

Up ahead of me there was a shattering burst of gunfire—it sounded like several guns going. They must have caught up with Judith.

I could hear the ones close by talking as I waited. They were hunting me out, but they could not see me, a fact due more to the rocks where I lay than to any skill on my part. After the sudden death of the man who had slid down among the rocks they were wary, hesitant to take the risk . . . and I was just as pleased.

Right about then I must have passed out for a minute. When I opened my eyes again I was shaking with cold. The wind had come up, and was blowing rain in on me. I didn't have what you'd call shelter, just the slight overhang of a slab of fallen rock.

My hands felt for my guns. I had both pistols, and I reloaded the one right there. All the time I was listening, fighting to keep my teeth from chattering, and the knowledge growing in me that it would be almighty cold up here at night.

Nothing moved; only the rain whispered along the ground and rattled cold against the rocks. Even if I couldn't get out of this, I had to find a safer place.

On the downhill side there was a scattered stand of pine, stunted and scraggly, along with the boulders and the low-growing brush. On the uphill side there was even less cover, but the gorge up which I'd been crawling ran on for sixty yards or so further, ending just off the ridge.

It stood to reason that if they wanted me they could get me crossing that ridge. All they had to do was hold their fire and let me get out on the bare rock.

But Judith, unless she was dead or captured, was up there somewhere.

So I crawled out of shelter, over a wet boulder and along the downhill side of a great old deadfall, the log all turned gray from the weather. Maybe I made fifteen feet before I stopped to catch my breath and breathe away the pain; then I went on.

I was nearing the end of the gorge. The only thing

for me to do now was break out and run for it. And I
couldn't run.

Only I had to. I had to make it over that ridge.
Lying there shivering in the cold rain, I studied that
ridge and the ground between. Thirty steps, if I was
lucky.

There was no sense in waiting. I came off the
ground with a lunge, stabbing at the ground with my
good leg, but hitting easy with the wounded one. I felt
a shocking pain, and then I was moving. I went over
the ridge and dropped beside a rock, and there they
were, the lot of them.

There was Judith too, her hands held behind her,
and a man's dirty hand clasped tight over her mouth
so she couldn't call out to warn me. There were six of
the Fetchen gang, with Black right there among
them—Black and Colby Rafin.

At times like that a man doesn't think. There's no
room for thought. I was soaked to the hide, bedrag-
gled as a wet cat, bloody and sore and hurt and mad,
and when I saw that crowd I did the last thing they
expected.

I went for my gun.

Oh, they had guns on me, all right! But they were
too busy feeling satisfied with themselves at setting
the trap, and there's such a thing as reaction time. A
man's got to realize what is happening, what has to
be done, and he has to do it, all in the same moment.

My right hand slapped leather and came up blasting fire. And almost at the same instant my left hand
snaked the other Colt from my waistband.

There was no time for anything like choosing targets. I shot into the man right in front of me, shifted

aim, and blasted again. I saw Judith twisting to get free, and pulling Rafin off balance.

Somebody else was shooting, and I saw Galloway, leaning on a crutch and his gun leaping with every spout of flame. And then, as suddenly as it began, it was over. There was a scrambling in the brush, then silence, and I was stretched out on the rocks and the rain was pounding on my back.

It seemed like hours later that I got my eyes open and looked around.

There was a fire in a fireplace, and Judith was sitting in front of it, watching the flames. I never saw anything so pretty as the firelight on her face, and catching the lights of her hair.

I was stretched out in a bunk in some sort of a low-roofed cabin, and the floor was littered with men, all apparently sleeping. Coffee was on the fire, and by the look of the coals we'd been here quite a spell.

I felt around for my gun and found it, but the rustling drew Judith's attention. She came over to me. "Ssh! The others are all asleep."

"Was that Galloway that showed up? Is he all right?"

"He's been hurt. He was shot three times, and has a broken foot. Pa's here, and so are Cap and Moss."

"Walker?"

"He's dead. He was killed, Flagan."

"Black?"

"He got away. He was hurt, I know that. You hit him once at least. He ran, Flagan. He turned and ran."

"That ain't like him."

"He was a coward," she insisted bitterly. "For all his talk, he was a coward."

"I don't believe it," I said. And I didn't believe it either. He was a lot of things, that James Black Fetchen, but he was no coward in a fight. He hated too much for that. He might have turned and run—she said he had, and she would tell me the truth—but I was sure there was more to it than that.

The old prospector's cabin where we had found shelter was on the eastern slope, not more than half a mile from where the fight had taken place.

We stayed right there a day and a half, until Evan Hawkes and Tom Sharp brought a wagon up Medano Pass. They built stretchers, and three of us came off the mountain that way.

Two weeks later I was able to sit on the porch outside the trading post and watch folks go by. Galloway was still laid up, but he was coming along fine. Though Costello was still sick, he was looking better. Cap and Moss, like the tough old-timers they were, looked about the same.

We got the news bit by bit. Three of the Fetchens had pulled out for Tennessee. Tirey was dead...he'd been killed up on the mountain. And they hadn't found the Reynolds treasure. Like a lot of folks who've looked for it before and since, they just couldn't locate it. They had all the landmarks and they had a map, but they found nothing.

"I've seen four maps of that Reynolds treasure," Sharp told me, "and no two of them alike."

Nobody saw any of the Fetchens around, but after a few days we heard they were camped over at the foot of Marble Mountain, with several of them laid up, and at least one of them in bad shape.

Galloway limped around, still using the crutch he had cut for himself up on the mountain. Costello filled us in on all that happened before we got there.

The Fetchens had just moved in on him and he had welcomed them as guests, although mistrusting their looks. Well, they were hunting the Reynolds treasure, all right, but they wanted his ranch and Judith as well.

Costello had had a lead on that treasure himself, but it didn't pan out, and so he had settled down to hunting wild stock and breeding them to horses brought from the East, the way Tom Sharp was doing.

"Reynolds buried some loot, all right," Costello said, "but whoever finds it will find it through pure dumb luck. I don't trust any of those maps."

"They aren't cured," Moss Reardon said. "There's supposed to be treasure in a cave up on Marble Mountain too. I'd lay a bet they're huntin' it now."

For the first time in my life I was pleased just to sit and contemplate. I'd lost a lot of blood and used myself in a hard way, and so had Galloway. As I looked around that country it made me wish I had a place of my own, and I said as much to Galloway.

"We get up and around," I said, "we ought to find us a place, some corner back in the hills with plenty of green grass and water."

James Black Fetchen seemed to me like somebody from another world. After a week had passed we never mentioned the big fight on the mountain, nor any of that crowd. One thing we did hear about them. The Fetchens had buried another man some-where up on Grape Creek.

My appetite came back, and I began thinking about work. Galloway and me had used up the mite of cash we'd had left and had nothing but our outfits. I mentioned it to Tom Sharp.

"Don't worry about it," he said. "You just eat all you're of a mind to. Those men would have caused plenty of trouble for us if you hadn't taken their measure."

The next morning we heard about the stage holdup over on the Alamosa trail.

Four men, all masked, had stopped the stage and robbed the passengers. There was no gold riding the boot on that trip, and the passengers were a hard-up lot. The robbery netted the outlaws just sixty-five dollars.

Two days later there was another holdup in the mountains west of Trinidad. That netted the thieves about four hundred dollars. There had been six of them in that lot, and one of the passengers had ridden the other stage and said they were the same outfit. One of them had been riding a big blaze-faced sorrel that sounded like Russ Menard's horse.

Sitting around waiting to get my strength back, I hadn't been idle. I'd never been one to waste time do-ing nothing, so while I sat there I plaited a rawhide bridle for Sharp, mended a saddle, and fixed some other things.

Costello rode out to his ranch. His place had been burned, even his stacked hay, and all the stock in sight had been driven off.

Galloway had taken to wearing two guns, one of them shoved down behind his waistband.

Then there was a holdup near Castle Rock, to the north; and word came down that Black Fetchen had killed a man at Tin Cup, a booming mining camp.

Meanwhile, Galloway and me were beginning to feel spry again, and we helped Tom Sharp round up a few head of cattle and drive them down to Walsenburg. There we heard talk of the Fetchen outlaws.

Those days Galloway and me were never far apart. We knew it was coming. The trouble was, we didn't exactly know what to expect, or when.

Costello hired two new hands, both on the recommendation of Rodriguez and Sharp. One was a Mexican named Valdez, a very tough man and a good shot who, as a boy, had worked for Kit Carson; and the other was Frank White, a one-time deputy sheriff from Kansas. Both were good hands and reliable men.

Judith was riding with me one day when she said, "Flagan, you and Galloway be careful now. I'm scared."

"Don't worry your pretty head. We'll ride loose and careful."

"Do you think he'll come back?"

Now, I was never one to lie or to make light of trouble with womenfolks. There's men who feel they should, but I've found women stand well in trouble, and there's no use trying to make it seem less than it is. They won't believe you, anyway.

"He'll come," I said. "He wasn't scared, Judith. He just wanted to be sure he lived long enough to kill

Galloway and me. I've got an idea he's just waiting his chance."

By now Galloway and me were batching it in a cabin on Pass Creek. We had built up the corral, made some repairs in the roof, and laid in a few supplies bought on credit at the trading post. Work was scarce, but we disliked to leave the country with Black Fetchen still around . . . and of course, there was Judith.

We had talked about things, even made some plans, but I had no money and no immediate way of getting any. Evan Hawkes had sold out and gone back to Texas. The loss of the boy had hurt him more than he had ever showed. We were just waiting, shooting our meat out in the hills and occasionally prospecting a little.

The showdown came all of a sudden, and by an unexpected turn.

A short, stocky man came riding up to the place one day, and he had a big, black-haired man with him. Both of them were dressed like city folks, except they wore lace-up boots.

"Are you the Sacketts? Flagan and Galloway?" the short man asked.

Now, I didn't take to these men much, but they were all business. "Understand you've had trouble with the Fetchen outlaws? Well, I've got to ride the stage to Durango, and I'll need some bodyguards."

"Bodyguards?" I said.

"I'll be carrying twenty thousand dollars in gold, and while I can use a gun I am no gun-fighter, nor is my partner here. We'd like to hire you boys to ride with us. We'll pay you forty dollars each for the ride."

Now, forty dollars was wages for a top hand for a month, and all we had to do was sit up on the cushions in that stage and see that no harm came to Mr. Fred Vaughn and his money. His partner was made known to us as Reed Griffin.

We taken the job.

CHAPTER 17

WALSENBURG WAS QUIET when we rode in and stabled our horses. We had come up a day early, for we both needed a few things and we hadn't been close to a town since the fight. The trading post at Buzzard Roost had most things a body could wish for, but we both figured to buy white shirts and the like to wear in Durango.

We found a table in a back corner of the restaurant and hung our hats on the rack. The food was good, and the coffee better. We were sitting where we could look out the window and down the street, and we were sitting there when we saw Reed Griffin come out of a saloon down the street.

"Might as well let him know we're here," I said, but when I started to get up, Galloway stopped me.

"Plenty of time for that," he said.

Griffin walked across the road and went down a passage between two buildings and disappeared.

It was quiet where we were, and we continued to sit there, talking possibilities. We figured to prospect around Durango a mite and see what jobs were avail-ble, if any. If there were none, we would use what cash we had to outfit ourselves and go wild-horse hunting. There was always a good market for saddle stock that had been rough-broken, and while many of the wild horses were scrubs there were always a few good ones in every herd.

Later in the afternoon we went across the street to the hotel and hired ourselves a room on the second floor, in back. Pulling off our boots, we stretched out for a rest. When I woke up it was full dark, but there was a glow coming through the windows from the lights in the other buildings.

Without putting on my boots I walked across the room and poured cold water into the bowl and washed my face and combed my hair by the feel of it. I had picked up my boots and dropped into a chair by the window when I happened to look out.

The door of a house on the street back of the hotel was standing open and there were two men seated at a table over a bottle. One of those men was Colby Rafin. The other was Reed Griffin.

"Galloway?" I said, not too loud.

He was awake on the instant. "Yeah?"

"Look."

He came over and stood beside me and we looked out of our dark window and into that open door. Reed Griffin was on his feet now, but as he turned away from Rafin he was full in the light.

"Now, what d' you know about that?" Galloway said softly. "I'd say we've got to move quiet as mice."

We ate at the restaurant that night, but we fought shy of the saloons, and in the morning, right after breakfast, we were waiting at the stage stop.

Mr. Fred Vaughn was already there. He had a carpetbag and a iron-bound box with him. The stage driver loaded the box as if it was heavy, then Vaughn got in and Griffin came out and joined him. We loitered alongside, watching folks come up to the stage. There was another man, a long-geared, loose-jointed man with a big Adam's apple and kind of sandy hair. He carried a six-shooter in a belt holster, and a Winchester.

The last man to enter was lean and dark-haired. He shot us a quick, hard look, then got in. His boots were worn and his pants looked like homespun. We had never seen him before, but he had a Tennessee or maybe Missouri look about him.

The stage driver was a fat, solid-looking man with no nonsense about him, and he was obviously well known to everybody else, if not to us. We got in last and sat down facing Griffin and Vaughn, with the Tennessee man beside us; the sandy-haired man was across the way. The stage took off, headed west.

We both carried Winchesters and our belt guns, but each of us had a spare six-shooter tucked behind our waistbands. Griffin and Vaughn wasted no time talking, but made themselves comfortable as possible and went to sleep. The sandy man settled down too, although he kept measuring us with quick looks, and the man beside us as well.

The road was rough. The stage bounced, jolted, and slid over it, and every time we slowed the dust settled over us in a thick cloud.

Both of us were thinking the same thing. Why hadn't Vaughn taken the train? It ran west as far as Alamosa now, and much of our route by train ran parallel to it. In fact, the stage line was going out of business soon. This made no sense...Unless there was something that could be done on the stage that could not be done on the train.

La Veta lay ahead. Once, not long ago, it had been the end of the railroad tracks, and a wild, wild town. Now the end-of-the-line boys had moved to Alamosa, although a couple of dives still remain there. To most people in this part of the country it was still simply the Plaza.

The hunch came to me suddenly, and my elbow touched Galloway ever so gently. I had noticed that Reed Griffin did not seem to be really asleep, though his eyes remained closed. My eyes went to Vaughn. He was also shamming sleep. The Tennessee man beside me was unfastening a button on his coat. Sandy was completely awake. He was watching me with bright, hard eyes, and his hand stayed close to his pistol butt.

When we got to the Plaza we changed horses, and I noticed that the Tennessee man disappeared into the stable there. Shortly after he returned, a man came from the stable, mounted a horse, and rode off down the road along which we would soon travel.

The stage driver stood by with a cup of coffee in his hands, watching the teams being switched. Strolling over to him, I said, "You size up like an honest man."

"I am that," he said coolly, "so don't make any mistakes."

"I won't, but some others will. Mister, if you hear a shot or a Texas yell from inside the stage, you let those horses run, d' you hear?"

He gave me a quick look. "What do you know?"

"I'm Flagan Sackett. That there's my brother. I think the Fetchen gang plan to take us, or kill us. And probably rob your stage in the process."

"Now I'm told. There's no law at the Plaza now."

"We'll handle it. You just run the legs off that team."

"All right," he said.

Indicating the sandy man, I asked, "Do you know him?"

"El Paso to Denver, Durango to Tucson. That's all I know. My guess is that he's a Ranger, or has been one."

He walked back inside with his coffee cup and the Tennessee man strolled over and got into the stage. Vaughn and Griffin followed. The sandy man threw down his cigarette and rubbed it out with his toe. I took one step over so he had to come up close to me, and when he drew abreast I said, "Stay out of it. The trouble's ours."

He turned his eyes on me. "You're a Sackett, aren't you? That's why you are familiar. I rode with McNelly at Las Cuevas. Orlando Sackett was there. He was a good man. I won money on him once when he fought in the ring."

"They've set us up," I said. "Everybody in that stage but you and us is safe enough," I said. "They'll stop us on the grade, I think, near Muleshoe."

The stage rolled out again, and the climb before us was a long one. Gradually the team moved slower and slower. Taking my hat from my head, I lowered it into my lap, and as I did so I drew out my waistband gun and eased it down beside my leg and out of sight, then I put my hat on again.

We went on, climbing steeply. The men across from me appeared to sleep again.

The switchback was behind us, and the stage

leveled out, then suddenly I heard the driver hauling on the lines, and I lifted my Colt and looked at the men across from me.

"Sit tight, if you want to live," I said.

Galloway had lunged against the Tennessee man and I saw him strip his gun from him. The Tennesseean started up, but Galloway laid the barrel of the gun alongside his skull and he fell across our knees. We pulled our legs back and let him go to the floor of the stage.

Vaughn and Griffin both started to complain, but I shut them up. "Unless you want a cracked skull," I said.

From outside we heard a familiar voice. "All right, pull up there!"

To the Texan I said, "You want to hold these boys for me? I've got some shooting to do."

"A pleasure!" he said, and meant it.

Catching the top of the door I drew myself out of the open window on my side, hesitated an instant, and dropped to the road on the balls of my feet.

Rafin walked up to the door of the stage on the other side. I could see his boots. "All right, boys," he said. "Trot them out!"

Galloway shoved the door open, knocking him back, and leaped into the road. At the same moment I stepped around the back of the stage.

Russ Menard was the first man I saw. He was on his horse, and he had a gun resting easy in his hand. Galloway had hit the dirt and, dropping into a crouch by the wheel, was shooting into Rafin. I shot over him and my bullet crossed that of Menard, who had been taken by surprise.

He shot quickly, his bullet hitting the edge of the stage-door window, and mine knocked his shoulder. Stepping wide of the door, I shot at him again. I felt the whiff of a bullet and, turning slightly, I saw Black Fetchen taking dead aim at me.

The muzzle of his gun wasn't three feet from my head and I dived at him, going under his outstretched arm. My shoulder sent him crashing into the side of the stage. I pushed my gun against him and fired three blasting shots, and felt his body jerk with every one, then whip free.

Menard had held his fire for fear of hitting Black, but now he fired, the bullet striking my gun belt such a blow that I was knocked staggering, and it exploded a cartridge in my belt that cut a groove in my boot toe. His horse had turned sharply, and for an instant his gun couldn't bear. When it could, I was ready and shot first, Galloway's bullet crossing mine.

Menard went off his horse, hit ground on the other side, and tried to get up. He had been hit hard, but his eyes were blazing with a strange white light and his grip on his gun was steady. I shot into him again and he backed up and sat down again.

Somewhere off to my right I heard the stage driver saying, "Careful now, you with the itchy finger. This shotgun will cut you in two. Just stand fast."

Menard was sitting there looking at me, one knee sort of drawn up, his gun lying across his leg. He had been hit twice in the lungs and every time he drew breath there was a frothy burst of blood from the front of his vest.

"I told him he should leave you alone," he said,

"but he wouldn't listen. I told him nobody could beat a man's luck, and you had it."

"So this is all for you," I said quietly.

"Looks like it. Pull my boots off, Sackett, and bury me deep. I don't want the varmints after me."

Not being a trusting man, I still held my gun on him while I tugged his boots free.

"You take the gun," he said. "It brought me nothing but trouble."

Galloway had come up to me. "Fetchen's dying," he said. "You tore him apart."

Taking Menard's gun, I backed off from him.

James Black Fetchen was not dying; he was dead, and there were two others besides him, one of them the man I'd seen at the stable.

The stage driver rolled his tobacco in his cheeks. "If you boys are through, we might as well bury 'em and get on. I got a schedule to keep."

———

AT THE PLACER-mining camp of Russell the stage pulled up and we got down. We took Reed Griffin and Fred Vaughn out on the street. "We agreed to see you safe to Durango. You had us set up for killing. Now, do you figure we've earned our money, or do we take you all the way?"

"You going to let us go?"

"Forty dollars each," I said, and he paid it.

"Ride out with the stage," I said, "and keep going."

So we let them go, the Texan riding along to see them on their way.

"Galloway," I said, "we'd better find some horses and ride back to that cabin on Pass Creek."

"You figure we should stay there?"

"Well, there's Judith. And that's pretty country."

"Hey, did you see that niece of Rodriguez' do the fandango? Every time I looked at her my knees got slacker'n dishwater."

We had come a far piece into a strange land, a trail lit by lonely campfires and by gunfire, and the wishing we did by day and by night. Now we rode back to plant roots in the land, and with luck, to leave sons to carry on a more peaceful life, in what we hoped would be a more peaceful world.

But whatever was to come, our sons would be Sacketts, and they would do what had to be done whenever the call would come.

GALLOWAY

LA PLATA RIVER
Contour Interval 200 ft.

Scale of Miles
0   1   2   3

LA PLATA MOUNTAINS

Benyin Pond

Madden Peak

Razor Peak

La Plata River

Baldy Mountain

Shalako

SOUTHWESTERN
COLORADO
SCENE OF *GALLOWAY*
Contour Interval 3000 ft.
Scale of Miles
0 20 40 60 80 100

Map by Alan McKnight

CHAPTER 1

THE OLD ELK walked up the knoll where the long wind blew. The wolves followed.

The elk realized what was happening, but he didn't know it was only a part of something that had been going on since life began.

He didn't know that it was because of these wolves or their kindred that he had been strong, brave, and free-running all his past years. For it was the wolves who kept the elk herds in shape by weeding out the weak, the old, and the inept.

Now his time had come, and the wolves were there. He no longer had the speed to outrun them nor the get-about to outfight them, and there were four wolves working as a team, not one of them weighing less than a hundred pounds and two of them nearly twice that.

All he had going for him was his wisdom, and so far he was making a fair country try in getting himself to a place where he could make a stand. You could see, plain as the snow on the mountains yonder, that he was heading for the rocks where he could get his back to the wall.

His trouble was that wolves, like Indians, are patient. They had hunted elk before, had seen all of this happen many times, and they knew they were going to get that elk.

They didn't know about me. Coming up as I had, they'd caught no wind of me, nor could they guess it was my work they were doing. For I was figuring on having most of that elk myself.

When a man has been on the run and hasn't had a bite in three days, he's ready to eat an elk—head, hoofs, and horns—all by himself. Trouble was, I'd no way of killing an elk...or anything else, really, and if those wolves got the idea I was as bad off as I was they might take right in after me.

A lobo is too smart to harry a man unless he's down and well-nigh helpless. They don't like the man smell, which always means trouble, but a wolf is born with a keen sense of something ready for the kill... which I was. Up to a point, I was.

My feet were raw and bloody, the flesh churned into a bloody mess by running over the broken rock, gravel, and stubble of the desert. My body was worn with hunger, thirst, and exhaustion to a point where I could scarcely walk. But there was that inside me, whatever it was that made me a man, that was a whole long way from being whipped.

The wolves could smell blood, they could smell a festering wound, but could they smell the heart of a man? The nerve that was in him?

That elk sprinted for the rocks and the wolves taken in after him, wary of his hoofs, shy of the vicious drive of those forefeet that could stab and cut a wolf to a cripple. The horns didn't worry them too much, but a wolf is a shrewd hunter and wants to lose no hide for his meal.

My instinct is for mountains. The Sacketts of our branch were mountain people, hill folk from

Tennessee, and when trouble showed it was our way to take to the hills again. At least until we got our second wind. That was why I pointed toward the mountains yonder.

Ever since I'd got shut of those Jicarilla Apaches I'd been heading for the hills, but they hadn't left me much to go on. I was making no complaints. If they still had me by this time I'd be dead...or wishing I was.

Somebody back yonder stirred up a pack of trouble and those Apache warriors had taken off like somebody'd set their breechclouts afire, leaving me with the squaws.

Now squaws are no bargain. They take to torturing with genuine pleasure. Thing was, when the warriors taken off they also took all the ponies in camp, so I just cut loose and started to run.

The squaws came close to catching me, with my hands tied and all. But I was a long-legged man, barefooted and stark naked and knowing what would happen if they caught me. When the warriors returned they taken after me, too.

By that time I was afar off and had gotten my hands free, and was just beginning to run. All that day and into the night I ran...maybe fifty miles... but an Apache is like a hound on the trail. So they were back yonder coming after me, and if I didn't get something to eat I was a finished man.

The elk had got the rock behind him and turned to fight, but for the time those wolves were just a-setting there, looking at him, their tongues hanging out.

There was scattered cedar where I lay, and I kept my eyes open for a club, a-wishing all the time for

Galloway to show up. But for all I knew he was miles away down in New Mexico.

Worming my way along the ground, I got closer to the wolves. It wasn't going to do me a sight of good to come up on them until they'd made their kill. I was sorry for the elk, but it was no use. If this bunch didn't get him the next would.

Sure enough, when I was still sixty, seventy yards away that elk turned too far after one wolf and another one slipped in behind and hamstrung him. The elk went down, making a game fight of it, but he had no chance. About that time I got to my knees, yelled, and threw a rock into their midst.

You never seen the like. That rock lit close to one big wolf with a cropped ear and he jumped like he'd been hit. Maybe sand from the ground stung him. Anyway, they turned to stare at me, waving my arms and yelling.

They backed up as I rose to my feet and started slowly toward them. I was holding two stones and I could fling passing well, so I let drive again and had the luck to hit one on the leg.

He jumped and yelped, so I flung the other and they backed up, getting the smell of me now. If those wolves taken a notion I was in as bad shape as I was I'd have had no more chance than the elk, but wolves have always feared man and these were no exception.

Just then I saw a dead cedar, limbs all spread like something had dropped in the middle of them. I picked up a branch longer than my arm and about as thick as my wrist and started on.

The wolves taken off.

They ran off a ways and I limped up to the elk. It was dead.

The wolves stopped a hundred yards or so off and sat down to watch. They hadn't given up by a long shot, but there was a whole lot about me that troubled them.

Naked as I was, I must have looked uncommonly white to them, and that was all wrong according to their notion of men. And they could smell the blood from my feet and maybe the festering that was there. One of the wolves had gone over where I'd been lying and was smelling around to see what his hillside newspaper would tell him. I could guess he was reading a lot out there that I wished he didn't know.

Yet I had a good club in my hands, my back to a cliff, and meat enough to feed me into health again if I could get it cut up. I also needed that hide.

The rock against which the elk had chosen to make his stand was about thirty feet high and sloped off another twelve feet or so that was mostly broken rock. Some of it was obsidian.

I found myself a good chunk of the right length and began chipping away at it with another rock. I'd seen Indians make arrowheads and when a boy back in the mountains had sometimes made small hunting arrows for my own bow. The Cherokees we grew up around showed us how.

What I wanted now was a knife, and I began chipping away. Those wolves weren't about to leave that much meat, but my chipping made them wary, as wild animals are of anything strange.

After I'd worked awhile on the knife I picked up some dried wood and put it together where it would be handy. My knife was still not in the shape I wanted, but it had a cutting edge and with it I started skinning the elk. When I had peeled back enough of the hide I cut two pieces off and tied them around my feet with strips of the same hide. Even looking at the condition of my feet made my stomach turn over with fear, for they were bloody, torn, and shapeless. But the covering of wet hide made it easier to stand on them and using my club for a cane, I began to hobble around.

The cliff where the elk had made his stand was a thirty foot drop-off at the end of a long, steep mountainside, and among the rocks at its base was all the junk that had fallen down the mountain. Plenty of dried wood, and a wide variety of rocks. What I hunted was iron pyrites, and I found several chunks and broke off two pieces to use in starting a fire.

Beside the elk I made a small pile of shredded bark, crumbled dry leaves and slivers, and then I tried striking the two chunks of iron pyrites together. The sparks came easy, but it taken nearly an hour to get one into the shredded leaves and bark. Then I coaxed it, blowing gently to get a flame going.

Once a tiny flame began I fed it carefully with more bark and then with some slivers of pitch pine until it was blazing nicely. When those flames leaped up and began to crackle I felt like morning on the first day. It was no time at all until I had a steak broiling on a stick propped over the fire. Then I went back to work on my knife.

The wolves showed no mind to leave, and I didn't blame them, so I cut out a few chunks of meat I wasn't going to want and threw them out. They sniffed kind of cautious, then gobbled them up, but they looked surprised, too. Nobody had ever fed them before, seemed like.

In the back of my thoughts there was knowledge of those Jicarillas. They'd be of no mind to give up, and my bloody feet had blazed a pretty easy trail for them.

Keeping my fire alive I skinned out the rest of that elk, scraped some fat off the hide, and cut out the best chunks of meat. I broke off a couple of pieces of antler because it makes a good tool for chipping stone, then I bundled those cuts of meat into the elk hide, whilst ever and anon I tossed a bone or something to those wolves whose kill I had taken.

I understood how they felt, for they had been hungry, too.

My eyes kept straying to the country south of me, but I could see no movement, nothing. With Apaches your first look is often your last one.

Putting out my fire, dropping the two pieces of iron pyrites into the hide along with the meat, I swung the hide over my shoulder and taking up my staff, I moved out. Following the face of the cliff, I started north. Behind me the wolves were snarling and tearing at the carcass.

"Flagan Sackett," I said to myself, "you owe those wolves. You surely do."

It was slow going. The meat and hide were a burden, and in spite of the elk skin on my feet it was all I could do to step on them. What I needed was a hideout, a place where I could rest up and let my feet heal...if they would.

The desert had run out behind me. Low green hills

broken by jagged outcroppings and covered by clusters of aspens or scattered pines lay before and around me. Twice I followed the crests of ridges, hidden by the scattered trees, scouting the land as I went.

It was a wild, lonely country with occasional streamers of snow in the shadows where the sun did not reach. The wind was cold off the mountains and I was a naked man with enemies behind me and nothing before me but hope.

Once I lowered my pack to gather some snakeweed that I found in a hollow, and blessed my mountain boyhood where a body had to scrape and scrabble to live.

When I could go no further I worked my way back into a willow clump where rising smoke would be scattered by the leaves and branches. Then I built a small fire of dry wood that gave almost no smoke, and made a vessel from bark. Dipping up some water from the creek I put it to boil on a stick suspended above the fire, and put some snakeweed into it. When the snakeweed had boiled for a time I bathed my feet with it, using a few handfuls of soft sage for a cloth. Meanwhile I broiled more meat.

The day had ruined my crude moccasins so I staked out the hide, scraped it some more, and cut out another pair made a little better.

After I'd eaten, during which time I moved my fire a few feet, I worked at my knife of obsidian, chipping away to get a good edge. I was clumsy. I'd seen Indians do it in a third of the time. Then I moved my fire again, scattered pine needles over the warm ground where the fire had been, and curled up there with the elk hide over me.

Just a-wishing wouldn't take me there, but my thoughts kept drifting back to the mountain cabin where I was born, back nigh to Denney's Gap, in Tennessee. That old cabin had been mighty comfortable, poor as it was, but unless some squatter had moved into it the cabin was alone now, and empty.

In the cold of dawn the birds were telling stories in the brush, and that spoke well of the neighborhood. As happy as they sounded it was unlikely there was anything hateful around.

My feet were sore and the muscles of my calves ached from the awkward way I'd walked trying to spare my feet. I got up, but my first step hurt so that tears came to my eyes. I sat back down, scared to think of the trouble I was in.

This was no place to stop. I had to start on again, no matter what. Suddenly the eye caught movement on the slope, and when I turned my head I saw the wolf.

It was the one with the cropped ear, and he was watching me.

CHAPTER 2

WHAT HAD BECOME of the others I did not know, but this one was there, and I remembered it well.

"Howdy, boy!" I said, and taking up a scrap from near the fire, I threw it out toward him.

He stood up then, started forward, then stopped. Turning my back on him I shouldered my pack, and taking my club in my hand, I started along the mountain.

When I came out into the open I looked back down the mountain. Far below and far away I could see something moving ... several men.

My throat kind of tightened up on me. They were still coming then, and that meant I hadn't a chance in the world. Not one.

If they stayed on my trail they were sure to get me.

The wolf had come up to where I had thrown the scrap of meat and was sniffing it.

My trouble started when Galloway and me decided to go to ranching. We wanted to find ourselves some fresh country not all cluttered up with folks. We wanted to settle somewhere in the mountains or with mountains close by, and we wanted land where there was grass and water.

We had us a talk with Tell Sackett and old Cap Rountree, and both of them told us about the country

face or beat me with sticks, sometimes for a b
at a time. All they got out of me was a lo
so they decided to try something really
Whilst they were setting around
over, I did some business on my
One of the youngsters had
he got tired of beating me
By humping myself
mouth, got it into
drops from th
toward my
At firs
but I
en

to t ... ...ns are notional, and it just might be that no shooting and a brave face might change their way to favor me.

So I just walked out to meet them, and when they showed up I cussed them out in Apache, as much of it as I knew, and told them that was no way to treat a friend.

Well, it didn't work. They bound my hands and feet and taken me back to camp. They were all set to find out how tough a man I was, and they began it by stripping my clothes off and staking me out in the sun. They hung a water bag close to my head with water dripping from it drop by drop within inches of my mouth, but they'd give me none of it.

The youngsters around camp and some of the squaws would come around and throw sand in my

alf hour
t of cussin',
good.

the fire talking it
own account.

dropped his stick when
and it lay across my chest.
p I slid it down toward my
my teeth and tilted it up until the
t waterbag were coming down it
outh.

most of the drops fell off onto the ground,
hung onto that stick like a bulldog and sure
ugh after awhile some drops began to get into my
mouth. Not that it was much, but when a body has
been so long without water the slightest drop feels
mighty, mighty good.

My jaws began to ache and my neck got stiff but I
daren't move for fear I'd lose the stick or the water
would start dribbling another way.

All of a sudden one of the Indians noticed what I
was doing and called the others. Well, sir, you never
heard such laughing and chuckling. They all gathered
around, pointing and talking. It was a new thing,
what I'd done, and they admired me for being game,
but that didn't change them none. After they had all
seen it one of the braves reached over and jerked that
stick from my jaws so hard he nigh taken some teeth
with it. I cussed him for a no-account coyote and a
dog-robber, and he kicked me.

All night I lay there, staked out on the sand with
no water and less hope. Once a tarantula crawled
across my belly, going about his own affairs, and the

ants found some of the cuts left from the stick beat-
ings. Come daylight they untied my feet and led me to
an anthill where they had stakes driven into the
ground, and I could see what they were planning.

Of a sudden there was a shot, then a yell, some
moaning cries, and every Apache in the lot jumped
his pony and rushed off after whatever it was.

And when they lit out, I did likewise.

We Sackett boys run to length, and I was always a
fair to middlin' foot racer, so I taken off like a scared
jackrabbit, paying no mind to the broken rock and
gravel underfoot. And those squaws came after me,
a-yellin' their lungs out.

Now the men were closing in on me, and with my
feet in the shape they were in I surely wasn't going far,
nor could I hope to outrun them. The only thing in
my favor was that we were heading right into Ute
country. Not that I'd be any better off in the hands of
Utes, but the Apaches didn't find any welcome in Ute
country, either. The further they got into Ute country
the more worried those Apaches were going to be.

Walking on pine needles was a lot better than rock
and the like, but what I needed was a hiding place,
and after that I needed some kind of weapon.

Deliberately I chose the steeper, less likely ways.
Climbing steps were no more painful than those on
the level, yet they would take me to places the Indians
could not follow on their ponies.

Pulling myself up through a narrow space between
two boulders I edged along a rim of rock and then
climbed a dry waterfall to the level above. My feet
were bleeding again, but I found some red clay that I
could mix with pinon gum and tallow from the elk fat

to make a salve often used by the Navajo to promote healing. Yet when I looked back and down I could see eight Apaches, close enough to see the color of their horses.

The Apache fights on his feet, and climbing that mountain after me would be no trick. They hadn't seen me yet but when they did, they'd come. Maybe I was a damned fool, my feet hurting the way they were. Maybe I should just quit and let them kill me. But there was no give-up in me. We boys in the back-woods weren't raised thataway. By the time I was fourteen I knew how to shoot, trap and skin, how to rustle my grub in the woods, and if need be to get along on less than a jackrabbit.

Mostly the boys I ran the hills with were Cherokee, and I learned as much from their folks as my own. We had only two books in our family, so Ma taught us to read from the *Bible* and *Pilgrim's Progress*.

One thing we learned. To make a start and keep plugging. When I had fights at school, the little while I went, I just bowed my neck and kept swinging until something hit the dirt. Sometimes it was me, but I always got up.

Right now I made a decision. Those Apaches weren't going to take kindly to leaving their ponies behind them in Ute country, so if they killed me they were going to have to do it on top of the mountain. That was where I headed.

Turning crossways of the trail I started climbing, using my hands as much as my feet. Stopping near a clump of aspen I looked back down. Far below I could see them and they could see me, and they were drawn up, staring at me.

There was no sense to shooting. Up hill thataway a body ain't going to hit much and I was a far piece off from them. I could almost hear them talking it over.

My hope was they'd decide I wasn't worth the trouble. But it was a slim hope, so I continued on up the mountain. It was a heartbreaker, almost straight up in places, although there were plenty of hand and foot holds. Then I crawled up on the ledge where lay a dead coyote, and I knew that Apaches wouldn't touch one. Taking it by the tail I gave it a good swing and let it fall toward the trail below, right across the path they would have to follow.

I doubted if it would more than make them uneasy, but it did give me an idea. To an Apache the hoot of an owl is a sign of death, and since boyhood I'd been able to hoot well enough to get answers from owls. Knowing sound would carry in those high canyons, I tried it.

They could no longer see me but I could see them, and at the first hoot they pulled up short, and when they reached the dead coyote they stopped again. So I started a couple of boulders rolling down the mountain. I wasn't likely to hit one of them, but it might worry them a little.

Of a sudden I came into a kind of scooped-out hollow in the side of the mountain. Some of it was meadow, but at the back leading up into the notch that led toward the crest it was mostly filled with aspen. And I knew that was it.

I just wasn't going any further.

Crawling back into those aspens where they grew tight and close together I covered my way as well as possible and just lay down. My feet felt like fire, and my legs hurt all the way up. Below the knees, from favoring the soles, the muscles were giving me hell. I just stretched out under the leaves and lay there.

They could find me, all right, but they'd have to hunt.

My club clutched in my hand, I waited, listened for the slightest sound. The aspens whispered and somewhere a bird or small animal rustled in the leaves, but they did not come. Finally I just fell asleep. I had no idea how or when . . . I just did.

Hours later the cold awakened me. All was still. I lay there for awhile, then slowly sat up. It brought kind of a groan from me, which I swallowed before it got too loud. I couldn't see anything or hear anything, so I just naturally lay back down, dug deeper into the leaves, and went to sleep again.

When next I awakened it was morning, and I was stiff with cold. Crawling out of the aspens I looked around, but saw nothing of the Apaches.

Gathering up my pack I limped out through the groves of aspen and began to work my way down into an interior canyon. After an hour, in a hollow under some trees and boulders I stopped, built a small fire of dry, smokeless wood and broiled an elk steak. Hearing a faint rustling among the trees I dropped a couple of bones near the remains of my fire, then went on down.

Later in the day I again bathed my feet in a concoction of snakeweed. Whether it was actually helping I did not know, but it felt good and eased the hurt.

For an hour I rested, then started down the stream. Later I found some bee weed, sometimes called stinkweed. The Navajo used it to start fires by friction as the brittle stalks, whirled between the palms, will start a fire in two minutes or less, especially if a little sand is added to increase the friction.

All the time I kept watch on the slope down which I'd come, but I saw nothing of the Apaches. Maybe the owl-hoot death signal had scared them off, or maybe it was the owl-hoot and the dead coyote together or the feeling they were getting into Ute country. Anyway, there was no sign of them.

Not that I was alone. There was something out there in the brush that was a-watching me, and it might be that wolf. A wolf has been known to stalk a man or an animal for miles, and this wolf needed nobody to tell him that I was in a bad way. He could smell the blood and the festering of some of the cuts on my feet. While I was wary of him and trusted him none at all, I still had no blame for him. He was a wild thing that had to rustle its grub as best it could, and I felt sympathy for it, which was the reason I tossed out those fragments of meat or bone.

Yet that night was the worst. The cold was cruel and my naked body could take no warmth from the remains of the elk hide. All night long I shivered, teeth chattering beside the fire that ate fuel like a famished beast so that I almost never ceased from the hunting of it.

Wild and weird were the snow-covered peaks around me, dark the gorge where I shuddered over my fire, the cold seeping through my bones, stiffening my muscles. A wind, cold and raw, came down the canyon, blowing my fire and robbing my body of the little warmth it had.

The night seemed to stretch on forever. Once I

slept, awakening to find the wind gone but my fire down to a few tiny coals, and with effort I nursed it back into flame. Something padded in the brush out there so I built my fire higher and kept my club and my stone knife closer.

How many men had crouched beside such fires in the years gone by? With no more weapons than I had?

At last the dawn came, cold and bleak, and I could see where wood lay without blundering through the brush. I built up my fire, then took the hide and cut a piece big enough for fresh moccasins. I buried the piece in the ground nearby to make it soft and pliable for the work to come.

I found some chickweed tubers and ate them and ate the last of the elk meat, throwing the few bones into the brush.

Hobbling up on the slope, I looked the country over with care. Now in most places a man can live if he knows something of plants and animals, and if he will take time enough to think things out. It is a man's brain that has removed him from the animals, and it is man's brain that will let him survive, if he takes time to think.

First, I needed a weapon. Second, I must have shelter and clothing. So I stood there, studying the land to see what it offered.

The canyon had high, rocky sides with forest climbing to the crest. There was a stream in the bottom of the gorge with willows around it, and a good bit of grass and some brush. On the ground not twenty feet away lay a well-seasoned branch fallen from a tree. By breaking off the small branches I could fix an obsidian point on it and have a lance.

The bushy-looking trees with scaly twigs and leaves, kind of silvery in the sunlight, were buffalo-berry. The Indians used to collect them to flavor buffalo or antelope meat. There were some wild roses there, too, and I could see the red of some rose hips. There was plenty of deer sign along the stream, and I might have time to make a bow and some arrows.

Limping down to the buffalo-berry bushes I started eating them, pits and all. I topped them off with some rose hips. They weren't any banquet but they would keep me alive. If no Indians found me.

This was Ute country, but both the Navajo and the Apache came here also.

And, of course, there was the wolf.

CHAPTER 3

THERE WAS A pole corral and two lights shining from square windows in the long, low log building. Galloway Sackett swung from the saddle and stood looking into the window for a full minute before he tied his horse.

It was little enough he could see. The window was fly-specked and dirty, but there was a bar inside, and several men. A half dozen horses stood at the hitching rail.

Four of the horses wore a brand strange to him, a Clover Three ... three figure 3's arranged like a three-leaf clover.

Galloway whipped the dust from his clothes with his hat, then started for the door. A glance at a powerful black horse stopped him. He looked at the brand and whistled softly.

Originally the brand must have been a Clover Three, but now it was a Flower. A reverse 3 had been faced to each of the other 3's, then another set had been added, a stem and tendrils to join the petals to the stem. The job was beautifully done, obviously by a rewrite man who knew his business and enjoyed it.

"That's a man I've got to see," Galloway muttered. "He'd wear a Sherman button to a Georgia picnic!"

He pushed open the door and stepped in, then walked to the bar. As he crossed the floor he saw four men sitting at a table together, obviously the Clover Three men. In a corner not far from the bar sat another man, alone.

He wore a fringed buckskin hunting shirt, under it a blue shirt, obviously either new or fresh. He wore a low-crowned black hat, and was smooth-shaved except for a reddish mustache, neatly trimmed and waxed.

The man in the buckskin shirt wore two pistols, one butt forward, one butt to the rear...a tricky thing, for a man might draw with either hand or both guns at once. On the table were a bottle of wine, a glass, and a pack of cards.

Aside from the scruffy-looking man behind the bar there were two others in the room, a man in a dirty white shirt with sleeve garters, and a hairy old man in soiled buckskins.

Galloway Sackett, who had as much appreciation for situations as the next man, ordered rye and edged around the corner of the bar so he could watch what was happening...if anything.

The four riders from the Clover Three looked embarrassed, while the lone man in the buckskin shirt drank his wine calmly, shuffled the cards and laid them out for solitaire, seemingly unconcerned.

Finally one of the Clover Three riders cleared his throat. "Quite a brand you got there, Mister."

Without lifting his eyes from the cards, the other man replied: "You are speaking to me, I presume? Yes, I rather fancy that brand." He glanced up, smiling pleasantly. "Covers yours like a blanket, doesn't it?"

Galloway was astonished, but the four riders only

fidgeted, and then the same man said, "The boss wants to talk to you."

"Does he now? Well, you tell him to ride right on in . . . if he has any horses left."

"I mean . . . he's got a proposition for you. After all, it wasn't him—"

"Of course it wasn't. How could he be expected to account for all the stock on his ranches? You tell your boss to come right on into town. Tell him that I'll be waiting for him. Tell him I've been looking forward to our meeting. Tell him I've been wanting to say hello and good-bye."

"Look, Shadow," the Clover Three man protested, "the boss just doesn't have the time—"

"That's right, Will. Your boss doesn't have the time. In fact he is completely out of time." The man called Shadow placed a card, then glanced up. "You tell Pasten for me that if he will turn his remuda loose, fire his hands and ride off the range with what he can carry on his saddle he can go.

"Otherwise," Shadow added, "I will kill him."

Nobody said anything. Galloway Sackett tasted his rye and waited, as they all waited.

Then Will said, "Aw, give him a chance! You know he can't do that!"

"Pasten robbed a lot of people to build his herd. Some of the cattle were my cattle, some of the cattle had belonged to friends of mine. Some of those people are no longer alive to collect what he owes them, but I intend to see that he does not profit from it. You tell him he's got twenty-four hours . . . no longer."

"Look here." One of the punchers started to rise. "You can't get away with that! You—!"

"Twenty-four hours, gentlemen. You ride out and tell him that. I am through talking." His head turned ever so slightly. "As for you, I would suggest you either sit down or draw a gun. The choice is yours."

He spoke mildly, as one might in a polite conversation, and without stress.

Slowly, carefully, the puncher sat down.

Galloway Sackett tasted his rye again and when the bartender came near he said, "I'm hunting a man who knows the San Juan country."

The bartender shrugged, then indicated Shadow with a gesture of his head. "He knows it, but I wouldn't start any talk about it now. He's got things on his mind."

"I also want a horse—a good horse and a couple of pack horses or mules."

"Talk to him." Then the bartender added, "That's a good country to stay out of. There's talk of trouble with the Utes, and the Jicarillas been cutting loose up thataway."

The four men at the table got up quietly and went out of the door, walking carefully. Galloway Sackett finished his drink, then walked over to the other man's table.

"Mr. Shadow? I'm Galloway Sackett."

"It is a name not unknown to me. Sit down, will you? What will you have?"

"I'm going to have some coffee and some grub, but what I really want is information. The bartender told me you knew the San Juan country."

"I do."

"About a week ago I run into a bunch of Jicarillas and they had my brother. They'd started to work on him. I was alone, but figured if I could create a fuss he'd cut loose on his own. I did, and he did."

"He got away?"

"He surely did. And dropped clean off the world. I hunted for him and they did. Those Jicarillas weren't about to lose him so they taken in after him. He was stark naked and had his hands tied, but he got away."

"He's dead, then."

"Not Flagan. We Sacketts don't die easy, and Flagan is a tough man. He's been up the creek and over the mountain. He's fit Comanches and Arapahoes on the buffalo plains, and about ever' kind of man or animal. He's a tough man."

"That San Juan country is tough. It's the most beautiful country in the world, but about two-thirds of it stands on end."

Shadow paused, waiting while the bartender placed coffee and food on the table. Then he asked, "What do you want me to do?"

"Tell me about it. How the streams run, the best ways to get through the mountains, where I'm liable to run into Indians. I'm going in after him."

"You're bucking a stacked deck, my friend. You'll need an outfit."

"That's another thing. The bartender said you had horses. I need a spare for Flagan to ride when I find him, and I'll need a couple of pack horses for grub and the like."

Shadow took a thin cigar from his pocket and lighted it. He studied the end of it for a moment, then said, "If I didn't have some business to attend to, I'd go with you."

"Twenty-four hours, you gave him. Do you think he'll move?"

"Yes."

Galloway glanced at Shadow thoughtfully. "He must know you, this Pasten gent."

"He knows me. He stole cattle and killed men in the Mimbres country. He wiped out a lot of us, then pulled out and drove the cattle clear out of the country. I took in after him.

"I lost the trail, then found it again. Meanwhile he'd settled down here, hired a bunch of reasonably honest hands, and then he cooked up that Clover Three brand. Guess he had an idea it couldn't be blotted, so I did it, just as a challenge. So he sent a hired man after me, but I remembered the man from Texas, and he did not remember me."

"How'd that happen?"

Shadow shrugged. "I was a teacher at Waco University. Our paths did not cross in a way he would notice."

"You were a teacher?"

He shrugged. "One does what one can. I needed the job, they needed the teacher. In fact, they wanted me to stay on, but the pay was small and I was restless. I had come to America to hunt for gold."

He glanced at Galloway again. "Are you related to Orrin Sackett?"

"He's kin."

"He defended me in a shooting case. My first one, in fact. It was a little matter of a horse. My horse was stolen. I hunted the man down and he drew a pistol and I shot him. Someone advised me to hire Orrin Sackett and I did...fortunately."

They finished their coffee, talked idly of various things, and then Shadow stood up. "I have a cabin down the road apiece. If you'd like you may join me. There's an empty bunk, and you're welcome."

The cabin was small but comfortable. There were Navajo rugs on the floors, curtains at the windows, and a couple of dozen books.

"I envy you the books," Galloway said. "School was a rare time thing for us. Mostly it was Ma teaching us from the Bible, and she read a couple of stories to us written by Walter Scott. Flagan an' me, we got our learning in the woods with our Winchesters."

"Your brother is a woodsman? Not just a cowhand?"

"We grew up in the Cumberland country. We learned from the Cherokees. Given a chance Flagan could get along most anywhere."

"Then he might make it. He might just be alive."

It was the first time he had slept in a bed in weeks, but Galloway slept well, and awakened with the sun. Shadow was already outside but a minute or two later he came in.

"I just had word. Pasten left the country. I've started some men rounding up my cattle, and the others."

Galloway Sackett dressed. Somewhere in the country far to the north and east his brother was either dead or fighting for his very existence. Somehow he must find him. The night before, Shadow had carefully outlined the lay of the country, how the rivers ran, the Animas, the Florida, and the La Plata, and Galloway, knowing his brother's mind as he knew his own, was trying to figure out what Flagan would have done when he got away.

He would have headed for the mountains, and the first trail he'd found had pointed north. It was Flagan's trail, but that of the Apaches following him as well.

Flagan would head into the hills, try and find some place to hole up. He would need some clothes, and he would need shelter and food. In the mountains, with luck, he could find what he needed.

"Sackett?" Shadow called from the door. "Get your gear together. I've saddled our horses and we're packed for the trip."

"We?"

"I'm going with you."

CHAPTER 4

FOR A WEEK I rested beside the creek, keeping hidden when possible. I treated my feet alternately with the salve I had made and leaves of the Datura, and the soles began to heal.

Twice I snared rabbits, once I knocked down a sage hen. There were yampa roots, Indian potatoes, and I found a rat's nest containing nearly a bushel of hazelnuts. The fare was scant but I was making out.

By the end of the week I'd completed a bow and some arrows, and had killed a deer. With the piece of elk hide, softened by its burial in the earth, I made moccasins. Marking out the soles by tracing my feet with charcoal, I then cut out an oval as long as my two feet, cut it in half, and in the middle of each squared-off end I cut a slit long enough for my foot to get into, then cut another slit to make a T. I now had the upper for each moccasin and using a thorn for an awl I punched holes to sew the uppers to the soles. Finally I punched holes along each side of the slit to take a drawstring.

One of the first things I'd done was to make a shelter hidden well back in a clump of willows. Crawling back into the middle of the thickest clump I could find, I cut off some brush, enough to make a sleeping space. Then I drew the willows together overhead and tied them, allowing others to stand up to mask what I had done.

This wasn't shelter I built all at once. First I had just crawled among the willows to sleep where I'd not be easily found, then I widened it for more room, and the willows I cut I wove in overhead and around the sides to make it snugger and warmer. After a week of work the tunnel was six feet long and masked by tying two growing willows a little closer together once I was inside.

Twice I saw deer just too far off to risk a shot. The one buckskin I had was not enough to make a shirt.

Living in such a way leaves no time for rest. Between the two slopes, the stream, and the narrow bottom of the canyon, I made out. Several times I caught fish, never large enough, and found clumps of sego lily and ate the bulbs. Gradually over that week the stiffness and soreness began to leave my muscles and my feet began to heal.

Yet I was facing the same thing that faced every hunting and food-gathering people. Soon a man has eaten all that's available close by and the game grows wary. Until men learned to plant crops and herd animals for food they had of necessity to move on... and on.

Most of what I'd done to make myself comfortable must be left behind, and it worried me that I had no better weapons. My feet were better, but the skin was tender and I daren't walk very far at any one time. I'd been sparing of the hazelnuts for they were the best of my food, but at last they gave out, too. On the ninth day I gathered my few possessions and started out.

Back up at the forks of the creek in Tennessee they

don't raise many foolish children, and the foolish ones don't live long enough to get knee-high to a short sheep. This was Indian country, so I taken it easy. My weapons weren't fit for fighting and my feet were too sore for running.

When I'd traveled about a half mile I sat down to study out the land. The canyon was widening out, and there was plenty of deer sign. Twice I saw tracks of a mountain lion, a big one.

By nightfall I'd covered four miles, resting often. The canyon had widened to a valley and the stream joined a larger river that flowed south. I could see the place where they flowed together, right up ahead. North of me the country seemed to flatten out, with towering snow-covered peaks just beyond. Those peaks must be the San Juans Tell Sackett had spoken of. I knew this country only by hear-tell, and when I'd been running ahead of those Jicarillas I'd not been paying much mind to landmarks.

Working my way over to the brush and trees that followed the canyon wall, I hunkered down to study out the land. And that was how I saw those Utes before they saw me.

They were coming up from the south and they had about twenty riderless horses with them, and a few of those horses looked almighty familiar. They passed nigh me, close enough to see they were a war party returning from some raid. They had bloody scalps, and it looked like they had run into those Jicarillas. Ambushing an Apache isn't an easy thing to do but it surely looked like they'd done it.

Trying to steal a horse ran through my mind, but I made myself forget it. My feet were in no shape for travel and I couldn't stand another chase. My best bet was to head east toward the Animas where I'd heard there were some prospectors.

Fact is, I was hungry most of the time. What I'd been finding was scarcely enough to keep soul and body together, and down on the flat it was harder to find what I needed. I found some Jimson weed and cut a few leaves to put in my moccasins. I'd used it for saddle sores and knew it eased the pain and seemed to help them to heal, but it was dangerous stuff to fool around with, and many Indians won't touch it.

Studying out the ground I saw a field of blue flowers, a kind of phlox the Navajo used to make a tea that helped them sing loudly at the Squaw Dance, and was also a "medicine" used for the Navajo Wind Chant. But I found nothing to eat until night when I caught a fine big trout in an angle of the stream, spearing it with more luck than skill, and then as I was making camp I found some Indian potatoes. So I ate well, considering.

When the fish was eaten I huddled by my capful of fire and wished for a cabin, a girl, and a meal waiting, for I was a lonesome man with little enough before me and nothing behind but troubles. Soon a cricket began to sing near my fire, so I made care to leave him be. There's a saying in the mountains that if you harm a cricket his friends will come and eat your socks. A hard time they would have with me, not having socks or anything else.

Galloway was no doubt eating his belly full in some fine restaurant or house, filling up on beef and frijoles whilst I starved in the woods. It is rare enough that I feel sorry for myself but that night I did, but what is the old saying the Irish have? *The beginning of a ship is a board; of a kiln, a stone; and the beginning of health is sleep.*

I slept.

Cold it was, and the dew heavy upon the grass and upon me as well, but I slept and the wind whispered in the aspen leaves, and in the darkness the taste of smoke came to my tongue, and the smell of it to my nose. Cold and dark it was when the smell of it awakened me, and I sat up, shivering with a chill that chattered my teeth. Listening into the night I heard nothing, but then my eye caught a faint gleam and I looked again and it was a dying fire, not fifty yards off.

Slowly and carefully I got to my feet. Indians. At least a dozen, and one of them awake and on guard. They must have made camp after I fell asleep, although it was late for Indians to be about, but come daylight they would surely find me. Easing my feet into my moccasins, I gathered what I had to carry and slipped away. When I was well away from their camp and in the bottom, I started to run.

The earth was soft underfoot, and the one thing I needed now was distance. They would find my camp in the morning and come after me. I ran and walked for what must have been a couple of hours, and then I went into the stream.

The moon was up and the whole country was bathed in such a white beauty a man could not believe, the aspens silvery bright, the pines dark and still. The cold water felt good to my feet but because the current was swift and the footing uncertain, I took my time. After awhile I came out on the bank and sat down, my muscles aching and weary, my feet sore. Carefully I dried them with handfuls of grass and clumps of soft sage.

Light was breaking when I started again. Within the hour they would be on my trail, and they would move much faster than I could. I did not know the Utes, but the stories I'd heard were mixed, and this was their country.

Now I moved from rock to rock, carrying a small flat rock in my hand to put down wherever I might leave a footprint. The rock left a mark but it was indefinite and might have been caused by any number of things. The Utes might find me, but I did not intend it should be easy, and I could drop the rock I carried and step from it to some other surface that would leave no mark.

Something rustled in the brush. Turning sharply I was only in time to see leaves moving where something had passed by. Crouching near a rock, I waited, but nothing came. Moving toward the brush, spear poised, I found only the faintest of tracks . . . the wolf.

He was with me still, a rare thing for a lone wolf to stalk a man for so long a time. Yet he was out there now, in the brush, stalking me for a kill. Still, there must be easier game.

Twice I made my way through thick groves of aspen, trying to leave no sign of my passing, yet always alert for a place to hide. By now they had found my fire, and were on my trail.

My feet were beginning to bleed again. I heard the cry of an eagle that was no eagle, and the cry came from where no eagle would be. One of them had found some sign I'd left and was calling the others.

They would find me now, for they could scatter out and pick up what sign I'd left. I was too slow, too tired, and the going was too rough for me not to make mistakes.

Suddenly, there was no place to go. There'd been no trail. I'd just been following the lines of least resistance, and now the mountainside broke sharply off and I stood on the brink of a cliff with a deep pool of water lying thirty feet below. I could hear water falling somewhere near, but the surface below was unruffled and clear. There was no hesitation in me.

This far I had come, and there could be no thought of turning back. So I dropped my gear into the water, and feet first, I jumped.

A moment of falling, then my body struck the water and knifed into it. There was intense cold. I went down, down, and then as I was coming up my head bumped something and it was the quiver of arrows I'd made. A few yards away was the bow. Gathering them up, I swam for the only shore there was, a narrow white-sand beach back under the overhang of the cliff from which I'd jumped.

No more than four feet long and three wide, it was still a place where I could crawl up and rest. As I neared it I found my spear and the hide with my few belongings in it floating near. After I'd beached the bow and arrows, I recovered them and returned to the beach.

Stretching out on that beach meant putting my feet in the water, and that was just what I did. That sandy strip was completely invisible from anyone not on the surface of the water, for the pool was rimmed around with smooth rock edges, and none of them seemed to be less than six feet above the water. Even if the Indians circled and got on the rocks opposite they could not see into my hiding place. Their eyes could touch only the water or the rock above me.

Nobody was likely to find me here, but the question was, and it was an almighty big question, how was I going to get out?

I'd no food left and not much strength, but for the moment I was safe. So I curled up on the sand, pulled the remnants of my hides over me and went to sleep.

And in my sleep I dreamed that I heard a sound of horses, the whimper of a dog or wolf, and the sound of falling water.

When I awakened it was a long time later. I was cold, shivering cold, and the water was gray with late evening. There was a waterfall near . . . not that it mattered.

This was one I wasn't going to get out of.

Galloway, where are you?

CHAPTER 5

T HERE'S A TOWN," Shadow said, "or what passes for a town."

"Flagan don't know nothing about a town. When he taken out he was stark naked an' running his heart out, but if I know Flagan he'll take to the hills. There's places to hide and a better chance of rustling some grub."

"Nevertheless, he's apt to come upon some tracks, and if he follows them he'll find some prospector's camp or a ranch."

"Ranch?"

"They're coming in. The Dunn outfit have laid claim to a wide stretch of range and they're bringing in cattle." Shadow rode around a tree, pulling up to let Galloway ride abreast. "There's some others, too."

"There's room for all."

"Not if you listen to the Dunns. They're a tough lot. From Kansas."

There was the shadow of a trail, long unused. It wound among the rocks and boulders, following the contour of the land. Under the trees it was shadowed and still. Occasionally they drew up to give their horses a breather, for the altitude was high.

"I was talking with an old Ute," Shadow commented, "and showed him a picture of the castle where I was born. He said there were bigger castles back in the mountains."

"Castles?"

"Big houses," he said, "bigger than any dozen houses he had ever seen, bigger than twice that many, he claimed."

"You'd never guess it. Not in this country. He was probably tellin' you a tall tale."

"Maybe."

Hours later they came down off the mesa into a wide, grassy valley. Almost at once they saw tracks. A dozen riders on shod horses had passed, and not too long before.

Nick Shadow drew up and studied the tracks. Then he looked north in the direction they had gone. "Some of that Dunn outfit," he said. "Stay away from them, Sackett. They're trouble."

"Isn't likely I'll run into them." They mounted a ridge as Galloway spoke and he pointed off to the west. "River over there?"

"The Mancos. Mesa Verde is just beyond. That's where the old Indian told me the castles could be found. Someday I'm going to ride over and have a look."

After a moment Shadow added, "You'd best not hope too much. Your brother didn't have much chance."

"He's a tough man. He's had his tail in a crack before this.

"If I know him he's a comin', and somehow or other he'll keep himself alive. Up to us to find him, no matter how long. No Sackett ever left another in a bind. Leastways, none from my part of the country."

They had turned eastward, and high upon the right, but back from where they rode, the mountains lifted, bold peaks, their rugged flanks streamered with snow, forested almost to the top. They rode cautiously, knowing it was Ute country but also that the Dunns were here.

"I've met none of them," Shadow said, "but they've a name for being a quarrelsome lot. Rocker Dunn killed a man over near Pagosa Springs a year back, and they say he'd killed a couple in Kansas before they came west. There's talk that several of them rode with Quantrill."

"Where's that town?"

"South of us. East and south. It lies over close to the La Plata. They've called it Shalako after one of the Kachinas."

Galloway was thinking of Flagan. Back in those mountains somewhere he was fighting to keep alive...if he was alive. Without weapons, in a rugged country where the only humans he found were apt to be enemies, his chances of survival depended upon himself and his own energies.

They had grown up together, fighting each other's battles, working together, struggling together, and no man could know another so well as Galloway knew Flagan. He knew what Flagan must do to survive because he knew what he would do. And there was no easy way.

Flagan would be struggling for every mouthful of food, thinking, conniving, planning. And he would be working his way north, staying with the kind of country where he could find a living, and slowly moving toward the destination for which they had set out.

SHALAKO LAY ON the flat with a backdrop of trees and towering mountains. The flat was green, dotted with clumps of oak brush, and the metropolis itself was composed of three buildings, two short stretches of boardwalk, one log cabin, a dugout, and several outbuildings of obvious intent.

"Now look at that," Nick Shadow commented. "It shows you how fast this country is growing. This town has increased one-third since I saw it only a few months ago. Somebody built a barn."

"Livery stable, looks like."

"Well, what more do you want? A saloon, a general store, and a livery stable. That's enough for any town."

"And looks like there's folks in town," Sackett commented. "Four, five horses in front of the saloon, and a buckboard yonder by the store. Business is boomin'."

"They're ruining the country," Shadow agreed. "A year or two ago a man could ride a hundred miles through here and not see anybody, or even hear anybody but the Indians who shot at him. Now look at it. You can hardly walk without falling over people.

"And by the way," he added, as he drew up before the saloon, "that's a Rocking D brand...the Dunn outfit."

They swung down, whipped the dust from their clothes, two tall men. Nick Shadow, man of the world, educated, refined, and immaculate...not even the long dusty ride had robbed him of that appearance. And Galloway Sackett, in a buckskin coat, a dark blue shirt, shotgun-fringed chaps and boots. On his head a black, flat-crowned hat. He wore his gun tied down, and carried a Bowie knife at his belt. The fact that he had another one, an Arkansas toothpick with a long slender blade, was not obvious. It was suspended between his shoulderblades, the haft within easy grasp below his shirt collar. This was a Tinker-made knife.

Tying their horses they crossed the boardwalk and entered the saloon. Outside it had a false front, behind it a peaked roof, and inside there was no ceiling, just the heavy beams overhead.

There was a long bar, a dozen tables, and chairs. The bartender was a broad-faced man with corn yellow hair, massive forearms resting on the bar. At the end of the bar was a wiry old man with a thin face and high cheekbones, in buckskins.

At a table were three men, obviously cowhands.

"Rye," Shadow said, "for two."

The bartender reached down for a bottle without taking the other arm off the bar and came up with the bottle and two glasses. He put the glasses down and poured, all with his left hand.

Galloway glanced at him thoughtfully, his eyes crinkling at the corners. "Good country around here," he said, speaking to Shadow. "I can see why Tell liked it."

"Tell?" the bartender asked. "You don't mean Tell Sackett?"

"I do mean him," Galloway said. "You know him?"

"Sure do . . . and a good man, too. You mean to say he's been in this country?"

"Several years back. Fact is, Tyrel rode through here one time, too. He'd taken off and was riding around the country, before he got married. And his pa was here long before that, back around 1840."

One of the men at the table, a pugnacious, curly-haired boy of about Galloway's age turned sharply around. "1840? There was nobody here that early."

"My uncle," Galloway said, "was a mountain man. He came down from the north with some other trappers, hunting beaver peltries. He described all of this country to us."

"As a matter of fact," Shadow commented, "there were many here earlier than that. Rivera was up here as early as 1769, and Father Escalante traveled right through here when he was looking for a trail to Monterey, in California."

The young man looked sullen. "I never heard of that. I don't believe it."

"Your privilege," Shadow said. "I realize that education is hard to come by in this part of the country."

The young man had started to turn back to his table. Now he turned sharply around. "What do you mean by that? You sayin' I got no education?"

Nick Shadow smiled. "Of course not. I assumed you were a rather bright young man, and you assumed I was mistaken about Rivera and Escalante. No doubt we were both mistaken."

Shadow turned his back on him, and Galloway said to the bartender, who was trying to hide a smile, "I'm hunting my brother. He got away from the 'Paches away down south of here and headed into the mountains. He'd be in mighty bad shape. Have you heard anything of such a man?"

"No. And I would have heard, I'm sure. There aren't many people around here. There's the Dunn outfit you were just talking to, and there's Lute Pitcher...he's got a place a couple of miles over in the hills beyond the river."

"If he shows up, lend a hand. I'll stand good for anything he wants."

The curly-headed man looked around. He had the feeling he had been made a fool of and it rankled. "An' who'll stand good for you?"

Galloway Sackett smiled. "Just me. I think that's enough."

"I don't think it is," the curly-haired one said, "I don't think that's enough at all."

"It is for me," the bartender said calmly. "Sackett is a respected name." And then he added, "Curly, I'd let it alone if I were you."

Curly Dunn got to his feet. "You ain't me, and I don't think much of the name of Sackett." He put his gaze on Galloway. "You want to make something out of that?"

Galloway grinned. "When I do, you'll be the first to know."

He turned to Shadow. "Shall we ride?"

They started for the door, and Curly Dunn shouted after them. "If you're thinkin' of land in this country, you'd better think again. This here is Dunn country!"

Galloway turned. "Are you Dunn?"

"You're durned tootin' I am!"

"Glad to hear it. I'm just beginning." He went out and let the door swing to behind him.

Crossing the street to the general store they entered, buying what supplies they needed. The owner of the store was a slender young man, loose-jointed and friendly.

"My first business," he said. "Pa, he doesn't think I can cut the mustard, but he offered to set me up. Well, I'd saved some, and the rest I borrowed under my own name. I plan to succeed without his help.

"Not," he added, "that there's trouble between us. It's just that I wanted to make it without his help." He grinned. "All I need is more customers."

"We're moving into this country," Galloway said. "We mean to run cattle."

Johnny Kyme glanced at him. "Have you talked to the Dunns about that? They say this is Dunn country."

"We met Curly over yonder," Galloway said dryly. "He sort of led us to believe they figured thataway, but we sort of left the thought with him that we figured to stick around."

Galloway explained about Flagan. "If he shows up, give him whatever he wants. It's good."

They made camp that night in a hollow alongside the rushing waters of the La Plata, with a scattering of aspen about them.

When they had their blankets spread Galloway pulled off his boots and placed them carefully beside him and within easy reach. "I take it kindly, Nick, that you've come along with me."

"I like to ride lonesome country. It's built in me, I guess."

"You born in a castle, and all, I'd figure you for the big towns."

"It wasn't my castle, Sackett. My father owned it and had the title. My mother was the daughter of a younger son who had gone off to sea, lost a leg in a sea battle and came back to set himself up as a wood-worker.

"My father had two legitimate sons who looked nothing like him, nor acted it, either. I was his image. His wife met me outside the town once where I was exercising a horse for a man. She asked me to leave the country. My mother had passed on, and I'd no taste for woodworking, and she explained to me that I was too much like her husband not to cause comment. She said she loved her husband, and she offered to give me a good sum of money if I'd leave.

"Well, I'd been wanting just that, though doubtful if I'd ever get it. I'd gone to good schools, but had no taste for business. So I thanked her, took the money and came to America.

"I've never told anyone else that, and probably never will again."

"How about your grandpa?"

"He hated to see me go, but he would have done the same. I'd have come to nothing there, unless it was trouble. I wrote to him, sent him money when I had it. He died a few years ago. The countess wrote and explained, asking if I wished to come back. One of her sons had been killed when he was thrown from a horse. Another got in trouble and left the country, and the third was not a well man."

"You could go back."

Shadow nodded. "She said my father would make me legitimate, which might mean I'd inherit. I'm no longer cut out for it, Sackett. This is my country.

Besides, I'd have trouble back east. There was a little affair in Missouri, a corpse and cartridge occasion ... his family was prominent and they would like to find me."

Neither man spoke for some time, and Shadow smoked in silence, then put out his pipe and crawled into his blankets.

"Sackett," Shadow said suddenly, "you've got to see the high country around here to believe it. There is nothing more fantastically beautiful. There are towering peaks, valleys no white man has ever seen, and streams that run to God knows where. I've seen the Alps and the Pyrenees, but there's nothing anywhere like these mountains."

Galloway was silent. Somewhere out in these mountains, perhaps even within a few miles, Flagan was fighting for his life, for his very existence. Slowly he began once more, trying to picture in his brain what must have been happening.

Flagan was a good runner, and he was always in excellent shape. He would have made good time, gotten enough of a lead so they would have a hard time catching up. Food would be harder to come by, but in the mountains they had often rustled their own food.

Somehow Flagan would survive. He must survive.

CHAPTER 6

FOR JUST A WHILE I lay there shivering in the cold. It was in that last hour before dawn, judging by the few stars I could see. My muscles were stiff and sore, and my feet hurt. I pulled myself painfully to a sitting position and took a slow look around my little island.

The only sound was the rustle of falling water, just loud enough to make it hard to hear anything else that might be stirring around. And then, far off over the mountains, I heard the deep rumble of thunder.

The last thing I wanted right now was a rain storm, me without any clothes, and cold as all get out. Worst of all, I seemed to be trapped in this place and from the looks of the cave walls around me the water in here sometimes rose several feet higher than I could stand. It didn't even have to rain right here to make trouble for me. The water coming down that waterfall I could hear would pour into this basin.

Time to time in my life I'd come up against trouble, but this here seemed about the worst. And my strength was drained by the poor food I'd had, and the beating I'd taken from both the Indians and the wilderness. I'd been bad off before, but at least I'd been out on solid ground where I could travel and maybe rustle a bite to eat. I'd gotten away from the Indians but I'd jumped right into a trap.

Thunder growled deep in the far-off canyons, and I turned my head and began a slow, inch-by-inch check of this place in which I was trapped.

I was on that small bit of sandy beach against the back wall of an overhang that seemed to be of solid rock. From where I sat I could see no break in the wall of the bowl into which I'd jumped, although as water poured into the basin, there must be a way for it to get out.

Finally, I slipped off into the water. Once in the water I was warmer than on the beach, and slowly I swam out into the open air. The rocky edge above me was only a rough six feet above the water, but the wall was sheer, polished by water and worn smooth. Here and there were cracks in the walls, but they were vertical, and there was no way I could see that I could hang on until I could catch hold with the other hand.

The largest one started a good four feet up the wall, and although I jumped a couple of times from the water my fingers wouldn't hold in the slippery crack, so I swam back and stretched out on the sand, just about all in.

Twice more I swam around that pool, trying to find a way out, but my only chance was that crack. Each time I went back to the beach I rested a little longer, for the days of scant food and struggling to cross the country and stay alive had about worn me out. Still, I always told myself, there was nothing a man couldn't get out of if he was sober and didn't panic, so I settled down to think.

The water I'd heard falling wasn't much of a fall, but the rock over which it fell was higher than the place from which I'd jumped, and the rocks were worn smooth.

It began to rain.

First there were scattered big drops, then a steady downpour that freckled the water about me. For awhile I just lay still, trying to get up energy to try again, and the falling water kind of lulled me to sleep. When I opened my eyes I was shaking with a chill and the water in that basin had raised by at least an inch.

Cold and shivering, I studied the walls again, but always I came back to that crack.

The bottom was a good four feet above the water, and the wall below it was smooth as silk. That crack was maybe four inches wide at the top, but it tapered down to nothing. If a man could have gotten up high enough to get both hands into it with his fingers pulling against opposite edges he might have worked himself to the top . . . he might have.

Toward the bottom there wasn't room to even get one finger into that crack, and I couldn't pull myself up with one finger, anyway.

There didn't seem to be any way out of this fix I'd gotten myself into, and I went back and stretched on the sand again. Seemed to me there was less of it, and the rain was falling steadily.

If I could just find something to wedge into that crevice to give myself a handhold . . . but there was nothing. Of a sudden, I thought of finding a stick, only there were no sticks, and my spear wasn't strong enough to hold my weight even if the crack was deep enough to thrust it in, which it wasn't.

If only there was something. . . . There was!

My fist.

If I could jump high enough out of the water to wedge my doubled-up fist in that crack I could hang by it. If I opened my hand I'd slide right back in the water, but if I could keep my fist closed I could muscle myself up high enough to wedge the other fist crossways in the crack, and then I could grab for the rim.

Something warned me that I had better try. The water running off the mountain in this rain had not yet reached the pool, but it would soon start pouring in from branch streams and runoff gullies, and I'd be forced to swim until I could swim no longer. My little beach would be covered within minutes.

Also, my strength was slipping away. I'd had nothing to eat, and much of my strength had been used up in running, climbing, struggling for life and for food. If this failed there was no other way, so it had to work.

Swimming across the basin I looked up at the crack, so close above me. Now when I was a youngster I'd managed to lunge pretty high out of the water many times in batting a gourd around the old swimming hole. This time I not only had to get about half my body out of the water but I had to wedge my fist in that narrow crack.

First I carried my spear close to the side and threw it atop the wall. Next I threw up my bow and the quiver of arrows.

On my first attempt I succeeded in hitting the wall and bruising myself. On the second my arm went high and my closed fist caught in the crack.

Slowly, flexing my muscles, I lifted my body. It was like chinning myself with one hand, something I'd rarely tried, but my body did come up out of the water and I got my other fist into the crack, but cross-ways as the crack was wider there. Another lift and I got my other hand on the edge. Pulling myself up, I flopped over on the rocky edge and lay still, the rain pounding on my back.

After awhile, shaking with cold and exhaustion, I got my feet under me, recovered my weapons and started into the woods. That night, cowering among the pine needles, without even the elk hide to cover me, I shivered alone and cold.

How much can a man endure? How long could a man continue? These things I asked myself, for I am a questioning man, yet even as I asked the answers were there before me. If he be a man indeed, he must always go on, he must always endure. Death is an end to torture, to struggle, to suffering, but it is also an end to warmth, light, the beauty of a running horse, the smell of damp leaves, of gunpowder, the walk of a woman when she knows someone watches...these things, too, are gone.

In the morning I would have a fire. In the morning I would find food.

The rain fell steadily, and in my huddle under the bushes the big drops came through and rolled coldly down my spine and down my chest.

Stiff and cold, I crept out in the gray dawn. The rain had stopped but the ground was soggy under my feet. Wearing only moccasins and a breech clout I hunted for roots. Starting across a clearing I suddenly heard a rush of movement and looked up in time to be struck by a horse's shoulder and knocked rolling.

Desperately, I tried to get up, to call out, but the wind had been knocked out from me.

A voice said, "That's no Indian! Curly, that's a white man!"

"Aw, what difference does it make? Leave him lay!"

It taken me a minute to get up and I called after him. "Help me. Get me to a ranch or somewhere. I'll—"

The rider called Curly spun his horse and came back at a run. He had a coil of rope in his hand and he was swinging it for a blow. Trying to step aside my feet skidded on the wet leaves and the horse hit me again, knocking me into the brush. Curly rode away laughing.

After a long while I got my knees under me and crawled to where my arrows were. The bowstring was wet and useless, but the spear might get me something. First I needed a fire. In a hollow near the river, I broke the dried-out twigs that were lowest on the tree trunks, gathered some inner bark from a deadfall and rigged a small shelter to keep the raindrops from my fire.

With my stone knife I cut out a little hollow in a slab of wood broken loose when a tree fell, then a notch from the hollow to the edge.

Powdering bark in my hands I fed the dust into the hollow, then used my bow and a blunt arrow-shaft to start the fire. It took several minutes of hard work to get a smoke and then a spark, but I worked on a bit, then managed to blow the spark into life. At last I had a fire.

It is times such as this that show a man how much the simple things like food and warmth can mean. Slowly my fire blazed up, and the first warmth in a long time began to work its way into my stiff, cold muscles.

Everything was damp. I'd nothing to cover my nakedness, but the fire brought a little warmth to me, and just having it made me feel better. My feet were in bad shape again, although not so bad as at first, and the bruises from the beating I'd taken showed up in great blotches over my hide. I huddled there by the fire, shivering, wishing for food, for warmth, for a blanket.

It was unlikely any wild game would stir during the rain, so I must wait it out or try to find what roots there might be, but looking from where I sat I saw nothing I could eat. Yet I had lived long enough to know that nothing lasts forever, and men torture themselves who believe that it will. The one law that does not change is that everything changes, and the hardship I was bearing today was only a breath away from the pleasures I would have tomorrow, and those pleasures would be all the richer because of the memories of this I was enduring.

It was not in me to complain of what had happened. A man shares his days with hunger, thirst and cold, with the good times and the bad, and the first part of being a man is to understand that. Leastways, I had two hands, two feet and two eyes, and there were some that lacked these things. The trouble was that I wasn't feeling quite right . . . I'd a sense of things being unreal, and of sickness coming on, and that scared me something sinful.

To be sick, alone, and in the woods, with the weather damp and cold . . . it was not a thing to favor the mind.

Of a sudden I was sweating, out there in the cold and rain, I was sweating where a short time before I'd been chilled and shaking. I burrowed down into the pine needles and leaves, and fortunate it was that here where I'd stopped the carpet was thick.

I'd stick out a hand from time to time to put something on the fire, scared of the time when it would be used up around me and I'd have to get out and go to hunting. There were willows near, and I peeled back the bark to get at the inner bark, which was good for fevers, and chewed some.

Along in there somewhere I sort of passed out. There was a time when I put a stick or two on the fire, added some leaves for lack of anything else.

Once I thought I heard a horse coming, and it was in my mind that somebody called out to me, but I don't know if I answered. My head felt light and my mouth was dry, and I was cold ... cold.

I've heard folks say that if you're down in a dark hole and you look up you can see the stars, even by day. Well, I looked up and saw a face looking into mine with wide eyes and lips parted, and it was like looking up out of that hole and seeing a star. Anyway, it was the last I saw for some time.

WE NEVER HAD much in the mountains. The fixings around the house were such as Ma contrived, or Pa when he was not too tired from work. Nothing fancy, just a few little things like curtains at the window, and flowers on the table, and Ma when she swept the floor and could keep us boys off it for awhile, she traced patterns in the dirt floor like you'd find on the finest carpets. Ma was good at that, and she liked things nice.

About the best we could manage was to keep them clean.

You don't make much on a sidehill farm in Tennessee. The country is right beautiful, and that is where you have to find what beauty there is, there, and in the singing. Most mountain folks sing. They sing songs learned from their grandfathers or other elders, and sometimes they change the tunes to fit the day, and change the words even more.

You get a hankering for nice things if there's much to you. It seems to me that first a man tries to get shelter and food to eat, but as soon as he has that he tries to find beauty, something to warm the heart and the mind, something to ease the thoughts and make pleasurable the sitting in the evening. About all we had was the open fire. It was the thing we set store by. Ma, she was too busy knitting and sewing just to keep us covered to have much time for fixing.

Opening my eyes like I done, in that bedroom with lacy curtains to the windows and a handsome patchwork quilt over me, I thought I'd sure come to in the house of some rich folks, or in heaven mostly, although I never did rightly know whether they'd have patchwork quilts. She set store by them, and she was always a saving of odds and ends she might use toward one. She never did get to make it. Pneumonia came too soon, and pneumonia to mountain folk far from doctors is nothing to feel good about.

There I lay, a long tall mountain boy in such a bed as I'd never seen, looking up at a painted plank ceiling...well, maybe it was whitewashed.

I turned my head and saw a dresser set against the wall with a mirror over it, and there was a small table with a pitcher and a washbasin. In a dish alongside the basin was a bar of soap. These here were surely well-to-do folks.

When I tried to set up I felt giddy, but the first thing I saw was that I was wearing a flannel nightshirt. I'd had a nightshirt one time, quite awhile back, but they were scarce. I was seventeen years old before I owned a pair of socks. We boys just shoved our feet down into boots.

We never had much, Galloway and me. First big money we made was on the buffalo range. We were shooters, me and him, and mostly we hit what we shot at. Back in the high-up hills a body didn't have enough ammunition to go a-wasting of it. When you shot at something you'd better hit it. Which led to our being good at stalking and tracking because we had to get close up before we chanced a shot. And if the animal was wounded and ran off, we had to track it down, for the needing of the meat and not wishing to leave any crittur to suffer in the woods.

That money we made on the buffalo range, that went to squaring Pa's debts, of which he'd left a few with men who trusted him. We never taken a trust lightly. It was a matter of deep honor, and a debt owed was a debt to be paid.

I lay there in that big bed, just a-staring up at the white ceiling and wondering how come I was here in this place.

There was a door opening to a sort of closet and in it I could see women's fixings and some man's shirts and pants. I could also see a holster with a gun in it. Gave me a comfort to have it near.

Footsteps were coming down the hall and then the door opened and a man came in. He was a square-shouldered man with a mustache and wearing a white shirt. He looked down at me.

"Awake are you? You've had a bad time of it, man."

"I reckon. How long have I been here?"

"Six . . . seven days. My daughter found you. How she got you on her horse I will never know."

I was tired. I closed my eyes a minute, thinking how lucky I was.

"You had pneumonia," he said. "We didn't think we could pull you through. At least, I didn't. Maighdlin, she never did give up."

"Where is this place?"

"It's on Cherry Creek, about six or seven miles from where you were picked up." He sat down in the chair he pulled up. "I am John Rossiter. What happened to you?"

It took me a couple of minutes to think that over, and then I explained about us hunting land, the Jicarillas, and my escape. I also told the part about the rider who wouldn't lend me a hand. "They called him Curly."

Just as I said that a mighty pretty girl stepped into the room, her face flushed and angry. "I don't believe that!" she said sharply. "You must have been out of your head."

"Could be, ma'am," I said politely, not being one to argue with a lady. "Only that horse surely hit me a

Curly Dunn. He's hard on his horses, and he's a
relsome man who's forever picking fights. M
ple are afraid of him because of Rocker."

"Rocker Dunn?" I knew that nam
many did. Rocker Dunn was said to
Quantrill, and for a time he'd b
down in the Cherokee Nation
was tough and strong and
a dead shot who woul
talking.

"That's the one.
"Yes, sir. I've
"Sackett,"
until you'r
outfit yo
we ha

well enough to travel. Why, you look half star...

"I can make out, ma'am. I don't want to stay
where I'm not wanted."

"You be still," she said. "I'll get you some soup."

When she had gone, Rossiter hesitated a moment
and then asked, "This man called Curly? Can you describe him?"

"Big, strong young feller, rosy color to his cheeks,
brown wavy hair and he favors them big Mexican
spurs. He was riding a handsome gray horse...no
cowhand's horse."

"Yes, that's Curly." Rossiter got up suddenly.
"Damn it, man, don't ever try to raise a daughter in a
country where men are scarce! I've heard talk about

quar-
lost peo-

...e, as a good
...have ridden with
...been a known man
...and in East Texas. He
... had the name of being
...sooner be shooting than

...You know of him?"
...heard the name."

...Rossiter said, "I want you to stay on
...strong again. When you're ready to go I'll
...u. We don't have much, but we'll share what
...ve."

He pointed toward the closet. "There's a six-
shooter in there if you should need it. It is an old gun
but a good one and I trust you'll use it with judgment."

After he'd gone I lay there awhile, just a-thinking.
Seems we Sacketts were never going to be shut of
trouble. We had started for this wild, new country to
build us a home, and it was country like nobody ever
saw before. It was mountain country, which suited us,
but the mountains were giants compared to what
we'd been used to. Clingman's Dome was a mighty
beautiful peak, but would be lost in the shadow of
most of those around me.

Running water, lakes, aspen, pines, spruce, and
so much fish and game the stuff fairly jumped at a
man ... there was hay in the meadows, flowers on the

slopes, and timber for the cutting. It was our kind of country, and here we Sacketts would stay.

I eased myself out of bed and started to stand up, but felt giddy of a sudden and sat down, my head all aswim. I'd have to take it easy. I'd have to wait it out. There was no place in this country for a man who couldn't walk tall down the trails or sit a saddle where the long wind blows.

The pistol was one of those made in Texas during the War Between the States. It was a Dance & Park percussion pistol, .44 calibre, that had been worked over to handle Colt cartridges. Somebody had worked on that gun who knew what he was doing. It had balance and felt right to a man's hand. The pistol was loaded and the loops in the belt were filled. I taken it down and hung it by the bed.

A good gun is a thing to have, and a body never knows when he'll need it.

There's a saying that when guns are outlawed, only the outlaws will have guns.

CHAPTER 7

I T WAS A mark of my weakness that I was almighty glad to get back into bed, and I dozed off after awhile and only awakened when Meg Rossiter came into my room with a tray to put on the bedside table.

Now this was a new thing for me. I'd never been waited on much. Not since Ma died. Or when I paid for it in some roadside eating place.

This here was something, to set up in bed with pillows propped behind, and good food there for you. "Ma'am, you could plumb spoil a man, doin' for him like this."

"You're sick," she said, and I figured there was a mite of edge to her tone. She didn't set so much store by me since I'd told what happened on the trail. But I'd no idea she was sweet on this Curly fellow...and it was too bad. Any man who would do to me what he'd done had something rotten inside.

All right. He had no cause to help·me, but he'd no cause to come back and knock me down, either. The first time might have been an accident, although I was no longer sure of that. The second time was not.

"I know you don't think much of me, ma'am, and as soon as I'm able I'll ride out of here. You'll be shut of me."

"But not what you said! You'll leave that behind! You'll leave it with Pa!"

"I only told the truth, ma'am, and when I spoke I had no idea you was sweet on him."

"I'm not! I'm not what you said! You probably think if Curly were out of the way I'd look at you!"

"No, ma'am," I said honestly, "I think nothing of the kind. I know I'm a homely man, ma'am, just a long tall mountain boy. Now Galloway...he's my brother...womenfolk pay him mind, but none of them ever looked twice at me, and I've come not to expect it."

She looked at me suddenly, as if seeing me for the first time. "You're not homely," she said. "Maybe you aren't handsome, but you're not homely, either."

"Thank you, ma'am. I reckon I decided long ago that I'd have to run in single harness. I like the high, lonesome country, so maybe it fits. Nobody ever wanted a home more than me, and nobody ever had one less, least it was Galloway. Gals like the high-spirited, high-headed kind, I've noticed. If they can break them to harness they aren't at all what the gal wanted in the beginning, and if she can't break them they usually break her. But that's the way of it."

She went back into the other room, wherever it was, and I ate my soup. It was good soup, and I thought how I'd lied in my voice if not in my heart. I did so think about her. When a big, homely man like me has a woman do for him it softens him up, and me being lonely like so much of the time, it was just natural I'd think of how fine it would be, but there's no harm in thinking, and I knew all the time it was impossible. Still, I wished it was somebody else than that Curly.

I wished it was anybody else than Curly.

After I'd eaten, I slept. What awakened me I don't know, but it must have been the sound of horses' hoofs in the ranch yard. Rising up on one elbow, I listened and heard voices.

Reaching over to that holster I drew out that Dance & Park pistol and brought it back into bed with me, taking it under the covers and alongside my right leg. With a man like Curly Dunn you have no idea, and after what he'd done I had a hunch that had he met me out on the trail alone he would have killed me . . . just for the hell of it.

With his friend along I guess he just didn't want to be that ornery. Nobody looks on cold-blooded killing with favor, not even those liable to do it themselves . . . a body never knows when he'll be the victim with a man like that.

Anyway, it gave me a right comforting feeling to have that old six-shooter under my hand.

There was talk in the other rooms that I could hear vaguely, talk and laughter and some singing. Meg was playing a banjo and singing soft and low, so I could not hear the words. It would have been a good sound to go to sleep by, only I daren't. Soon or late she was going to tell him about the man she found alongside the trail, and he would come to look.

Suddenly I heard footsteps and then the door opened. Curly stood there, looking across the room at me. I was setting up.

"They were fools to take you in," he said. "They've no idea who you are."

"Neither do you," I said. "But they're good folks,

who'd help a man who was hurt...not ride him down."

He chuckled, but it was a mean kind of humor. "You looked funny," he said, "topplin' over thataway. Like a rag doll."

He started toward me, dropping his hand to his gun. "You're the kind who might commit suicide," he said thoughtfully, "a man as bad off as you are. It wouldn't surprise anybody."

"It would surprise my brother Galloway," I said, "and the rest of the Sacketts. But don't you worry none. I'm not figurin' on it."

"But with a little help?"

He meant it, too. There was a cruel streak in the man, a mean, cruel streak. He taken another step toward me and then almost by accident his eyes fell on the empty holster hanging to the bedpost.

It stopped him.

That and my right hand under the covers. Did I have the gun? He didn't know, but I could see him begin to sweat. The beads just stepped out on his forehead like water had been thrown at him.

He looked at me, and toward the blanket where my right hand was hidden, and I could just see him wondering if I'd draw that gun from under the covers in time, so I said, "Now no man in his right mind draws a gun from under blankets when he can shoot right through them."

He looked at me, his eyes all hot and bright, the sweat still on him, his fear fighting with his greed to kill or maim. "You've got a gun?"

"Have I?" I grinned at him. "It's a good question, isn't it? I didn't have one out on the trail, bein' stark naked as I was, but Mr. Rossiter might have given me one."

"He wouldn't be such a fool. You might murder them all."

"Maybe he thinks they're in less danger from me than from you."

That hit him. He liked being what he was but he did not like having it known, or guessed.

"What's the matter?" I asked. "Was it Rocker's name that got to you? You probably decided you could kill more men than he could...only Rocker generally shoots them standing up. Or so I've heard."

He kind of drew back. He had decided he did not like the odds. He might have tried it, at that, and then tried to convince the Rossiters it had been suicide. Such men often believe the impossible because it suits them to believe, or because they have big ideas of themselves.

Just then we heard the click of heels and then Meg was in the room, her pa right behind her.

"Oh! Here you are! I went to put fudge on the dish and start some coffee and when I got back you were gone."

"He came back to pay his respects, ma'am," I said dryly. "It was the only polite thing to do."

She shot him a quick glance, then looked hard at me. Curly Dunn looked as bland and innocent as a newborn baby, but I expect that was how he always looked. Only when he glanced at me his eyes took on that greasy look.

When they had gone Rossiter remained behind. "What happened?" he demanded.

I shrugged. "Nothing. Nothing at all."

Rossiter's eyes went to the empty holster, then to my right hand under the covers. "You're a careful man," he said.

"My grandpa," I said, "lived to be ninety-four. It was a caution to us all."

We talked the evening away, mostly of cows and ranching, Indians and the like, and all the while I was learning about this country, the prettiest I'd ever seen.

"In the country north of Shalako," he said, "there's high mountain parks the like of which you've never seen. Running streams everywhere, waterfalls, lost canyons, and good feed for stock. I've seen outcrops of coal, and there are stories that the old Spanish men mined for gold up there."

"I'll be riding out," I said, "but I'll be coming back ... with Galloway."

He glanced at me. "Curly says he's met your brother. That Galloway Sackett backed down from him."

"Galloway," I told him, "hasn't any back-up in him. He probably didn't figure it was the custom of the country to kill somebody that isn't dry behind the ears yet."

He left me finally, and I eased down into the bed and stretched out. It felt good, real good. I was warm, I had eaten, and I could rest. Yet I did not let myself fall asleep until I heard Curly Dunn ride off.

Rossiter had a small operation going for him, a herd of no more than three hundred head, mostly breeding stock, but he was a prosperous man and had come into the country with money. He had no need to sell stock, and could hold off and let the natural increase build his herd. Although I expect he had the notion of picking up a few head when buying was possible. A man with ready cash can often make some good buys of folks who just can't cut the mustard.

He had built a strong five-room house of logs with three good fireplaces, one of them big enough to warm two rooms and which could be fed from both. He had a weather-tight stable and some pole corrals, and he had a dozen head of good horses and two cowhands. In the house he had a Mexican woman for a cook who looked strong enough to handle both of the cowhands in a rough-and-tumble fight. But she could really throw the grub together.

She brought me breakfast in the morning, and then she brought me some clothes. The pants were a might short in the leg as I am two inches above six feet, and the shirt was short in the arm, but it felt good to have civilized clothes on again. They hadn't no spare boots but they did have hide, so I set to work and made myself a pair of moccasins.

Meg stopped by to watch. She set down on the porch beside me whilst I cut them out and shaped them to my feet. "You have done that before?"

"Often. I can make a fair pair of boots, too, given the time."

"Have you?"

"In the Sackett family if a boy wanted boots he made 'em himself. That is, if he was over twelve. Before that we mostly went barefooted. I was sixteen year old before I had me a pair of store-bought shoes. I saved 'em for dancin'."

She hugged her knees and looked at the line of trees beyond the ranch-yard. "What were the dances like?"

"Well, most often they were at the schoolhouse.

Sometimes they'd be in somebody's yard. The word would go out and folks would tell each other, and each would fix up a basket and go. Other times it would just be sort of on the spur, and they'd come from all over.

"Most of the boys weren't so much for dancin' but if they couldn't dance they could hold the girl whilst she did. There'd be a fiddle, sometimes some other instrument, but a fiddle was all anybody expected or needed.

"A lot of courtin' was done at those dances, and a lot of fightin'. Mostly the boys came for the fightin'. Galloway always had some girl who'd set her cap for him, but he paid them no mind. Not serious, anyway.

"Sometimes there'd not be enough for dancin' so we'd set about an' sing. I liked that because I just plain like to sing."

"What are you going to do now?"

"Hunt us a piece of land and go to ranching. I reckon right now the thing to do is head for Shalako and team up with Galloway."

"You'd better be careful. The Dunns will think you're crowding them."

"It's open range, and there's enough for all."

"That isn't what they think, Mr. Sackett. There are six of the Dunn boys, and there's their pa, and they've a dozen or more men who ride for them."

"Well, there's two of us Sacketts. That should make it work out about right. Of course, if need be there's a lot of us scattered around and we set store by our kinfolk."

I completed the moccasins and tried them on. They felt good on my feet, which had healed over, although the skin was still tender.

I looked down at the girl. "Ma'am, you're a right pretty girl, and the man that gets you will be lucky, but don't you go wasting yourself on Curly Dunn. He's as poisonous mean as a rattler."

She sprang to her feet, her face stiff with anger. "Nobody can be nice to you! The first time I try to talk to you you end up by criticizing Curly!"

"If I hadn't been armed last night, he'd have killed me."

"What kind of talk is that? You mean he'd have tried to kill you right in my own house, with Pa and me close by? That's ridiculous!"

"Maybe. He said it would look like suicide. Ma'am, you may hate me for this, but I'd be less than a man if I hadn't told you. That Curly is sick. He's sick in the head. You'd better understand that while there's still time."

Scornfully, she turned from me. "Go away. And I don't care if I ever see you again! Just go away!"

"Yes, ma'am. That's why I told you. Because I am going away and I don't figure to see you again too much, and you and your pa have been almighty kind. I've warned you just like I'd warn folks if there was a hydrophoby wolf in the neighborhood."

I limped to the corral and roped the *grulla* mustang Rossiter had agreed to loan me. I saddled up with the borrowed gear, then went to the house.

Rossiter met me at the door. "Sorry to see you go, boy. If you come back this way, drop in."

"I'll return the outfit soon as I can rustle one. Galloway has a little money. I lost all mine back yonder."

"No hurry." Rossiter stepped down off the porch

and lowered his tone. "Sackett, you be careful, riding out of here. I think you have made an enemy."

"If he stays out of my way, I'll stay shut of him. I'm not one to hunt trouble. An' Mr. Rossiter, if you ever need help, you just put your call on a Sackett. You'll get all the help you need, an' quick. You help one of us and you've helped us all. That's the way we figure it."

The *grulla* was a good horse, mountain-bred and tough. He was a mite feisty there at first but as soon as he found that I intended to stay in the saddle and take no nonsense he headed off down the trail happily enough. He just wanted to settle as to who was boss.

Shalako wasn't far down the road. I kept to the trees, avoiding the trail, and at noontime I watered in the La Plata River a few miles below the town. When the *grulla* was watered I taken it back under the trees and found a place there with sunshine and shadow, with grass around, and a place for me to rest, and I rested while the *grulla* cropped grass.

Fact is, I wasn't up to much, and what lay beyond I did not know. There might be folks at the town that I wanted to see, and some I'd rather fight shy of.

Somehow the thought was in my mind that I was coming home...this country felt right to me, and I even liked the name of that town.

Shalako...some Indian name, it sounded like.

Then, for awhile, listening to the cropping of grass and the running water, I slept.

CHAPTER 8

THE TOWN LAY off the road with the most beautiful backdrop of mountains you ever did see, and the La Plata was down off the bench and under the trees, hidden from the town, but close by.

Now when I say "town" I mean it western style. In this country we folks call anything a town where people stop. First off there's a stage stop or a store or maybe only a saloon. Out California way there was a town started because a man's wagon broke down and he just started selling whiskey off the tailgate.

Generally towns in this country, like in the old country, began at river crossings or places where the trails crossed. Folks like to stop at rivers, but the smart ones always cross the river first, and then camp. The river might rise up during the night and hold them for days.

London, folks tell me, began at the only good crossing of the river in many miles. At that place there was a gravel bottom. The same thing folks tell me was true of other cities about the world, but how Shalako came to be, I had no idea.

It was mid-afternoon when my mustang ambled up the one street of the town. With the mountains reared up against the sky in the background there were three buildings, two on one side of the street, one on the other. I swung down in front of the saloon and tied my horse, sizing up the place.

Across the street was a general store and as soon as I could round up some cash I figured to go over there and buy myself an outfit, including boots. Meanwhile I'd tackle the saloon.

Now a western saloon wasn't just a place to belt a few. It was a clubroom for the men, a clearing house for information, and often as not more business was done at the bar than anywhere else around. A man could go into a saloon and find out how the trails were, whether the Indians were on the warpath, or just about anything he needed to know. And I needed to know plenty. Mostly where I could find Galloway.

So I pushed past the swinging doors and went in. It was cool and quiet inside. The bar ran across about two-thirds of the end of the room, and by the end of the bar there was a door. That bar was polished and in mighty fine shape. There were a dozen tables, a beat-up music box, and a man leaning over the bar.

"Howdy," I said, "I'm Flagan Sackett. I'm hunting a brother of mine and somebody who'll stake me to a bait of grub."

"Your brother Galloway Sackett?"

"That's the one."

"He and his partner rode off up country. They said to give you whatever you needed, so the grub will be ready. You want a drink?"

"Thanks. I don't shape up to be much of a drinking man, but I'll have it."

Now I didn't shape up to be much of anything right then. Like I said, those clothes I had on fit me a mite too soon. The pants ended above my ankles and the shirt sleeves only came down below my elbows. The shirt was tight across the chest and back, and of course, thin like I was from lack of eating, I looked like the skeleton had come out of the cupboard.

Just then the doors swung open and two men came in—cowhands from somebody's outfit. They wore chaps and they bellied up to the bar and then one of them saw me.

"Look what the cat dragged in," he said. "Mister, next time you swipe somebody's pants you better make sure they fit."

"That would be hard to do," I said, "judging by what I see around. I don't think there's a man-sized pair of pants in the outfit, letting alone the bartender."

One of those gents was a stocky, redheaded gent with square shoulders and freckled hands...fists right now. He taken a step toward me and said, "Let's see who fills the biggest pants around here."

"Mister Red," I said, "I'm in no shape for a fight. I've come off the mountain after a most difficult time with Indians and such. You just hold that head of steam for a week or so and I'll take you out and punch your head into shape."

"I think you're yella," he said.

"No," I said, "although I can understand your viewpoint. But I don't aim to give myself none the worst of it and I'm in no shape to fight. Right at this moment I couldn't whip a sick kitten."

The bartender came through the door from the kitchen pushing a tray loaded with grub ahead of him. "Here you go, Sackett," he said. "This'll put meat on your ribs."

That redhead stared at me. "Is your name Sackett? You related to Tyrel?"

"Cousins," I said, "although the only time we ever met was down in the Tonto Basin awhile back. Do you know Tyrel?"

"I know him. He's hell-on-wheels with a gun."

"Runs in the family," I said. "We all take to shooting like we do to girling or eating. Comes natural. I cut my teeth on the butt of a six-gun."

"We had trouble, Tyrel an' me."

"Must not have amounted to much," I said, "that trouble you speak of."

"Why?"

"You're still alive, ain't you? The way I heard it Tyrel don't waste around. When he has a job to do he does it. If I were you I'd forget all about that trouble. And whatever you had in mind here, too. I don't want nothing to take my mind off this grub."

So saying I straddled a chair and cut into that meat. Hungry as I was it could have been an old saddle and I'd have eaten it, stirrups and all.

Red brought his beer over and sat down opposite me. "Truth to tell," he said, "Tyrel could have pinned my ears back, and he didn't. I was tied in with a rough crowd and I was feeling my weight. I never did get nowhere bucking Sacketts."

"Then it's about time you either stayed out of the fights or got in on the right side."

"Which side is yours?"

"One not hunting trouble. We came into this country hunting land. We figure to settle down and raise cows and families. You got anything against that?"

"No . . . but the Dunns might."

Well, I didn't want to talk about it. Seemed to me there'd been too much talk already. What I wanted was some shut-eye, now that I was stowing away this grub. I wanted a rest and then an outfit. I'd need blankets, a poncho, saddlebags, a rifle, and some grub. It was a lot to ask, but no more than I could pay for, given time.

The saloonkeeper left his bar and crossed over to my table with a beer. "Mind if I join you? Name's Berglund."

He was a big, tough-looking man with yellow hair, a wide, battle-scarred face, and massive shoulders, arms and fists. "Glad to have company," I said. "You been here long?"

"Nobody has. I was driftin' through the country, headed west. I suppose I was huntin' gold, and did make a pass at it now and again, but then I came up on this bench and I decided this was where I wanted to stay. The fishing was great and the hunting was even better, so I bought an axe and an adze and built myself a saloon. I figured that was the easiest way to find company.

"In the good months I fish and hunt, and in the winter I sit by the fire and read or talk. I'm a talkative man, Sackett. I like people, and enjoy their company. Nothing like a warm fire when the weather's turning bad to get folks to sit up and talk."

"It's a risk meeting folks," I said. "You never know which one is a danger to you. It's like coming to a crossroads where you pull up and look both ways and your whole life may change if you take the wrong direction. One thing you can be sure of...your life wouldn't be the same."

"I do[...]
takes trou[...]
"Well," I s[...]
Curly Dunn first[...]
And I'd no idea I'd[...]
Rossiter taken me ho[...]
middle of the target."

When I finished that mea[...]
ment, enjoying the contented [...]
me down. I sorely needed an o[...]
I'd no desire to get my feet under [...]
there. Nor was there pleasure in the t[...]
ing my sore feet down into new boots.

"There's folks a-coming in," Berglund sa[...]
of them prospectors, but there's a few farm[...]
cattlemen coming, too. This here's a growing lan[...]

"The Dunns come in often?"

"Nearly every day. They spend money, but I don't
care for them. And the worst of them isn't Curly, either. He's small calibre compared to Ollie Hammer or
Tin-Cup Hone. Tin-Cup got his name from the mining camp they call Tin-Cup. They had a way of running marshals out of town or killing them, and Tin
was one of the worst of the lot. Then he ran into Ollie
and they teamed up and came down here and signed
on to punch cows for Old Man Dunn and his boys.
That's a mean lot."

Getting to my feet I thanked him and walked
outside. The sun was still bright on the mountains
although it would soon be hidden behind them. I
walked across the street, limping some, and went into
the store.

Galloway had been there before me and told them

n't know," Berglund argued, "I think a man
ble with him."
aid, "*I surely didn't* want trouble when
came up on me. He brought it to me.
ever see him again, but when Meg
me she taken me right into the

I just sat there for a mo-
feeling that was settling
outfit, but right now
me and walk over
bought of push-

aid, "most
rs and
d."

one'd never look twice at me," I said. "But I'll tell
you what I want to do. I want to write a letter. You
got the makin's?"

So Berglund fixed me up with paper and pen, and
en went to stirring up a fire. Fine as it was in the
ime a body could always sleep under a blanket
Shalako, which suited me.
r I wrote was to Parmalee. He was a
t, folks of which we'd heard tell but
e with until that trouble down in
en Tyrel and Parmalee Sackett

Those flatland Sacketts
f, and Parmalee had

been to school and all. It never affected his shooting, though, so I reckon school is a thing to be wished for. Wishing never done me any good.

Parmalee had cattle, and this here was fine grazing land, and Parmalee had something else he'd need. He had nerve.

When I'd finished the letter to Parmalee, telling him of the range, I suddenly had a thought. We were shaping up for trouble with the Dunns, and that was excuse enough to write to Logan.

Now Logan was a Clinch Mountain Sackett, and those boys from Clinch Mountain are rougher than a cob. There were those who called Logan an outlaw, but he was family, and he was handy with a shooting iron.

I wrote to him, too.

Trouble was, the shooting was likely to be over and done with before any of those boys ever got here, unless it was Parmalee, who was down in New Mexico, not far south of the line.

He might make it in time. And of a sudden I had a hunch we'd need him.

This country was shaping up for war.

CHAPTER 9

LEAVING MY GEAR at Berglund's place, I mounted that *grulla* and rode down off the bench into the river bottom of the La Plata. It was very still. There was grass, and everywhere a body looked there were the tall white trunks of the aspen. Stopping at the river I let the mustang drink from the cold water that ran down from the melting snows on the mountains.

Across the stream I went up through the trees beyond. There was a plateau over there with good grass, a few clumps of oak brush here and there, but a fresh, green country lying at the foot of the mountains.

There were pines along the mountain slopes with thick-standing clumps of aspens of a lighter green. The aspen was usually the first tree to grow up after a burn, and the aspen groves provided a lot of food for wildlife.

Riding slowly along the edge of the mountain and up under the trees along the slope, I knew this was my country, this was where I wanted to be. This was the land I'd been looking for and no amount of Dunns would keep me off of it.

I headed back to Shalako.

The first person I saw when I walked into the saloon was old Galloway, and I never laid eyes on anybody that looked better.

"You look kind of peaked," he said, grinning at me. "I declare, the first time I leave you alone you make out to get yourself killed, or nigh onto it.

"Flagan, this here's Nick Shadow . . . a good friend."

"Howdy."

"My pleasure."

We all sat down together at a table and went over what had taken place, and we came to agreement on Curly Dunn. Galloway looked me over mighty curious when I talked about Meg Rossiter, and I felt myself flushing. More because he was looking at me than anything else. It was no use him thinking there was ought between us, nor me thinking it either.

The only thing she wanted from me was distance, and I had no ache to a shoot-out with Curly Dunn over a girl that couldn't see me for dust. What I had to tell them then was about the land I'd seen, and they agreed.

I taken to Shadow. Galloway and me, we see things about the same, and anybody I liked he liked and the other way around. Nick Shadow was a tall, handsome man but one who had judgment as well as education, and the two don't always accompany one another. I've seen some men who were mighty bright in their books who couldn't tell daylight from dark when it came to judging men or the condition of things.

Now I hold by the Good Book, but in some ways I am closer to the Old Testament than the New. I believe in forgiving one's enemies, but keep your hand on your gun while you do it, mentally, at least. Because while you are forgiving him he may be studying ways to get at you.

I like my fellow man, but I also realize he carried a

good measure of the Old Nick in him and he can find a good excuse for almost any kind of wrongdoing or mischief. I wanted no trouble with the Dunns, and would avoid giving them cause, but at the same time I had common sense enough to realize they might not feel the same way. A man who starts imagining that others think good because he does is simply out of his mind. I've helped bury a few who did think that way... nice, peaceful men who wanted no trouble and made none.

When feeding time comes around there's nothing a hawk likes better than a nice, fat, peaceful dove.

"We can lay claim to land," I said, "but we'll have to have cattle on it. I've written to Parmalee."

"I've got a few head," Shadow said. "We might include them in the drive."

We spent the evening talking about the ranch we wanted, the cattle drive to come, and the future of the country. There was or had been a fort over on the Animas, and Berglund told us there was a house over there if you wanted to call it that. So we were not alone in the country. There was an Irishman named Tim McCluer who had moved into the country and he was getting along with the Utes... which showed that it could be done.

McCluer told Berglund that the Utes and the Jicarillas usually got along, so the bunch who had been hunting me were likely to have been renegades, prepared to plunder anyone who crossed their trail. The Indians had men like that as well as the whites.

We stabled our horses in the livery barn and camped in the loft. Falling asleep that night I dreamed of my own outfit, and slept with the smell of fresh hay in my nostrils.

We moved over west of the town, and west of the La Plata, and we made camp there in a grove of aspen, a splendid country spread out before us. We decided we'd all spend some days working on the beginnings of a spread, and after that Nick Shadow would take off for the south to meet Parmalee and to round up his own cattle to join the herd.

"I don't need to tell you boys," he said, "but keep the Dunns in mind. They're a tough, lawless outfit and they won't take lightly to our being here. Especially after both of you have had words with Curly."

First off, we built a corral, and then a lean-to. We built them back into the woods with a screen of trees between us and the open flat. Then we went back into the trees and cut some limbs here and there, and a whole tree yonder to scatter amongst the other trees and make a sort of crude barrier for anybody who tried to come up behind us.

There was nothing that would stop anyone, but nobody could come up through those trees without arousing us.

Galloway and me, we weren't like the usual cowhand, who'd rather take a whipping than do any work that can't be done on a horse. We were both planting boys from the hills, who could plow as straight a furrow as the next man, if need be, so we spaded up a corner of ground, worked over the sod and went down to the store to buy seed. We planted potatoes, carrots, pumpkins and corn, to start. We had no idea how they'd grow, but if they did they'd be a help. Starting a home in a new land is never a bed of roses, but then we didn't come looking for it to be easy.

Work pleasures me no more than the next man, but if a body is to have anything there's no other way, although we found excuses enough to get up in the saddle and go perambulating around the country. Of course, that was necessary, too.

We'd chosen to locate near the opening of Deadwood Creek, with a mighty big ridge rising to the west of us, and Baldy Mountain to the east.

We had to hunt or gather for our grub, and we Sacketts were born to it. And that Nick Shadow—he might have been born in a castle, but he knew his way around with an axe, and took mighty fast to what we showed him about rustling up grub in the forest.

Working about the place and rustling for grub as we did, we kept out of sight. We didn't see anybody or even their tracks. Each of us would take a ride sometime during the day, and at night over the fire we'd tell of what we'd seen, so within a few days we were getting a fair picture of the country around.

Sometimes of a night we'd set about the fire and talk. Nick Shadow had education, but he never tired to hear our mountain expressions. We'd lost a few of them coming west, but an argument or a quarrel we still called an upscuddle, which seemed almighty funny to Nick.

"We don't have so many words as you," I told him, "so we have to make those we have stand up and do tricks. I never figured language was any stone-cold thing anyway. It's to provide meaning, to tell other folks what you have in mind, and there's no reason why if a man is short a word he can't invent one. When we speak of beans that have been shelled out of the pod we call 'em shuck-beans, because they've been shucked. It's simple, if you look at it."

"Learning," Galloway added, "isn't only schoolin'. It's looking, listening and making-do. If a man doesn't have much or if he's in wild country he'd better get himself to contemplate and contrive. Pa always taught us to set down and contemplate, take our problem and wrassel with it until there's an answer. And then we contrive. Back in the hills we couldn't buy much, and we didn't have any fancy fixin's, so we contrived. We put together what we could find and added it to something else."

Nick, he knew a powerful lot of poetry, and like most lonesome, wandering men we liked it. Sometimes of a night he'd set by the fire and recite. He knew a lot of poetry by that fellow Poe who'd died about the time I was born. He used to live over the mountain in Virginia...over the mountain from us, that is, who lived on the western slope of the hills.

We'd never paid much mind to Nick Shadow's talk of gold. There'd been Spanish people in Colorado from the earliest times, and for awhile there'd been French folks coming west from New Orleans when Colorado was part of the Louisiana country. The story Nick told us about the gold he knew of was known to others, too. But treasure stories come by the dozen in gold mining country, and everybody you meet has got a mine worth a million dollars or many millions, depending on how many drinks the owner's had.

One night he said, "Finding the big caches, where they hid the millions would be accident now, because nobody knows exactly where it was hidden, but there's another treasure that might be found, so I'm going to tell you about it.

"My grandfather had a brother who trapped in this country nearly fifty years ago, and much of the sign left by those early French and Spanish miners was plainly visible when he arrived in the country.

"The others had never heard the stories of the gold found in the La Platas, nor the less known stories of diamonds found there, and Arnaud was not the man to tell them of it, but he kept his eyes open, and he had an idea where to begin looking.

"No need to go into all the details, but I figure we're not more than ten miles from that gold right now."

"Ten miles is a lot of country," Galloway suggested.

"They were headed up the La Plata, planning to take an old Indian trail that follows along the ridge of the mountains, and Arnaud was counting the streams that flowed into the river. Just past what he counted as the sixth one he saw what he was looking for . . . a dim trail that led up into the peaks.

"They continued on a mile or so further and then he suggested they stop and trap out a beaver pond they'd found. Arnaud volunteered to hunt meat for them and he took off along the river, and as soon as he was out of sight of the others he started back, found his trail and started up.

"It was a steep trail, unused in a long time, and he figured that in the two miles or so of trail he climbed about three thousand feet . . . he was judging in part by the change in vegetation. He reached a high saddle, crossed over and started down. He was looking for a creek that flowed out of the mountain, and he could see the canyon down which it flowed, but there was no longer a trail. That had played out when he reached the crest of the ridge.

"It was very cold, and the going was difficult. He had to move slowly because of the altitude. He crossed over the saddle, as I've said, but he had no more than started down when he heard a shot where he had left his friends. A shot, and then several shots.

"As you can imagine, he was in a quandary. If he went back to help his friends, it would take him the better part of an hour, moving as he would have to, and by then any fight would be over.

"Or perhaps they had merely killed a deer. In the final event, he continued on, found the head of the creek and found the marker, a piece of a ramrod thrust into a crack in the rock. The gold was cached just below it and to the right, and when he removed the stones he found a dozen gold bars, several sacks of dust, and one small sack of diamonds.

"It was too much to carry and now that he knew where it was he could come back any time. He took one sack of dust and dropped a couple of the diamonds in it and thrust it into his pack. Then he recovered the gold and started back.

"There had been no more shooting, but when he came near the bottom of the hill he took great care, studying out his trail in advance. He was still some distance from the beaver pond when he saw Mohler. He was lying face down in the grass with five arrows in his back, a golden carpet of dandelions all about him.

"Arnaud watched for several minutes but there was no movement from the body, no sign of life. From where he lay he could see the dead man still had his rifle and tomahawk, so the body had not been looted.

"Easing back into the brush he worked his way around toward the pond, and there near a fallen log he saw another one. He couldn't make out who it was, but this body had been stripped, scalped, and mutilated.

"The fact that the one body had been stripped and the other had not implied the Indians were still around, so he moved back into the brush and lay quiet, listening.

"He stayed there all day without moving on the theory that if he did not move he would make no sound and leave no tracks. Several times he saw Indians, but each time they passed some distance away, and finally they mounted up and rode away.

"When it was dark he went down to Mohler, but the man was cold in death and had been stripped and robbed in the meantime. The others, if any remained alive, were busy getting away from there, and that was what he decided to do. The Utes had gone downstream, so he went upstream with the idea of striking the highline trail. He did, found one of the others of his party still alive, and together they got out of the country."

"But the gold is still there?"

"The gold and the diamonds. Of the two he got out with, one was worthless. The other was an excellent stone, however, and with the results he bought a small farm in French Canada."

"He never came back?"

"He decided to let well enough alone. He married, had children, but none of them were inclined toward adventure. I gathered they did not have much faith in their father's stories. Their own lives were rather prosaic and his stories were unbelievable to them... but not to me."

"Well," I said, "it won't do any harm to look. You say the place is close by?"

"Right back of that peak yonder. The start of that trail can't be three miles from here." He glanced over at Galloway. "Now you know why I was so willing to come along. I've been up here before, but these rivers were named when Arnaud was in here, and I wasted time on the Florida and the Animas before I realized they had to be wrong."

We brought our horses in from their picket-ropes and after watering them, turned them into the corral. Then we bedded down and went to sleep.

There for a few minutes I lay awake, considering that gold. If we had it we could buy more cattle, fix our place up better, but I wasn't counting any gold we didn't have. A lot of folks had their hands on that gold and it hadn't done any of them much good.

The fire died down to coals, and I could hear the rustling of the aspens and the faint sounds the horses made in the corral.

I wondered, suddenly, what had become of that wolf.

CHAPTER 10

MANY A CAMPFIRE dies down with talk that doesn't count up to much in the sunlight.

Around the fire is the time to talk of treasure, and ha'nts and witches and such, but come broad day there's work to be done. Somewhere back down the line Parmalee Sackett should be starting north with a herd, and it was time for Nick Shadow to ride down to meet him.

It was also time for somebody to ride down to Shalako and burden themselves with grub for the next two weeks of work, and it spelled out to be me for that job. The past few days had helped a sight when it came to my strength catching up to itself, and I felt a whole lot better. Still, we didn't want to leave our place alone too long. Not that we had anything there. Galloway, he said to me, "Flagan, let's ride this out for awhile. Let's sleep out and see what they do. If there's to be a fraction over this let's not have anything they can burn." . . . So we hadn't.

Nevertheless the thought of that gold was in all our minds, and it was in our thoughts to ride up there someday and have a look for it. Right now we had to pin down the things that were sure or that we were trying to make sure.

Shalako lay still under the afternoon sun when I

rode into town. I was still wearing the moccasins because my feet were not quite well, and they were almighty tender around the edges where the flesh had been broken and torn and mashed by rocks, but otherwise I was dressed pretty well for the time, and for a working cowhand.

The first thing I saw was the buckboard from the Rossiter outfit, and Meg about to get down, so I swung my horse alongside and stepped down in time to take her hand and help her down.

She smiled, but I'd say it was a might cool, but when she taken my hand to step down she done it like a real lady, and I could see she set store by such things. Fact is, I set store by them myself. It pleasures a man to do graceful things for a lady, and if she's pretty, so much the better. We'd be a sorry world without the courtesies, as Ma used to say.

"My!" Meg said. "I would scarcely know you!"

Me, I blushed like a fool, which I have a way of doing whenever a woman says "I, yes, or no" to me. And the blushing makes me mad at myself, which makes me blush all the more. So I stood there, all red around the ears like a dirt-kicking country boy.

"I got me an outfit," I said finally. And then I added, "We're fixing to go ranching, me and Galloway and Nick Shadow."

"How nice!" she said primly, and then with a little edge to her voice she said, "I'm surprised you have the nerve after the way you backed down for Curly Dunn."

Now I never backed down for no man, and she knew it, but girls like to put a man in a bad place and she had done it to me. Like a fool I started in to argue the question, which I shouldn't have done. "I never backed down for him," I said, "or any man."

She turned away from me. "If I were you," she said, "I'd leave while I could. Curly is going to meet me here."

Well, now. Common sense told me that I should go, but her throwing it up to me like that...well, I couldn't go then. So I just turned and walked off feeling like I'd come off a pretty poor hand, but then I never was much at talking to women.

In the store I laid out to get the things we needed—flour, salt, coffee, and whatever. They had dried apples, so I laid in a stock of them, and this time I was able to pay. I'd lost whatever I had when the Indians taken me, but Galloway was carrying a good bit right then, as I had been, and whatever either one of us had the other could have. But these supplies were for all of us.

Adding to the list I bought four hundred rounds of .44-calibre ammunition.

The storekeeper, he looked up at me. "You planning a war?"

"No, sir, I ain't. But if anybody comes a-looking I wouldn't want them to go away disappointed. It ain't in my nature to leave folks a-wanting. Meanwhile we have to hunt our meat."

"The Dunns have been around. They've been talking against you."

"Talk never scratched any hides," I said. "They've got to do more than talk."

"That's what we came to town for," Curly's voice said from behind me. "I'm going to whip you right down to your socks."

"You'd have trouble," I said, "because I ain't wearing any."

And then he hit me.

He caught me as I was turning but he'd not been set proper and the punch never staggered me. I just unbuckled my gun and handed it to Berglund, who had just come in.

I think Curly was kind of surprised that I was so ready, and that I didn't get flustered and mad. So he was a mite slow with that second punch and I saw it a-coming. Now I never did want to tear up any man's store, so when that punch came at me I just ducked under it and taken him in the belly with my shoulder, wrapping one arm around his legs and rushing him right out the door.

At the edge of the porch I dropped him and he staggered so I hit him.

Now we Sackett boys grew up a-sweating with an axe, shovel, and plow. We'd worked hard all our lives and my fists were big and hard and backed by an uncommon lot of muscle, so when I fetched him a clout he went back into the middle of the street and fell down.

Stepping off the walk I walked toward him and he got up. He was big, maybe twenty pounds heavier than me, and he was in a whole lot better shape because he'd not been through what I had, but also he was a drinker, and drinking whiskey isn't what you'd call proper for a fighting man.

He came at me, a little wiser now, because that clout he'd caught had carried some power. But he wasn't worried. He'd won a lot of fights and saw no reason why he shouldn't win this one.

Me and Galloway had grown up fighting in the mountains and then we'd knocked around on riverboats and freight outfits and most of what we knew we'd learned by applying it that way.

He came in and he taken a swing at me which I pulled aside from, and when I pulled over I smashed my fist into his belly. It taken him good—right where he lived. I saw his face go kind of white and sick and then I hit him again.

He went down hard into the dust, and the next thing I know there's a crowd around yelling at him to get up. Without them I don't think he would have done it. Meg was there, too, her face all kind of white and funny, staring at him like she had never seen him before, but she didn't look scared, nor did she look altogether displeased.

What I didn't know until later was that both Ollie Hammer and Tin-Cup were in that crowd, just a-watching.

Curly had his friends behind him and he'd made a lot of brags no doubt, so he had it to do. His first punch missed but the second caught me a rap alongside of the face and I staggered. He came on in, swinging with both hands and hit me again. We clinched and I threw him with a rolling hip-lock, and stepped back.

I was just learning how much that time in the woods had taken out of me, for I'd no staying power at all. He came at me, swinging. Again I made him miss one but caught the other one on the chin, and it hurt. So I bowed my neck and went to punching with both hands. I missed a few but some of them landed, and when they landed he gave ground.

We fought up and down in the dust for maybe three or four minutes, and then he remembered about my feet, and he stomped on my toes with his boot heel.

It hurt. It hurt me so bad I thought I'd go down, but I stayed up and seeing it had hurt, he came at me again. This time when he tried to stomp I hooked my toe under his ankle and kicked it up and around and he fell into the dust. When he did that I ran in and grabbed him by the collar and the belt, whirled him around and let go, and he hit the water trough all spraddled out.

He got up though, his face bloody and him shaken. Me, I was all in. I had to get him now or never, so I walked in and swang on him. I threw it from the hips and it caught him in the mouth and pulverized his lips. My next one split his ear and then I threw one to his belly. He pawed at me, but I had it to do now or never, and I brushed it aside and hit him with an uppercut in the belly.

His knees buckled and I went in on him, got my forearm under his chin and forced his head back, and then I swung on his belly.

Somebody grabbed me from behind and then Berglund yelled, "Lay off, Hammer! Back up now, or I'll drop you!"

He was up there on the porch with my old Dance & Park in his fist and they taken him serious.

Well, I stepped back and let Curly fall into the dust, and he just lay there, his shirt all tore up and his face bloody, as much as I could see of it.

I staggered some, and almost fell into the water trough, but splashed water on my face and chest.

When I turned around nobody in that crowd looked friendly. I could see by their faces looking like Curly that two or three of them were Dunns. "He asked for it," I said. "Now take him home."

A powerful big older man sitting a bay horse spoke up. He had a shock of hair on a big square head and he looked like he'd been carved from granite. "Boy," he said, "I'm Bull Dunn, and that's my boy. You get out of this country as fast as you can ride and maybe you'll get away. If you stay on here, I'll kill you."

"Mister Dunn," I said, "I'm staying, and you've got it to do."

He turned his eyes on me and for a moment our eyes held. I was in almighty bad shape and not wishing for any trouble with him right now. My fists were sore from the fight and I wasn't sure if I could use a gun if I had one, and I was afraid I was going to have to try.

It was Red who walked out of the saloon and leaned against a post. "Mister Dunn," he said, "you'd better give it some thought. I was with an outfit one time that tried to buck these Sackett boys and we came out at the small end of the horn."

Bull Dunn did not even seem to notice him. He merely repeated, "Get out while you can ride." Then he turned his horse and the others followed. Right there at the end Ollie Hammer turned and grinned at me, but it was not a pleasant grin. And they rode on out of town.

The storekeeper he came out on the boardwalk. "You'd better get another hundred rounds," he said. "It does look like war."

Well, sir, I went on inside the saloon and dropped

into a chair, and I was in bad shape. That fight had used me up. I was getting my strength back but I was a long way short of being the man I had been.

Berglund, he brought me a drink, and it did me good. Then he brought some coffee and he began to work on my face, patching up a couple of cuts. He had handed me back my gun when I came inside and I kept flexing my fingers, trying to get the stiffness out of them.

"You watch yourself, Sackett," he said. "They've dry-gulched more than one man."

After a long while I began to feel better, and the fresh, hot coffee helped.

They had probably been watching us, and they were sure that Nick Shadow was gone. Probably they had not guessed why he was going, but they certainly knew they had but two men to contend with, and to them that must seem like nothing at all.

Right now Galloway was up there alone, and they might choose this time to cut the odds in half. Only my brother was no pilgrim, and coming up on him unexpected was not an easy thing to do.

"I've got to get back to camp."

"You need rest," Berglund protested.

He was right, of course, but his rightness did not help. Galloway was up there alone, and while he might choose to withdraw up the mountain or up Deadwood Gulch, it was more likely that he would refuse to be pushed.

Loading supplies on a borrowed packhorse, I prepared to start back. My body was stiff and sore, and I wanted nothing so much as sleep, yet I had to get back. Even now they might be preparing an attack on Galloway, and they were a tough, mean, bitter lot.

It would be days, perhaps weeks before the others arrived, and until then we must somehow defend our position, or at least keep it open for the arrival of Parmalee Sackett and the return of Nick Shadow.

Mounting the *grulla* I rode into the bottom of the La Plata, then cautiously worked my way upstream. Several times I came upon the hoofprints of horses. They had been here then, no doubt studying what they must do. The tracks were several days old.

Galloway was nowhere in sight when I rode up the last few hundred yards to the corral, but he came out of the woods, Winchester over his arm. He glanced at my face.

"That must be quite a town," he commented, affably. "Seems to me they hold out a welcome."

"You should try it some time. I ain't what you'd call mincy about towns but this here one is about to try my patience."

"Who was it?"

"Curly . . . and but for that saloonkeeper in yonder they might have salted me away."

"You whup him?"

"I ain't sure. I feel like it was me got whupped, on'y when it was over he lay stretched out. I bruised him. I reckon I did."

Well, I got down and like to fell off my horse. Galloway, he taken my horse back in the woods whilst I set by the fire, my head hanging. It was aching something awful and my mouth was cut inside, and my face sore.

"I didn't think he had the sand," Galloway commented.

"He didn't. It was those fool friends of his, urgin' him on. I think he wanted to quit but he was scared of what would be said, and I was scared he wouldn't quit before I had to fall, I was that all in."

Galloway was making soup. He got that from Ma. Anytime anybody had anything happen, birth, death, fight or wedding, Ma made soup.

Suddenly I saw something at the edge of the woods. There for a moment it looked like a wolf. He was looking back the way I had come, so I turned my head to look also.

A rider was coming up the draw. He was right out in the open but he was coming right on, walking his horse. He had a rifle in his hands.

CHAPTER 11

EVEN BEFORE THE old man came close enough for us to make him out, I could see he was an Indian by the way he sat his horse. He came on slowly and when he drew up facing us he sat looking upon us thoughtfully.

He was the shadow of a man who had been great. I mean in a physical way. The bones were there, and the old muscles showed how once they had stretched the skin with power, and the look was there yet, in his eyes and in his carriage. He was a proud man.

"We're fixing to have some soup," I said. "Will you set up to the fire?"

He looked at me for a long minute, and then said, "Are you Sak-ut?"

The name came out short and blunt.

"We both are," I said. "We're brothers. In thinking as well as in blood. Will you get down?"

He put the rifle away and swung down. Maybe he was a mite stiff, but not enough to bother. He dropped his reins and walked to our fire with dignity. I held out my hand to him as he came up. "I am Flagan Sackett. This here is Galloway."

"Howdy," Galloway said.

He wasn't missing a thing, his eyes going from my moccasins to my face. When he turned toward me again I saw there was a scar on the left side of his face from what seemed to be a powder burn.

After we had eaten, Galloway dug out the tobacco sack. Neither Galloway nor me ever taken to smoking but most Indians did and it was handy for trade. After he had puffed away for awhile he looked up and said, "I am Powder Face. I am Jicarilla."

He let that set with us for a few minutes and then he said, looking right at me, "You are warrior. I am warrior. We can talk together."

"I have heard of Powder Face," I said, "and to talk to him is an honor."

His eyes glinted, but after a few puffs at his pipe he said, "You escape from my people. You are good runner."

"I am a good fighter, too," I said, "but your folks left me without much to do with."

"You are like Indian," he said, "like Jicarilla."

Well, that was all right with me. What all this was leading up to, I didn't know, but I was willing to set and listen. Raised around the Cherokee like I was, I have some savvy for Indians and their ways, and all things considered they make out to be pretty fine folks. Their ways are different than ours, but the country was different, then.

"I come to you because you think like Indian. You fight like Indian. Maybe you will talk to Indian."

"I'll talk," I said, "and I'll listen."

"I am called renegade," he said. "My tribe is small. Some are Jicarillas, some are Tabeguache Ute. We fight, we do not surrender. Finally there are few of us, and we hide in high mountains."

He paused for a long time, but finally he said, "Our

people are few. There are many Indians south or north, but we wish to fight no more. We have watched from the peaks as the white men come. A long time ago I rode far to the east, and I have seen the towns of the white man. In the north I have seen the wagon that smokes. The white man has strong medicine.

"We are twenty people. We are six warriors, seven women, and seven children. Soon there will be two more. The winter will come, and the game will come down from the peaks and we will starve.

"We do not wish to go with the Jicarillas. We do not wish to go with the Utes. There may again be war and we do not want to fight." He looked up suddenly and mighty proud. "We have been great warriors. For our lives we will fight, but we cannot leave our young ones to starve in the cold.

"You are white man. You are warrior. You are strong against pain and you know the Indian way. I come to you as to an elder brother. You will tell us what we should do."

Well, now. He was an older and no doubt a wiser man than me and he had come to me for advice. One thing I had he did not have ... at least, not quite so much. I had knowledge of the white man. And all of what I knew wasn't good, but that was true of his people, too. We all had our good and our bad. The white man had broken treaties and the Indian had killed innocent people, and without warning. The white man had done his share of that, too.

There was no need to talk to Galloway. We two understood each other as if we were of the same mind. I didn't know what Nick Shadow might think but that we'd have to work out as best we could. I just knew what I was going to do.

"We are going to ranch here." I swept a wide gesture at the hills. "We are going to raise cattle and horses. We are going to need help. Can your young men ride?"

"Our old men can ride, too," he said proudly.

"Suppose you bring your folks down and camp over yonder." I indicated an area back against the mountain. "Your people can live here and your young men can ride for us.

"There's one more thing: your people must stay close to here at first. There are some men around who will not like it that you are here. Stay close to the ranch or in the mountains until they get used to the idea."

The old man bedded down not far from us that night, and in the morning he was gone. Galloway he looked over at me and chuckled. "You sure bought trouble," he said. "I never seen the like."

"What would you have done?"

He grinned at me. "The same thing. Only I'd not have asked him if his young men could ride. That was like askin' if a fish can swim."

"I was really asking them if they would ride," I said. "That there is what is called a rhetorical question. At least that's what Nick Shadow would call it."

"What'll he think about this?"

"He'll buy it. Nick will buy anything that's contrary to the prejudices of people around him. He's just like that. He's just naturally contrary, and he don't give a damn whether school keeps or not."

There was plenty to do before the cattle came. We

scouted the range we figured to use, and we gathered wood. Usually we would just throw a loop around a log and drag it to where we could use it come snow time. There were a lot of deadfalls around, and we gathered a good many knowing a long winter was ahead and there wouldn't always be time for hunting firewood.

Then we set to notching the logs for a cabin, and we built a stoneboat for hauling stones for the fireplace. In between times one or the other of us would ride out afar from home to get an elk or a deer for meat. There were a good many beaver along the branches but we didn't figure to worry them. The pools they make back of their beaver dams help to control floodwaters and keep the water where it's needed, right on the land.

All the time we kept an eye open for that Dunn outfit, but none of them showed.

Galloway he rode down to Shalako after some extra grub and when he came back he said, "The Dunns are bringing in a boy that Berglund was telling about. He's a youngster, about twenty-one or twenty-two, and he's hell on wheels with a rifle.

"Seems that Red was in and dropped us the word, to be passed on by Berglund. This youngster is a dead shot and he's the kind that lays up in the country and watches for a good shot. He says the Dunns came into this country from a real mean fight, and this kid done half their killing for them. His name is Vern Huddy."

Now there's no safe way when a sharpshooter is coming against you. He's only got to find himself a place and wait until he gets his shot and he usually needs only one. First off, all you can do is try to keep him from getting that one shot. Don't set yourself up for him, don't skyline yourself or stand still out in the open, and when you ride, keep your eyes open and watch your horse. He'll usually know before you do if anybody is around. Always keep a good background for yourself, something that swallows you up, sort of.

However, we taken to scouting the country. We'd been doing that, but now we were even more careful. We skirted our area about a hundred yards around, checking for tracks, then a circle about three hundred yards out, and then out to a quarter of a mile.

And then I saw the wolf.

I had killed a deer and cut it up to take back to camp, when I saw that wolf, so I taken a piece of the fresh meat and tossed it to him. He disappeared, but a moment later when I glanced back the meat was gone.

There was something peculiar about that wolf. Why had he left the others and taken to following me? Did I have the smell of death on me?

When I was almost back to camp I happened to turn in my saddle and caught just a glimpse of the wolf as he dodged into the brush, so I fished another chunk of meat from the hide where I carried it and dropped it into the road. Why I did so I've no idea. Maybe I figured it was better deer meat than me meat.

Galloway had moved our camp about a hundred yards back into the brush. He was making sourdough bread when I came in and he had a pot of beans setting in the outer coals. "I don't like it, Flagan. Our boys should be showing up by now. I don't like it a-tall."

"Come daylight I'll cut across the hills. I'll study the trail."

"You ride wary. Trouble's shaping up. I can feel it in my bones."

The sun wasn't up when I mounted the *grulla* and taken to the hills. The old Dance & Park six-shooter was shoved down in its scabbard, but I carried my Winchester in my hands. It was not yet light, so I rode right back into the trees, riding up through the timber until I struck an old bear walk.

This was no regular trail, but even so I didn't hold to it long, suddenly starting up the hill on an angle, and so it was that I glimpsed something down below in the brush. It was that wolf, and he was keeping ahead of me.

Of a sudden he brought up short. He lifted one foot, then ducked into the brush like a shot.

My feet kicked free of the stirrups and I went off that horse like I'd been shot, and I almost was. As my feet hit dirt I heard the boom of a shot and I threw myself forward in the brush, then scrambled up and ran in a short dash to where an outcropping thrust up from the mountain. I was just in time to see a man legging it for his horse and I could see the horse, so I threw up my rifle and shot at the tree it was tied to. I made a wild guess as to where the reins would be tied, and either cut one or the horse broke it with his lunge when fragments of bark stung its face. Anyway the horse broke loose and when the man lunged into view again I put a bullet where he should have been but he dove into the brush.

Taking a running jump I hit the saddle as the mustang took off and we went down that slope just a hellin'. Another shot cut close to me and I let drive with two, firing my rifle off my hip into the brush and when that mustang hit the brush it went right on through. Out in the open beyond a man was legging it down the slope. He stopped, whirled around and came up with a rifle, and I let go at him again and he spun around and dropped.

When I came up on him he was sitting there, holding his side, an ugly look in his eyes. "You played hell," he said. "They'll kill you for this."

"That's what you tried to do to me," I replied. "Are you Vern Huddy?"

"*Me?* No, I ain't. Lucky for you, I ain't. He ain't here yet. If I'd been Vern Huddy you'd be dead. I'm Jobe Dunn, if you want to know, cousin to Curly."

His rifle dropped when my bullet hit him, but he was still wearing a six-shooter. Either he'd forgotten it or he was hoping I had. "Take it out," I said, "with two fingers. Throw it just as far out as you can. And don't try anything funny unless you want to feed the buzzards right from where you're at."

He drew that pistol and dropped it, and I swung down and gathered up his pistol and his rifle.

"Now you get on your feet and start for home, and don't stop this side of there."

"Hell, that's a good eight miles."

"It must be," I agreed. "Make a nice walk for you. Better not pass out along the way or you might die before somebody gets to you."

"You just ain't a kindly man," he protested.

"Nope. No more kindly than I'd be if I was lyin'

up there on that slope dead from your bullet. I guess you figured you'd kill me your ownself and then go back and brag how you'd done it. How you'd beaten Vern to the punch."

"*Vern?* You're crazy! I wouldn't cross Vern for all the tea in China. He's meaner than you are, and a whole sight better with a gun."

"Maybe."

When he set off a-walking I went back up through the trees and found my trail.

And it surely wasn't intentional that when nightfall was coming on I saw the lights of the Rossiter place. Took me all of a minute to decide to ride down there and share potluck with them. There was a chance that I'd run into Curly, but a good chance that I'd not, and a few good home-cooked vittles wouldn't go at all bad . . . or seeing Miss Meg, either.

However, before I decided to settle in for the night I'd just make sure Curly wasn't there. No use stirring up trouble on their doorstep. It was bad enough that I had shooting to think of without worrying them.

Rossiter was just unsaddling a gray gelding when I came into the yard. "How are you, boy? Light an' set."

"Don't mind if I do, only there's been shooting trouble and there'll be more, so I'd better ask. Are you expecting Curly Dunn?"

"No."

"All right then. I'll stop and gladly."

"Now just a minute. I said I wasn't expecting him, and I am not, but that doesn't mean he might not show up. He's coming over here every few days."

Nevertheless, the warmth and comfort of a woman-kept house was too much for me to turn down, so I stripped the gear from the mustang and turned it into the corral.

We walked side by each up to the house and he spoke of the shooting trouble. "I knew there were hard feelings, but I didn't know it had come to that." So I told him about Jobe taking a shot at me.

"Was he hurt bad?"

"I didn't examine him. Looked to me like a burn along the ribs, and he may lose a good deal of blood. Maybe I nicked the inside of his arm, too. He was holding it mighty odd."

We went in the door and Meg was there and she said, "Pa, supper's ready. Who're you talking to?" And then she seen me.

"Oh . . . *you?*" she said disdainfully. "I was hoping it was Curly."

"If he's got over his beating," I said, "I'll bet he wasn't able to kiss you for a week, with those mashed-up lips of his."

"That's probably why you hit him there," she accused.

"Are you funnin'? I never gave it no thought. Why should I care who he kisses? Anyway, we weren't fighting over you. We were fighting because he had an awfully big opinion of himself and he figured to teach me something."

"I don't care why you fought," she said irritably. "You were like two animals! Now sit down and eat."

So I sat down. And she could really fix grub. I told her so. "Ma'am, for a woman with a harpy's tongue you can surely put vittles together. I declare, it's a wonder some man hasn't sweet-talked you into marrying him."

"I've never heard any sweet-talk from you!"

"No, ma'am, I was never given to it. I reckon I'd just have to bundle a girl up in my arms and kiss her real good. I wouldn't be much for talking."

"Why pick her up?" she demanded. "That's no way to do."

"Well, now. If she was as short as you—"

She stepped right up to me. "I'm not all that short!"

"Maighdlin!" Rossiter said sharply. "Put the supper on the table."

She finished putting supper on the table and she had no more to say all through it, but while Rossiter and me talked of cattle and beef prices and how a herd might increase, I kept a-thinking that maybe she wasn't that short. Especially if she stood on tiptoe.

CHAPTER 12

IT DIDN'T DO me any good to stall around the next morning, although I never taken so long to saddle a horse in all my born days. Nor so long over breakfast, either. I was hoping Meg would show up but she didn't and after awhile I swung into the saddle and rode off up the trail.

When I was maybe a mile off and away higher up I glanced back in time to see a small figure come running from the ranch house and stop there in the yard, and I lifted my arm and waved, but surely she could not see me at the distance and against the mountain.

Two days of riding it needed before I came up with the herd. I saw their dust long before I rode up to it, but when I came near I swung off to one side so's not to turn them. Whoever was riding point had gone off somewhere, but that big old brindle steer in the lead needed no help.

Halfway down the herd I came up to Parmalee, looking like a dude. He pulled in and thrust out his hand, and dude he might be but he had power in that grip. I had a feeling those flatland Sacketts had much to be said for them other than money, for they were all well off. Nick Shadow rode up from the drag and allowed he was glad to see me. It had been a hard drive.

"You're coming into good range now," I said, "but

nothing like what your headed for along the La Plata."

"We'll need some hands," Parmalee said. "Most of these just joined up for the drive."

"You got anything against Indians?"

"No . . . why?"

"I've just taken on a whole set of them. Tough old warrior and some followers of his. He came to me hunting advice, and looking for a place to light."

"So you took them on," Shadow said. "Good for you."

He looked at my face, which still carried a few scars. "You've had trouble, then?"

"I had a difficulty with Curly Dunn. I was in no shape for it, but I whopped him. A couple of days back I had a run in with Jobe. I scratched him with a bullet, but don't take them lightly, old Bull Dunn is a tough man."

"Old?"

"Aw, you know! He ain't that old. Maybe forty, but he must weigh about two hundred and fifty pounds and I don't think any of it is fat."

We rode along together, the three of us, talking things over and reminding ourselves of other days, other cattle, other drives. Time to time I kept looking back into my mind for pictures of Meg, knowing I was a damned fool all the time I was doing it. She was like every other girl that age who likes to flirt and think about love and such. Curly had the inside track there, and I knew it, but that couldn't keep a body from dreaming, and dreamable girls were almighty scarce in this country.

It was on that drive that I learned that Shadow

was one of the best hands with a rope I'd ever come across. He used the rawhide rope, the *la reata* that Americans have cut down to lariat. He'd learned it from the Californios, and he worked with a rope sixty feet long. He could really make that rope stand up and perform. He never tied fast, though. A man who ties fast with a rawhide rope is in trouble. When a big steer, say a thousand pounds give or take a few, hits the end of that rope something's got to give. A hemp rope will stand the gaff better, but Shadow liked rawhide and he stuck with it, and I never saw anybody who could rope any better.

He was a good hand with stock and he never shied from doing his fair share of the work. They had brought eighteen hundred head of mixed stuff, and a few of them were Texas longhorns, big, rangy beasts who could walk the legs off any other kind of cow crittur and most horses. They'd brought the herd along carefully and they didn't seem to have lost much weight on the trail.

Aside from Parmalee and Shadow there were just four hands and the cook, which was nowhere near enough even after the herd was trail broke. Seven hands were all right as long as there was no trouble. Now that I had come along there were eight and that extra man meant all the difference.

"I can't figure it," I said that night at the fire. "Bull Dunn told everybody he was going to run us out. He's made his brags, now he's got to make good, so why hasn't he done something?"

"Maybe he was waiting until Galloway was alone," Parmalee suggested.

"He's waiting for the cattle," Shadow said. "What

does he gain by running you out? He keeps the country to himself, but is that enough? If he runs you out after you have your cattle brought in then those cattle are going to run loose on the range, and after a respectable time he'll just start slapping his brand on them all. And who's to stop him?"

"If that's the case," Parmalee suggested, "he'll stampede our cattle as soon as we're close to his range ... or sooner."

Morning came bright and clear, and the cattle started off well. Maybe it was the smell of fresh water, maybe it was the grass, but the cattle wanted to go. We had the towering wall of Mesa Verde on the east and Ute Park on the west, and soon we would start bearing east to strike the trail to the ranch.

Suddenly one of the cowhands rode up. "Sackett," he said, "we're being watched." He pointed toward the distant ridge. "Indians!"

Sure enough, there were several Indians watching us from the ridge, and as we moved along they kept pace with us, watching our every move.

THE DUNN RANCH house was long, low and built of logs. Cornered against it and forming a right angle was the bunkhouse, where there were bunks for twenty men, and thirty yards away, forming another side to the loose square, was a barn or shed, also low-roofed and built of logs. The fourth side of the square was the corral.

Inside the house, seated at the table, was Bull Dunn. A huge man with bulging muscles, he slouched at the table with a pot of black coffee and a jug of whiskey, staring at Curly with narrowed eyes.

"You listen, and you listen damn well," he said—then his eyes swept the room—"and this goes for you all. I seen countries change. I ain't so young as you, and I seen them grow up. Well, when they do those folks who hold land are the ones in power, they run things. Those who don't have nothin' are shoved out.

"This here's the end of it. We're going to latch onto a big chunk of this country and we're going to hold it. We're through bein' movers. Here's where we make our stand.

"The Sacketts are bringing in a herd. That's fine, because we'll need stock. There's two of them and this Nick Shadow. I happen to know the cowhands comin' in with the herd won't stay. Anyway, there's only four of them.

"We're goin' to hit that herd of a night, and we're goin' to scatter it to hell an' gone into the breaks of the canyons, and we're going to kill the Sacketts and Shadow. If one of them goes down from a fall or is hurt in the stampede, just leave him lay. We want this to look as right as it can be...not that there's much chance of anybody nosin' around up here.

"Curly, you been sparkin' that Rossiter gal long enough. Marry her, with old Rossiter's let-be or not. You latch onto her, then you be the nice lad and you go over there and work for her papa, and you work hard. I want Rossiter to tell folks what an all-out fine son-in-law he's got. Then if anything happens to Rossiter nobody will ever think you had a hand in it.

"Then I want ever' last one of you to file on claims,

grazing land or mining claims, just so you claim title to it.

"We been wanderin' around the country long enough, and the land is fillin' up back east and we might as well have ours while we can. This is closed-off country, and if we move right it'll be our country and sooner or later we can freeze out anybody who moves in."

Ollie Hammer rolled a cigarette, touched the paper with his tongue and folded it over. "Maybe you're cuttin' a wide swath, Bull. These Sacketts have the name of bein' rough."

"So are we. On'y we're rougher and meaner. I got Vern comin'   and when he gets here he'll take to the hills ai   anything we left over.... As for the stampede, we blame it on the Utes."

He downed his whiskey and refilled the glass to the halfway mark, then took a gulp of the black coffee.

"We done this before, and you all know what to do. I want nobody *seen*. And get this into your thick heads. We ain't outlaws no more...we ain't renygades...so when you go into Shalako or any other town, you act like gents. If you can't hold your liquor, don't drink.

"Get this—" Bull Dunn pointed with a stiff middle finger, "some folks are goin' to complain...let 'em. But if we mind our p's an' q's we'll end up with a good many folks on our side.

"Now they can't have more than three men on the night ridin' job, and three ain't goin' to stop any herd of near two thousand head. If we can stampede those cattle right over their camp, so much the better...we might just take out a Sackett in the process.

"But remember this. I want nobody *seen*! An' Curly, as soon as ever this is over, you ride hell bent for election back here, get you a fresh horse and go on over to Rossiters' place. Tell 'em your horse spooked a couple of times, and you think there's Indians about. Rossiter will likely get up, but you offer to set up with a rifle.

"Above all, if one of them Sacketts should show up over there, you be friendly. You put yourself out to do it. And you act the gent, see?"

When all had scattered, Bull Dunn drained his glass, gulped another cup of black coffee, then stretched out on his bed. He was not worried. His outfit had scattered or rustled herds across seven states in the past dozen years and nobody had ever caught up with them yet. Of course, there was a lot of places where they could not return, but they had no idea of going back, anyway.

This place he liked, and here he was going to stay. He chuckled in his beard. More than one old-time cattleman had rustled a few head and then put on the coat of respectability, and so could he ... and he would enjoy it, chuckling all the time at how he had fooled them.

Curly worried him. Rossiter was too shrewd a man to fool, so as soon as ever Curly was married up with that Rossiter girl, they'd have to do something about Rossiter. In this rough country with half-wild horses and cattle, with dangerous trails and rough winters, a lot of people disappeared.

He was tired of moving, and this was the best country he had found. Right here he would stay.

The Sacketts' herd moved north and then turned

east. In the mountains, their horses grazing nearby, the Dunns played cards, slept, or talked in a desultory fashion as they waited.

Galloway Sackett saddled a horse to ride into Shalako. With a trail herd coming there'd be more hands to be fed, and they would need more grub.

Far to the east, at a stage stop not far from Pagosa Springs, a big man on a sorrel horse rode up to the hitch rail and dismounted. The hostler, his team ready for the incoming stage, glanced at the horse.

"That's a mighty fine animal, but you're riding it hard."

"I got a ways to go." The big man with the shaggy hair had a bullet hole through his flat-brimmed hat, and he wore a low-slung gun, tied down. "You got a horse you want to swap? I'd want as good a horse as I'm trading."

"Only one around is a strawberry roan over in the stable. I don't know if the owner would swap or not. But he might sell. He's in a poker game and he's losing ground fast."

The big stranger walked across the hard-packed yard. He wore a beat-up sheepskin coat and striped pants. His boot heels were run down. He walked into the stable, glanced at the horse, then untied the knot and took it outside where he walked it around a good bit. When he retied the horse he walked back. He took the stub of a cigar from his pocket and put it between his teeth. He lighted up, then squinted over it at the hostler. "That man in there? He's surely losin'?"

"He was unless it's changed in the last five minutes.

Mister, you'd not go wrong on that horse. It can run and it can stay."

"I figured it. Will you hold mine for me? I'll be comin' back through in a few days. I got me a little business to tidy up...family business."

The big stranger walked into the stage station. In one corner of the room near the ticket window three people were sitting, concerned with their own affairs, luggage on the floor beside them. At the other end of the room was a bar and there were several tables. A poker game was going on at one of them.

The big man walked to the bar and ordered a beer, and taking it in his hand, strolled over to where the game was being played. The owner of the horse was immediately obvious.

His brow was beaded with sweat and he was peering at the cards he held close to his chest. Two of the players had dropped out of the hand, and the two remaining were obviously card sharps. The big man knew both of them by sight but it was none of his affair. A man who played poker should not play unless he could pay, and if he played with a pair of card mechanics it was his tough luck.

The man with the diamond scarf pin tossed two chips into the pot. "Up twenty," he said. The other card sharp did likewise.

"Now wait just a minute," the loser said. "I'll raise the money. I'll—"

"I'll let you have twenty for your horse," the gambler with the scarf pin suggested.

"And I'll give him thirty-five," the big stranger said. "Cash on the barrelhead."

The gambler looked up, his eyes level. "You were

not invited into this discussion," he said pointedly. "Mr. Liggitt and I were discussing a business deal."

"And I put in my bid," the stranger said, and he was not smiling.

"Look here!" Liggitt objected. "That's a fine horse! That horse is worth a lot of money!"

"He's worth what I say he is worth," the gambler replied harshly. "And you've got just two minutes. Put up, or shut up."

"My offer at thirty-five stands," the big stranger said.

The gambler's gaze was deadly. "I am getting a bit tired of you," he said. "Just a little tired."

"Wait a minute!" Liggitt said. "I'll take that bid! Thirty-five it is."

The gambler's eyes remained on the big man's. "I told you," he said evenly, "that I was—"

The gambler was not really a gambler. He was a man who played with marked cards and loaded dice, and when he used a gun he did not gamble either. Suddenly a little warning bell was ringing in his ears. This big man was too confident, too ready...and he wasn't worried. Not the least bit.

"Give him the thirty-five," the gambler said, "and let's get on with the game."

The big man thrust his hand into his pocket and the gambler went for his gun. By ordinary standards he made a good try. The only visible gun on the big man was in a holster on his leg, his right hand was in his pocket.

The stranger drew and fired...drew a gun from his waistband with his left hand and shot the gambler through the third button of his vest.

There was a moment of silence and the acrid smell of gunsmoke. Liggitt slowly pulled back from the table, his face a sickly white. "I'll be goin'," he said. "I guess I'll be goin'."

"Wait." The big man put thirty-five dollars on the table. "A bill of sale for one strawberry roan with a white stocking and a Rafter Open A brand."

"The game's over. There's no need for me to sell."

"You agreed. You taken my offer." The big man looked around. "I leave it to you all. He taken my offer, didn't he?"

It was unanimous. Liggitt looked around, sweating. Reluctantly he made out the bill of sale and picked up the thirty-five dollars.

"That horse is worth a lot more," he protested.

"That he is," the big man agreed, "so I suggest that as long as the game is over, and nobody knows how it would have turned out, you take half of what's on the table."

The other gambler recovered his voice. "Like hell!" he said. "I won this fair and square! I—"

The big man's smile was not pleasant. "My friend," he said, "my advice is to let well enough alone. If you get half of this it will give you a road-stake, and that's more than you're entitled to. Now don't make me start reading from the Book. You ain't even very good at what you've been doin', so let it ride."

The gambler sat back carefully. "All right," he said to Liggitt, "fifty-fifty."

The hostler had come in and was standing near the door. "I put your saddle on the roan. I'll hold your horse for you until you come back."

"Thanks."

The big man watched while Liggitt and the other gambler split what was on the table, then he turned and went out, his spurs tinkling softly as he walked.

There was a silence when he left, then the gambler sighed. He looked over at the hostler. "Did you know that man?"

"No, sir, but I seen him before. I seen him a couple of times. That was Logan Sackett."

The gambler looked at his hands, they were trembling. Then he glanced at the body of his partner. "You damned fool!" he said softly. "You poor damned fool!"

The sound of hoofs pounded away into silence, and the bartender came around from behind the bar. "Jim," he said to the hostler, "you take his heels."

CHAPTER 13

THE WEATHER TURNED off hot, and riding to the windward of that herd was plain murder with the heat coming off their bodies in a wave. Nobody wanted it much or long, and me no more than the others.

Me or Shadow held to the point a good part of the time for we alone knew the trail. It was work. The cattle had turned ornery with the heat and just plain didn't wish to travel, nor to be guided when they did travel.

They seen the mountains yonder and wanted to hole up in some of those shady canyons close upon a running stream, and I felt as they did, but necessity demanded we march along.

The Indians who had followed us along the Mesa Verde cliffs disappeared. Maybe they'd come to a place where it was no longer possible, and maybe they had something else in mind. I hoped they weren't figuring on a scrap. It was too blamed hot.

The way ahead was narrowing down some and beyond there it widened out with a lot of broken country to north and south, and the Mancos River ahead. Pulling up I let the herd roll by and waited for Parmalee to come up.

First time I ever saw him look dusty. But only a mite. He reined in and we let them go by, and he said,

"We'll water this side of the Mancos? Didn't you say there was a creek?"

"If there's water in it."

"If not, then the Mancos."

Parmalee had his rifle in his hand, and he pointed with it. There were Indians coming, right down the slope from Mesa Verde, but this was no raiding party. There were only seven... no, eight of them.

It was Powder Face.

"Hold it," I said to Parmalee, "these are the Indians I hired."

Powder Face stopped and the others gathered around him. Two of them were mere boys, not over fourteen. "We come work if you see proper."

I started to welcome them and then had a hunch. "Powder Face," I said, "you can do us more good if you hold off until night.

"I think," I added, "somebody is going to try to stampede our cattle, and steal them. Once everybody is in camp, three men will be on guard, then when the night is half gone they will sleep, and three more will ride. I want you to hide out, then move in at night and help guard the herd.

"This herd," I added, "is your winter meat as well as ours, and it is meat for many seasons. If the cattle are driven off, I cannot feed you."

"We watch," he said. "You ride."

Like smoke they were gone, leaving nothing but a scattering of tracks. To anybody who watched it would have seemed they had tried to beg beef and we had turned them away.

We bedded the herd down on a little branch about five miles west of the Mancos, with good grass all around. They grazed for awhile, then lay down. Parmalee, Munson, and the two Tyler boys taken the first night-herd, with me, Nick Shadow and Charlie Farnum, a breed, taking the second.

It was one of those still, beautiful nights when a body could hear a stick break a half-mile away. I didn't hear anything. I was dog-tired and wanting a bath and so hungry I couldn't finish my grub. I just went and crawled under my soogan and was asleep in no time.

Parmalee woke me up at one o'clock. "We stood it another hour," he said, "as it was quiet. The wind's coming up, so be careful."

Tugging on my boots I said, "See anything of those Injuns?"

"We won't, will we?"

"Prob'ly not. They're probably off in the woods fast asleep." But I was joking and Parm knew it. Those Indians were out there, and they were hearing and seeing everything.

Squatting by the fire I tried to blink the sleep from my eyes while pouring a cup of coffee. It was hot, and black as the hinges of hell, but it tasted good. I picked up a chunk of sourdough bread and some jerky and chewed on it while waiting for Shadow.

He was a sullen man on being awakened in the night and wanted to talk to nobody. In the night I always felt good and took to awakening at any hour with no problems. I also could do a fair job of sleeping at any hour, given the chance, which was rare.

Charlie Farnum never talked much at any time so he and Nick were suited. And I had sense enough to keep my trap shut. We all sat around the fire staring at it with blank faces like so many bumps on a log, slowly letting the coffee take the kinks out of us. After awhile I got up and went out to throw my kak on a little buckskin I was using for a night horse.

It could move like a cat and see like one, and was a horse I trusted for night work, and she seemed to take to me. It nuzzled at me and I fed it a chunk of carrot I had swiped from the chuckbox.

In the western lands a man had best be good friends with his horse or he may never have another friend or need of one. A man afoot in wild country is a man who may not live out the day...which is why horse-stealing was the major sin. In many cases if you stole a man's horse you condemned him to death, a much less pleasant death than if you'd just up and shot him.

The buckskin humped its back a couple of times to show me it was in good shape and ready for work and also that it would take no nonsense from its rider. That horse wanted to know I was wide awake, and after those bumps she gave me, I was.

Shadow and Farnum followed and we rode out, checking in with the riders we relieved and saw them drift off to the fire. They'd probably have coffee, chew the fat a little and then hit the sack, for they were a tired lot. Cattle drives don't leave a man much in the spirit of playing the night owl. There's nothing like a long cattle drive for making a good Christian out of a man...for at least as long as the drive lasts.

That little buckskin taken out, moving around the herd. Things look different at night, so on the first couple of trips around I was mostly locating landmarks and spotting the known troublemakers among the steers. This being a mixed herd it was more apt to stampede than had it been one or the other, but we had a couple of steers and one cow that were plumb flighty, ready to jump at the slightest noise.

We sang to 'em. Then they hear your voice coming and aren't startled by you. Ride up quick on a steer and he's liable to jump right off the ground and run clean out of the county. My voice isn't much, but I often used to tell folks I was a singer, and that I'd sung for crowds of up to three thousand. I didn't tell them I was talking of cows, but they had heard my voice and probably guessed. Galloway might have made 'em believe it, he was that much of a singer.

Shadow stopped to talk when we met the second time around. "The breed was telling me he thinks it's too quiet. Nothing stirring out in the brush, and there should be."

"Well, let's play it that way," I said. "Let's stay on our toes."

"What do you think about it?"

"Look," I said, "if something starts them running we got to keep them off the boys so they won't get tramped. Let's make it so each time we pass the camp we slow up so there's somebody in position most of the time. Then if the cattle start to run, try to keep them headed east and out of the canyons. If they get into those canyons and up into the breaks we'll never get them out before snow flies, and that means we'll never get them out."

It was still over an hour before daylight when all of a sudden somebody stepped out of the trees and stood there. Rifle ready, I rode up, although waiting for me like that he wasn't apt to be an enemy. It was an Indian.

"Powder Face say tell you man come...maybe ten, twelve man."

"Thanks," I said, but the Indian did not fade into the brush.

"Powder Face say he thinks they try Indian trick. Use mountain-lion skin."

And that time he did disappear, but it was a comfort to know they were close by.

Nick Shadow closed in. "Was that you talking?"

So I told him. He knew the trick as well as me. The Indians used to do it with a fresh puma hide. They'd get in close and wave the skin and the cattle would get that smell of cat, and then one of the Indians would imitate the scream and those cattle would be gone.

We started on and I was almost to the camp when I heard that scream, and those cattle came off the ground with a lunge. They made a break toward the camp and I jerked out my pistol and let go with a shot into the air and a wild, Comanche yell. Some of them veered, but some of the others I couldn't reach and they went through camp just a hellin'. Pots and pans went every which way. I heard a pistol shot and then another and then a scream, and all of a sudden that herd was gone. All that was left was dust and the sound of thundering hoofs.

They were headed for the Mancos River and that was one of the reasons I'd stopped where I had. If they had a run of several miles and then reached the river they might stop to drink. This bunch was pretty fat anyway, and they weren't like a bunch of wild longhorns all hungry for water who might run for hours.

Wheeling around I rode into camp. It was a shambles. First off I saw a man on the ground or what had been a man. It was one of the Tyler boys. The only way I could tell was by the silver conchas he wore on his belt.

Even as I swung up, Parmalee came down out of a tree. The cook came out of the rocks, and the other two had taken shelter behind the wagon. My pistol shot had come just in time to give them a split second.

"Tyler," I said, "you and Cookie take care of him." I indicated the dead man. "Parm, you'd best go help with your cattle."

"What about you?" he asked.

"I'm going to ride up the canyon. I want to read some sign."

"I'll go with you."

"No. I'll take Charlie Farnum. Unless I'm mistaken you'll find your herd at the river and my Indians will be there too."

Nick Shadow had gone down after the cattle, but I'd heard Farnum's horse slow down and I figured he had the same idea I had. I rode out from the camp and he was a-settin' there waiting for me.

"Figured you might like to look around," he said, and we started walking our horses slow, keeping to the open ground where we made less sound. Once we drew up to listen, and after a moment Charlie said, "Why you do that for those Indians?"

"They're good folks," I said, "and this was their country. It's nobody's fault as to what's happened. Wherever there's open country there'll be people coming hungry for land, and it wouldn't have made much sense to let a lot of folks in Europe starve to death when there was miles and miles of unused land awaiting.

"The Indian would have had a better deal, and should have but for a lot of greedy white men and because of a few scalp-hungry Indians. There was right and wrong on both sides. I'm doing no crying for the Indian. He made his fight but he never could get enough guns and ammunition and the white men kept moving in, but when old Powder Face came to me he came honest, and he told me who he was and what he'd done, and I made him welcome. I figure those boys will make good hands and as far as I'm concerned they're here forever."

After that we shut up and rode on, and pretty soon we noticed our horses' ears go up like they saw something or smelled something, and sure enough there was a fire, and a half dozen men around it, and one young feller had that cat hide in his hands and he was laughing at the way the herd took off. The rest of them must have been off following the herd. I figured Powder Face and Nick Shadow would take care of them.

"Charlie," I said, "you shoot the first one that moves."

When I spoke I spoke loud and you never saw a bunch of men come to stillness any swifter. Then I stepped down there and I looked at the tall blond ranny with the hide in his hands and I said, "You killed a good man tonight, a better man than you'll ever be. So you drop that hide and go for your gun."

"Can I put the hide down first?"

"Any way you like," I said, "but have at it."

Me, I was mad clear through. They'd tried to wipe out our camp and kill us all. It was pure-dee luck that they hadn't done it.

"You're a Sackett," this tall ranny said. "Well, Sackett, I'm Abel Dunn, and I'm going to save Rocker his job."

He let go the hide and his hand swept down and closed over that six-shooter and my gun stabbed flame at him twice, so close together they looked and sounded like one. And he folded and went down.

"That's for Tyler," I said. "Now old Bull Dunn warned me out of the country. You take Abel back to him wrapped in that cougar hide, and you tell Bull Dunn he can leave the country or stay, it don't make me no mind, but if he stays he better start goin' to Sunday School and actin' like it."

"You talk big," one of them said. "Wait until Rocker hears about this."

"You tell him," I said. "You just ride fast and tell him."

"You're the one better leave. You got no more herd than nothing."

"You wasted your time," I said. "My herd's down at the Mancos right now, and its all in one piece and my boys are with it. You started your victory party a mite too soon."

I could see several bottles around camp so I put bullets in them, and when one of them thinking my gun was empty started to reach, Charlie Farnum put a bullet through his arm.

Right there in front of them I shoved the shells out of that old Dance & Park pistol and loaded up again.

And then I went in there and emptied their guns, dropping the shells into the fire and throwing their guns into the brush. Then I taken off.

In about a minute shells began to pop and those Dunn people scrambled for shelter.

Charlie Farnum and me we started east for the herd, riding together. When we were a few miles off we started to sing, and we sang a dozen songs before we shut up and left it to the coyotes.

That Charlie Farnum had a better voice than me.

For that matter, so did the coyotes.

CHAPTER 14

ON THE SECOND morning after the stampede, and knowing nothing whatever about it, Galloway Sackett headed for town.

He chose a new route, avoiding the trail they had used, and crossing the La Plata well above Shalako. He stayed in the trees and brush, keeping out of sight until close to town, then he emerged from the woods behind the livery stable and rode around in front of Berglund's place.

Crossing the street to the store he swung down and tied his horses. Inside he ordered rice, beans, flour, and whatever it seemed likely they would need. He sacked it up and loaded it on the packhorse.

The town was empty and still. Occasionally the music box from the saloon would brighten the day with tin-panny music. In the distance there was snow on the mountains. Galloway paused in tying his pack and stared at it, thinking he'd like to go up there. He'd never been that high up in the mountains. It was then he remembered Nick Shadow's story about the gold and diamonds.

He glanced thoughtfully toward the peaks. Now if he could just take a little trip up there...

The rope came snaking from the shadows beside the store and the loop dropped over his head, pinning his arms to his sides. He swore at himself for day-dreaming at such a time and made a desperate attempt to reach his gun. A jerk from the rope sprawled him on the boardwalk, and then another loop fell over his legs. He heard a laugh boom out and another rider rode out from behind the store leading three horses.

He started to speak and they jerked him into the dust, dragging him a few feet. Then one of them walked over and drew Galloway's gun from its scabbard and thrust it behind his own waistband.

Curly Dunn still wore the fading blue marks left from the bruises Flagan had given him, and there was a scarcely healed cut over his eye.

"We got us a Sackett, boys. Let's take him over into the tree and give him the Injun treatment."

Arms and legs held tight by the nooses, there was not a thing he could do. If he made a move they would jerk him and drag him, so he waited. Inwardly, he was desperate.

Flagan was miles away with Nick Shadow and Parmalee. He could expect no help from the towns-people who were trying to stay out of the trouble, and for which he did not blame them. They could do nothing against the Dunns, who could simply burn them out and ride on. Nor had he any reason to be-lieve they even knew of his situation. In any event the total population of Shalako at this moment num-bered just five people.

There was nobody to help him. He must not strug-gle, but must bide his time, hoping to catch them off guard. If he struggled they would only jerk the ropes tighter, making escape more difficult.

Curly swung his horse and started for the trees, the others following. Suddenly one of them pulled up.

"Curly, we should ought to have us a bottle. This here may take some time, and his sweatin' may make us thirsty."

"All right, go get it then. You got money?"

"I have," the other one broke in.

"You two go an' get the liquor, but hurry back. You don't want to miss the fun. Alf, you loosen that rope around his legs. I want him to walk to it."

Galloway made no move as Alf loosened the ropes. The two turned then and went toward the saloon. Curly grinned at Galloway. "Here's where I get a little of my own back. We're goin' to see how loud a Sackett can yell."

"You'll wait a long time," Galloway said quietly.

Curly laughed and started for the trees. Galloway had to trot to keep up. Once he fell and Curly dragged him several yards before he stopped and allowed him to rise. And then just as he was on his feet, Curly jerked him sharply so that he hit the ground hard. Curly laughed. "How's it feel, Sackett? That ain't nothin' to what's comin'. How do your toes stand up to fire? Pa tried that on a Yankee one time who wouldn't tell us where he'd hidden his proud-ofs. He told us soon enough, but pa let the fire burn for awhile just to teach him a lesson."

They were well into the trees before Galloway saw his chance. Suddenly he darted to one side and ducked around a tree, taking a quick turn of the rope around the bole. The move was so sudden that Curly, who only had dallied the rope around the saddle horn, was caught unawares. Curly was no cowhand, although he had worked cattle to some extent, and he was careless by nature. Galloway's quick move in snubbing the rope around the tree not only brought his horse up short, but gave Galloway the instant he needed. Holding the snub tight with one hand he hastily kicked and shook the rope loose.

Curly wheeled his horse with a yell, but Galloway had ducked around a tree with others growing close beside it and it took Curly just a minute to find a hole through which he could guide his horse.

Curly grabbed for his pistol but a branch interfered. Galloway shook off the rope and ducking around the tree, jumped for Curly. Trying to pull back from the tangle in which he found himself, Curly felt a sudden heave on his stirrup as his leg was thrown up. He started to fall and tried to grab a secure hold on the pommel, but Galloway hacked at the fingers and Curly lost his grip.

He hit the ground with one foot caught in a stirrup and the frightened horse, backing and rearing, swung out of the trees and broke into a run.

Galloway staggered back, caught himself against a tree and slowly recovered himself. The horse went racing back toward the town, with Curly bouncing at every jump.

Glancing quickly around, he found Curly's pistol where it had fallen among the leaves. Hastily he checked the cylinder. Only three cartridges. Damn a man who didn't reload!

Holding the pistol in his hand Galloway started back for Shalako, only some two hundred yards away. He limped as he walked for his leg had been badly bruised when he had been dragged over the edge of the boardwalk.

He came into the head of the street and saw Curly's horse stopped in front of the saloon. Alf and the other Dunn were unfastening the rope. Berglund was kneeling beside Curly.

Galloway was within forty yards of them before Alf looked up. "I want my gun, Alf. Take it out mighty careful and put it down on the boardwalk."

Alf Dunn looked at Galloway. Hatred burned within him. At his feet lay Curly, dragged, torn and battered, injured badly, possibly dying. Always before the Dunns had had it their own way, and his hatred was filled with frustration and disbelief. This had never happened to the Dunns, it could not be happening.

Success corrodes, and the Dunns—always brutal, always cruel, always fighting a hit-and-run battle—had enjoyed success. Before their enemies could gird against them they were gone, miles away and with no idea of returning. In those swift strikes at unprepared ranches or communities they had been swaggering, triumphant and confident. Then Curly had been whipped by Flagan Sackett, a man who had just gone through a punishing ordeal, Jobe had been wounded, and the old Bull himself ignored. Now Curly had been terribly hurt in their moment of triumph, and here came the man who had done it, ordering him to throw down his pistol.

It was more than he could take. Alf said, "Pete, let's take him." Berglund left the ground in a long dive that carried him across the body of Curly and into the sparse grass beyond.

Alf and Pete with one accord had gone for their guns. Galloway's gun came up and fired. Alf turned halfway around and Galloway fired a second time. Alf Dunn backed up and sat down and Galloway's gun covered Pete even as Pete's gun came up. "Don't do it," Galloway said. "I'll kill you."

"And if he don't," a new voice said, "I will!"

Berglund, sitting up now that he was out of gun range, looked at the shaggy-haired big man in the faded red shirt and the black vest. A sheepskin coat was tied back of the saddle and there was a Winchester in the boot. The big man looked unkempt and almost unreal, for there was about him a wild savagery that was somehow shocking.

Galloway backed off a few steps to where he could see the newcomer. "Howdy, Logan! Nice to see you!"

He swung his eyes back to Pete. "You'd better take Curly home," he said, "and you tell Bull Dunn we want no more trouble. You brought it to us and by now you ought to have your belly full."

Pete snorted. "You think the old Bull will take this? He'll come in here a-foggin' it, mind you."

"His funeral. You tell him what I said. There's no need for all this shootin' and shoutin'."

Berglund got up slowly from the ground. "You two come in and I'll buy you a drink." He glanced at Logan. "I take it you're a Sackett?"

"Logan Sackett, from Clinch Mountain." He jerked his thumb toward Galloway. "He's a Cumberland Sackett. They're good people, too."

At the bar Berglund poured the drinks. "I think you boys are going to straighten out that Dunn outfit. They were riding roughshod over everybody."

"We want to ranch," Galloway said. "All we want is to make a home. If we get settled in, Tyrel and Orrin are coming up here. We'll have the whole family together."

BULL DUNN SAT at the table in the long house and poured his tin cup half-full of whiskey, then replaced the jug on the table. "Stir up that fire," he said, speaking to no one in particular. "I want my coffee *hot*!"

An hour before, Pete Dunn had come in with the battered, half-alive body of Curly Dunn, and the body of Alf in which no life remained. And then, just a few minutes ago, Rocker had ridden in, leading the crew Bull had sent down to scatter the Sacketts' cattle.

Bull didn't need anyone to tell him they had failed. His eyes swept over the group of men wordlessly leading their horses into the corral.

"Where's Abel?" he asked, as Rocker swung off his horse in front of him.

"Dead. I wasn't there when it happened."

Bull turned on his heel and walked into the house. Now he was sitting at the head of the table, looking at what was left of his family and the few others he could trust.

The old Bull was shaken. For the first time in years things were going against him, and he was sure he knew why... because he had elected to stop.

Why stop? Was he getting tired? He tasted the raw whiskey, then turned the glass in his fingers.

That Curly... he couldn't do anything right. He

goes into the woods with a tied-up man and comes out with his horse draggin' him.

"Vern," he glanced down the table at the sallow-faced young man, "you got it to do. Cut 'em down, one after the other."

Vern Huddy batted his eyes and looked sour, but offered no immediate comment. He had been studying out the country and he knew what he could do.

"That big man," he suggested, "the one Pete told of. That'll be Logan Sackett. He's an outlaw gunfighter. You all lay off him. He's a tiger."

"Let's have it," Bull said suddenly, "how did they get through with those cattle? I want to know."

"They had more men than we expected," Rocker spoke quietly. He was a young man of medium height, medium build, who carried himself with pride. "One of them, at least, was an Indian."

"There were several Indians," Ollie Hammer said. "They seemed to come right out of the ground and they kept those cattle running straight right down to the river. We never had a chance to scatter them."

"What happened to Abel?"

"He tried to draw against a Sackett. It was Flagan, the one who whupped Curly. Tin-Cup and me was with Rocker going after the cattle. There was no one else there who could take on Sackett."

Rocker had been toying with his cup. Now he lifted his eyes to his father. "Pa, we lost Abel. Curly is done up. If he lives he won't be any use to us until this here fight is all over. Jobe has got him a crippled arm. Alf is dead . . . I figure we'd better rattle our hocks out of here."

For a moment there was dead silence. Several stole

looks at Bull, all were shocked. It was the first time any of them had dared suggest such a thing, and Rocker was the only one who could say it without a blow.

"You're talkin' crazy. When did we ever run from a fight?"

"Never. But nobody but a fool bucks a stacked deck. Pa, you don't know these Sacketts. There's a good many of them around the country, and when one of them is in trouble, they'll all come. We haven't seen anything yet."

"Vern will whittle 'em down."

"Maybe."

Vern's eyes came up sharply at the implied doubt. He started to speak, then held his silence.

"The Sacketts aren't nesters," Rocker continued. "They aren't just cow ranchers. Every one of them is a woodsman. They grew up feuding and fighting and they know all the tricks. I've heard about them for years. Tyrel and Tell are probably the best hands with guns, although Logan may be as fast.

"Flagan, Galloway, and Orlando are all good. I don't know about Parm Sackett, the one who bought those cattle they are bringing in."

"Rocker," Bull said impatiently, "that's fool talk."

"Maybe. But why buck a stacked deck? I think our luck's run out."

Bull glared at Rocker, but he made no reply. He gulped whiskey, took the coffee chaser, and waited. Something would come to him. It always had.

This country was too good to leave. He had hated the flat plains of Kansas, although he knew it was great cattle and wheat country. He liked eastern

Colorado and Texas no better. He had wanted to stop nowhere until he rode into the valley of the La Plata.

It had looked easy. The country was wide open to settlement. The town of Shalako was small enough to be comfortable, and there weren't too many people around. They could move in, take what they wanted, and settle down to raise cattle and families. Controlling the largest number of voters he would be able to elect his own sheriff or marshal.

In just a few years they'd have some herds built up, stealing them down in New Mexico or Arizona if necessary, and they could hold this valley like a private place.

Then the Sacketts came in. They were warned, only they did not go. Curly had gone and picked himself a fight and gotten whipped, and that had been a blow. Bull Dunn knew how important is the reputation for invincibility, and the defeat of Curly by a man in bad physical condition threw a shadow over that reputation.

Suddenly everything had gone wrong.

Worst of all, Rocker was failing him, and Rocker had always been the smartest in the lot, the smartest and the quietest. The rest of them, well they were a wild lot, obeying nobody but him, listening to nobody but him. And until now they had believed nothing could whip them. Bull Dunn was not that kind of a fool. It was good for them to believe that as long as he, who was the boss, knew better. Bull Dunn had seen quiet communities suddenly rise up in anger, and suddenly the trees began blossoming with hanged men.

He knew all about that. He had left Virginia City,

up in Montana Territory, just before the hanging started.

Just a hunch that he had, a sudden waking up in the morning with an urge to ride...and he had ridden.

When the news reached him that Henry Plummer and the rest of them were left dancing at the end of a rope he had known he was right.

Had his senses dulled over the years?

Was that what Rocker was feeling now? The Rocker had always been cautious, however. He was good with the six-shooter, probably the best Bull ever had seen, but he had a tendency to caution the others scoffed at, but not in front of the Rocker.

"All right, Rocker, you've been right before. We'll make one more try...just one. If that doesn't work we'll ride north out of here, head for Brown's Hole."

Rocker Dunn was uneasy, but he knew there was no use arguing, as even this concession was more than he had hoped for. And of course, the old Bull might know what he was talking about.

Yet he could not but remember the broken, bleeding body of Curly...he had never liked Curly, brother or no. There was something unhealthy about him. Nonetheless, to see him come in like that... what was it about those Sacketts?

There was that Texas Ranger, McDonald, who said, "There's no stopping a man who knows he's in the right and keeps a-coming."

Maybe that was it.

CHAPTER 15

THE CATTLE CAME in before noon of the day following the fight in the streets of Shalako. They came in bunched nicely and moving well. Parmalee had brought them over the trail losing no flesh and ready for a final polish before cold weather set in.

Yet the work had just begun with the bringing of the cattle, and while the Indians rode herd, I taken Galloway, Nick, and Charlie Farnum out to make hay.

There were high meadows where the hay was good, and we bought extra scythes at the store in town and went to work. Galloway and me, we'd had a spell of this as boys, and we went down the line cutting a wide swath, swinging the blades to a fine rhythm. Nick and Charlie were new at it and made more work of it.

We kept our guns handy, and usually one or two of the Indians were on lookout. We used the boys for this. They were sharp-eyed and eager to be helping, and lookout was warriors' work, so they loved it.

We saw nothing of the Dunns.

My thoughts kept a-turning toward Cherry Creek and the Rossiter place but there was just too much work for any one of us to shake loose. Anybody who thinks that ranching is just sitting and watching cows grow fat has got another guess a-coming. Ranching is mostly hard work, can-see to can't-see, as we used to say. Daylight to dark, for pilgrims.

Parmalee came out with a scythe on the third morning and threw us all a surprise. He was maybe the best of the lot at mowing hay. When it came to that, a body could see why. Down there in the flatlands they had more hay to mow than we folks on the uplands. Why, where I came from even the cows had legs shorter on one side than the other from walking on the sidehills!

The peaches and apples we grew on those mountains were so accustomed to the downhill pull you could only make half a pie with them because they insisted on slipping over to one side.

Bats and birds taken from those mountains down to the flatlands used to have to set down in the grass, they'd get so disoriented. They were used to flying alongside the land instead of over it.

If a man took a wrong step when plowing he was apt to fall into his neighbor's pasture or maybe his watermelon patch, which led to misunderstandings.

Church was down in the valley, so we never walked to church in the morning, we slid. We had the name of being good Christian folk in our part of the Cumberland because we just couldn't be backsliders.

Even Logan came out from town and took a hand at the haying. He was a powerful big man and he cut a wider swath than any of us. He'd put in a full day's work by morning and then he'd set by the fire and make comments about us being so slow. But we got the hay down and we got it stacked, and Logan proved a hand at that, too, but nobody could top off a stack as well as Parmalee.

Parmalee was a great one for reading, too, and he

went nowhere without his books. I never could see why he needed them for he could remember nigh all he read, and it was a-plenty. Of a night by the fireside when somebody would start to tellin' stories of ha'nts and such, he would recite poetry to us. He'd set there like he was telling a story and it would just come a-rolling out.

He'd read poetry by Greeks even, and some by the Frenchies, and he had a way of saying it that was a caution. He and Nick Shadow would sit there spoutin' poetry at each other, sometimes for hours. Whenever one of them didn't start it, Logan would. Where he picked up book knowledge I don't know, and he always pleaded that he knew nothing, but he did know a surprising lot. One time he admitted that he was snowed in one winter with five books of which he read them all, over and over. One of them was the Bible. He knew all the stories but didn't seem to have picked up much of the morals.

Logan Sackett was from Clinch Mountain, and those Clinch Mountain Sacketts were rough, lawless boys. They were fierce feuders and fighters and they went their own way, most of them lone-wolfing it until trouble showed to another Sackett.

He was a story-teller when it came to that, and could yarn on for hours about country he'd seen or about bad men. Mostly in those days our world was small. Folks got around a good bit and so we exchanged information backwards and forwards of the country. We knew about trails, marshals, bad men, bad horses, tough bartenders and the like in countries we'd never seen because word was sort of passed around.

Guns, riding, and cattle were our business, so we heard plenty of stories about tough old mossy-horn steers, about bad horses and men who could top them off. Every outfit had at least one man who was salty with a gun, and each one had a bronc rider. We bragged on our roping or cutting horses, not often the same ones, and how tough were the drives we made. We ate beans, beef, and sourdough bread, and we had molasses for sweetening. We slept out in the open, rain or shine, and we rode half-broke horses that could shake the kinks out of a snake.

It was a rough, hard, wonderful life and it took men with the bark on to live it. We didn't ask anything of anybody and as long as a man did his work nobody cared what else he was or did.

Logan Sackett wasn't a bad man in the eastern sense. Out west he was. In the west a bad man was not necessarily an evil man or an outlaw...he was a bad man to tangle with. He was a man to leave alone, and such a one was Logan. He was mighty abrupt with a six-shooter, and if you spoke rough to him you had better start reaching when you started speaking, and even then you'd be too slow with it.

Logan had the name of being an outlaw. I suspect he'd rustled a few head of steers in his time, and maybe his stock didn't always wear the brands they'd started out with. I wouldn't be surprised if here and there he hadn't stood some stagecoach up while he shook the passengers down. About that side of his life I asked no questions. However, I'll bank on one thing. He never done anything mean or small in his life.

We'd all heard about Vern Huddy, but like everybody after awhile, you get careless. We'd been keeping an eye on the hills and the Indians were looking around for us, but all of a sudden one day there was a rifle shot and one of our Indians was down in the dirt and dead.

He was standing not three feet from me at the time and I had just moved over to dip up some beans from the pot and he had stepped up where I had been and was waiting with his plate. I was sure that shot had been meant for me, and Vern Huddy had sighted in, then maybe had taken his eyes away when he cocked his rifle and had squeezed off his shot before he realized there'd been a change. At least, that was how I figured it. I was sorry for that Indian, but glad for me.

We moved our camp deeper into the brush and all of us stayed clear of clearings.

"Somebody's got to go up there after him," Logan said.

"I'll go. I'm the best Indian. Every man has a pattern, I don't care who he is. Rifle shots are among the worst for that sort of thing. He's developed himself a style. If I study the places where he has been I can find the sort of places he likes to shoot from."

It made a kind of sense, so from that day on, I took to the hills.

Stalking a killer is no job for the weak-nerved. Sooner or later your killer is going to know he is being hunted and then he becomes the hunter.

If I found him soon I'd be lucky or unlucky, depending on who saw who first. The chances are it would only be after a painstaking search. So I taken a sight on the hills after dark. I set up a forked stick out there and a prop for the butt of my rifle and I figured the height of that Indian who was shot and where the bullet hit, then I sighted right back along my own rifle and pin-pointed the area from which that bullet must have come.

Now I was sure Vern Huddy wouldn't be in that spot. He'd have moved, found himself a new location. Maybe he did not know he hadn't killed me, and maybe he did. By day I borrowed Logan's spyglass and studied the mountainside where the bullet had come from.

Only one thing I did do before I took to the woods. I went to Shalako to pick up a few things and ran smack-dab into Meg Rossiter.

She had come to town with her pa for supplies and the like. Town was town, even when it was so small, and a girl like Meg simply had to come in.

She had come up the steps to the store just as I rode up, and we stopped there for just a minute, she holding her skirt up just a trifle to clear it from the dust, and me just about to get off my horse. Finally I said, "Howdy, ma'am!"

"How do you do?" she said cool as you please. And when I swung down and stepped up on the porch she said, "I suppose that brother of yours is proud of himself."

"Galloway? What for?"

"For nearly killing poor Curly Dunn. That was just awful! He should be ashamed!"

Astonished, I said, "Ma'am, you don't have the right of it. Curly got the rope around Galloway unex-pected, and was taking him into the woods. Curly was talking torture and the like. Galloway got free of him and Curly's horse dragged him, that's all."

"Galloway got free of him! That's likely, isn't it? Who helped him?"

"He was alone, ma'am. The rest of us was miles away with the herd."

Her eyes were scornful. "That's your brother's story. I don't believe any of it. Curly was not that kind of boy."

"I'm sorry, ma'am, but that's just the way it happened." Getting kind of irritated, I said, "Curly ain't much. He hasn't the nerve that Alf had or any of them, and he wouldn't be a patch on his old man. He's just kind of pretty and he has a real mean streak in him."

She just glared at me and turned away and flounced into the store. Well, I just stood there mentally cussing myself and all the luck. Here I'd been setting myself up, shaping up all kinds of meetings with her in my mind, but none of them like that. I never figured that Galloway's fracas with Curly would bother her none, least ways where I was concerned.

I guessed she was just fixed on Curly. She'd set her cap for him and she wasn't giving any thought to anybody but him.

Well, she could have him. I told myself that and stood there on the porch, wanting to go in the store and afraid she'd think I was following her, and wanting to follow her all at the same time. But I had to go in. That was what I'd come to town for.

Finally, I gave my hat brim a tug and ducked my head and went on in. Johnny Kyme, the storekeeper came over to me and said, "What can I do you for, Sackett?"

"About thirty feet of rawhide string," I said, "and a couple of those thin-bladed hunting knives." I also bought an extra hatchet and a few nails, with a few other odds and ends. I also bought me a pair of homespun pants (the brush doesn't make any sound when it rubs on them like it does on jeans, or even like on buckskin). I also bought a woolen cap with earflaps, although I wouldn't be using them. Where I was going a hat would be falling off, and I needed the bill of the cap to shade my eyes for good seeing.

Meg was coming right past me although she could just as well have gone the other way. She had her chin up and she was flouncing along, and suddenly I taken nerve and turned on her. "Ma'am, I'd admire to buy you a coffee over to the saloo——I mean, the restaurant, if you'll be so kind."

For a moment there she appeared about to turn me down, but I had something going for me that wasn't me. It was that she was in Town with a capital T, and a girl when she came to Town ought to see a boy. To sit and have coffee would be nice and she could think of herself as a great lady in Delmonico's or some such place.

She looked right at me, cool as you please. "Thank you, Mister Sackett. If you will give me your arm."

"I'll be back for all that," I said to Slim over my shoulder, and walked out of there, proud as could be, with that girl on my arm like we were going to a ball or something.

Now you have to understand about that saloon. It was a saloon, but one side of it was set up for an eating place where ladies could come if they wished, and when they were present the men kind of toned down the loud talk and the rough talk. Fact is, most of the men liked to see them there, added a touch of home or something, and most of us were a long way from womenfolks.

We went up those steps with me all red around the gills from not being used to it, and trying not to look like this was the first time or almost.

Berglund, he came over with a napkin across his arm like he was one of them high-class waiters and he said, "What's your pleasure?" So we both ordered coffee, and he brought it to us, and then I'll be damned if he didn't fetch some cupcakes with chocolate highgrade all over the top. I never even knew he had such stuff.

When I said as much he replied, "Why, surely you understand that we only cater to the carriage trade? To the most elite clientele?"

I didn't know whether I was an elite clientele or not or if it was something I should shoot him for, so I tried to look stern and unconcerned all the same so he could either think I knew what he was talking about or irritated because he said it.

We sat there, sipping coffee and eating those cakes and talking. She started in about the weather just like we hadn't had those other words at all. I asked her about her Pa, and she asked me about Parmalee and Logan, and then somehow she got started telling me about a poem she'd been reading called the *Idylls of the King,* by somebody named Tennyson. I knew a puncher back in the Cherokee Nation by that name but it couldn't be the same one. The last time I saw him I don't think he could even read a book, let alone write one.

From all she had to say it was quite a book, and she

was taken with this here Lancelot who went around sticking things with a spear.

There wasn't much I could say, not having read the book except to comment that it must take a mighty big horse to carry a man with all that iron on him. I don't think she thought that comment was very much in the line of her thinking. And she kept talking about chivalry and romance and her eyes got kind of starry until I began wondering where I could buy myself one of those suits.

Anyway, we had us a nice talk and I was right sorry to finish the coffee and those little cakes, but it did look like we were going to part friendly when all of a sudden she says, "You aren't the only pebble on the beach."

What she meant I didn't know for awhile, and then she said, "Mr. Huddy has been calling on me. He's very nice."

And before I thought what I was saying I said, "He's the one who has been trying to kill us. He hides up in the hills and shoots at us. He killed one of our Indian boys the other day."

Her face went kind of white and she jumped up so quick she almost upset the table, and then she said, "Flagan Sackett, I never want to see you again!"

And she left out of there.

Berglund, he was polishing a glass and he said, looking at nobody, "It's better to have them mad at you than indifferent."

"Oh, shut up!" I said politely, and walked out of there, mad at me, mad at Berglund, and mad at Meg Rossiter.

CHAPTER 16

WHAT I SAID was true, but that didn't make any difference and it was the wrong thing to say right then, and to her. Meg Rossiter was a lone girl in a country filled with men, most of them older than her. There weren't any parties or dances or box-socials or the like to go to. She hadn't much chance to be a girl or to flirt.

Dumb as I was about women I'd watched them enough to know they like to play one man off against another, and like to feel wanted even if they ain't. Now Meg had set her cap or seemed to for Curly Dunn, and right away I come around saying he doesn't amount to much, and then Curly set to to prove me right.

No matter what she said to me she must have heard talk at the store. Johnny Kyme was a married man and his wife was a friend of Meg's and there was no nonsense about her. She knew what a skunk Curly was, but that didn't help Meg. Then we have a nice get-together like, and then she springs this Vern Huddy on me. Maybe she wants to make me jealous, maybe she just wants to feel courted, but right away I have to go make him out as bad as Curly or worse.

Back in the woods next morning we got together for a bit. Logan was there, Parmalee, Galloway, and Nick Shadow. Charlie Farnum came up as we started to talk. Everybody knew what I was starting out to do, and everybody knew it was a life-and-death matter. I was going into the woods after a man who was a dead shot, who moved like a cat, and had the senses of a wild animal, or so we'd heard. One was going to be dead before I came out of the woods. I knew it and they knew it.

He seldom shot, almost never missed, and of the few reported to have lived after he shot them, none could say they had seen him or even knew he was about.

We talked a mite of everything else and then I got up and taken my rifle. "I'm not going to take a horse," I said. "When you have a horse and you leave it you've got to come back to it and the killer knows it. I don't want to be tied to anything."

It was early morning and a mist lay in the valleys. All was very still. At such times every sound in the forest seems magnified if there is a sound, but I heard nothing, moving carefully, taking my time. The route I chose was roundabout. Where Vern Huddy would be I had no idea, only that he would likely not be where I would expect to find him.

My first destination was the spot from which he had fired. I wanted to see what he liked in the way of firing positions, and if possible pick up a clear track so I could recognize it at any other time. So far I was working blind.

Taking my time, I worked my way through the woods to the north, found the mouth of Little Deadwood Gulch and worked my way across it, checking for tracks. I found the tracks of elk, deer, and some smaller game, and started up the gulch, moving a few yards at a time. Part of that was the need to study the mountain to use the best cover, and part because of the altitude.

Just short of timberline, which I figured to be about ten thousand feet up, I crossed the gulch and worked my way along the flank of the mountain. By noon I was holed up in a clump of spruce looking over at Baldy.

For over an hour I sat there with Logan's spyglass, which I'd borrowed, studying the side of Baldy from the bottom of Deadwood up to the top. First I swept it side by side at ten-foot levels, searching for life. Twice I glimpsed deer feeding quietly. Birds occasionally flew up, but none seemed disturbed.

Then I checked for possible approaches to Baldy, found a good one and promptly discarded it. Undoubtedly he had seen it, too, and would be watching it and occasionally making a sweep of the hillside. There was nothing.

Keeping low, I worked my way down into the gulch and up the other side. It needed an hour to find his firing position. He had built up a mound of earth on which to rest his rifle and he himself had a comfortable seat while he was waiting.

He had a good field of fire with no obstructions, and the actual distance was about four hundred yards, give or take a few. He had made no effort to conceal the fact that he had been here, probably doubting anybody would ever make a hunt for him or find the place. Or he might have left it for bait.

That idea hit me as I squatted on my heels and I just let myself go and hit the ground on my shoulder and rolled over into the brush just in time to hear the echo of a shot. It wasn't until I was thirty feet off and still moving that I remembered hearing that bullet. It had been a close thing.

He knew where I had disappeared and I had no idea where he was shooting from so I worked my way, moving swiftly but with no sound down the slope, then along the flank below his first firing position.

Was he pulling out? Or stalking me? No sooner had I asked the question than I knew the answer. He was stalking me. This Vern Huddy was confident. He might even be cocksure. He figured he was better at this game than anybody else, and maybe he was. If he was, I was a dead man.

Crouching for a moment in a sheltered place, yet one from which I could watch around me, I considered the situation. There was a good chance that after firing the shot that killed the Ute, he had pulled back to the slope above and just waited. He figured that somebody would come looking and he would get another one.

Some time passed and he had probably begun to relax. Maybe he was beginning to think nobody would come, and somehow I had slipped in and he hadn't seen me at first...which was almighty lucky for me. Or else there'd been a branch or something in the way of his shot and he had to wait until I moved.

There was nothing about this I liked. He was hunting me and that wasn't the way I wanted it. He'd probably had a few days to study that slope of Baldy and knew it better than me.

How about the back side? Maybe he knew nothing about that part of the mountain and mayhap I could just lead him around there and get him into country strange to both of us. To do that I had to stay alive long enough.

The worst of it was, he was above me. Like a ghost I moved along the mountainside, careful to break no stick, to let no stones rattle, to let no branch snap back. My clothes were soft, and the leaves brushing me made no sound that could be heard more than a foot away.

Did he have a horse hidden somewhere? Did he stay on the mountain at night?

One thing I had going for me. He had visited Meg Rossiter, and that could mean he moved on and off the mountain. There was every chance I could intercept him. Working my way on I went through a grove of aspen, circled some spruce, and then changed direction, going back and up on a diagonal line.

It almost worked. Suddenly, not a hundred yards off I saw a foot, gray moccasin, gray buckskin. My rifle came up and I fired . . . just as the foot was withdrawn. Instantly I put two shots into the brush above where I'd seen the foot, then slid thirty feet down the mountain, got up and ran through the brush. I ran swiftly and silently, swinging around to get above him.

There was no sound. My heart was pounding. Running at that altitude was not the thing to do, even though I'd spent a good time in the high-up mountains, nobody runs long up that high unless they've lived there for years.

There was small chance I'd hit anything. The shots into the brush were fired as much to make him wary as to hit. Of course, I wanted to nail him—I had to—but the chance of scoring was small.

When I'd gotten my breath back I listened, then went on up the slope, using all the cover I could find, until I was at least a thousand feet higher up the mountain. Then I studied the terrain all around me.

Timberline was close above, which cut down my room to maneuver, but which also trimmed down his chance of getting around me.

My position was good. Only a thin line of wind-torn trees and rocks separated me from the barren top of the mountain. On my right the mountain was also bare for about four hundred yards, beyond that a clump of brush and trees, low growth, but enough to conceal. It was an island, however, and farther down, the slope was bare.

Before me was a weathered outcropping covered with lichen, the gnarled trunk of a weather-beaten spruce and low brush.

For a long time nothing moved below me, then suddenly a bird flew up. It might mean anything or nothing at all. I waited, rifle ready. Taking a piece of jerky from my small pack I began to chew on it while watching the slope.

Suddenly, I heard a rock strike, then a trickle of gravel. It was on the slope to my right, but nothing moved there. Flattening out, I studied the terrain to my left, and an instant later I caught the movement. He darted, just a shadow in the brush, running to get a little closer. I led him a little and fired. He hit the ground and I fired again and again. Gravel rattled on the slope below, but I did not move. If he was dead it did not matter, if he was alive he would be waiting for me to come to check on the results of my shots, and I would do neither.

An hour passed...soon it would be sunset. Below me I heard a muffled groan, but I remained where I was. If he was dying, he could die without me. If it was a trick, and I was sure it was, it would not draw me out. Yet the coming sunset worried me for the sun would be setting just beyond that patch of brush and there would be a period when I could not see in that direction due to the glare of the sun.

It was time to move. Swiftly and silently I went along the mountainside in the opposite direction, avoided the beginnings of Sawmill Canyon, crossed over it and through a grove of aspen, some of the largest I had ever seen. While I rested there I reloaded my rifle.

We could dodge around these mountains for weeks taking potshots at each other, so something had to be done to bring it to an end. I'd dusted him a few times, I was sure of that, and I had done it to worry him. I wanted to force him to great activity, for when a man moves he takes a chance.

Night was coming on, so what would he do? If I had a girl like Meg waiting I'd get shut of this black old mountain and ride over there. He'd have to go back across the La Plata to get over to Cherry Creek and the Rossiter place, and there was a good chance he'd left his horse over there, safely out of the way.

Well, I went down off that mountain fast. Circling around, I got to our camp, got my horse and headed for Cherry Creek. Getting my horse back into the brush out of the way, I watched the ranch. Sure enough, it wasn't more than an hour before that there Vern Huddy came a-riding up like a Sunday cowboy all slicked out in a fresh shirt and a black coat. He left his horse at the rail and went up the steps.

I thought for a minute of finding myself a place out there in the brush and pickin' him off when he came out. That's what he would have done to me. But drygulching just wasn't my way. I never could have faced up to Galloway and Parmalee if I'd got him that way...not to mention Meg if she ever found out. And she probably would...I'm not much good at keepin' quiet about something I'm ashamed of.

I got up and led my horse down, watered it, and led it to the hitch rail and tied it right alongside his. Then I went up the steps and rapped on the door.

Rossiter answered it. "Howdy there, boy! Good to see you! You're just in time for supper!"

He led the way into the dining room and you never saw such a picture. Vern Huddy's mouth must have opened a good bit when he saw me. His face went kind of pale, he was that surprised. And Meg, she was surprised, too, but she wasn't surprised for more than a second and then she was pleased. Here she had two men a-courting her at the same time. Of course, she knew nothing about what had gone on up on the mountain that day.

"Mr. Sackett," she said primly, "I want you to meet Mr. Huddy."

Me, I grinned at him. "I've been looking forward to meeting Mr. Huddy," I said. "In fact, I've been thinking about him all day."

"You have?" Meg was puzzled.

"Oh, yes! He's the kind of man to keep you thinking about him. I can understand why a girl might give a good deal of thought to him, but ma'am, if you'll accept my word for it, he's a mite hard to pin down."

"Mr. Huddy and I," she said primly, "only met a few days ago."

"You'd better tie to him whilst you can," I said. "He may not be with us long." I was feeling good. I'd surprised them both and thrown them off balance and I was feeling in the mood for fun. Anyway, this was a chance to size him up a little. I'd never actually seen him before.

He was well set-up but a mite on the thin side, with a narrow, strict-looking face and not much sense of humor to him. It made him look a little older than I knew he was. He was mad now...I could see that plain as anything. I could also see that he thought well of himself and liked folks to fear him. Kill me he might, before this was over, but make me fear him he couldn't. He was just another man with a gun, and I'd seen a-plenty of them.

When he turned his head I saw a burned place on his forehead...it could have been from a branch but was more likely from a bullet. Had I been wrong about that groan I heard? Had he been knocked out and lying there all the time?

"Mr. Huddle," I said, "looks to me like you ran into something in the dark. Best be careful."

"My name is Huddy," he said testily, "and I shall be more careful. But I don't think the job I am doing will take me long. It is almost too easy."

"Now that's the way a man should look at his work," I said heartily. "I like to see a young man with ambition. That's what it takes to get ahead." Meg went for another platter of meat and I added, cheerfully, "Full of lead."

His eyes were ugly. He didn't find me much fun, I'm afraid. "You're easy," he said, "there's nothing to you, tomorrow—"

"Why not tonight?" I suggested. "We can ride

down the road together, take our distance and shoot it out. You can have it as you like."

"I'm not a fool!" he said angrily.

Meg walked in then and smiled at us both. She was enjoying herself, and if she sensed anything in the air it surely didn't show.

"It's a real pleasure," I said, "meeting Mr. Huddle. I don't know many people in the San Juan Basin yet, and I'm most anxious to get acquainted." I looked over at him and smiled. "I understand you're connected with the Dunn family. Good neighbors," I continued. "Why the other night when we were driving our cattle in, the whole lot of them waited for hours in the dark so they could be there to help us drive them in. And we've scarcely met. I call that neighborly," I said to Meg, "don't you?"

"I hadn't heard about it"—She was wary of me now. Something was going on and I knew she was remembering what I had said about Vern Huddy. He was no good at hiding his feelings either. A blind man could track the anger across his face—"but I would say that was very nice of them."

"I thought so. Especially as we didn't even know them, you know. All twenty or more of them waiting there in the dark, anxious to surprise us with their help. Fortunately we already had recruited some Indians to help us, so we had to express our appreciation an' run along about our business."

Rossiter was sitting there, saying nothing, missing nothing.

He was no fool and he had heard some of the talk that was going around. Also, the facts were obvious. We Sacketts had brought cattle into the country, a big herd and good stock, and we had shown every evidence of settling down.

The Dunns had built cabins but nothing else, making no effort to improve their land.

"We're going to build," I said to Meg, "and when we have the barn-raisin' we'll have all the folks over. We Sacketts sing ... not me, I'm not much good at that, except for myself when I'm riding an easygoing horse ... but the rest of them. We were Welsh and Irish away back, and we brought the singing notion with us.

"We'll have a barn-raisin', a house-warmin' and a sing. We've got some fiddlers amongst us, and we like a good time. Now I'm the serious one, me and Cousin Tyrel, I reckon, but Galloway, he's right amusing, downright amusing."

"I'd love a party!" Meg said. "Nobody's had one since we've been here. There are scarcely enough people, I think."

"Ma'am, a western party never lacks for folks. I've seen cowboys ride from sixty, seventy miles away just to look at a pretty girl, let alone dance with her, and ma'am, you sure are the prettiest!"

Now like I've said, I ain't much on saying things to girls. I get tongue-tied and all, but being here with Vern Huddy across the table, and sort of ridin' him a mite, I just got shook loose and took to talkin' like Galloway or somebody. Maybe it was the excitement. I don't know much about causes and things, but I did not like Mr. Huddy. I've used a gun, but never to hunt a man down and kill him in cold blood. It's been in defense of life or property and when I'm forced to it. And I had doubts that Mr. Vern Huddy could meet anybody face to face.

Meg looked surprised and pleased, but she was also looking as if she couldn't believe it was me that said it. Neither could I.

"Nice to have new folks in the Basin, Mr. Huddle," I said. "We need folks who can help to build, to make this a better place to live. I look forward to the time when we'll have schools, churches and homes around about here. I suppose you're a prospector?"

"No, I am not." Vern Huddy looked up, his eyes on mine. "I am going into the cattle business."

"He's joking," I said, cheerfully. "At least I took him for a prospector. He was all over Baldy today, knocking on rocks, beating through the brush... he was surely looking for something and I am equally sure it wasn't cattle."

He ate with small appetite, while I felt good. Meg could really cook, and she was a right fine girl when it came to that, and I did justice to her food.

When the meal was over, Huddy got up. "I am sorry, but I must go." He was a little stiff and very angry.

"I reckon I'd better go too, then." I glanced at Meg. "You know, ma'am, there's been some shooting from the dark around here, and I think we'd be better off if we rode two together. Nobody's so apt to start shooting if there's two men."

"Oh!" she was disappointed. "Do you have to go?"

"Mister Huddy can stay if he wishes," I said blandly. "I have to be a-gettin' off down the road."

He had no idea of staying after I did and giving me the chance to lay for him beside the road, or to follow him to wherever he was going. So we walked out together.

Rossiter and Meg came with us. He gripped my hand. "It's been good to see you, Sackett," he said. "Come back any time."

He glanced over at Huddy. "Goodnight, Mr. Huddle," he said, and I chuckled. Then he and Meg went inside.

Vern Huddy wheeled his horse around and dropped his hand to his gun. Mine was covering him.

"Temper, Mr. Huddle," I said, "and there's a matter of common politeness. Never shoot anybody in somebody's yard who has been entertaining you."

My draw had been so much faster than his that he never cleared leather, and I know he thought I was going to kill him as he certainly would have killed me. "Now you ride out ahead of me, and don't try anything fancy."

He rode quietly until we neared the first bend in the road, then suddenly he was around it and running, and I let him go.

We knew what was coming, both of us, and the showdown would be tomorrow, in the mountains.

To follow down that trail now with him maybe laying for me would be crazy, so I turned off. There was a dim trail that led into the high-up hills just a mite west of Starvation Creek, so I taken it.

It wasn't until I was well up in the breaks before I realized that the head of Starvation Creek was where Nick Shadow's gold and diamonds were supposed to be hidden.

CHAPTER 17

WHEN LOGAN SACKETT rode back to Shalako after the haying, Berglund's saloon was sporting a new sign—*The Gold Miner's Daughter*—and a painting of a well-endowed young lady in a flaming red dress and rings in her ears.

Berglund was standing outside looking at it. "Now there," he said, "is a work of art!"

"Who's the painter?"

"Who, he says. I am. Pat Berglund."

Logan studied it. "You better go back for more lessons," he said, "and I don't mean in painting."

They went inside and Berglund set out a bottle of beer. Despite the fact that the year was growing late, the day was hot. The beer was cold.

"How'd a Swede ever get the name of Pat?" Logan asked.

"My mother was Irish. I'm named for her brother who was a policeman in Boston."

He glanced at Sackett. "What are you named after? A berry?"

"A preacher...a circuit-ridin' preacher. He gave me a prayer book at my christening."

"You ever read it?"

"Sure. I know all the prayers. Trouble is, I never used 'em enough. I can quote the Bible by the chapter. My ma was a great one for camp meetings."

"You come to town alone?"

"Why not? I don't need any help."

"You may. Here come the Dunns."

Logan Sackett glanced out of the window, then finished pouring his beer. "There's only five or six of them. No use spoiling the fun by having Galloway along."

"You're not entirely alone," Berglund said. "I just saw Nick Shadow step into the store."

Bull Dunn got down off his horse. Ollie Hammer looked slowly around, then got off his horse.

Logan took a swallow of the beer. "Berglund, if there's anything in this place you don't want busted you better duck it out of sight. I have an idea those Dunns are hot for trouble."

The first one through the door was Tin-Cup Hone. He saw Logan Sackett and stopped dead.

"Howdy, Tin! You're a long way from home, and you've got a horse."

"What's that mean?" Hone said warily.

"A man with a horse who's so far from home ought to be riding it," Logan said cheerfully.

"I'll stay."

"All right. When I go to funerals I always admire to see a handsome corpse. They'll fix you up real pretty, Tin."

Red had come in from the back door. "Take his advice, Hone. I got that advice one time and I pulled out. I ain't never been sorry."

"He's alone, ain't he?"

"No, Tin, he ain't. Nick Shadow's down the street, and Nick is just plain poison with a six-gun and he's one of the kind who just don't care. He's like the mule who butted his head into a tree, an' somebody asked if he couldn't go around it and they answered sure, but he just didn't give a damn. Shadow is like that. Did you ever buck a man who just plain don't care? Everybody dies but him. I seen it before."

Hone walked slowly to the bar. "There's six men out there and four more a-coming up. Not even Logan Sackett and Nick Shadow can buck them odds."

Red chuckled. "You ain't countin' me. I been on the wrong side too often. This time I'm on the right ride. I think I'm as good as you, Tin.

"And I'll tell you something else. Galloway was cuttin' a tree down in the breaks by the river and when he came out he saw you Dunns a-coming. Right now him and Parmalee and that breed of theirs, Charlie Farnum, they're right over yonder in the livery stable."

"Gimme a beer," Tin-Cup said. "It'll be thirsty, riding."

"Drink it on your horse," Logan said, "they're going to open the ball."

Bull Dunn came through the door. He saw the back door closing after Tin-Cup Hone and he turned his cruel eyes on Logan. "Heard about you," he said.

"I usually fight with a gun," Logan said, "but this time I'm going to whip you with my hands."

Dunn glanced at him, disgusted. "Don't be a fool. Nobody ever came close."

"Maybe they didn't do it right," Logan said, and hit him.

He had put the beer down on the bar and he simply backhanded Bull Dunn across the mouth, smashing his lips. Bull Dunn was huge and powerful, but Logan Sackett, while considerably lighter, was almost as tall and a man with huge shoulders and chest. His blow did not even stagger Dunn when it mashed his lips, but Logan let the impetus of the blow turn him, so he threw a left hand at Bull's head. The bigger man pulled his head aside and grabbed Logan with his huge arms.

Logan shoved the butt of his palm under Bull's chin, forcing his head back, then he struck him twice in the ribs and shoved him off. Dunn struck out hard and knocked Logan into the bar, then charged him, head down and swinging. Logan rolled free, smashed a wicked short right to the side of the face that split Bull's ear, showering him with blood.

Bull turned like a cat, landed left and right to the head and rammed in again, but Logan slapped a hand down on Dunn's head, thrusting it down to meet Logan's rising knee. Dunn staggered back, his nose and mouth a gory wreck.

Then toe-to-toe they began to slug, smashing punch after punch, neither man trying to evade, each one soaking up punishment. Logan was a little the faster, Dunn the heavier and perhaps the stronger. It was rough, brutal, and beautiful to watch. People crowded into the room. Up and down they went. Logan pulled free and knocked Bull Dunn down with a smashing right, but the big man lunged up from the floor, grappled Logan about the hips and lifted his body clear of the floor, then slammed him down across a table, which crashed beneath them. Bull dove at him, but Logan hit him with a short right to the face, then heaved him off. Both men came up together. Dunn swung a kick for Logan's groin, and Logan brought his knee up across in front of him, blocking the kick.

Then he walked in, smashing blow after blow to Dunn's face. Bull broke away, charged again and threw Sackett hard. Dunn jumped for Logan's face with his boots and Logan rolled aside. He got to his feet in time to meet Dunn's rush. Again they stood slugging, grunting with every punch. Shirts torn and faces bloody, they swung and swung, but Logan was slowly pushed back by the larger man's brute strength. Back he went down the room, then suddenly he seemed to weaken, and fell back against the bar.

Seeing victory, Dunn set himself and drew back his fist for a finishing punch, and Logan Sackett, who had faked his weakness, threw a short inside right. It dropped like a hammer to Dunn's chin inside of his swing, and stopped the big man flatfooted. Stunned, Bull Dunn stood, his fist poised, and then Logan Sackett punched short and hard with both fists—a left to the face, then a ripping right uppercut to the midsection.

Dunn's knees sagged and Logan Sackett whipped another right to the face.

Bull went down. He hit the floor on his knees and Pete Dunn screamed as if stabbed. "No! No, pa! They can't lick you! Nobody can!"

Bull Dunn lunged up, dazed and shaken, staring blindly for his enemy. Logan Sackett was pouring beer into a glass, and Dunn lunged at him. Logan Sackett lifted a foot to fend him off—boot against Dunn's chest, knee bent. Then he straightened the knee and Dunn staggered back and fell again.

Logan Sackett rinsed his cut mouth with a swallow of beer, then gulped it down. "Stay down, you damn' fool," he said. "You're game enough."

Bull Dunn stared up at him. "I wish . . . I wished I could get up, damn you, I'd—"

"Have a beer," Logan said. "You fight pretty good."

He walked over and taking the bigger man's arm, helped him to his feet where he half fell against the bar. Logan shoved a beer in front of him. "It's cold," he said. "Tastes good after a fight, and before a long ride."

Bull looked at him. "You don't need to grind it in," he said. "I should have listened to Rocker."

————

IT WAS HOT in the street outside. Nick Shadow stood in front of the livery stable, well out of sight. Galloway was in the doorway, staying in the shade to see better. The sound of fighting from the saloon was finished.

"Somebody won," Shadow said, "and somebody lost."

Parmalee came from the store. "I guess it's all over," he said.

"Not quite," Ollie Hammer said, "not quite."

"Why not?" Parmalee suggested. "It's finished in there. If your people won they'd be out here in the street, looking for the rest of us."

"What about your crowd? Won't they come out?"

Parmalee smiled. "They know we can handle it," he said calmly.

"You? You dude? You're leavin' it to Shadow, or that cousin of yours, or whatever he is."

"Second cousin, I believe. Oh, they could handle it all right, Hammer, but if you prefer me, I'm at your pleasure. Draw when you will."

"Now there's the gent," Ollie Hammer said, " 'draw when you will' " he mimicked. "All right I'll——"

His hand flashed for his gun.

Parmalee's gun was an instant faster, his shot smashed Ollie's gun hand and the gun fell into the dust. "And to show you that was intentional," Parmalee said, and he fired again, the bullet smashing the gun's butt as it lay in the dust. "I really don't want to run up a score, Hammer," Parmalee said. "I'm a ranching man, not a gunfighter."

"You ain't seen the last of this," Ollie Hammer said. "Huddy is still up on the mountain. When he's finished there won't be a Sackett left. And then there's Rocker."

Parmalee put his gun back in the holster and walked across to Galloway. "What about it? Shall we go up there and help Flagan?"

"Flagan don't need help. And right now he knows he's up there alone. He can shoot at anything that moves. If we go up it'll just complicate things. Leave him be."

He hitched up his pants. "Let's all go home. We got some siding to build. We're goin' to have a barn-raisin' soon, and we're going to build us a house."

Galloway gestured toward the hills. "I want to come out of a morning and look up at those hills and know nothing can be very wrong as long as there's something so beautiful.

"My pa used to say that when corruption is visited upon the cities of men, the mountains and the deserts await him. The cities are for money but the high-up hills are purely for the soul.

"I figure to live out my life right here where I can hear the water run and see the aspen leaves turn gold in the autumn and come green again with spring. I want to wake up in the morning and see my own cattle feeding on the meadow, and hear the horses stomping in their stalls. I never had much chance for book learnin', but this here is a kind of book anybody can read who'll stand still long enough. This here is the La Plata country, and I've come home."

CHAPTER 18

THE WIND SANG a broken song among the
sentinel trees. Below the scattered outposts
were massed the dark battalions of the pines like an
enemy ready to march against me, and somewhere
along the lower edge of that black line lay the man
who held the rifle that had shot me, and the bullet
with which he intended to kill me.

Vern Huddy had the taste of blood upon his lips,
and was a-thirst for more, and I lay with my body
torn by his bullet, shuddering with every breath, my
coat gone and night a-coming on, waiting for him to
make his move.

Only thing good about it was that he didn't know
exactly where I was. His bullet got me most of an
hour before as I dove for shelter, but I'd wormed
and scrambled and crawled some little distance since
then.

I gouged snow from the almost frozen remains that
had backed up against a rock near me. I let a handful
melt in my mouth and felt the delicious coolness of it
going down my throat, through my body.

Moving stones from under me I piled them
around, digging myself deeper against the cold and
Huddy's bullets. The weakening was upon me, and
for two hours before the bullet hit I'd been driven
and outflanked at every turn by a man who was a

past master at his trade, and who knew now that I was somewhere along timberline with nowhere else to go. In his heart he was sure he was going to get me.

This was my last stop. Whatever happened must happen here. I told myself that and I believed it. I could not go back because it was a wide-open space and even in the night there would be enough light to see me against that gray-white expanse.

The hole made by the bullet I had plugged with moss, and now I was waiting for him to come in for the finish. If he came before I passed out I might get him, and if not he would surely get me.

It was growing dark. Down in the valleys below it was already dark and people were sitting down to their tables to eat warm suppers in pleasant surroundings. Meg Rossiter was down there preparing supper for her pa, or helping, and around the campfire my brother and the others would be wondering where I was.

Easing my long body to a better position, I waited. He did not know where I was and I did not know where he was, and each needed to know. Squirming deeper into the gravel, I shivered against the cold. It was growing late in the year and at this, nearly twelve thousand feet of altitude, it could become icy by night.

This was a different peak from the night before, unknown to both of us. They called it Parrott or Madden . . . the two were side by side and I was not sure which we were on. I didn't know the country that well.

Digging a fragment of jerky from my pack, I began chewing on it. That pack of mine was almost flat, just a place to carry a few pieces of bread and meat to sort of tide a man over.

I'd lost a good bit of blood and the shock of the bullet had been great. It seemed to have struck the top of my hip-bone, knocking me down and numbing my leg, but then it had glanced into the flesh and had gouged a deep hole.

Even if Huddy did not get me I'd be lucky to last the night. The blood drained from me and the icy cold would take care of that. Suddenly something moved, and leaving my rifle alone I drew my pistol ... how could he have come so close!

There was a low whine ... *that damned wolf!*

How could he have followed me up here? But why not? He seemed to be haunting me. Now I've known wild animals to do some strange things. I heard of a panther one time who followed a boy two miles through a dark forest only a few feet behind him, the boy talking to it all the while thinking it was his dog. Then he called out to the house and when they opened the door they all saw the panther ... it ducked off into the brush.

I taken a small bit of the jerky from my pack and said quietly, "Here, boy!" And tossed it out there.

Eager jaws took it, and I could hear the chewing. I began talking to it in low whispers, and calling it to me. After a long while it did come, crawling over the bank on its belly as if it knew enough to keep down, and then waiting while I talked to it. Suddenly it crawled closer.

Seen up close, even in the almost dark, it looked like a wolf and yet not quite like one. In fact, it might have been half dog.

My hand reached out to it. The wolf growled a little, but warningly rather than threateningly, then it sniffed of my fingers, seemed reassured and crept closer. I put a hand on it, then listened, but heard nothing. My hand brushed the thick ruff and started to scratch.

"My God!"

The expression was startled from me, for around the neck of the wolf was a collar, a collar so tight the poor animal was almost strangled!

"Why, you poor devil!" I reached for my knife and talking to it all the while, slipped the knife under the collar. The wolf began to gag and choke, but he seemed to know I was trying to help, and then that razor-sharp blade cut through the collar and it came loose.

The effort taken a good bit from me, but I lay there, whispering to that wolf that he'd be all right now. The poor thing had been follerin' me around for all this time, figuring I could help it. Must be that some man had at one time had it for a pet, had put the collar on when it was small, and the wolf had gone back to the woods or maybe the man had died. Then the wolf had grown and grown until the collar was choking it. No wonder it was so hungry for the small fragments I threw out. It could swallow them.

I kept my hand on the ruff and kept talking to it, and oddly enough, the wolf showed no idea of leaving. He crept closer, and even licked my hand. And the first thing I knew I'd fallen to sleep.

It must have been the warmth of the big animal lying close thataway, and part of it was that my attention had been torn from the main issue and I forgot about staying awake. Anyway, I slept.

And then I heard a low, ugly growling alongside of me and suddenly I was awake. Just the glimpse of the stars showed it was past midnight.

"Quiet, boy!" I whispered, putting a hand on the wolf, and it quieted down, but its ears were pricked and it was looking right straight ahead.

Me, I eased my pistol out and rolled away from the wolf so if I drew fire it would not get hit.

He was coming in. I heard a foot grate against gravel and then he was there, black against the sky.

The wolf suddenly sprang away and his gun came up and I said, "Don't shoot. It was just a wolf."

"A *what*?"

"A timber wolf," I said. "He's a friend of mine."

"You're crazy," he said. "Out of your head."

"You going to kill me now?" I asked, conversationally.

"And enjoy it," he said, "and then I'm going down to see Meg. Nobody will ever find you up here. I'll just leave you for that wolf or whatever it is."

My pistol was in my hand but he hadn't seen it. He was standing about a dozen feet away and he had a rifle and he was holding it in one hand pointing it at me. It began to look like a Mexican stand-off, with both of us dying up here.

"Ever see a wolf come to a man before, Huddle?" I said. "If you'll stop and think, that there's impossible. Up in the mountains of Tennessee we know all about wolves and such, like ha'nts and werewolves."

He was suddenly still, like he almost stopped

breathing. "That's fool talk," he said. "I'm going to kill you, Sackett."

"If you do," I said, "you'll never get off the mountain. That there's what the Indians call a medicine wolf. He'll get you sure. Tear you to bits... unless you got a silver bullet."

"You're lying!"

There was a low growl from the bushes to his right, and as he spun slightly toward the sound I lifted my gun and shot him.

His rifle went off and spat sand into my face. His movement must have deflected it just by a hair, just enough to save my bacon.

He was down, but I could see the glint of the rifle barrel as he moved it toward me. I shot him again.

The rifle fell from his hands as he rolled over on his side. I stood up. "No! No!" he whispered. "Oh, no, *no*!"

"You gave it to a good many, Huddy," I said. "You shot that poor Indian who worked for me, shot him when he didn't even know, and when no enemies were around. He never had a chance to lift a hand. Now you know how it feels."

"No... not me." He was whimpering like a child. "Not me!" And I had it in me to feel sorry for him. Somehow his kind never figure it will be them. They always kill; they are never killed. That's the way they see it.

Taking up his rifle I backed off a little, still wary of him because he was packing a six-shooter, but I needn't have been because he was dead.

The wolf moved out there in the dark and I said to him, "Come on, boy, we're going home now."

Picking up his collar because I wished to see it by daylight, I started down the mountain in the first gray of dawn, and the wolf—or dog-wolf which he seemed to be—fell in behind me. Not too close, not too far.

Looked like he'd been lonesome for a man to belong to, and when he saw me and I tossed him that meat back yonder he figured I might be the one to help him out of the trap that was sure to kill him sooner or later.

We started down the mountain, but we stopped down there where Starvation Creek flows out of the rock, and I hunted around for that gold and found it. Taken me only a few minutes and I had to rest, anyway, with my wound and all.

I was in bad shape again, but this time I was going home and I had a friend with me. The gold was heavy so I only taken one sack of the stuff, just to throw on the table in front of Nick Shadow, and say "This what you were lookin' for?"

The sky was all red, great streaks of it, when I walked across the meadow toward the fire. Soon as I felt better, I was going over to see that Meg girl. She'd want to hear about my wolf.

The boys came out and stood there staring at me. "It's Flagan," Galloway said. "I knew he'd be coming in this morning."

"Boys," I said, "you got to meet my wolf. Take good care of him, I—"

Well, I just folded my cards together and fell, laid right down, dead beat and hurt. But it was worth it because when I opened my eyes, Meg was there.

About Louis L'Amour

*"I think of myself in the oral tradition—
as a troubadour, a village tale-teller, the man
in the shadows of the campfire. That's the way
I'd like to be remembered—as a storyteller.
A good storyteller."*

IT IS DOUBTFUL that any author could be as at home in the world re-created in his novels as Louis Dearborn L'Amour. Not only could he physically fill the boots of the rugged characters he wrote about, but he literally "walked the land my characters walk." His personal experiences as well as his lifelong devotion to historical research combined to give Mr. L'Amour the unique knowledge and understanding of people, events, and the challenge of the American frontier that became the hallmarks of his popularity.

Of French-Irish descent, Mr. L'Amour could trace his own family in North America back to the early 1600s and follow their steady progression westward, "always on the frontier." As a boy growing up in Jamestown, North Dakota, he absorbed all he could about his family's frontier heritage, including the story of his great-grandfather who was scalped by Sioux warriors.

Spurred by an eager curiosity and desire to

broaden his horizons, Mr. L'Amour left home at the age of fifteen and enjoyed a wide variety of jobs including seaman, lumberjack, elephant handler, skinner of dead cattle, assessment miner, and officer on tank destroyers during World War II. During his "yondering" days he also circled the world on a freighter, sailed a dhow on the Red Sea, was shipwrecked in the West Indies and stranded in the Mojave Desert. He won fifty-one of fifty-nine fights as a professional boxer and worked as a journalist and lecturer. He was a voracious reader and collector of rare books. His personal library contained 17,000 volumes.

Mr. L'Amour "wanted to write almost from the time I could talk." After developing a widespread following for his many frontier and adventure stories written for fiction magazines, Mr. L'Amour published his first full-length novel, *Hondo,* in the United States in 1953. Every one of his more than 120 books is in print; there are nearly 300 million copies of his books in print worldwide, making him one of the bestselling authors in modern literary history. His books have been translated into twenty languages, and more than forty-five of his novels and stories have been made into feature films and television movies.

His hardcover bestsellers include *The Lonesome Gods, The Walking Drum* (his twelfth-century historical novel), *Jubal Sackett, Last of the Breed,* and *The Haunted Mesa.* His memoir, *Education of a Wandering Man,* was a leading bestseller in 1989. Audio dramatizations and adaptations of many L'Amour stories are available on cassette tapes from Random House Audio Publishing.

The recipient of many great honors and awards, in 1983 Mr. L'Amour became the first novelist ever to be awarded the Congressional Gold Medal by the United States Congress in honor of his life's work. In 1984 he was also awarded the Medal of Freedom by President Reagan.

Louis L'Amour died on June 10, 1988. His wife, Kathy, and their two children, Beau and Angelique, carry the L'Amour tradition forward with new books written by the author during his lifetime to be published by Bantam.